The Sun at Noon

A Quarter of Mankind
Asia Awakes
East Meets West: Singapore
The Long March 1935
The Future Role of Singapore
The Neutralisation of Southeast Asia
Mao Tse-tung in the Scales of History (editor)
Mao the People's Emperor
The Great Wall (co-author)
When Tigers Fight: The Sino-Japanese War 1937–1945
Chou: The Story of Zhou Enlai 1898–1976
Another Bite at the Cherry: The European View of Japan (in Japanese)

The Sun at Noon

AN ANATOMY OF
MODERN JAPAN

by

DICK WILSON

HAMISH HAMILTON

LONDON

First published in Great Britain 1986
by Hamish Hamilton Ltd
Garden House 57–59 Long Acre London WC2E 9JZ

British Library Cataloguing in Publication Data

Wilson, Dick, *1928–*
    The sun at noon : An anatomy of modern Japan
    1. Japan—Social conditions—1945–
    I. Title
    952.04'8   HN723.5
    ISBN 0-241-11839-5

Typeset by Rowland Phototypesetting Ltd, Bury St Edmunds, Suffolk
Printed in Great Britain by
St Edmundsbury Press, Bury St Edmunds, Suffolk

To K.F.

Contents

A Note on Japanese Names and Words

The Japanese put family before self, so it is logical for them to put a person's family name before his or her given name – Smith Mary, so to speak, rather than Mary Smith. But many western institutions or publishers reverse that order, to bring a Japanese name into line with European or American expectations, and many Japanese voyagers to the West voluntarily change their name around for the same reason. It becomes dogmatic in a book like this to insist on the correct Japanese order, and so the names are printed here with the given name first, the family name second, to ease the burden of unfamiliarity. Readers are alerted, however, to the problem they may face in pursuing further research.

At the back of the book are some notes giving references for quotations in the text, further reading in a few instances and identification of people whose views are cited. The reader will also find some acknowledgements there. Meanwhile, for convenience, the English meanings of a few common Japanese words used in the text are listed here:

gaijin:	foreigner	*shimbun*:	newspaper
geisha:	traditional entertainer	*shogun*:	ruler under Emperor
haiku:	three-line poem	*sogo shosha*:	trading corporation
harakiri:	suicide by disembowelment	*sushi*:	raw fish
		tatami:	rush matting
kabuki:	traditional theatre	*ukiyoe*:	wood block print
kimono:	full-length dress	*yakuza*:	gangster
sake:	rice wine	*yen*:	unit of currency
samurai:	warrior	*zaibatsu*:	cartel
sayonara:	goodbye		

Key Dates in Japan's History

about 1000 BC	First migrations from Korea, China, Southeast Asia and Pacific islands.
660 BC	Emperor Jimmu founds present dynasty, according to legend.
400 AD	Japanese scholars bring script from China.
about 550 AD	Buddhism introduced from China and Korea.
794 AD	Kyoto capital of Japan (until 1868).
about 1000 AD	*Tale of Genji* by Lady Murasaki, world's first novel.
1158–1868	Japan ruled by Shoguns 'on behalf' of Emperors.
1542	First European (a Portuguese) enters Japan.
1549	Francis Xavier lands at Kagoshima.
1600	Will Adams, first Englishman in Japan, arrives.
1638–1853	Seclusion of Japan, foreigners not admitted.
1853	Commodore Perry brings his 'black ships' from US to open up Japan to international intercourse.
1868	Meiji Restoration overthrows Shoguns, institutes western-style reforms under Emperor Meiji with new capital at Tokyo.
1894–95	Japan wins first Sino-Japanese War, takes over Taiwan as colony.
1902–21	Anglo-Japanese Alliance (Japan fought with Allies in First World War).
1904–5	Russo-Japanese War, first modern Asian victory over European power.
1910	Korea annexed as colony.
1923	Great Kanto Earthquake (almost 135,000 dead and missing).
1926	Emperor Hirohito ascends throne.
1931	Japan invades Manchuria (in north China).

1936	Japan and Germany sign Anti-Comintern Pact.
1937, 7 July	Marco Polo Bridge Incident starts second Sino-Japanese War (to 1945).
1940, September	Tripartite Treaty with Axis powers, Germany and Italy.
1941, 7 December	Japan's surprise attack on US Navy at Pearl Harbor in Hawaii, entry into Second World War – in course of which Japan conquers Philippines, Malaysia, Burma, Hongkong, Singapore, Indonesia, Thailand, Vietnam and parts of Papua New Guinea as well as the important areas of China.
1945, 6 August	Atom bomb on Hiroshima (and three days later on Nagasaki).
1945, 2 September	Unconditional surrender to US and Allies.
1945–52	American Occupation of Japan.
1947	New western-style Constitution.
1951	Peace Treaty signed in San Francisco, also first Security Treaty with US.
1956	Japan enters United Nations.
1960	Second Security Treaty with US.
1964	Tokyo Olympic Games.
1968	Yasunari Kawabata becomes first Japanese writer to win Nobel Prize for Literature.

Introduction

ON 6 AUGUST 1945 the atom bomb exploded on Hiroshima. A month later General Douglas MacArthur landed near Yokohama to begin his seven-year term of supreme power as Japan's 'blue-eyed *shogun*'. The two events symbolized the destruction of the old Japan and the creation of a new Japan.

The Japanese yield to no one in terms of pride, and yet for forty years they have subjected themselves to an American constitution and been governed by an American-style legislature, with an English-style cabinet and constitutional monarchy, the whole system being operated by American-style political parties. They have accepted an American-imposed restriction on their defence forces and have heavily geared their economy towards trading with American and European partners. Under these foreign trappings the Japanese surprised everybody by producing in the 1960s an economic miracle of unprecedented dimensions, but they did so by keeping an unnaturally low profile – not only in world affairs where they have made little diplomatic impact as yet but even in the East Asian region where they used to be mightily feared before 1945.

Today, forty years on, this unnatural situation is threatened. The Japanese organism shows belated signs of rejecting the American transplant. The needs for which those foreign institutions were imported in the 1940s are now replaced by a bigger and tougher agenda of political decision-making. It looks as if indigenous styles may gradually take over, and as if Japan may therefore begin to project a rather different character on the world scene.

Much of the traditional pre-war Japan, both body and spirit, was flattened in 1945, and MacArthur's American reformers were only too eager to substitute western-style* values and institutions. As the

* 'West' and 'western' are used in this book as a kind of shorthand to indicate ideas, values and behaviour commonly found in the mainstream of European and North American life, especially where these contrast with Japan. I recognize that such countries as Italy and Spain have social structures somewhat between the British and the Japanese, just as there are enormous variations within Japan itself. But this book would be uncomfortably lengthened by definitions being spelt out in every case, and I ask the reader to indulge the shorthand.

1950s unfolded, two facts became clear. The Japanese had buckled down to the basics of economic survival and were going to rebuild their economy. And in so doing they assimilated the massive dose of westernization which MacArthur had injected into their society (vitally reinforcing the earlier administrations of 1858–1920).

English became the major foreign language, and Westerners were pleasantly surprised to find that they could fly into Tokyo and talk to large numbers of people without having to learn Japanese. The Japanese to whom they talked were predisposed to western ideas by virtue of their having mastered some English, but that did not seem to matter at the time. It was possible to conclude that Japan was going through a kind of microwave 'colonial' experience which could render the country as accessible and amenable to the West as India and Southeast Asia already were.

Then in the late 1960s Japan's economic recovery programme went into overdrive, and Japan's living standards started to approach those of Southern Europe. The West called it a 'miracle' at first, but found itself wanting words to describe what happened in the 1970s as the Japanese economy began to overtake the countries of Northern Europe in quick succession. The flagging West had then to take the Japanese economy seriously, finding numerous points of contention which led to bitter arguments, cultural* clashes and racial insults. Actually the rising sun of the Japanese economy has reached its noon in relative international terms, but there is a time-lag in other countries' perception of this.

If Japan had, indeed, become westernized to the same degree as her economy was modernized during those forty post-war years, the tensions might have been contained within an agreed framework, similar to those between Britain and America, or France and Germany. But it transpired that the Japanese did not want to become culturally internationalized; the western idea that they could ever do so had been shallow and superficial from the start.

At the beginning, Japan had to obey American orders. When the Occupation ended in 1952, Japan was caught up in the American-dominated international capitalist system and could not easily extricate herself, lacking the economic and political power to pursue an independent role. There was no alternative to taking on board as much westernism as possible, but only to provide Japan with the

---

* 'Culture' is used throughout this book to signify the intangible aspects of behaviour which a society teaches its individual members, from language and expression to family and social relationships, from values and beliefs to education and arts. Race or ethnicity is physical, inherited and immutable: culture is learned only from infancy.

equipment needed to protect her interests in an alien world, not as an instrument to change the Japanese personality.

As the economic miracle unfolded, the incentive to follow western ways dried up. Some of what had been injected took hold, and in other cases the mere fact of the modernizing of Japanese society, irrespective of alien cultural values, caused certain indigenous traditions to become no longer appropriate or comfortable; these gaps were filled by a natural process not at all, or not exclusively, influenced by western models.

Japan has thus become a richly complicated mixture of indigenous and foreign elements but, whereas the trend in the first twenty post-war years was broadly towards westernization, the trend since about 1965 has been more selective, more discriminating, and more solicitous of traditions – not the whole of the tradition, only those parts of it which contemporary Japanese generally admire and enjoy, or those parts which have been continuously modified from within to cope with the changes in material life.

In cultural terms a re-discovery of Japanese values is going on, rather similar to what has happened in other countries, like India, that came too close to the West for comfort. The social currents are contradictory, some individuals and institutions developing towards international modes at some times, busily reinforcing elements of the tradition at others. Westerners, recalling guiltily their failure to study the language and culture, now find Japan difficult to interpret. So much so that pessimists wonder if the open door which Japan has held out to the world in the past forty years might shut again, heralding a repetition of the closed periods of 1639–1853 and again from 1930–45. There are indeed intimations of a change of course in Japan, and there is no doubt of the intense nostalgia that Japanese feel about their cultural tradition, or of their strong desire to assert their cultural identity. In order to modernize, Japan has had to suppress some of her cultural instincts and behave to a certain extent in alien ways in dealing with the outside world. Now there is something of a reaction to that going on.

Yet the Japanese brain tells the Japanese heart that the open door periods were times of material success, whereas the most recent closed door has brought disaster. And there is no visible way of altering Japan's minority in a club of world managers who are all white, all Christian, and all rooted in European culture. In the long run, other Asian and even African states will join the club, and then the primacy of Anglo-Saxon values will be challenged, but that is still a long way ahead. Meanwhile, Japan's only course is neither to exclude the West, nor surrender to it, but to continue the process of interaction and synthesis – as a result of which Japanese-ness will change considerably, while Western-ness will be modified by the Japanese contribution only very slightly (one laboratory for that being California).

The precise nature of this compromise which Japan will strike is controversial. Japan's older generation has swallowed its pride for forty years in order to rise again in the world. But younger Japanese, born after the war, do not share the guilt and remorse which their parents feel about what their country did in the 1930s and 1940s, and they take their modern progress for granted. They are superficially more cosmopolitan, but, as with time they come to dominate the population, the Japanese body increasingly rejects some of the western vaccine. For example, the contradiction between western-style parliamentary democracy and Japan's cultural preference for consensus-unanimity, avoiding majority votes, is becoming more obvious.

This book seeks to explain where the Japanese stand today in the most important aspects of their lives – especially their sense of individuality, their family and social relationships, their politics and economics, and their links with the outside world – and the direction in which they appear to be heading. It would be impossible to cover such ground in one book without cutting corners and skipping over reservations and caveats which would have to be entered in an academic work: it is presented as only the briefest of introductions. It is an interpretation of Japan to help Westerners in the late 1980s and 1990s, and the content of western values is therefore taken largely as read. The goal is to present the minimum fact and opinion which a Westerner newly interested in Japan would want to know for a basic all-round understanding.

The interpretation of the character of the Japanese people is something which arouses fierce passions and partisanship. Japanologists in western universities shy away from it. Western writers who dwell on the traditions, the 'backwardness', the values of the old Japan, are criticized for perpetuating the myth that Japan has got stuck, socially speaking, on the escalator to modernization. Others who highlight the ways in which contemporary Japanese, especially young ones, are similar in tastes, activities and values to their counterparts in the West, are felt to gloss over the differences.

The conviction behind this book is that no one can understand Japan without first gaining some idea of its traditions, but that having got that under his belt, he should plunge firmly into a study of the contemporary scene where those traditions vie with all the features of modern material life already familiar to a Westerner, to produce a unique mix. That mix is impressionistically portrayed in these pages, not to show the Japanese in any preconceived light as good or bad, old-fashioned or innovative, but simply as they appear to one observer who likes them, is deeply committed to their participation in world affairs, but has no axe to grind and is not in the least committed to their government or their national goals.

The cross-currents, the cyclical contradictions, the opposing influences at work on Japanese life are tortuous. A trend among 120 million people can, after all, leave several tens of millions doing the other thing. But one has to start somewhere. In a very general strategic sense the Japanese personality (with all due reservations about reducing 120 million individuals to that term) seems to be moving very tentatively towards an international cosmopolitan norm – in company with others, like the western, arriving from different directions.

Tactically, however, there seems now to be a reaction to the dizzy speed of internationalization of recent years, so that Japan may appear in some respects to be 'going backwards' – not, however, to unwanted and rejected aspects of the past, like aggressive militarism or social inequality or severe restraints on individual freedom, but to such basics as what to eat and how to eat it, what to wear and when to wear it, whom to associate with and on what terms, and in the very human wish to cease to feel apologetic about expressing these cultural values.

The counterpart of this book would be the volumes which Japanese writers produce about England or France. Like them, this book is culture-centric but I would feel chagrined if it were judged ethnocentric. Before writing it, I read as many books by Japanese writers as western, and sought the views of as many Japanese intellectuals as western. I cannot, and do not wish to, escape my English-ness, and am not among the growing number of bi-cultural writers whose testimony will sooner or later prevail on questions of international understanding. But I do chafe at many restrictive features of English society – its puritanism, immobility and class distinctions, for instance – and relish their relative absence in Japan, which I have visited almost forty times since 1953, staying in many Japanese homes and making dozens of staunch friends.

It is concern at the unnecessary insults exchanged between Japan and my own country over trade frictions, and at what they portend for the future political relationship, that made me undertake this book in the first place. And the motivation is not just to improve relations with Japan, important though that may be, but to try to persuade Britain and other western countries to cultivate now the more equitable and culturally tolerant attitude they must eventually take to the Asian nations which will ultimately assert their majority in world affairs.

*

This book is about the Japanese people. But they are moulded by their soil and landscape, more than most societies, and a reminder of the particular qualities of the land where they live may be in order.

Leaving tiny islets aside, the distance to the nearest mainland is about one hundred miles, which helps to explain why Japan was so isolated in her history. The Japanese islands are part of what geographers call the ring of volcanic fire which circles the Pacific Ocean. Volcanic eruptions and earthquakes are endemic. In the Bay of Shizuoka, just south of Mount Fuji and an hour or two's ride from Tokyo, two giant plates meet underground, grinding into each other at a rate of six inches a year and creating a springboard tension which will one day thrust up the surrounding soil and seabed.

The last big earthquake in the Tokyo area was in 1923, and scientists expect the next one some time around 1990. They agree that, this time, the city of Tokyo is not likely to be badly hit, since the epicentre will be more to the southwest. The Japanese are philosophical about the inconstancy of the rocks beneath them. An old legend tells of a giant catfish that lives underground, shaking the soil every time it stirs. Yet a sensational novel called *Japan Sinks* was a best-seller in the 1970s, hinting at morbid fears behind the calm.

It follows that architecture is necessarily impermanent. Temples and houses are built in such a way that they are easily restored. Temples apart, the oldest building extant dates only from 1648. Until twenty years ago, it was not permitted to build more than ten storeys in Tokyo: now Tokyo is studded with sky-scrapers, all of them expensively made to withstand earthquakes of the intensity of 1923, with specially reinforced, flexible or floating structures.

The land itself is so mountainous that only one-sixth of its area is flat enough to live on or farm. It may look big on the map, but in terms of useable land, Japan packs the equivalent of the British and French economics and populations combined, into the space of Italy. The average farm is little more than a couple of acres, one-twentieth of the European and one-sixtieth of the American norm. The need to irrigate small and often terraced plots probably explains why the rice farmers co-operated rather than competed in the first instance, setting Japanese society on a different track from Europe's.

Land scarcity means population density; some 4,000 people are squeezed together in every habitable square mile. With the seventh largest population in the world (almost 120 million), Japan has a density of population twice that of Europe, and the denizens of metropolitan Tokyo are packed three times more tightly into their living space than Greater Londoners. A premium attaches therefore to mobility – one feature of the Tokyo scene, for example, being mobile massage parlours, known as the 'Pink Shuttle'.* And the Japanese still live in what an EEC official once mockingly called 'rabbit hutches'. A few years after the war a businessman lived with his wife and child in one tiny room in Tokyo where they had to hang their bicycle from the ceiling over their bedspace because there was nowhere else to put it. If the spirit of competitiveness were to be encouraged, one Japanese professor warns, the herding of people together could lead to madness.

The worst human coagulation comes on the commuter trains at rush-hours. 'If pigs were crammed in this tightly,' Professor Yutaka Sasayama observes, 'they would all die within thirty minutes . . . If American or European commuters were treated in this way there would be violence.' There is a full-time occupation on the railway called *shiri-oshi* – 'bottom-pushers', men whose task it is to shove the last would-be travellers into their carriage so that the doors can close before the train departs. Once inside such trains, there can be no policing and morality visibly sinks. Groping has become an institution, and overt masturbation has been reported.

With so many people trying to run a miracle economy in such a small space, pollution is widespread. Toxic substances used to flow freely in rivers, and it was recently found that the Japanese have sixty times the hair mercury of the Germans. Fifteen years ago the police were predicting that Tokyoites would have to go to work carrying gas masks, but then anti-pollution car regulations improved things.

The tightness of land denies Japan room for growth within her borders, so that leaders sometimes talk desperately about building an entirely new island out at sea through reclamation (or by assembling an offshore steel metropolis), buying West Irian (or various Pacific islands or the American desert), or getting a UN mandate to develop New Guinea.

The land dictates the diet. Japan has never been a meat-eating country, taking fish as its staple food. Its gourmets distinguish twenty kinds of oyster. Even when western foods are introduced they tend to be Japanized – pizzas topped with squid or eel – and there are now *sushi*† takeaway chains. But rice and fish have virtually given way

---

* 'Pink' in Japanese carries a connotation of sexual titillation.
† A small piece of raw fish with cold rice and possibly seaweed or pickled ginger.

to bread and meat in Japan's post-war revolution of the dinner table. Meat overtook fish in tonnage consumed in the mid-1970s. The Japanese have greatly increased their fat, animal protein and fruit intake in the past twenty years, and eat less rice as a result. The other vital ingredients in the Japanese diet are soya beans and seaweed.

The traditional liquor is rice wine, called *sake*. James Bond got it wrong in *You Only Live Twice* when he said it should be served at 98.4° Fahrenheit, but it is served hot. Alcohol has a bigger role in Japanese life than in European, and for a good reason. An evening spent drinking together, the old saying went, yields friendship for a hundred years. What you say or do while drunk is not held against you in Japan; the whiff of alcohol might save you from a parking fine. Liquor gives legitimate release to the many emotions which Japanese have to suppress in social life. Some equate its role with that played by psychiatry in the West.

'I think we would explode without it,' says a businessman. Dr Hiroaki Kono, an expert on the matter, adds, 'We are the most permissive people in the world as regards alcohol. We consume it with abandon.' The average consumption is fifteen gallons a year. The average Japanese gets drunk once a week and schoolchildren imbibe to survive the pressure of exams. The custom goes a long way back: a Chinese historian of the third century noted, rather as contemporary Romans used to record the quirks of the savage English, that the Japanese 'loved their liquor'.

The explanation is that most Japanese have a physical make-up that luckily saves them from alcoholism. They lack two enzymes which in European bloodstreams help break the alcohol down into chemicals that can be quickly absorbed. A European can sink larger quantities of alcohol without discomfort, but when most Japanese drink, the alcohol tends to pass neat into the bloodstream. They get drunk more quickly, on a smaller intake, and are less vulnerable to becoming addicted.

The land neither feeds the people nor fills its glasses. One quarter of what the Japanese eat by weight (nearer a half by calories) has to be imported – a higher dependence on foreign supplies than any western country faces. If those imports were to stop, Japan would revert to the mass hunger of 1945, and this is therefore a powerful factor in her foreign policy.

The same goes for underground resources. Japan produces less than one-tenth of her energy needs, and three-quarters of those needs are supplied by Middle East oil. 'The Day Japan Dies for Want of Oil' was the heading of a magazine article in the 1970s, and Westerners who feel apprehensive about Japan's becoming aggressive again might ponder the fact that the stocks of oil held by Japan on the eve of Pearl Harbor in 1941 (50 million barrels) would today last only a week. An imaginative government official wrote a novel called *Yudan* (*Negligence*) fifteen years ago predicting that, if Middle East oil were cut off for six months, up to three million Japanese would die. With other minerals the story is similar: one-twentieth of the iron and half of the coal for Japanese industry have to be brought in by ship from other countries.

The climate instils in the Japanese a certain liquidity of mood. It rains three times as heavily as in Europe, but at fixed seasons, so the Japanese know the sun and the snow as well as the rain. Poets and novelists typically see their country as floating, misty, covered with soft ambiguous dampness.

> In the eyes of poets
> The whole world liquefies

says one of them, Hitoshi Anzai. The Japanese respect and admire nature, and have carried this into their modern lives more affectionately than the industrialized societies of the West. The words for rice, water and tea are given honorific prefixes, and rain is such a personality in its own right that there are more than twelve different words for it in all its moods.

From their forbidding land base the Japanese people derive a tendency towards intuitiveness, ambiguity and naturalness of emotion. The land's habit of frequently breaking up and burying everything inspires a certain fatalism, and the challenge of growing large amounts of food on tiny and difficult plots of ground has conditioned the people to co-operativeness and group consciousness rather than individualism. That is the contribution of the Japanese earth.

1

Pale Shades of Yellow
The Japanese Race

THE JAPANESE were so long protected from the hurly-burly of international conquest and migration that they think of themselves as a distinct race only when confronted by foreigners – and the first pang of such occasions is their short stature. They have to look up to almost everyone else on the planet, only five inches or so in the case of Westerners, but enough to dent their self-assurance. 'The average Japanese body', an official pamphlet warns European businessmen, 'differs from that of Westerners, so clothing for export to Japan should be modified accordingly. Specifically, arms and legs are shorter in proportion to body height, the head is larger, and feet are shorter and wider.' The average height of 17-year-olds is only 5 feet 4½ inches.

The Japanese are all too often laughed at in other countries because they appear so tiny – the Chinese unkindly called them 'Eastern Ocean dwarfs' during their recent war. When Liza Dalby, the American *geisha*, went out in Kyoto in her correct formal dress, Japanese men often took her as another Japanese man in drag, because of her height. Shuji Terayama complained in his book *Making the Rounds of America's Hells* in the 1960s that American urinals were higher than the average Japanese navel. This sensitivity to height makes short Westerners exceptionally popular. Japanese executives working in factories in South Wales disarmingly confess that one reason why they prefer it to other European locations is that the people there are 'not so tall'.

There is another difference. 'The Westerner', an American martial arts expert explains, 'is muscle-centred on the chest and arms, while the source of the Japanese athlete's strength is in his stomach, his waist and his loins . . .' *Hara*, or stomach, plays an important role in Japanese life. It is considered, among other things, a seat of intelligence and communication. Better diet since the war, especially the addition of meat, eggs, butter and milk to the menu, has put some of those missing inches on the height of the younger generation, mainly in the leg. Post-war youngsters are also more used to chairs, and cannot sit for long with their legs folded underneath them in the way their elders can for hours on end. Sports teachers report that greater height has brought with it weaker back muscles. It will be a few more decades before Japan's sensitivity over height is overcome, and by then western visitors may be spared those cramp-inducing invitations to squat on the rush-matting floor for dinner.

Besides their shortness, the Japanese can also distinguish themselves from most foreigners by skin colour. The West thinks of them as yellow-skinned, and yet Marco Polo in 1307 called the people of *Chipangu* 'white, civilized and well-favoured'. True, he had never been there, but one of the first Europeans who did visit confirmed that 'the Japanese are white, . . . not excessively pale as the northern nations but just moderately so': a few of them are white-skinned still, but the boys are teased at school as womanly.

Yet the Japanese think of themselves as yellow only when they have jaundice. If they do use a colour to describe their own skin, they commonly say 'white'. The association of white with beauty, and black with ugliness, goes far back into Japanese history. White skin is essential to feminine beauty and, as long ago as the eighth century, women at court were putting white powder and rouge on their faces – to be imitated in the twelfth century by aristocratic men as well. People made fortunes selling medicine claiming to 'turn the skin as white as the snow found on the peaks of high mountains'.

In the seventeenth century the novelist Saikaku Ihara idealized women whose skin was 'a faint pink colour'. One of the most popular heroines of the twentieth century, Naomi in Junichiro Tanizaki's novel *The Love of an Idiot*, had skin 'white to an astounding degree . . . all the exposed parts of her voluptuous body were white as the meat of an apple'. So the mass-circulation newspaper *Mainichi Shimbun* could say in its women's column in the summer of 1965: 'Blessed are those white in colour . . . How can you become a white beauty? You should be careful not to expose your skin directly to the ultra-violet rays in sunshine . . . never forget to carry a parasol . . .' Vitamin C and hydrogen peroxide packs were prescribed instead of the nightingale dung that country crones used to recommend.

In the last few years the Japanese have permitted themselves more realism. A feminine suntan is now envied because it suggests that you can afford a winter skiing holiday – and if you tan with gloves on it shows you can afford those soaring golf club fees. Young women these days distinguish between two equally attractive male types, one white-skinned and delicately featured like a *kabuki* actor, aesthetic but a little 'feminine'; the other darker-skinned, energetic, masculine, dependable and assertive. In pre-war times darker skin was associated with crude peasant features, bold lips, well-developed muscles and an extrovert personality. But today things are more egalitarian and more complex. The Japanese are now much-travelled, and begin to see themselves with different eyes as a result. A Japanese mother in the USA explains that her daughter is considered very 'white' by their compatriots. 'Looking at her face, I often say to myself how white she is. As a mother I feel happy. But when I see her among Caucasian children in a nursery school, alas, my daughter is yellow indeed.'

Another trade-mark of the Japanese is their straight black hair. Wavy hair used to be considered a mark of immorality, while red hair was supposed to mean drunkenness. On my first visit to Tokyo I was advised by my host's very charming five-year-old daughter to eat as much seaweed as possible, so that my hair would turn really black – and then I would be able to speak Japanese! A schoolboy about to emigrate with his family confessed, 'I am afraid to go to Brazil. Will my hair turn red?' But it is now sixty years since some Japanese women first began to perm their hair, and in the 1970s it became the fashion for a woman to use a little red tinting, so the old stereotypes are bending.

The single hemless eyelid, shared with the Chinese and Koreans, is another major physical feature of most Japanese; it displays an edge which looks as if it had been slit with a knife in the tightly stretched skin. Lafcadio Hearn described its beauty: 'The ball of the eye is *not* shown – the setting is totally hidden. The brown smooth skin opens quite suddenly and strangely over a moving jewel.' In most Japanese the machinery of the eye is veiled. Yet countless Japanese women have undergone operations to remove this feature, misled into believing that they have to look like Brooke Shields to attract the eligible bachelors of today's Japan.

So much for how the Japanese see themselves. They are conscious of themselves as a race, with the Hitachi company song invoking 'the honour of our people', and the Yomiuri Giants priding themselves on their 'pure-blood' baseball team (whereas rival squads take advantage of the two foreign players each is allowed to sign up). They are also sensitive to the way other races see them. One of the Japanese prisoner-of-war books about the Burma campaigns cites a British pamphlet warning Allied troops that they were about to encounter Japanese soldiers who were ugly, small-eyed, flat-nosed with projecting teeth and short bandy legs. Professor Eiichiro Ishida comments that probably all Europeans at that time 'considered the Japanese as physically repulsive'. A streak of racial masochism is suggested in the case of the young radical Japanese terrorists who massacred passengers at Tel Aviv airport in 1972: they had originally planned to mutilate their faces before committing suicide, erasing the signs of their being Japanese in the hope of becoming Arab heroes.

Physical characteristics do vary across Japan, reflecting the confluence of two distinct streams of pre-historic immigrants – taller, white-skinned, delicately-featured tribesmen from Manchuria or Korea, and more squat, better-muscled, light-brown-skinned men from Southeast Asia or the Pacific Islands. The first type of Japanese, the aristocrat of the two, may feel a distant kinship with North China, the second, more Polynesian, type with Malaysia, Indonesia or the Philippines. The two types can still be distinguished, though not always.

That is the background against which the Japanese confront the outside world and the various foreigners who come to boss, despise, enjoy, teach, convert and, increasingly, learn from them. The Japanese bring to these encounters a traditional view formed over long periods of historical isolation. 'Foreigners', says the psychologist Hiroshi Minami, 'are not only different people of different race and nationality coming from outside, but they are also people of higher status and stronger power, coming from above.' The Japanese feel shy towards foreigners, and are sometimes ready to feel inferior, certainly towards Westerners, as well.

Whites are called *gaijin*: the word means literally 'outside country people' but incorporates whiteness by association, so that the Chinese, for example, are excluded from its definition. White, symbolizing virtue and purity, was already the colour to which the Japanese aspired long before the first European landed there in the reign of Henry VIII. Because of this ancient association, a post-war Japanese student who slept with a white prostitute could find her 'pure white' skin 'somewhat incongruent with her nature'. Shusaku Endo described in his first novel his sense of physical inferiority when sleeping with a French girl. 'Besides the gleaming whiteness of her shoulders and breasts . . . my body looked dull in a lifeless dark yellow colour . . . The two different colours of our bodies in embrace did not show even a bit of beauty or harmony . . . I suddenly thought of a worm of a yellow muddy colour, clinging to a pure white flower . . .' In their proud moments Japanese intellectuals can assert themselves as the 'golden race', metallurgically superior to the 'silver' Europeans, but the reality of physical engagement has been steeped in shortcoming.

Japan's artists are perhaps more reliable on this sort of question: they endowed their first Portuguese and Dutch visitors with grey, pinkish or light brown faces, some nearly white, others darker. They exaggerated the nose, double eyelid, moustache and beard, to make their visitors larger than life, and these things, together with the Europeans' height and their red-brown hair and hairiness of body, made a far greater impression on the Japanese than their skin pigmentation. The Dutch were at first called *komojin*, or 'red-haired people'.

All kinds of scare stories ran round Japan in those very early days. The newcomers had bushy tails, no ankles (because, apparently, of their heeled shoes) and eyes like cats or monkeys. They lifted one leg to pee like dogs and were masters of sexual technique. The Dutch seamen, an astonished Japanese caller reported after an early visit on board their ship, had 'dark, sallow faces, yellow hair and green eyes. They seem to appear from nowhere, and are just like goblins or demons. Who would not run away from them in fright?' When Japan's rulers asked how 'animals' from overseas could produce such excellent manufactures and medicines, Toshiaki Honda, the eighteenth-century scholar, wryly replied that even animals were capable of surprising skills. By the nineteenth century Europeans were no longer so frightening, though they still created an aura of impurity on Japanese soil. Queen Victoria sent her second son, Prince Alfred, Duke of Edinburgh, to be the first foreign dignitary to call upon the new Emperor Meiji in the 1870s. When the Prince crossed the bridge into the Imperial Palace compound he was subjected to a purification ritual. He took the formality in good part, but an American envoy crossly commented in a report home that the ceremony showed how the Japanese regarded foreigners as a lower order of animals, below human beings.

These memories can flood back when needed, as in the Pacific War of the 1940s when Americans were called *chikusho*, or beasts. And the aesthetic judgements are not dislodged. The skin texture of most Europeans is still deplored – 'rough' in one description, 'full of wrinkles, spots and speckles'. A 1954 novel mentions how a cinema screen close-up revealed ugly freckles on a white actress's face – and gold hairs on her lover's caressing fingers 'shining like an animal's bristles'. A teacher tells his class that 'hog' means a big pig, whereupon a boy explains: 'I know, like a foreign woman!' They all laugh and agree. Yet what the Japanese associated with this ugly, hairy, animal-like European body were the very desirable properties of vitality, energy and sexuality. He would instinctively defer to what he supposed to be their greater power. A Japanese woman scholar cannot recall 'ever having read any stories, novels, essays or scholastic works from my childhood down to the present day in which white people were shown as inferior to Japanese'.

Their poise and *savoir-faire* added to their purely physical charms to render European and American girls fascinating to Japanese men. One of Japan's first envoys to the United States told the niece of President Buchanan in 1860 that he preferred American women to Japanese because 'their skin colour is whiter'. One of his colleagues was bowled over by young American girls at a ball: 'Their skin with its natural beauty was whiter than snow and purer than jewels.' He compared them with 'fairies in wonderland'. Tanizaki in *The Love of an Idiot* describes a Russian beauty as so 'extraordinary white' that the violet-coloured blood vessels under the skin were 'faintly visible like the veining of marble'. Other Japanese are more critical. One says that what he can see in a European is 'the whiteness of the fat under the skin, not the whitness of the skin itself . . .'

When the French sent the Venus de Milo for exhibition in Japan in 1964, some 1,750,000 Japanese (a world record) came to worship. Shusaku Endo had already written: 'I do not know why and how the standard of human beauty . . . stemmed from the white body of the Greeks and has been so maintained until today. But what I am sure of is that in respect of the body, those like myself . . . can never forget miserable inferiority feelings in front of people possessing white skin, however vexing it might be to admit it.'

Another sign of this racial obeisance is the fact that cars cannot apparently be sold without the presence of a Hollywood star. It seems that seeing a smart and sexy European caressing a watch, tape-recorder or glass of whisky makes a Japanese feel envious – and that is how to sell a product. The logical conclusion has already been capitalized upon by the British firm Display Club of Vauxhall, which is supplying mannequin models of Caucasian dimensions to Japan under a £3 million licensing agreement. A similar phenomenon is the popularity of magazines with English titles – *More, Big Tomorrow, President, Will* (the names themselves suggest the underlying psychology). Finally, an endearing survival of the good reputation of some early European visitors is the fact that doctors pioneering new methods and establishing better communications with patients are known as 'Redbeards' after the Dutch doctors who were so influential from the late sixteenth century in helping to modernize Japan's medical care.

With some, the sense of inferiority runs deep. A Japanese commentator on the Russo-Japanese war of 1904–5 praised the chivalrous conduct of Japanese soldiers as proving they had 'white hearts under a yellow skin'. Another Japanese more recently confessed to the feeling that 'the white skin of the Caucasian tells me that after all I am an oriental and cannot acquire everything western, however westernized I might be. It is the last border I cannot go across . . .

symbolized by the white skin.' On a highly practical plane, a 1977 discussion about overseas investment in the monthly magazine *Bungei Shunju* refers to the fear in some Japanese minds that 'orientals are bound to run into trouble if they try to employ whites'. According to opinion surveys over half of the Japanese regard their own race as inferior to western races.

Back in the real world, the Japanese are thus baffled, feeling disadvantaged before Europeans in one way, contemptuous in another. 'They are basically different beings,' a Japanese complains. 'There is . . . a definite discontinuity between us and the Caucasians.' When there is a close encounter, as in the prison camps and battle-fields of the Second World War, or its aftermath, ambiguity remains. Michio Takeyama's novel *Harp of Burma* (beautifully filmed by Kon Ichikawa) showed the British as more humane than the Japanese. Yuji Aida in *The Ahlone Camp* conceded he was neither beaten nor kicked by his British captors in Burma, but instead they did worse, they never treated the Japanese as human – 'British soldiers never spoke to us, they only ordered us about by pointing with their chins or feet; they thought nothing of feeding us with the same rice that was used for the livestock; British women thought nothing of being completely naked in front of young Japanese prisoners . . .'

Sex is one kind of contact with Westerners of which the Japanese thoroughly approve. One who enjoyed Russian prostitutes in Manchuria in the 1920s recalled the feeling as 'different from what one has with an Asian woman'. Sex with a white woman made his comrades feel 'more masculine'. It was not all smooth sailing. Taijiro Tamura describes in a novel a meeting with a Russian prostitute in China before the war: 'When I sat next to her, the volume and weight of her whole body made me . . . think that I was a race physic-ally smaller and weaker . . .' Dancing alarmed him: 'Her chest was . . . too broad. It did not belong to the category of chest that I had known from Japanese women. It . . . wriggled in an uncanny way.'

But the obsession with white skin continues. Hundreds of young European and American girls are tempted into club entertainment contracts leading to prostitution, in a recruitment operation 'as close to white slavery as you'll ever get,' in the words of an American detective. Issei Sagawa actually shot his Dutch girlfriend in his Paris flat in 1981 and ate her, piece by piece (the author sent to write the story for fascinated Japanese readers observed that he was not especially shocked to learn of Sagawa's deed but 'more interested to know what it felt like and what parts of the body he had eaten').

Marriage was not so popular as an entrée to the western world. A hundred years ago thinkers like Arinori Mori and Yukichi Fukuzawa urged Japanese students abroad to marry Caucasians in order to 'improve' the Japanese race. Many did so, but with results that were not always happy. White men, said Endo in his novel *Up To Aden*, would allow him to 'wear their clothes, drink their wine, love a white woman', but 'they could not accept that a white woman loved me'. Perhaps that was one of the rationales of Herbert Spencer, the British social Darwinist who advised the Japanese government in 1892 that, among other things, 'the intermarriage of foreigners and Japanese . . . should be positively forbidden'. The Meiji authorities did not need to go so far. In Ogai Mori's novel *Maihime*, published in 1890, the hero gave up his German mistress, a beautiful dancer, in order to return home and take up a promising conventional career: the love-sick girl followed him to Japan in the hope of marrying him, was snubbed by his family and went mad. Such attitudes were representative.

'The Japanese . . .' wrote a British resident before the war, 'were as unalterably opposed to, and as ultimately contemptuous of, a mixed marriage as the most fanatical Anglo-Saxon.' A Japanese is happy to have an affair with a European girl, but becomes upset if his sister wants to marry a white man. A young Dutch woman living in Japan tries to rent a house with her Japanese boy-friend, only to meet animosity and the tired refrain, 'Full up.'

The real victims of prejudice against marriage with Westerners are often their progeny. 'My children look foreign although their mother is Japanese,' remarks a former Jesuit missionary. 'Sometimes other children call them names and mistreat them.' Lafcadio Hearn feared for the acceptability in Japan of his son, who was 'everything I would wish – except one thing. After all, he is going to be fair-haired and fair-eyed and not much like a Japanese.' At this level the racial prejudices of the Japanese can be cruel indeed.

If justification were needed, there is plenty of ill-informed prejudice on the part of Europeans and Americans to be reciprocated. Congressman John D. Dingell, Democratic Representative for Michigan and effectively for the automobile industry of Detroit, beleagured by Japanese competition, once referred to the Japanese in a closed-door discussion as 'little yellow people'. Challenged by his fellow-Democrat from California, Congressman Norman Mineta (of Japanese origin), Dingell could only raise the lame comment: 'Well, I wasn't talking about you, Norm.'

Europe has been just as hurtful. Soseki Natsume, one of the great novelists of his day, was quite dejected in his Camberwell digs in

London in 1901–2, 'living a miserable life among British gentlemen like a shaggy dog among wolves'. The English way of freezing someone who does not fit was most effective with the over-sensitive Soseki: 'I feel very sorry, you British gentlemen, for walking around Westminster like a beggar . . .' At about the same time, a Japanese philosopher studying in Kiel suffered from the wave of anti-Chinese feeling in Germany and Kaiser Wilhelm II's apocalyptic warnings about the Yellow Peril: 'They hate . . . the yellow race. When we walk in the street, children throw stones at us and shout abuse.' Even Hitler, their ally for a few years, called the Japanese 'little yellow Aryans'.

'Jap', a harmless abbreviation in itself, was a monosyllable into which British wartime newsreel commentators could pack a payload of contemptuous hatred, and that is the context in which the Japanese learned to resent it. When the *Guardian* recently introduced a story about the market in twenty-year-old British motorbikes with the phrase: 'Now you can indulge your nostalgia for the Jap-free '60s', it could legitimately be accused of raking up wartime memories to make a point about a current trading dispute.

A special case in Japan's attitude to other races concerns the Jews, whom many Japanese admired. Some 17,000 Jewish refugees from Germany were allowed to settle in Japanese-occupied Shanghai between 1938 and 1941, and there were senior Japanese officers who hoped to harness their power and wealth to the Greater East Asia Co-Prosperity Sphere. It had been a Jew, Jacob Schiff, appalled by the Tsar's repression of Russian Jews, who lent money for Japan's war against Russia in 1904–5 when other western bankers were still sceptical about Japan's viability. Something about the Jews' long history of being rejected and persecuted, their sense of uniqueness and their drive to achieve things, attracts some Japanese to the extent of identification. A huge impact was made on the reading public a decade ago by a book called *The Japanese and the Jews* where Isaiah Ben-Dasan compared Auschwitz with Hiroshima and admired the trusting humanity of the Japanese. Actually, it is a Japanese writer who lurks behind this Jewish pseudonym, finding it effective to pretend that his criticisms and recommendations about Japan come from another race that has succeeded in influencing the whole world without losing its distinctive way of life.

No such impact would be made by using an African pseudonym. It is sad how the Japanese have inherited the same stereotyping about black being bad, and white good, as the Europeans. In comic books for girls, the Japanese villainess will shed her devil's tail and evil heart at the end of the story, exchanging her black locks for golden

hair in order to enter heaven. Blacks have exercised a morbid
fascination for the Japanese, ever since a sixteenth-century Portuguese found his Negro drummer attracting all eyes, and the Jesuits in
Kyoto had their door broken down by eager Japanese wanting to see
their black slave. (The Shogun summoned him and made him strip to
see if the colour was genuine.)

An eighteenth-century Japanese writer said that blacks became so
by the scorching of the sun, describing them as stupid, flat-nosed,
'uncivilized and vicious'. Yet it is an oddity of history that the historic
first letters from an American President to the Emperor of Japan
were for some reason of US protocol physically handed to Prince
Toda in 1853 not by Commodore Perry, commander of the 'black
ships' which ended Japan's 200-year isolation, but by two tall and
well-armed black American sailors, 'the best looking fellows of their
colour that the squadron could furnish . . .'

Seven years later the first Japanese mission to the West called on
the African coast on the way home and found the blacks looking 'like
devils', with the 'physiognomy . . . of a monkey'. There is little
change: a Japanese in post-war America admits to a 'biological
repulsion' to the presence of blacks. One writer describes the body of
a black GI as 'cylindrical, like a monkey's', another comments: 'Only
the close-trimmed beard appeared civilized.' Surveys show blacks as
the second most disliked kind of foreigner in Japan, after Koreans. In
an essay called 'We Cannot Marry Negroes', Taisuke Fujishima
recalls the 'sickening body odour at Nairobi airport' and suggests that
racial discrimination is triggered by 'the physiological repulsion
caused by this striking odour'.

In Kenzaburo Oe's short story *The Catch*, a black US airman is
captured in wartime by villagers. One of them, observing his reactions, remarks: 'He's just like a human!' Some local boys take him
for a bathe in the spring:

> Suddenly we noticed that the Negro had a splendid, a heroic, an
> unbelievably beautiful phallus. We gathered around him clamour-
> ing, bumping our naked bodies against each other, and when he
> grasped it, and, taking up a fierce threatening stance, gave a great
> bellow, we dashed water on him and laughed until the tears ran
> down our cheeks.

Blacks like that, full of vitality, can prompt misgivings about the
Japanese physique. The boy befriending the captured airman catches
sight of himself in a mirror, with 'pallid bloodless lips, an utter
nonentity of a boy' by comparison with the magnificent black. (It is
reported, incidentally that an American condom manufacturer used

to make smaller ones for the Japanese than for anyone else in the world.)

Genuine fellow-feeling does inform the Japanese attitude to blacks from time to time. The first *Nisei** or Japanese American was the son of a Japanese gold-digger who married a black girl in Sacramento in the 1870s. *Not Because of Colour* by Sawako Ariyoshi depicts a Japanese woman married to a black American in Harlem. 'Living long enough among the Negroes,' the heroine muses, 'one comes to realise how human their faces are, . . . how gentle.' But the children of such romances may be found upsetting. When Ariyoshi's heroine takes her half-yellow, half-black daughter to visit other Japanese, they exclaim: 'Indeed it is black, even when it is young,' or 'She must have taken only after her father. So black. Poor thing.' Some old-fashioned Japanese even believe that such a baby 'blackens' the womb, so that the mother's later babies would be 'stained' even if fathered by Japanese.

The most shocking story is the fate of the hundreds of half-black Occupation 'orphans' left behind in Japan by American forces. Nobody wanted to know about the problems and needs of these sad children, whose mothers were often unable to care for them properly. Nobody, that is, until Mrs Miki Sawada, an enlightened and compassionate Christian, opened a home for them. She fought valiantly for their welfare, but, as a former Japanese ambassador concedes, 'there were absolutely no openings for them in race-conscious Japan' (save as entertainers or sportsmen). Nor in the US, for that matter, and most of these unwanted people are now living in Brazil, one of the few countries where yellow and black are both good colours, where Mrs Sawada bought land for them.

In the real arena of contemporary world politics the rivals to the Japanese are the whites, and in seeking out the weak points of the whites the Japanese can make common cause with blacks. A Japanese who travelled in the US, an Oxford graduate, was assured by his Pullman porter before the war that 'all the Negroes in the South will revolt' and join Japan when it declared war on the US. Black leaders in New York say that Japan did offer arms to them in the 1930s. But a post-war observer wonders whether Japan's 'surface concern for the Negro conceals concern for the Japanese himself, concern lest he too be numbered among the inferior races'.

---

* *Nisei* means 'second generation', and in strict correctness one should say '*sansei*' for a third-generation Japanese American, and so forth. But in practice *Nisei* seems to be used by Americans generally as a term for all Japanese Americans.

These attitudes to blacks are muted now. The government and corporations conduct a vast programme of aid, trade and investment in black Africa. The latest fad among *avant-garde* Tokyo girls is to date black GI's in the discos, paying all the expenses to enjoy, as one GI puts it, 'our skins, our beautiful bodies . . . and our long history of slavery, which appeals to the Japanese taste for sentimentality'. But Japanese sometimes warn their close European or American friends about the dangers of letting blacks take over their cities, factories and commercial enterprises, with the consequence of lowered standards. Such Japanese cannot understand why Britain in particular has been so liberal in allowing black immigration, and they believe the British will soon pay a heavy price for this.

From all this it must be clear that the Japanese do not readily accept the 750,000 or so foreigners (less than 1% of the total population) who live permanently in their country. The oldest colony of non-Japanese are the aboriginal Ainus in the north, apparently Caucasian and called by anthropologists the hairiest people in the world. But they are so few after centuries of intermarriage that their survival as a separate race and culture is in doubt.

Next come the 50,000 Chinese. They are not descended from the mediaeval immigrants who brought learning and technology, because those became Japanized and only certain surnames like Hata (the silk-maker) may remind the present generation of their origins. Those who now regard themselves as Chinese came, like the Koreans, when Taiwan and Korea were colonies of Japan in the first half of this century. Today they are thinly scattered, the older generation running restaurants, laundries, saunas and pinball parlours, though many are active in the import-export trade. The younger ones seek to enter business and the professions. Public opinion surveys show that Japanese feel friendly towards China as a country, but prefer to have Europeans or Americans as individual guests in their homes.

At the bottom of the heap stand the 650,000 Koreans, unreasonably disliked and blamed for everything, from wartime atrocities to contraband, tax evasion, cadging from public relief funds and general lawlessness today. 'The wall of prejudice against Koreans,' a Japanese writer admits, 'is thick, high and formidable.' An American living in Japan reckons it 'makes the black-white thing in America look like kindergarten'. Today, a Japanese confides, a father who might accept a western son-in-law would move heaven and earth to prevent his daughter marrying a Korean. Can a Japanese tell a Korean by sight or speech? The story of Kim Kyong-dok provides the answer. 'When I was young,' wrote Kim in a petition to the Supreme

Court in the 1970s, 'I struggled to erase all traces of Korean-ness from my personality. By the time I finished university, behaving like a Japanese was second nature. However the charade of playing Japanese in order to avoid discrimination took its toll, exacted in much agony and suffering.' In the end, weary of the constant anxiety over being found out, Kim 'came out'. He refused the last hurdle, that of naturalization in order to practise law, and persuaded the Court to let him keep his Korean citizenship.

Westerners also suffer discrimination when they live in Japan, though they mostly have the status for that not to matter so much. They are not accepted as full members of society, and most live alongside their own kind in certain cosmopolitan districts of Tokyo, Yokohama or Kobe. But that is largely because they do not learn Japanese in the way that almost every foreigner in Britain would learn English. The few who do learn Japanese have wider options, and could easily fall in love with the country. Lafcadio Hearn took not only Japanese citizenship but his wife's family name during a period of teaching and writing from 1890 to 1904.

Gifted or assiduous Westerners like Hearn are still treated kindly, but not assimilated into Japanese life. They are always honourable guests. That is a kind of discrimination; it is not how most other countries treat foreigners willing to 'go native' in speech, dress and custom, and the few Westerners concerned feel rightly frustrated. 'I have lived in Japan for twenty years,' one explains. 'I have married a Japanese lady. I speak Japanese. I eat Japanese food . . . But no matter how doggedly I try . . . I cannot hope for the Japanese people to treat me as a Japanese.' Another, a German, says after fifty years in Japan, 'my face does not fit'. The status of a person as a foreigner overrides whatever individual impression he may succeed in making as someone you could in fact relax with, forgetting about his origin.

Sadly, those entitled to lodge this complaint are very few. The language is difficult and so are the almost telepathic means of communicating feelings without words, by look and body language, and by all kinds of noises like sucking in the breath and those 'Ahs' and 'Ohs' with which Japanese pepper their conversation. 'Only a handful' of Westerners, an official report recently noted, can be said to have mastered the language. If you ask a Japanese intellectual to name the Westerners who can speak Japanese 'like a native', as well as any Japanese can, he may start with two or three foreign professors at Sophia University (the Christian university) but then run dry.

Immigration is more tightly restricted than in any other industrial country. Apart from businessmen, it was rare, until very recently, for foreigners to be allowed to work in Japan. Artistic and intellectual circles are largely closed to them save in a few isolated institutions like Sophia University. Even when full employment loomed in the 1970s, there was no relenting, except for the employment of Koreans and Southeast Asians on Japanese ships. Outstanding foreigners are regularly recruited by the richer football and baseball clubs, but now that two successive Americans (one Hawaiian, one Samoan) have come to dominate *sumo*, the peculiarly Japanese form of heavy-weight wrestling, there are murmurings of dissent. The Samoan had his likeness in straw nailed to trees at midnight in a Shinto shrine (a traditional curse), and a *sumo* writer warned that 'foreigners with black hair are tolerable, but . . . blond topknots and blue eyes would be resisted'.

When riots struck Britain and France in the 1970s, sparked by unemployment and immigrant labour, the Japanese congratulated themselves on their foresight. They had 'never thought of giving the dirty jobs to members of another race,' boasts Professor Kanji Nishio of the University of Electro-Communications, preferring instead to 'let robots have them.' Nor will Japan have much truck with that *in*voluntary immigrant, the refugee. Europe can treat Indochinese boat people as special cases of immigration, for which a framework already exists. In Japan foreign labour is taboo, so each refugee case has to be debated on its merits. Harassed Foreign Ministry officials explaining to the outside world why Japan can absorb only a fifth of the refugees Germany has agreed to take – one twentieth of France's quota, less than one per cent of America's – fall back on desperate arguments. Japan is not a territorial state like the European coun-tries, they say, but historically racially-based. The government can get jobs for refugees but cannot settle them into the community. It is a policy, the former Ministry of International Trade and Industry (MITI) Vice-Minister Naohiro Amaya glumly admits, 'lacking in humanism'.

Will it change? Minor rationalizations can be imposed on this provincial attitude by a government uncomfortably mediating west-ern demands that Japan behave more like other countries. But from below it looks entrenched, with contradictory trends visible. On the one hand, the Japanese have more exposure to foreigners than before. The young in particular are shedding the old sense of inferior-ity and discomfort and are much more at ease with outsiders. Yet the opinion polls display another face, that two in three Japanese do not want any dealings with foreigners, and two in five would veto their brother, sister or child marrying one. When they *have* to socialize with a foreigner they can do it better than before, but they would still prefer everyone to leave them alone, thank you.

So where does modern Japan fit in the racial atlas of today? It seeks on the world stage what its individual citizens search for in their own society: a group to join. It went first for the western club, and still remembers the Anglo-Japanese Alliance of 1902 long after most Britons have forgotten all about it. That was spoiled by the victors of World War I, who rebuffed Japan's request for a racial equality clause in the peace treaty. America's refusal to accept larger Japanese naval power in the Pacific advertized that the Anglo-Saxons were not going to give up their old privileges over newcomers, and so Japan turned to the only other available club, namely Asia – fighting her way in to secure her membership.

Today the Japanese realize that their behaviour in the China and Pacific Wars made more enemies than friends in spite of having made it difficult for the European colonialists to get their empires back afterwards. The idea of being 'Asian' in a world run by whites still pleases, as it did the schoolchildren who wrote letters to the press protesting against the American war in Vietnam. 'I cannot bear to watch the sufferings of fellow-Asians,' said one. But for the past forty years the Japanese have enjoyed what they had really wanted all along, and what suits them, namely a close alliance with the USA.

Intellectuals may fight it: Kenzaburo Oe, the novelist, mocks the tendency of the Japanese to 'submit to mastery by the Westerner with smiles and shouts of *hello* while he maliciously snubs his oriental brothers'. But the fact is that fellow-Asians, certainly the darker-skinned like the Indians or Malays, are as strange to the Japanese of today as Westerners are. With the Chinese he shares some ideo-graphs and ancient cultural influence, but they still seem to him unmodern, unsmart and poverty-stricken. Westerners are unpredict-able, brash and extraordinarily ignorant about Japan, but at least they can be talked to in the language of modern consumer society – about sport, popular art, business and technology. The alien-ness may be about equal. After all, Fukuzawa in 1865 had seen his countrymen as honorary whites, at one and the same time Asian and Western.

Europe has been correspondingly puzzled about the niche of the Japanese in its racial scheme of things. Raffles in 1812 declared them 'much nearer to Europeans than to Asiatics,' but Kipling could not place them so surely. 'The Jap,' he complained on his first visit, 'isn't a native, and he isn't a *Sahib* either.'

It is all very difficult for Japan. An Englishman touring Japan on his own does not come to doubt his very English-ness, but a Japanese alone in a foreign country can often feel depressed, ineffectual and unsure of his identity, needing to confirm that identity by mixing with other Japanese.

That the Japanese can over two or three generations assimilate into other cultures and nations is proved by Senator Daniel Inouye of Hawaii, Sessuo Hayakama, the argumentative California judge, Kazuo Ishiguro the British novelist, and the tens of thousands of other descendants of immigrants into America and Europe. The first generation immigrant is amazed by the ease with which his child or grandchild can discard not only the language but also the gait, customs and culture of the homeland. Such people are sometimes a source of pride to the Japanese, but more often they are despised in the spirit of Kanzo Uchimura, the Christian leader, who grumbled that 'a Japanese who becomes an American or an Englishman, or an amorphous universal man, is neither a true Japanese nor a true Christian'.

Many Japanese Americans and other Westerners would concur. The Japanese as a race were 'totally unassimilable into Western culture', the *San Francisco Chronicle* proclaimed in 1905, and the reason why the futurologist Herman Kahn qualified his original prediction about the twenty-first century's being Japan's century was a question-mark over the exportability of Japanese culture.

There are plenty of Japanese who believe that they can never enjoy a meaningful talk with a foreigner even if the language gap is bridged. Chie Nakane, Japan's leading sociologist, goes further in saying that the overly self-conscious view of society in Japan, in which foreigners are always at arm's length, constitutes a 'barrier to Japanese internationalization'.

The Japanese race is not unique. It shares many physical features with neighbouring Asian countries from which its ancestors set out millennia ago to emigrate. But it was sheltered from subsequent invasion and has developed a unique culture, so that a kind of homogeneity has formed which now proves almost impervious to external change, at least in essentials. It is more a case, perhaps, of 'yellow hearts under a white skin'.

For a long time it will not be as easy for other major countries to work with Japan as to collaborate with each other. Of all people in the world the Japanese are about the most difficult for an outsider to get to know. Those ready to take on the challenge stand to win the closest and most loyal friendships that could be imagined. Those who lack the time or the incentive must wait until the slow processes of social change eventually achieve a greater autonomy for the Japanese individual.

2

Drive a Nail of Gold
The Japanese Individual

A MEDIAEVAL head of the Mori family summoned his three sons to his death-bed. Taking an arrow out of a quiver, he broke it in half before them. Then he had three arrows bound together and invited each son in turn to break them. They could not do it. The message of family unity did not need to be spoken. Every Japanese knows the story and has its lesson imprinted in his heart.

To most Japanese it is more comforting to stick together with family, friends and workmates than to chase after a vulnerable individuality. Europeans and Japanese both compromise between self and society, but the European balance tilts towards the self, the Japanese towards society. At the cost of being less assertive than his European counterpart, a typical Japanese gains more organized help from others in attaining goals which he shares with them. He also moves within society by particular empirical rules rather than the universal principles which the European would apply to all comers.

It is the squeaky wheel which gets the grease, an American would say. But one of the commonest Japanese sayings is that a nail which sticks up gets hammered down. Inconspicuousness is a virtue. When a Japanese walked into an American university politics class, to find the professor firing questions and students firing back, he was shocked. 'I had never experienced debate. I felt sick . . . I thought how ill-mannered American students must be, and how terribly disrespectful they were towards their professors.' Debate is thus an early victim of Japanese conformity. If a group of businessmen or engineers goes to visit a company in the West and one of the younger ones asks a lot of questions, instead of being commended afterwards for his initiative, he will be rebuked by his seniors for being opinionated, presumptuous, exhibitionist, conceited and a general pain in the neck.

This traditional system is today under attack, however. Japan has been modernizing herself, though not in the same way as Europe, for the past three centuries, leaving individuals more scope for self-expression than before. Western influence has also been at work, superficially in the first century of contact that ended in 1639, intermittently during the following two centuries when Japan kept the world out, and in a flood after 1853 when Perry's 'black ships' brought that seclusion to an end. The fundamental relation between individual and society is now slowly changing, leaving some people awkwardly caught between a sometimes suffocating tradition and a 'modernity' which can make them feel lonely.

A Japanese needs to be seen in double focus, therefore, if a foreigner is to understand him – in both his traditional and modern aspect. Neither alone gives a complete guide to his behaviour, but both are necessary for an outsider to interpret him. Take first the old-fashioned half of the picture.

The traditional Japanese individual seeks the companionship of the small group, not just for play but for the serious goals of life as well. The physical man whose animal parts the modern European system fails to nourish is thus well satisfied, though less expression is available for the intellect or imagination, for creativity and individuality. To oversimplify, the Japanese feel that an individualistic society based on competition and merit is too painful for all concerned. If you openly challenge others and lose, you ask for humiliation: why not close your eyes to the incompetence of other people, and give them the benefit of the doubt, instead of painstakingly evaluating and distinguishing between them? Why publicize the differences between people, when you can perfectly well preserve the fiction that they are all the same? How can you stop individualism degenerating into selfish arrogance?

A Kyoto psychiatrist, Dr Keigo Okonogi, argues that by recognizing each other generously on equal terms, the Japanese form a maternalistic society to be contrasted with the father-ruled West. Mother loves all her brood equally, regardless of ability; father wants to know who is the brightest. Mummy has become the saviour of the modern Japanese family, taking over Daddy's role since he is out at work all day and every evening, and too tired at the weekend to assert his authority. A lawyer specializing in family conciliation finds that more men are becoming 'abnormally' attached to their mothers, especially the over-protected only son who telephones Mummy for guidance and encouragement even from his honeymoon hotel.

A maternal society forgives its citizens, a paternal one punishes them. When a Japan Air Lines 'plane was hijacked a few years ago, a middle-aged Japanese woman hostage expressed sympathy for the young Japanese who were responsible. 'Shouldn't we just forgive them?' The press supported her: why not welcome future hijackers home and forgive them in the traditional Japanese way? 'In a maternal society,' says Dr Okonogi, 'one mustn't kill anyone, and maintaining human life has an absolute value. In the case of a 'paternal' society like West Germany's, one starts with the question "What is right?".' In a mother's world, you do not have to compete with your betters, and if you do anything wrong you will be forgiven. 'I am sorry' is the trump card for leading a trouble-free life. To a Westerner, apologizing so quickly without serious appraisal of the wrong you have done or the need to make it good may sound insincere or slapdash.

The closeness to mother may explain why psychoanalysis plays such a minor role in Japan. When Dr Heisaku Kosawa introduced this new practice many years ago, he alarmed his patients' relatives by appearing to boost their sense of individualism. It seems that his successors learnt the lesson: Japanese psychiatrists are now criticized by western colleagues for the opposite tendency, for actually tightening their patients' bonds and reinforcing their sense of belonging to their group. Even when frustrated, the Japanese do not like to cut their ties to their families. Psychoanalysis has few devotees. The borderline between the conscious and unconscious is in any case blurred. The unconscious hovers near the surface to play a bigger role than in Europe in everyday life, which once prompted a Frenchman to conclude that, 'no one whose [richly associational] language is Japanese needs to be psychoanalysed'.

The old-fashioned Japanese sees himself not as standing alone in the world, but as a member of a little club of other individuals who reflect his self back to him, a club whose pooled efforts can more successfully realize the shared goals of all the members. His personality can be absorbed in such groups. He knows that he cannot live alone, and having a small network of intense, trusting relationships is one sure way of getting his human needs sensitively met – even if the price is giving some of himself back to meeting those other needs reciprocally.

These are not those casual detached acquaintanceships which Westerners go for, but emotional compacts of total dependability, more akin to Chinese or Malay friendships. A Japanese instinctively gives them priority. 'I think of my community or family, parents, company or group,' a businessman explains, 'before speaking to outsiders, and I will stop speaking out if it may harm my group, even if I know it is true.' It is not so much that the individual is suppressed within his group, but rather that he can use it as a more effective framework within which to achieve his own ends. Naturally, once you have surrendered your individual autonomy in order to achieve your goals in this way, it is difficult to retreat. The group becomes addictive.

This traditional system could appear highly civilized to European visitors who saw it in its prime. Lafcadio Hearn, who took a Japanese wife and gently subsided into provincial Japanese life, was delighted to be among people not constantly striving to expand their own individuality at the expense of others. 'I . . . must confess that the very absence of the individuality essentially characteristic of the Occident is one of the charms of Japanese social life . . .' But the cost of all this was the frequent stifling of the individual, the cult of conformity and the emergence of what a leading newspaper could recently call 'a society of human alienation'.

At another level, conformism leads the Japanese into orgies of fads, crazes, fashions and bandwagons, usually very ephemeral but on a mass scale. It is partly a matter of 'keeping up with the Kono's', by buying your colour TV aerial first, for instance, before the TV set itself, to impress the neighbours. A literary critic notes the Japanese feeling that 'acting differently from others is unwise. There is a just-like-everybody-else way of thinking.' The compulsion for Vuitton handbags and Gucci shoes is carried further than in the West, and the sacrifice of more important priorities in order to appear in the latest socially required activity, whether it be motoring or golfing or foreign holidays, exceeds the Western practice.

A scholar of the Shogunate warned in 1825:

> The weakness of some for novel gadgets and rare medicines, which delight the eye and enthrall the heart, have led many to admire foreign ways. If some day the treacherous foreigner should take advantage . . . and lure ignorant people to his ways, our people will adopt such practices as eating dogs and sheep and wearing woollen clothing . . .

When Europeans did arrive to influence Japan in earnest in the 1870s, there were so many things to undertake, and the Japanese solemnly took them up one by one and *en masse*. In 1873 it was rabbits, in the following year cock-fighting. Later successive national crazes were for subscription editions of dictionaries, boating on the river, velocipedes, whist, waltzing, mesmerism and planchette, wrestling, joint stock companies – and so the list could go on to the 1980s.

The Japanese, in his old-fashioned persona, takes it for granted that people need each other, and goes on from there to cultivate the art of successful dependence, or how to remain individual while indulging the craving to be looked after. To that end the jolly naturalness which his ancestors used to have, and which is now revealed only at certain times and occasions, had to be tamed.

Zen Buddhist priests used to teach what Yoshisaburo Okakura

described in *The Japanese Spirit* as 'the self-control that enables us not to betray our inner feelings through a change in our expression, the measured steps with which we are taught to walk into the hideous jaws of death . . .' What began perhaps as a religious luxury became a political necessity in the seventeenth and eighteenth centuries, when the *shoguns* consolidated their power and public order by an almost inhuman policing system in which thousands of people were paid to inform on the misdeeds of their colleagues.

The first rule in this elaborate game of selective suppression is to keep quiet. The Japanese admire a man who senses what others are thinking or wishing, without uttering a word himself; who avoids hurting others' feelings by blurting out the answer to a question prematurely; and who remains ambiguous if he cannot give a favourable answer, in the hope that the other person will understand his true meaning without his having to use the blunt and hurtful western 'no'. As John Morris noted in *The Phoenix Cup*, the Japanese habit of not saying exactly what you mean 'is not done with intent to deceive; it is largely a question of good manners – a method of sparing a man's feelings'. Indeed, one ingenious scholar wrote a paper on 'Sixteen Ways to Avoid Saying "No"'.

This has repercussions throughout society and the economy. It means that if you ask a friend or neighbour to sign a petition, they will often do so even if they disagree with your purpose. No one likes to spoil the atmosphere, and there is a tacit understanding that you may interpret signing merely as a proof that you have seen the petition. The same kind of make-believe goes on in offices about documents needing to be stamped with the seals of executives. In other words, it is nicer to say what other people are expecting or wanting you to say than to come out with what you actually mean. It is the same thing with saying sorry and accepting responsibility for mistakes. When you are late at the office, you do not explain how the 8.25 train was held up by a cloudburst, you merely express your deepest regret in the hope of forgiveness – just as a manufacturer will not evade responsibility for delay by blaming the late delivery of components from other firms.

The heavy suppression of feeling provides a rich source of misunderstanding with Europeans, who find the bland exterior of the Japanese hiding his emotions insincere. The Japanese themselves read body language and are usually aware of the other person's underlying attitude, whatever his face may appear to show, and so their need for sincerity is quite differently handled. Europe equates sincerity with spontaneity, Japan gives the two feelings different fields of play.

Europeans and Japanese both repress their emotions, of course, that being a necessary part of life in a sophisticated society. Indeed, the basic emotions – grief, joy, fear – are more successfully hidden behind the stiff upper lips of the English than on the 'wet' features of the Japanese, whose faces all too often give them away in spite of the myth of 'inscrutability'. What can go wrong are the subtle signalling systems about intentions, which are sufficiently different to mislead.

Stratagems for preserving other people's self-respect are inculcated young. Yukichi Fukuzawa, Japan's most famous teacher, never forgot the impact which a school book had made on him urging him never to 'show joy or anger in the face'. A Japanese who misses his train will often grin, instead of scowling. His face, a Japanese writer explains, is normally without expression. All ill-bred emotions are held back behind the surface. But the strain of keeping your face like that needs to be relieved occasionally, when no one else is looking, for example, or perhaps when something unexpected happens and you are momentarily taken aback. At such times you may *appear* to smile, but a Westerner might misread the signal. The Japanese smile certainly succeeded with Hearn when his horse-drawn carriage was struck by another and his horse injured. Hearn angrily hit the offending other driver, a Japanese, with the butt of his whip. 'He looked right into my face and smiled, and then bowed. I can see that smile now. I felt as if I had been knocked down. The smile utterly nonplussed me – killed all my anger instantly.'

One sanctuary for the uninhibited self is drunkenness. No one is held responsible for his actions while under the influence of liquor, as a cursory look at the Tokyo Ginza scene late at night would confirm. A scholar from the time of the *shoguns* is remembered for his *bon mot* that slander and liquor make delicious companions; drinking can lower the mask and is deliberately used to get closer to colleagues, customers and clients, or as a safety valve for pent-up irritation with bosses and other superiors.

What it comes to is that you speak your mind (*honne*) to your real buddies but hold back to strangers (*tatemae*). The individual who submits to this traditional system has to be intuitive, unjudging and sensitive to the feelings of others. Is there perhaps a feminine quality to such an individual? The word is not mine, but that of the psychologist Ohtski, who finds the Japanese lacking in masculine attributes, quintessentially feminine.

The traditional system creates stress, and the private self, driven further back behind the surface, can become compressed to explosion point. When aggression does happen, it comes not on the low-level widespread scale of Europe, but spectacularly and quite beyond any social rules. After all, there is no designated escape in a conforming society, no way out. The possibility of going into exile, for example, does not suggest itself to most Japanese. There were only two notable political exiles during the Pacific War, Sanzo Nosaka in China and Ikuo Oyama in America.

Suicide, which has a respected place in the Japanese tradition, is one acceptable escape. Yukio Mishima's sensational disembowelment (*seppuku*) in 1970 was perhaps the last example of a man performing this particular ritual to score a social point as well as resolve his internal conflicts. Was he insane? Was it the act of a disconsolate homosexual lover? Was it perhaps sheer exuberant exhibitionism? Or did Mishima wish to warn Japan to be more patriotic, more careful of its heritage?

'He must have gone mad,' the Prime Minister commented, reflecting the general disapproval. One newspaper, *Mainichi Shimbun*, called it 'an impermissible act of violence', while another newspaper feared that foreigners would be confirmed in their suspicion that 'innate Japanese savagery and primitiveness' was ineradicable. Yet Mishima was only following, though in a more dramatic mode, a distinguished line of literary geniuses who committed suicide at the height of their careers – including some of the greatest authors of the past century, Ryunosuke Akutagawa and Osamu Dazai – and the Nobel Prizewinner Yasunari Kawabata was treading on his heels.

A safety engineer committed suicide after a mine accident in which several men were killed. Yet the record showed that he had repeatedly warned the owners about the dangers. There is a novel in which the heroine almost sets her house on fire by accident, and reflects that if it had spread to neighbouring houses she would have had to commit suicide by way of apology. One can hear the apologetic tone, too, in the note which the marathon runner Tsuburaya left after his suicide: 'I can't run any more.'

The most famous suicides are those whose name has passed into international currency, the *kamikaze* pilots of the Pacific War. *Kamikaze* was the 'divine wind' which miraculously beat back the Mongol would-be invaders in the twelfth century, and the single-manned bomb-laden planes of the 1940s were similarly intended to keep the Americans out of Japan. What is interesting is that some of the *kamikaze* pilots could not bear the tension and terror of waiting, and killed themselves the night before their mission. Individualism was caged before 1945. The Ministry of Education spelled it out in a wartime directive: 'It is unforgivable to consider private life as the realm of individual freedom where we can do as we like . . . Nor are we purely in a personal capacity when at play or asleep.' Even in the late 1960s the far from fascist cabinet could go on record as criticizing a White Paper on national welfare prepared by civil servants because it asserted that 'the life of the individual is of first importance. But this is a dangerous way of thinking: without the nation there is no life of the individual.'

If, under the old system, you were to have projected a strong, idiosyncratic personality, you would have courted suspicion and distaste. Much religious teaching held that a strong personality was bad, and the hero in history was portrayed as someone who illustrated his time rather than stamped his imprint upon it, being a mere vehicle for the impersonal forces at work. A Japanese businessman explains that his people are not creative because 'the creative mind is peculiar, and we Japanese don't like anything peculiar. We believe that everyone should be the same.' American baseball players report that Japanese players do not think for themselves but only carry out what the manager or coach tells them. 'One must be capable of classification as a type in order to be accepted in Japan,' according to James Kirkup, the English poet and teacher who lives there. 'If one is not typical of something, one is nothing.' One has to be average to be socially acceptable.

This short-measuring of self can be traced into language, where personal pronouns are commonly left out. Edward Seidensticker reveals that his worst problem when translating a Japanese author is to 'find his subjects'. In a status-conscious society where you pick your I's and you's from a bank of pronouns all with differing honorific value, Japanese often choose not to sound them at all. If a tradition-minded man does choose to say 'I', he might use *'papa'* to his daughter, *'boku'* to his wife, *'keigo'* to his parents, *'watakushi'* to his office staff, and so on. Individuals do not speak to individuals, rather roles to roles. You should use honorific speech to your superiors in status, informal constructions to your inferiors and neutral forms to those in between. An able fifty-year-old department head may feel obliged to use linguistic honorifics to a newcomer in the office half his age, if the younger man is a high-flyer from a prestige university with a rich education and the right family background to go on to be chairman. A disrespectful pronoun can provoke anger or proclaim rebellion, as undergraduates did in the 1960s unrest by addressing their professors as *te mae*, instead of *anata* (both mean 'you', but the latter is more respectful).

Actually, the hard edges of mediaeval rules of speech are being softened. 'Respect language', the use of obsequious ways of speaking to your superiors, is now on the wane. The old 'flowery' style is mostly used by friends who know each other well, and also by people who have never met before, and for special occasions. But for routine purposes and among the younger generation less formal speaking is becoming acceptable. Honorifics are heard less and less on the radio and TV. 'Young people's spoken Japanese,' three Tokyo University teachers observe, 'is characterized by wholesale retreat of honorifics, and instead new intonations have been adopted as a means of self-assertion.'

One of the two words for individualism in Japanese carries overtones of selfishness, even of nihilism and anarchism. It is widely seen as a destructive philosophy which frees people from responsibility at society's expense. There is no general admiration for a value system which lets you look after yourself while neglecting your old parents. In Europe a machinery of inner control was developed which allows the legitimate self-seeking of one individual to leave scope for the self-seeking of others, but that kind of restraint has not been constructed in Japan. Many of today's young Japanese see individualism merely as in a way of becoming free from the pressures of their parents and teachers. Individualism in Japan is in a sense negative. It can be portrayed by traditionalists as something which promotes conflict between individuals competing to satisfy their own appetites and fantasies. So the contemporary novelist Ryotaro Shiba can declare that 'the private "I" is a shameful thing, to be hidden, like going to the lavatory'.

It might be thought that the traditional system is so riddled with weaknesses that its end cannot be far off. Actually, it is so creatively strong that new forms of groupism and dependency have arrived which are suitable to modern conditions. One of these relates to the reincarnation of the patron, a role which evidently takes a lot of burying. In the days of the *shoguns*, a Japanese would frequently use his work and family connections to attach himself to a patron, and mutual loyalty made the arrangement useful to both sides.

Today the rationale for this might appear to have gone, with giant factories and corporations beyond the range of a single 'fixer'. Yet the old role attaches to such key men as the trade union organizer or father-of-chapel, the factory foreman or the head of department in a commercial office. A newcomer anxious about finding his feet in an impersonal organization may offer to depend on such a patron, in return for being guided and protected by him.

The new forms of collectivity can be vast. Ronald Dore, the British sociologist and expert on Japan, talks of Japanese individuals transferring during the industrialization process of the past 100 years 'from the cosy womb of group solidarity in family and village straight into the cosy womb of corporation solidarity in a big firm, a big office' – an explicitly maternal metaphor. Japan is also subject to the same new collective phenomena as other industrialized countries, such as nationalized industries, state welfare services, mass media and commercialized fashion, and the Japanese succumb the more easily to their attractions for having jumped from feudalism to industrial capitalism virtually in one go.

Critics have begun to realize that advertisers are now exploiting their freedom to create a new kind of conformism (far more pervasive than in the West) in which an individual consumer may believe that he is expressing his own opinion, but is actually following the social trend. The symbol of such people is Hideki Noda, Japan's 'angry young man' who wrote *The Lowbrows: People Without A Standpoint*. Young people do go after minor brands and customized goods, but these are still values coming from without. A research institute recently concluded that today's young people are more group-oriented than their recent predecessors, because they cannot select from the barrage of information and choice presented to them. Rather than make their own judgements, they float along and use the group to give them a discernible identity.

The old ethic of dependence on the group and upon superiors has not yet disappeared, while the rules governing economic development have been imposed from above instead of being worked out in the stress of conflicting individual wills as was the case in Europe. Precisely because the individual has just won free to some extent from pressures of family or village, he may need the compensating security of a larger belonging and thus be more vulnerable than ever to the forces of conformism on a wider scale.

The ultimate star which many Japanese, seeing their country as a late entrant in the race to modernity, would like to follow, is socialism. Yet intellectuals seem happy to skip over the tiresome process of reforming the individual personality, and to omit the baptism of liberal individualism, epitomised by the Victorian era in England, in order to carry straight through to the security of a socialist order where many of the traditional Japanese needs could still be met. But without a revolution in individual attitudes, social change is bound to be elusive.

So much for the resilient traditional system of individuals meeting their needs in groups. The other half of the picture is composed by the individualizing forces at work, from within Japanese society as well as from outside. The faceless mass of mutually conforming Japanese has always been relieved by a small number of individuals who succeed in establishing their authority, eccentricities and all. Those few gifted Japanese with the strength to pursue a lonely road to power, enlightenment or artistic expression stand out as exceptional in all epochs.

Most of the architects of Japan's modernization, the leaders of the Meiji Restoration, rose from the relatively humble ranks of *samurai*. The Japan of the tight family is also the country where the woman poet Yosano could declare:

> Into the edifice which humanity
> Has been building
> From time immemorial,
> I too drive a nail of gold.

There are other achievers in Japan without the advantage of the artist's articulacy or the politician's flair for self-advertisement. Think of Kenichi Horie who at twenty-three sailed a 19-foot boat across the Pacific in ten weeks, or Katsuichi Honda's scholarly sojourn in an Eskimo village in the interests of research, or Tadashi Nagase's walk across Africa in 1982 – or the many Japanese explorers and mountaineers who have scaled the Himalayas and opened up Antartica.

The religious leaders, many of whom committed continuous social treason with equanimity, should also be counted as individualist models. A countryman described Daisetsu Suzuki, the famous twentieth-century Zen Buddhist, as being 'quite devoid of the habit, common among many Japanese people, of smiling for no particular reason or behaving with almost uncomfortable politeness. He remains profoundly compassionate and emotionally impassive, refusing to make any display of meaningless politeness.'

That mindless and time-wasting deference is still rampant in Japan despite the efforts of many reformers to restrict it. An example of how it works was once retailed by James Kirkup. He was saying goodnight to a crowd of teachers and students in a restaurant on the top floor of one of the new hotels in Tokyo. There were three automatic lifts, and each time one arrived its doors would open for a few seconds, during which time Kirkup would try to make his farewell bow, to which all the others responded, only to find that by the time he had finished his reciprocal bowing, the doors had shut again. When the next lift arrived, he had to start bowing all over again, trying this time to back gracefully while doing so. Again he was baulked, and only when the third lift arrived could he succeed in retreating into it, bowing still from its interior, receiving 'a nasty blow on the head as I bowed for the final time and the door collided smartly with my left ear. This disrupted the mechanism of the elevator, and I had to get out and start bowing all over again.' Japanese politeness, another

English writer has observed, has little connection with consideration for others: it is simply ritual.

Even ordinary people can feel themselves more in control of their lives than the traditional system may seem to allow. One writer, Takashi Oshio, explains having to cope with different personal pronouns or roles in life by comparing himself with the railway signalman at a busy station. 'I myself am the force that skilfully changes the switches at lightning speed . . . this does not mean that I am selfless, without character and irresponsible, as the Europeans claim. On the contrary, I am a huge ball of energy.'

Multiple roles can also express individuality. A newspaper once reported that a well-known figure had been converted to Roman Catholicism. A pained letter of correction came from the Protestants: it was their faith to which the gentleman had subscribed. But the Catholics insisted that the report was correct, so the gentleman himself was asked to settle the matter. He innocently explained that both religions had been recommended, each had its good points and so he had been converted to both. It is not uncommon for individuals and families to take on a completely new name in the hope that it will change their luck, or for voters to belong to two parties at once. The present Prime Minister, Yasuhiro Nakasone, had to reprove a member of his Cabinet for recruiting Opposition party members, including Communists, to his local supporters' association. After which it can come as no surprise to find the president of an industrial company carrying two different name cards around with him, one giving his former title as chairman of the company trade union, and another showing him as company president: he could present himself in whatever colours were most suitable.

More important than these long-standing loop-holes for individualism in the traditional system is the intrinsic break-down, only just begun and proceeding very slowly, of the groups which govern it. The family is becoming less cohesive. Five generations ago its income came typically from its members' co-operative work on the farm. Today, each individual is paid a wage by a different company or organization. Free compulsory schooling is available to a child in its own right, not requiring action by its parents. The wartime obligation of military service was placed upon the individual and not, as in the days of the *shoguns*, the family. Taxes are paid by individuals, public offices are filled by the election of individuals, and Christianity is a religion for individual rather than family conversion.

Instead of sheltering all his life under his family's umbrella, the contemporary Japanese will have spent his impressionable years in the classroom, the factory, the office and (in wartime) the army. He will have learnt there to engage with other people not involved in a hot-house emotional relationship with him, and to see other people, even his own relatives, in a more impersonal light where he can consider how to get them to do what he wants, rather than merely lubricate their self-respect. This change has been spreading across Japan very slowly for more than a century, and the next stage has now been reached: the glue that holds these groups together is beginning to weaken. After a protracted forced diet of belonging, the Japanese are beginning to resist what they find unpalatable.

The groups, however, hold a trump card in their capacity to blunt the impact on the individual, who would be powerless without such mediation, of the swelling bureaucracy of Japan. And the group may pragmatically come to terms with the new climate, by recognizing the individual's new-found need to have some room for manoeuvre and becoming more tolerant if he departs from the collective opinion on some question. These days, individualism is occasionally permitted, as long as it does not become the rule.

Such changes create particular tensions between generations. Old people still live out the idiom of mutual dependence, trying to communicate with young people who may believe they have banished such ideas. An old-fashioned Japanese is thoughtful about the other person's point of view, refrains from asserting his own rights, forgives the other's selfishness (magnanimously interpreting it as a 'request to be dependent') and hopes that eventually the other person will feel first guilty and then grateful. But the older Japanese also feels frustration, called upon to suppress his own self-assertion, practising an unrewarding masochism instilled into him as a child, in order to support vast numbers of younger people who seem quite indifferent. Many a youngster treated in this way by an elder disregards the considerateness, seeing it as an attempt to meddle in his life, and keeps his distance.

Communication sometimes fails, therefore, across the generations. But even a young person may well be sufficiently affected by tradition to want subconsciously to avoid hurting other people through his behaviour. He may carry away from an encounter with elders, however outdated he may think them, a secret burden of anxiety or guilt, which then serves as a new psychological bond to keep Japanese society together. Individuals in Japan may seem to be following their own desires with every appearance of satisfaction, but deep down they still worry, as the pioneer generation in this experiment, about 'whether it is really all right to live this way'. There is a nagging fear that the new freedoms will some day disappear, the old authorities re-emerge.

Okonogi believes that some Japanese, trying to assimilate what they see as the desirable individualism of the West, have cut themselves off from their traditional system before there is a working alternative to meet their needs. This disorients them, making them feel they belong nowhere. Hence the apathy of many young Japanese whose only goal seems to be to extend their youth indefinitely, free of responsibilities. This introduces the second major source of change in the status of the Japanese individual, namely the powerful influence of western life and thought that flooded over Japan from the middle of the nineteenth century, reinforcing the domestic agents of change. It was the writers and artists of the Meiji period who explored these new avenues of individualism most eagerly.

Soseki Natsume, the influential novelist, wavered in his convictions. In 1910, in his early forties, he explained: 'As I believe in myself, I do not believe in God. Nothing is more valuable than myself in the entire universe.' But he later conceded in his masterpiece *Kokoro* that the price which his generation had to pay for its liberty was loneliness. And while first promoting the self to be 'master of the house while all others are guests', he finally allowed the state an entrée through the back door. 'When the state faces a crisis, individual freedom contracts . . . that is only natural.' In his last work, Soseki Natsume moved from the idea that an individual must fight the outer elements in order to liberate his self, to the ultimate logic that he must conduct a conscious and aggressive conquest of other selves in order to fulfill his own self to the limit. The Japanese were horrified by this book, *Meian*, and it still frightens them.

The intelligentsia of Japan's Edwardian era were saturated with individualism, culminating in Katai Tayama's novel *Futon*, whose hero hovers maunderingly between the young girl whom he loves and the wife and family to whom convention ties him, and Ogai Mori's *Vita Sexualis*, an autobiography of exaggerated individualism. This generation of writers did not know how to use the intoxicating new freedom imported from Europe except for their personal gratification. They 'biologised emancipation', in the later accusation of Tatsuo Arima, 'instead of socialising it.' The novelist Saneatsu Mushakoji wrote in the 1910s, 'I am the only man given to me by nature. Unless I have a desire to fulfill this life of mine, how could I care for the lives of others? . . . Tolstoyism and socialism try to place on me a burdensome social responsibility. If I had quietly assumed such a burden, I would have been immobilised.'

Japan's intellectuals seized upon the beguiling decadence of Oscar

Wilde before having absorbed the self-help precepts of Samuel
Smiles, quaffing the heady *fin-de-siècle* wine without first swallowing
the Victorian stodge to sponge it up. Akutagawa was surely satirizing
the whole movement when he observed that, 'Life does not equal
even one line of Baudelaire's poetry.' The artists still lead in the post-
war quest for individualism. 'I want to be an individual . . . first,' the
painter Sugai insisted, 'and a Japanese second.' He gave his compatriots in Paris in the 1950s the cold shoulder, professing unconcern for
the 'petty problems of being Japanese, because first and foremost I
belong to a far greater entity: myself'.

Of all the writers and artists of our day, Yukio Mishima was the
most colourfully individual. Body-builder, militarist, novelist, bi-
sexual and above all showman, he exhibited a richly idiosyncratic
personality, so much so that when a compatriot gave him a Rorschach
test a few years before his suicide, he deduced from it that Mishima
was 'a foreigner with Japanese tastes'.

It was all blatantly overdone. Even General MacArthur, who could
have decreed the most radical of reforms across Japan during the
American Occupation, had qualified his proclamation of fundamental human rights in the new Constitution with the warning that
individuals should 'refrain from any abuse of their freedom and rights
and shall always be responsible for using them for the public welfare'.
Yet one eager young businessman set out to build his post-war life
entirely on the new principles of rationalism, contract and individual
rights, defying all his traditional group commitments. His fate was
instructive: he first went bankrupt and then committed suicide.

Why did Japanese intellectuals go overboard about individualism?
The psychiatrist Keigo Okonogi suggests that, in order to assert
independence, a Japanese has to make himself into 'a heartless
ingrate who ignores and scorns guilt feelings. In order to make the
break at all, one feels compelled to go to extremes and utterly
debauch oneself.' One interpretation could be that Japan's intellectuals are still critically digesting their initial over-indulgence of
western culture. Alternatively, western individualist culture may
have come to be tolerated as a permanent option for the intellectual
élite – as long as the vast majority of Japanese society underneath was
left free to pursue its basic traditions.

The literary and artistic obsession with the West is reinforced by
hard-headed political and economic calculation about the need for
international communication. Everyone avoids unnecessary friction
with others, the Europeans by following generalized rules of behaviour, the Japanese on a more conscious case-by-case basis. At the
interface between Japan and western countries this difference can

cause trouble. The Japanese instinct to pretend to agree with somebody, in order to make him feel good, works where the other person
is also Japanese and knows what the real score is. It does not work
with a European who will feel betrayed when the truth comes out
later.

There is an unusual bureaucrat called Shinsaku Sogo, who sometimes acts as a one-man cultural shock-absorber between Japan and
the outside world. He put his finger on this problem by calling
on Japan to 'admit that disagreements exist between people and
countries, because otherwise we're going to have more serious
problems without having time to think of the compromises to solve
them'. Japanese are trained to detect the true message of a
compatriot underneath the prettied-up one, but this does not work in
the outside world of integrated communication. This is an incentive
for the Japanese government and business apparatus to take some
individualism on board. As Dr Okonogi puts it, 'Our system does
not work in the outside world, so we have to assimilate western
individualism.'

It was a titillating shock for the Japanese to see Margaret Thatcher,
for example, performing on their TV screens: 'One would find few
politicians in Japan,' a viewer commented, 'who could talk so persuasively, projecting such a sense of personality.' Japan will lose out
in the world, and is already doing so, without its own native versions
of such western personalities.

Mrs Thatcher makes headlines in Japan because it is unimaginable
for a woman to become Prime Minister there. Only in 1946 were
women able to vote, and the thirty-nine who were then elected to the
Diet have never since been exceeded. Prime Minister Hayato Ikeda
appointed two women Ministers to his Cabinet a quarter of a century
ago, but his initiative was not maintained and it is still rare to see
women succeeding in politics or the professions.

The sex established a separate Japan Women's Party in 1977, but
even that has yet to make its mark. Only one woman in fifty keeps
step with the men at university or college, and she could usually hope
to draw only half a man's salary afterwards. Only in 1986 did a
reluctant government enact (in order to satisfy international opinion)
a mealy-mouthed Equal Employment Opportunities Law. There is
only one woman ambassador representing Japan in the world and,
even more disgraceful, only one woman professor at the senior
university – and it is said that she had to mouth the 'respect language'
of a man in order to win her chair. The Vice-Foreign Minister was
recently barred from a diplomatic golf match because the club
excluded women at weekends.

This is not because of ingrained anti-feminism in the Japanese make-up. There were outstanding women empresses in mediaeval times, and Japan can claim in the eleventh century the world's first true novelist of either sex, Lady Murasaki, author of *The Tale of Genji*. It was women who developed the *kana* script a thousand years ago for grateful men to take over afterwards, and it was a woman who first established sexual passion as a motif in Japanese poetry.

Before the nineteenth century women did not have to abandon their own family irrevocably when marrying, and several well-known men took their wife's surname on being adopted into her family through marriage. There were places in Japan where women wrestled, and where male prostitutes staffed brothels to serve them. But by Victorian or Meiji times, the treatment of women had become repressive. Sons were always preferred in a family, and the woman poet Hosho, being a third successive daughter, had to be boarded out by her mother until a brother could be born to satisfy the angry father. Chikamatsu, sometimes called the 'Shakespeare' of Japan, made his female characters use thirteen different degrees of honorific language on stage.

It may not always have been so, but in the nineteenth century women were virtually excluded from intellectual life. Politics, literature and science were closed books, and the poet Sakutaro Hagiwara could write as late as 1929 that 'women are all primitive and very simple mechanisms, while men are delicate engines with a complicated system'. During the war a woman's cigarette ration was smaller than a man's, and even now she has to endure such discrimination as having to wait longer than a man to remarry after divorce. Until the new 1985 Nationality Law she could not pass her nationality to her child if her husband was foreign, and she has to give chocolates to the boys on St Valentine's Day! This explains why many Japanese girls go abroad and stay abroad, where they are treated as women (or even as persons) instead of as mothers, wives, mistresses, or players of other roles. One girl who came back from America recognized that she had acquired attitudes and behaviour there which her friends and family considered deviant. 'I am a kind of outsider now in Japanese society.'

But modern life has greatly benefited Japanese women. It is typical for a husband to give all his salary to his wife for her to dispose of, and to leave the management of the home entirely to her. The Parent-Teacher Association introduced by the Americans after the war provided an unexpected forum for feminine individuality, 'turning out', a commentator notes, 'a new breed of woman that is willing to question authority'. Only a generation ago most women said they would prefer to be reborn as men, but today most are content with their gender. There is a popular strip cartoon in the mass-circulation newspaper *Asahi Shimbun* whose heroine, a new post-war wife, tells her husband to 'call me by my name,' rather than summon her with an 'Oi!'

The traditional view of the woman's role is still defended, fiercely and by women themselves. A woman teacher, Hiroko Hara, explains that Japanese women handle not only 'the family finances, but all the delicate and extremely important personal relationships involving the family, the community and often the business or professions . . . In these . . . men depend on *us*.' Another woman writer challenges the assumption that women in Japan lack individual dignity. They are, she says, often satisfied in their family role, contributing to the group's happiness instead of competing with men to earn money. 'The commitment of Japanese women to their role . . . is not necessarily from mere force of habit but grows out of a carefully calculated choice of options.' Indeed, some women rejected the Equal Employment Opportunities Law as a submission to 'white race values' which threatened Japan's 'cultural ecology.' The idea that there might be different choices made by different individual women still seems far away.

Some Japanese women actually welcome their being called too 'feminine' by foreign critics. They will take it as a compliment and argue that Japanese women are more skilful at handling men, more sensitive about when to assert themselves and when to give in. This picks up in a modern context the old tradition whereby Japan produced the most sophisticated courtesans in the world, and its houses of pleasure carried the notion of femininity to the ultimate degree. That kind of thing is dying out, but the same idea informs the cosmopolitan saying of today, popular in Japan as well as other countries, that any man's ideal would be to have a Japanese wife, in a western house, with a Chinese cook.

It also feeds male chauvinism of the kind revealed by the head of the Cultural Affairs Agency in 1984. Asked why he went jogging, this leading civil servant explained: 'It would be a shameful act for a gentleman to rape women, but it is shameful that a man does not have the physical strength to rape a woman.' He poured fuel on the flames by later remarking, 'I wish rapists would attack promiscuous women.' He had to apologize in the Diet, but such notions are widespread.

Japan's first women militants were premature when they wrote on their new journal *Bluestocking* in 1911 the motto: 'In the Beginning there was the Sun, and it was Woman.' This was a correct rendering of Japanese legend, but woman's inequality remains. Selfishness, aggression and untidiness is indulged in young boys but not in girls. It seems that boys have a more fragile ego which girls must learn from an early age to shore up. It is still common in schools for language to diverge according to sex, the girls beginning at about ten to use the more respectful women's language while the boys continue mouthing the rougher idiom which custom allows them. The decorum instilled in a Japanese girl may extend even to the bed, with instruction from her elders in how to control her body while asleep.

But the ultimate degradation is surely the fact that so many Japanese women feel physically uncomfortable with their bodies, envying the western stereotype – 'with large, rounded eyes', as a Japanese girl defines it, 'preferably with a large, rounded bosom and long shapely legs' – for which Japanese men yearn. This is why so many women undergo surgery to have their eyes westernized and their breasts enlarged.

To sum up, the individual in Japan is restricted by tradition, but is slowly becoming more free. It is something for a Japanese to put a sticker on his car window saying 'I am somebody', but we await the stage when he will no longer need to do so. The change that is going on is not a simple one from the traditional Japanese to the modern European model. There is a more complex process of inner evolution, of convergence and mutual influencing of models going on. After a century of observing the individualism of Wilde and Zola, Wagner and Picasso, the Japanese are becoming more aware of the ways in which their individuality can already find expression within their own tradition.

In the old-fashioned rural Japanese family a child was sufficiently loved for his life to take on meaning without need of the universalistic values that permeate a western household. The family in Japan stayed put as a constant shelter for its members when things went wrong for them, and also as a keystone for social values to guide those same members when they ventured out into the world. In this way Japan's modernization could succeed through individuals acting with markedly less independence than had been the case in Europe. The Japanese is still ready to tailor the gratification of his own self to the expectations of others. An Osaka University professor, Esyun Hamaguchi, calls it contextualism, in which mutual reliance in interpersonal relations becomes an end in itself.

A century of eager Japanese participation in the creative and imaginative life of European civilization has not changed fundamental values. Individualism is perceived in Japan as a person's right to pursue his own interests even against those of his group, and at the expense of his duties to others. 'To be honest,' Shusaku Endo recently said, in reaction to the whole discussion, 'I have doubts about all this post-war talk of individuality. Put bluntly, there are other things that are more important.' Only three Japanese in ten say they would dare to do what they believe right, even against the prevailing social opinion.

Another psychiatrist, Professor Takeo Doi, poses the question in a different way, as a philosophical issue. The Japanese, he says, have penetrated below the superficial excitement about changing the role of the individual, and are now anxious to know at a deeper level why European individuals have become as autonomous as they are. He poses the question from the Japanese viewpoint: have Europeans already gained that vital inner certainty of being loved once and for all, or have they outgrown the need for dependency altogether? How did individualism come to develop in the West in the first place? What aspects of it are culture-bound, and inappropriate to Japan, and what aspects universal, for Japan to develop as soon as may be comfortable?

These questions are asked in the knowledge that the West itself is not as certain as before about its goals. Western society provides a framework in which individuals can give and take, retaining their essential autonomy yet still following basic rules of social behaviour to allow others the same privileges. In the milieu of Rousseau's social contract this may have worked splendidly, reaching its apogee in some respects in the Victorian age, but with the new modernity of giant mechanized industry, mass communications and mobility for the asking, it does leave many individuals floundering.

Ronald Dore once suggested to British legislators, by way of disarming the criticism of Japan's conformism, that Britain had perhaps pursued things to a point of almost neurotic individualism. A Labour MP indignantly rebuked him: 'That is not the way we characterize individualism here. It is almost a gospel.' But to pit yourself against everybody in sight, including the members of your own family, takes confidence which many Japanese do not have, and implies risks which they have so far preferred to avoid. Lafcadio Hearn was ahead of his age in decrying the West's 'cultivation of pure egotism', but gradually more and more Westerners have come to feel that limits should be placed on individualism. A British manager in a Japanese firm, John Buchan of TDK, describing how the Japanese work together in a company instead of fighting each other in the classic British union-management manner, adds: 'By comparison, Westerners are . . . totally self-contained and mostly confident individuals, but I wonder whether the western world can continue to remain individualistic?' It serves little purpose to slam the Japanese for dilly-dallying on a road whose end is not yet clear for the West itself.

These are some of the strands which make up the Japanese individual. But he is formed in the first instance by his family, and the family's influence on behaviour is longer-lasting than in the West. 'So-called Japanese individualism', one writer has observed, 'was born of the ego of the son tormented within the framework of the family.' What is this family, which the Japanese goes on cherishing long after his Anglo-Saxon counterpart has snapped the strings?

3

Lions or Lambs?
The Japanese Family

THE JAPANESE used to trundle through life in a comfortable old family charabanc with lots of room for the old folks and the children. The generations were linked, the young could soak up social ethics in the most natural way imaginable and each passenger received a clear set of roles in life. One destination and one route was chosen collectively by the family elders, one driver led these dozens of human individuals, and one common set of landmarks stirred them all. From this commodious vehicle a Japanese went out to try his luck in the world safe in the knowledge that, whenever he was tired or defeated, sick or dying, he could go back to it for unquestioning refuge.

Now the bus has shrunk abruptly into a two-door mini. The 'small family' based upon one couple has arrived. These frail-looking vehicles tackle the road with varying power and conflicting senses of direction. Children spend little time with their great-grandparents or grandparents, uncles or aunts or cousins, so the transmission of experience is cut and respect for the old expires. Are the Japanese crossing a cultural bridge, some European observers wonder, over to the side of individualism and westernization?

The contemporary Japanese household does outwardly resemble the small modern European model of two adults and the one or two children they may bear. But there are important differences. Change overtook Japan much faster than Europe, so it is less easily absorbed; and, while the Japanese have been released from the worst social restrictions of their past, they have not been simultaneously reprogrammed for vigorous self-asserting individualism. The result is sociologically confusing.

The little suburban home may look like Sanderstead or Brunoy, but the relationships within it have a more traditional colour. The young Tokyoite may still call the boy in the next bed *oniisan* (honourable elder brother), rather than Kazuo or Hiro, just as his old-fashioned father might still refer deprecatingly to his wife in front of guest as *okusan* (back-of-the-house person): in the Japanese family one's special role seems more valuable than any abstract

individuality unrelated to family realities, and so the personal name
which is a Westerner's badge of individuality is not used so much.
There may also be a grandparent – usually the husband's mother –
living in. Mother looms larger than life in a Japanese man's world: it
always used to be said that, if your family were ever swept away in a
flood, it was your mother you should save first – you could *always* find
another wife . . . In the old days, when her son married, a mother
would conduct a ritual rivalry with the new daughter-in-law over the
right to ladle out the steamed rice at meal times. The modern fiancée
tries to negotiate easier arrangements with her intended, and the
ideal catch for the liberated girl became a man *ie-tsuki, car-tsuki,
baba-nuki* – 'with house, with car, but without mother-in-law'.

Feelings of guilt as well as practical economics intrude all the same,
and today there are more than a million old people living with their
married children. Japan has just overtaken Iceland to lead in the
world longevity stakes: the average grandpa or grandma can now be
expected to live to seventy-seven. Diet, demography and drugs
destine Japan to contain the highest proportion of aged persons in the
world. Her population will have 'greyed' in the second half of the
twentieth century in only a quarter of the time it took for European
countries similarly to re-order their age cohorts – a disconcerting
consequence of modernizing so fast.

Torn between honouring elders in the traditional way and pursuing
the increasingly demanding work of factory, office or home, harassed
middle-aged workers and housewives and their passive self-oriented
children may now show resentment and inconsiderateness towards
the old. Sadly the living-in forebear often commits suicide, chilled by
the coldness of the new-style small family wrapped up in its own little
tasks and tensions. If a grandfather wants to remarry, his grown-up
children may stop him registering the union, to keep their own
inheritance safe. The exhortation of the Edwardian novelist Katai
Tayama – 'For us children they did everything they could afford.
What have we done for them?' – falls on deaf ears these days.
Grandparents are victims of modernization, as in other countries,
only the social loss is greater in Japan because the big family
household was so recently abandoned.

Now that elders are neither automatic nor necessarily popular
members of the household, more depends on the father – and yet he
too suffers from the new truncated system, wielding only what
authority he can create by his own efforts in his reduced household.
This is made difficult by his being away at work so much ('Mr Early
Morning', his loved ones may call him after those endless 'business
evenings' at bars or nightclubs). Even if the economic recession

begins to shorten his working hours to allow him more time at home, he may pretend to be detained in order to save face with the neighbours. Some husbands become little more than boarders in their own home, second in line for space and attention after examinee-children. 'Why,' one housewife recalled after twenty years of marriage, 'I hardly ever had to give him much service like cooking special meals—or even having sex.'

Today it is the young wife who manages the household and controls its assets, often choosing her husband's clothes and doling out pocket-money for him to spend. She takes the responsibility for the children, who see her not in her pre-war role as mediator between them and their father but as the central figure and final arbiter in their upbringing. Japan has almost become, in the words of the psychologist Takeo Doi, a fatherless society. Children have surprisingly little to do with their fathers. 'They tend to consult with friends when they need advice', a Government survey sadly concludes, 'rather than with their fathers.' Another report finds that one father in three has no communication with his offspring. 'I cannot ever remember touching my father or being touched by him,' one boy confesses.

Since the father was so all-powerful before the war, this is a big change. Crown Prince Akihito has set a good example by helping his wife wash up, but not every family follows his royal lead. The latest trend for newly-weds is claimed to be 'kiss in the morning and take it in turns to wash up', but more convincing is the tale of the husband who claps a lordly hand for his wife to serve drinks when guests come, but cannot wait to set up the ironing board once they have gone. 'It lets him forget all his office problems,' the wife explains, 'he just loses himself in ironing . . .' The public gauleiter so admired by friends turns closet houseworker in the bosom of his family when his two worlds are cleanly separated – that is a characteristically Japanese manipulation of roles. Social pressure to maintain a macho image is amazingly strong. Your workmates would think you a hilarious sissy if you telephoned your wife to ask if she would mind your stopping off for a drink on the way home.

A couple has more privacy now than before, though not as much as Europeans would expect. A young child may still sleep on the *tatami**

---

* When Carla Rapoport opened a *Financial Times* article in 1985 by saying that in the world's third richest country more than half of the people 'still sleep on the floor,' she roused a storm of indignation. Many Japanese sleep at floor level, but only on *tatami* – rush matting which is not treated in the way Europeans treat their carpets, but kept free from dirt by the custom of taking off shoes at the entrance and putting on slippers or proceeding in socks or bare feet indoors. It is as good a bed as any European could wish, the only difference being that it is not raised from the level of

rush matting next to one of its parents, or between them. No special tension is set up by the idea of an adult boy sleeping in the same room as an adult girl.

'We all sleep together,' a widow with a grown-up son and daughter explains, 'sharing everything and keeping nothing from each other. It's happier that way.'

When parents in such a household want sex they have to choose a time, therefore, when the children are out, or else do it surreptitiously – on their sides, quietly, with little foreplay. Sociologists report that Japanese couples have sex about five times a month, only half as frequently as the British. Privacy was not valued in the old Japan where the group always came first; today many Japanese would like to have it, but shortage of housing space and surviving habits of family sociability frustrate them. Hence the popularity of the expensive new 'Love Hotels'.

Some Japanese intellectuals believe that only when their countrymen are brought up in separate, lockable, sound-proofed bedrooms will the idea of individual responsibility and democracy take root. The bricks and mortar, the composition of the household, the material and economic life-style may be similar to London or New York, but the preferred sleeping arrangements and intangible relationships within the home can still remain distinctively Japanese, reflecting the strength of age-old traditions which survive because they satisfy human needs.

This may explain why Japanese psychiatrists regard what they call the 'Ajase complex', rather than the Oedipus complex, as the key to childhood emotions. This refers to the story of a queen in ancient India who so longed for a son that she consulted a fortune-teller. He predicted that, when a certain forest sage died, he would be reincarnated in her womb. Impatient for the event, the queen killed the sage and, sure enough, the boy Ajase took shape in her womb soon afterwards. Frightened at what she had done, however, she tried to abort him, and even after giving birth to him she tried to kill him in case she was cursed. When Ajase grew up and learned the story, he hit his mother in anger. Overcome in his turn by guilt, he succumbed to a foul-smelling disease, which he threw off only with the help of his

---

footnote continued.
the floor. And that of course makes for economy of space in a space-short nation, because the bedclothes can be rolled up in the daytime and put in cupboards to release the room for eating and working – until the next evening. The loss is of privacy, not comfort or cleanliness. The twelve-year-old son in Junichiro Tanizaki's novel *Some Prefer Nettles* always slept between his parents in the same room.

mother's devoted nursing. This dissolved their mutual anger, they forgave each other and were reunited in love.

This cycle of unity-resentment-forgiveness is central to the Japanese image of a mother-child relationship. Heisaku Kosawa, Japan's first Freudian psychologist, argued to the master himself in Vienna in 1932 that the guilt of Ajase, rooted in remorse and the knowledge that he had been forgiven by his mother, was qualitatively different from the crude Judaic concepts of punishment and retaliation underlying the western sense of guilt. Shamed guilt was surely nicer than frightened guilt. Unlike Oedipus, Ajase committed neither parricide nor incest.

The Ajase theory helps to illuminate how the Japanese organize their emotions. After the Pacific War many a Japanese sincerely repented of his military misdeeds and, assuming that forgiveness would follow, acted as if they had never happened. He was surprised and bewildered to find Chinese, Americans and Southeast Asians who were prepared neither to forgive nor to forget.

Sex was less important than other ingredients in an old-fashioned Japanese marriage. Intimate companionship was not expected, which meant that both parties could feel more secure – less anxious in case some fickle alteration in chemistry came to destroy the entire household (American women striving to keep themselves constantly sexy and beautiful right through their marriage are therefore pitied by Japanese counterparts). Japanese men, who are already out at work all day and evening, seem to find it natural to seek sex outside the home. Many wives accept this, even welcome it. The external durability of the practical domestic relationship is more important in Japanese values. The old *haiku* poem put it in five words:

> Loved
> By my wife? –
> Disgusting!

Only recently have the women's magazines, following the western lead, begun to stress the desirability of orgasm, and this may gradually encourage wives to demand more. The insidious power of the media, acting upon the unfailing curiosity of the Japanese, may here succeed in engineering a change towards westernization in the long run.

Love used to be thought effeminate: the masculine part was to control such emotions. Now modern couples display the mutual affection forbidden by law in pre-Victorian times, and Prime Minister Yasuhiro Nakasone even urges them to hold hands more often in public. He gives a better lead than his predecessor, Eisaku Sato, who went out with *geisha* girls and frequently beat his wife in front of their son: not surprisingly Mrs Sato confessed later to having 'no special liking for him'.

Extra-marital affairs are still popular. Six husbands out of ten were once said to be conducting such liaisons, according to their statistically-minded government. Emperor Hirohito's father was himself the product of one, and the actor Toshiro Mifune delighted some admirers (but upset others) by taking a pretty young mistress in place of his estranged wife to an official dinner given by the visiting President Gerald Ford for Hirohito in 1974. A few years ago Masashi Sada took a song to the top of the Japanese hit parade in which he commanded his wife to

> Go to bed last, be first up in the morning,
> Cook tasty food and wear pretty clothes
> – And if I have a little affair, just put up with it!

His female fans drooled at the reappearance of macho man with all those traditional Japanese virtues. Now wife-swapping has reached Japan, carried by fervent missionaries over the Pacific, so that extra-marital sex is at least becoming a little more democratic – another minor advance into Western ways.

The trouble is that husbands and wives can still have surprisingly little in common. Even if they share a bed and the kitchen sink, they are liable to lead separate social lives. This can be taken to an extreme if a wife refuses to go with her husband to another city where his company may have transferred him. It is not even necessary to plead that the children be spared a change of school which might set them back in exams, or that the wife should keep her own job – if she is also working – and its pension. She may simply dig in her heels and say she likes the house and her neighbourhood friends and will not go. Many thousands of families are now separated in this way, further depressing the authority of the father.

Possibly marriages may get closer as the element of choice widens. Instead of being a job of work, as it was before the war, or mere personal gratification as sometimes in the 1950s, marriage is nowadays a subtle mixture of arrangement by others (*miai*) and true romance (*renai*). Very often a girl will allow her parents, brothers, sisters or even a professional matchmaker to select a boy, while keeping a right of veto if, after going out with him a few times, she feels no enthusiasm. For a young man it is often the other way round: he may initiate the choice on the basis of sexual attraction, indicate the girl he has fallen for, and only abandon her if his parents find weighty reasons against. The parents' criteria will include breeding,

physical and mental health, education, wealth and social and occupa-
tional attainments. The young man's requirement, apart from good
looks, may be virginity, thus excluding the girls he may have been
playing about with earlier. Both generations may unite in wanting the
marriage to harmonize families as much as delight individuals.

Akio Morita, Chairman of Sony Corporation, tried to block his
son's marriage to a pop singer because he feared her career would get
in the way of the boy's playing his full part in the family business. But
we are a long way from the days of the nineteenth-century novelist
Ogai Mori, whose mother fastidiously selected not only his first wife
but his second – and even the mistress in between!

If the young are content to retain an element of parental involvement in their choice of partner, it is less because they genuinely value
the voice of experience, more because they feel morally uncomfortable flouting their parents on such a central family question. Young
idealists, tempted to make a love match frowned upon by elders,
pause longer than Europeans would at the thought of nursing lifelong guilt towards their parents. Literature is full of double love
suicides where the generation gulf could not be bridged. The novelist
Osamu Dazai actually made three attempts, each with a different girl.
Today's parents are more reasonable, expecting to allow children
some say in choosing their marriage partner.

Meanwhile there is a record number of divorces, sometimes
dignified by ceremonies where the guests pay for their food and drink,
the rings are formally returned and the couple apologize to all.
Divorces happen at the rate of twenty every hour, higher than ever
before in Japan, though still proportionately fewer than in Europe or
America. The children are a major delaying factor: two out of every
three mothers say they would keep their marriage going despite
estrangement in order to protect their children's upbringing.

A Japanese living in London at the time of Prince Charles's
wedding was surprised to see both the stepmother and the natural
mother of Princess Diana present at the ceremony: 'In Britain divorce
is a matter between husband and wife, and does not concern even the
children. There is no room for the Japanese notion that a child
cements a marriage.' An exaggeration, no doubt, but the children are
certainly a bigger consideration in Japan.

Sons to continue the family line have always been important in
Japan; that is why adoption is so frequent. Such famous writers as
Ryunosuke Akutagawa (author of *Rashomon*) and Soseki Natsume
(*I am a Cat*) were adopted as children. If you had an only child who
was a daughter, you would think of marrying her to a man whom you
could then adopt as your own son to carry on the family name: Prime

Minister Kakuei Tanaka did just this. Two of his predecessors, Nobusuke Kishi and Eisaku Sato (they happened to be impoverished blood brothers) also took the surname of their respective in-laws in order to marry rich wives – which may explain why Sato used to beat his better half so much!

It was the younger sons, called *hiyameshikun* (people who have to live on cold rice), who got the thin end of the deal under the pre-war primogeniture system. One of the standard explanations of Japan's success in industrializing in the late nineteenth century was the enterprise of these younger sons, pushed out of the family home at an early age with the challenge of making their own living. The American Occupation saddled Japan in the 1940s with an imported 'democratic' law of equal inheritance, but farmers and landowners hated to see their land – their own best security – divided, and so many of them persuaded their younger children voluntarily to renounce their rights in favour of the first-born.

Strangely enough, the unpopular American reform made possible an almost perfect, if unintended, solution of the land inheritance problem. If the eldest son does not want the responsibility, the children can renounce in another brother's favour – the one who is best at farming, or finds it most convenient to live on the family estate instead of in the city, or simply the one that volunteers. In a very Japanese rescue of an American mistake, an occidental element of democracy has been firmly introduced, giving freedom of choice to the individuals within the family, but without fractionizing the property on which the family is based – so that an important cultural and economic value is preserved.

But survival of the family name and lands is now the concern of a dwindling minority. Most Japanese parents have only one or two children to cope with, and their worry is how to bring them up into adulthood without those useful elder brothers and sisters, cousins, uncles and aunts against whom a pre-war child could test himself and construct his own identity. Pessimists in Japan fear that the torpid, myopic, selfish little monsters produced in many of these new small households will render their country a benighted and leaderless jungle in a few more decades – and some would blame the lack of any post-collectivist ethos like Christianity or the 'true' self-reliant individualism of the West which the Japanese, beguiled by the superficial glamour of Latin Quarter egotism, never took on board.

Uchi benkei is the traditional ideal of the Japanese child – 'a lion at home, a lamb outside'. The baby was smothered in affection at first, unwittingly monopolizing the love which its mother was not supposed to exhibit towards its father. 'A Japanese woman,' two British residents commented in Edwardian times, 'never expects to love anyone but her own baby; she must serve and obey everyone else.' There was a physical side to this: a baby might be much handled by its mother in the belief that this was how to develop its brain, and suckling used to be prolonged – you can meet men who fed at their mother's breast till the age of seven.

This intense physical closeness to the mother probably explains why so many Japanese feel such a lifelong tie to Mummy; why, innocent of puritanism, they regard their body as a natural object of self-gratification (in the *ofuro*, or hot bath, for example); why they grow up passive and accepting of their environment; why the men are said to be more sensitive than Europeans, even 'feminized' by comparison with them; and why Japanese rarely experience psychosis. (There is, however, a Mother House in Tokyo where businessmen under stress can go back to babyhood for a while – complete with dummy and nappy – for around £100.)

The mother-bond is sufficiently special for Stanley Levine, an American living in Japan with a Japanese wife, to have insisted that their son should not become 'tied sexually' to her: 'I've seen too much of the way some Japanese mothers hold their boys to them. They don't use apron strings; they use bands of steel.' (Yukio Mishima found time just before his suicide at the age of forty-five to bequeath the copyright of two of his best-sellers to his aged mother.)

Sleeping on the *tatami* in the same room as its parents offers a child good companionship if poor psychology. A girl of thirteen recently wrote to a newspaper advice column after seeing her aunt have sex with her married lover: 'When the man comes to my aunt, my heart begins to beat and I cannot sleep well because we have only one room and we sleep together.' Now most children have their own tiny rooms.

To sleep on the same rush-matting does not mean, however, that a child necessarily comes to terms with its parents' sexuality. Europe has the privacy of separate rooms, yet a couple there may still kiss and caress throughout the house in front of the children. Japan demands more restraint, and the moment when a child is forced to see his parents abandoning their social roles to act towards one another as mere individual man and woman is delayed as long as possible. The concealment makes the ultimate discovery all the more shocking, all the more resented. A teenager or young man feels betrayed when his mother 'comes out' as a woman, especially, of course, if there is any question of divorce or remarriage. 'My only pleasure', commented one ten-year-old stepson sourly, 'is raising hamsters. At least they don't betray you.'

A mother seeks to buy her baby's compliance without force or struggle. In Japan the universal drama of potty-training takes the form of a child's becoming aware of its own discomfort and of society's demands for cleanliness, and being helped by its mother (who is careful not to identify with the demands or to reinforce them) to alleviate that discomfort and meet the requirements with the least possible upset. This is an area where British practice has swung towards Japanese traditional permissiveness in recent years. Mother avoids acting and speaking for the mysterious outside authority, appearing instead in the role of a welcome ally to help cope with it.

A child will typically receive heavy cuddling until it is five or six. With such an upbringing, what infant would feel a compelling need to develop a will of its own? The early indulgence and absence of punishment encourage it to do what society expects of it, without pricking up its ears to any interior voice of conscience. When such children grow up they may be sunnily placid, but the over-protection and closeness they enjoyed at home can leave them scared of being alone or of asserting their own convictions. Their fate is sheep-like conformism. Worse, if maternal protection defuses the rebellion which every human being has to wage against his parents, the child may emerge either overly submissive and obedient at one extreme, or in a state of potentially violent delayed rebellion at the other. Japan, too, has that badge of modern society, the 'battered mother syndrome'.

'Today's parents,' a leading newspaper proclaimed, 'bear a lot more responsibility in their children's upbringing than did the parents of larger families, and yet they are exercising less.' It is almost as if many of today's mothers never imbided the art of motherhood. 'Our children', complains one mother, 'are completely in the hands of the teachers and television.' The older traditions of intense protection are still in the majority, though a little emasculated, but when they do break down there is no safety net of alternative groupism or culti-vated individualism to catch the unfortunate and unprepared child.

After the smothering comes the prodding. A couple goes to extraordinary lengths to ensure its child's success at school and university, even robbing it of the stimulus of self-reliance. A classic example in the 1950s was the violinist Yoko Kubo, whose parents actually divorced solely to further her education. Living in Okinawa, they were advised that she should train in Tokyo if her talent were to flourish. Travel was then restricted to special cases, such as people in need of urgent medicine or divorced wives going back to their parents' home. Although the Kubos were Catholic, their priest agreed to give them a token divorce enabling the girl to go with her mother to Tokyo.

After all, the 1872 Education Act, the bible of modern schooling in Japan, had declared definitely that 'everyone should subordinate all other matters to the education of his children'. Lavish gifts are showered on teachers, and, when a husband is posted to another part of the country or abroad, one out of two couples prefer to split up so that their children's progress through local schools is not interrupted. Failure is a social, not just a personal lapse: an Osaka father who gassed himself when his boy failed to get into a good secondary school was not thought unusual.

Closely knit in life, the family may carry its solidarity to the grave. When Toshio Hattori, driving drunk and uninsured without a licence, knocked an innocent young woman down on the road, he signed his entire family's death warrant. The stress of finding the money he agreed to pay the girl, aggravated by the burden of helping look after her at the hospital and guilt at consequently neglecting their own young daughters aged six and eight, led the Hattoris to tie themselves and their children up and then jump into a deep river.

As smaller groups of kinsmen are thrust into greater intimacy, violence becomes more visible and less restrained in the family and young teenagers increasingly take it for granted. A seventeen-year-old stabs his mother to death for telling him to turn his radio down; a boy taking the entrance exam for Tokyo University kills his parents with a baseball bat after a scolding; a father chokes his teenage son to death for no apparent reason – such tragedies occur in all countries, but are nowhere more distressing than in partly-Confucian Japan where family values are cardinal.

Where is the family structure heading? Trends are difficult to pinpoint, because the cement that bonds the family together is neither strong and particular like the moral authority radiated by the traditionally autocratic Jewish or Chinese father, nor diffused but articulated like the mutual affection that keeps many a European or American family together. It is something less definable, namely a network of reciprocal rights and duties whose content depends on the particular relationship – you must do this for your mother, that for your elder brother, something else for your younger sister, and all these obligations are sweetened and made bearable by the duty of those others to do things for you. When a Japanese feels guilt, it is not because he has broken a rule laid down by some Moses or Confucius, but rather because he senses that he has let the people in his immediate family down, failed their expectations.

This is neither authoritarian, since there is no arbitrary dictator in the family circle, nor democratic, since you cannot get out of the obligations. But whatever label may be found for it, the system works. It has produced not only social order but a degree of mobility and flexibility invaluable to Japan's industrialization. Its form continues, despite the miniaturization of households. Does the substance hold?

True to their innate fatalism, the Japanese themselves are pessimistic on this score. A journalist finds that, 'Brothers and sisters have lost the affinity and solidarity of a 'family' and pay no attention to the affairs of their relatives. The fibres of kinship have disintegrated . . .' Hiroshi Iwai, a Professor of Medicine, feels that teenagers have rejected their old vertical relationships with parents. 'Is our society,' he asks rhetorically, 'doomed to become a jungle where isolated animals, having lost their common humanity . . . separately stalk their own selfish ends?'

Government social welfare has, of course, eroded the sense of obligation to aged parents felt by working children – who now refuse sometimes to take their demanding elders back in the house after a spell in hospital. Surveys show that many young people find no significant meaning in their family life. From such an unpromising start, can tomorrow's parents create homes with love and protection from outside forces and at the same time satisfy one another as small-family companions and lovers? It will be a tough assignment for the Japanese family, needing all the supportive help of the best of the old tradition as well as self-confidence in rejecting harmful aspects of the western example. But the despondency of some Japanese writers should not be too infectious: there is a good chance that Japanese society will survive these changes without lapsing into anarchy.

The Japanese family is changing with modernization, but the negative changes – smaller households, fewer elders living in the home, parents having less time to bring up children – are easier to chart than the positive ones. The spread of privacy, for example, seems ambiguous as a factor for social progress, making for more satisfied parents and teenagers, but also for less worldly-wise and socially embosomed small children. There are gains, nevertheless, such as the slow but perceptible growth of individualism and the increasing presence of love in marriages that in the old days were largely arranged by totally unromantic criteria. There is even evidence that some married couples, reacting against the trend, are beginning to favour the three-children family and three-generation household again.

These gains are likely to colour the future of the Japanese family more than might be guessed from the defeatist commentaries of the

Japanese themselves, caught in the whirlwind of breakneck change without any balanced point of reference. Selectivity in Western social imports should combine with the sheer rugged vitality of the tradition to ensure the survival of the essential nucleus of those family values that still appeal to the Japanese personality. The old family charabanc has been taken out of service, but the little minis which instead fill the motorways remember their predecessor and retain some at least of its good points, as well as incorporating the new facilities offered by the material progress of their own society and the envied features of foreign models.

4

Life Below the Navel
Sex in Japan

WHAT TWO people do beneath the bed-quilt is private, a less obvious candidate for cultural change than family life itself. Cosmopolitan connoisseurs of the *shunga** of Japan's classical pornography and modern cinema, rank Japan high in the sexual arts. They would say Japan has more to teach the West about sex than the other way round. Yet subtle changes are taking place, not in the act of love itself but in the social climate surrounding it.

The Japanese used to be marvellously free of that solemn puritanism which darkened Europe in the Christian era. Before Meiji there was a tradition of bodily pleasure that was relaxed, open and free. Far from chivvying the act of love into dark corners, society actually approved it. Sexuality was frankly acknowledged, without cynicism and in all naturalness. No one was shocked by the hero in a Tanizaki novel who died of too much sex.

When Japan began consciously to modernize herself in the late nineteenth century, fuddy-duddy foreign experts advised her not only to acquire new industrial technology, but also to 'clean up' her morality – from clothing habits to sex – in order to follow the successful example of Europe. A shallow wave of Victorian prudishness then flowed over Japan, but did not destroy her underlying preference for more open and tolerant attitudes. Following the western example, an 'official', slightly sanitized view of sex gained ground in Japan. The Meiji state in the late nineteenth century, trying to grind down some of Japan's sturdy artlessness in the name of 'keeping up with the West', stopped people from taking their summer baths outdoors, for example, so that Westerners would no longer laugh at their nakedness.

A Japanese grasps more readily than a Westerner the opportunities presented by everyday life to gratify the basic physical pleasure of being legitimately close to other human bodies and literally in touch with them – in the family or public bath, for example, in bed, or while nursing patients or taking care of children. If a sexual feeling were to

---

* Erotic 'spring drawings' in the *ukiyoe* style, usually exaggerating the genitals.

steal into such domestic situations, it would complicate things and spoil the innocent enjoyment. The custom is, therefore, for both parties to ignore it or exclude it in some way – or deflate it with a joke – in order to prolong the simply physical pleasure of sexless bodily contact (something western society has largely forgotten about).

Nakedness was not shameful in the old Japan. 'They wash twice a day', reported a seventeenth-century Portuguese missionary, 'and do not worry if their privy parts are seen.' Nudity was such a cliché that some lovers found a frisson in 'dressing up' for sex. Today, people try out of courtesy not to expose themselves in full frontage to others. When you are washing at the baths, you cannot avoid this, so others will studiously look past you. Even so, while walking about or sitting in the bathhouse, you will primly dangle a modest little flannel over the parts you prefer not to inflict upon the vision of others of either sex.

In the summer, people used to walk home stark naked from the baths, even into the twentieth century, and others would ignore such nudity in appropriate circumstances. 'Nakedness,' it was said, 'is to be seen but not looked at.' Only a downright prude like the British Bishop George Smith (in the 1860s) could censure the intermingling of ages and sexes at the baths 'in one shameless throng', and go on to condemn the Japanese as 'one of the most licentious races in the world' – exaggerating the licence and underestimating the shame. The Japanese, be it noted, who did not think twice about mixed bathing in the nude, reeled in horror when first exposed to the 'unnatural' and 'unclean' American-style invention of putting a lavatory and bath together in the same room. 'A device that sets your own sewage out in front of your eyes,' a character in a Tanizaki novel complains, 'is highly offensive to good taste.'

What Japanese also enjoy about the public bath, besides its purely physical pleasure, is the way it breaks down barriers between people, facilitating the human relationships which are life's great goal. 'Psychologically,' a housewife comments, 'I feel I am expanding myself in the tub . . . You can talk more freely . . . It is not only the steam, but you are free from clothes . . .' An American immigrant enlarges the sentiment: 'Being in the bath with my wife was one of the things that helped free me sexually. Nobody in America knows how close you can feel to a woman when you are in a Japanese bathtub with her.'

Another natural phenomenon which enjoys a better status in Japan than in Europe is farting. The poet Sakura wrote a *haiku* guaranteed to appeal to all schoolchildren:

> The lady teacher
> Does not look as though
> She would ever fart.

Such natural irreverence is not just a thing of the past. There is a post-war film by Yasujiro Ozu where children compete to see who can fart loudest and longest. And when the atom bomb was dropped in Nagasaki, a schoolboy rallied his colleagues by comparing the noise with an emperor's fart in a witty parody of an imperial edict: 'Know ye, our subjects, we broke wind involuntarily; you . . . must find it malodorous, but pray withstand it for a second.'

Urination fails to shock, too. A leading politician and candidate for Prime Minister was recently caught by a press camera pee-ing against a gingko tree in the gardens of the Diet. It did him no noticeable harm. Yet another example of naturalness is over the fact that a man's testicles hang low when he is relaxed: during the crucial naval battle with the Russians in 1905, the Japanese Chief of Staff apparently tested Admiral Togo's composure by putting a hand out to feel the position of his balls. He was relieved to find them hanging down, and passed the fact on to appreciative colleagues. On the other hand Okamoto, the terrorist who shot up an Israeli airport in 1972, was chagrined to discover, when the time for his exploit arrived, that his testicles had contracted.

None of these non-sexual natural phenomena raises a puritanical snigger in Japan – and sexual sensuality is not the target of scorn either. One might expect elderly Anglo-Saxons to respond to any kind of sensual delight with strait-laced repression. A Japanese, by contrast, will squirm with innocent joy under, for instance, the masseur's hands. He believes that the stiff upper lip does not suck the best from life. (Here again, Europe is now moving towards the more tolerant Japanese position.)

Consider these random examples from contemporary Japanese life:

– In a film about a striptease dancer, she notices a member of the audience masturbating happily, his eyes fixed on her crotch. Touched, she leans forward to ask tenderly: 'Doing OK, dear?' at which he gently nods. There is no sleazy coarseness of the kind that would inform such a scene in a European or American movie.

– A pop record poster widely displayed in Tokyo shows a sexy young male singer making a provocative gesture underneath the slogan 'Tonight from Inoue Yosui – 7 inches!'

– A tent manufacturer distributes 25,000 company magazines every

month unashamedly devoted to sex, because he finds that is the way
to get its name and product known.
– A teenage girl's magazine runs a letter from a reader complaining
that her brother had surreptitiously photographed her while she
was masturbating. The agony column editor's advice was: get even,
do the same to him!

This is not the climate of a society that has lost touch with nature.
One curiosity is that the Japanese, who so admirably tolerate sex in
real life, can be troubled by it when depicted by writers or artists. As
Fosco Maraini has neatly observed, Japan admits nudity in life but
not in art – the converse of the European approach. It is rare to see
fully naked lovers in the *shunga*, where it is often only the penis and
vagina, enlarged in loving detail to perhaps ten times life size (for the
highly practical but restricted purpose of privately enlightening or
stimulating lovers), that are unclothed. When Yukio Mishima had
himself photographed in the buff for his last book, the publisher
virtuously cut him off just below the navel.

It was Seiki Kuroda, the Paris-trained painter of the 1890s, who
offered the first Japanese nudes to be taken as serious art rather than
utilitarian pornography. Scandalized bureaucrats put the matter to
the Supreme Court – which judged that anything aspiring to be art
should show no genital details or pubic hair. This is still broadly the
official policy, though with a little relaxation. The French government recently had to lodge an official protest when the Japanese
Customs, following these curiously out-of-character rules, banned a
collection of Man Ray photographs intended for exhibition – because
they showed the dreaded pubic hairs.

Even stranger was the postwar course of literary censorship. *Lady
Chatterley's Lover* and de Sade's *Juliet* were judged obscene by the
same Supreme Court in the 1960s (both publisher and translator were
found guilty). The former contained passages 'that one would hesi-
tate to recite to the family circle', serving only to 'excite and stimulate
sexual desire'. Despite the long line of distinguished Japanese pornography catering for precisely that need, and those endless classical
novels celebrating the '108 appetites of the flesh' in the indulgent
Buddhist canon, Japan's unconfident censors forbid foreign pornography. They do so apparently because *foreign* opinion has already
judged it shocking, and they feel Japan should keep up with the
blue-pencilling Joneses of the West. Nagisa Oshima, the avant-garde
film director, took no chances with his masterpiece *Empire of the
Senses* (containing the famous scene where a jealous woman cuts off
her lover's penis): the negatives were all sent to Paris for developing,

to escape the Japanese censor. After their millennial love affair with nature, the Japanese have a high resistance to being inwardly shocked by any human phenomena. But their authorities try to protect them from what, it is felt, *ought* to shock a modern enlightened people, even if it signally fails to do so.

The irony is that what ordinary Japanese first found shocking about Western sex habits was not the explicitness of D. H. Lawrence or the morbid imaginings of Sade but such public behaviour as open kissing and dancing, a man and woman walking arm-in-arm, a woman wearing bright colours and make-up, the casualness of divorce. These were what offended ordinary Japanese when the American Occupation forces were showing off in Japan in the late 1940s and 1950s. Intellectuals and professionals were receptive to Americanism, but the man in the street was more Victorian, at least towards marriage, the family aspects of sex and public appearances.

Hollywood has made the kiss a central sacrament of the Western sex relationship. But the Japanese used unromantically to call it *kuchi-sui* or mouth-sucking, and some of them believed it was an import. 'The mouth', a *geisha* insists, 'was not intended by nature for contact with another person's, only for eating and speaking.' It was 'gentlemen from abroad' who invented 'this extraordinary perversion'. A mother similarly warned her daughter before visiting America to beware 'the custom among foreigners to lick one anothers' faces like dogs'. The kiss that accompanied or immediately preceded the sexual climax, caught in many feelingly-composed *shunga*, was an involuntary response to approaching orgasm, not a deliberate and separate action. As another *geisha* puts it: 'We do not kiss casually in the Western way. We Japanese eat and drink our kisses, making them part of the whole act of love.'

For the milder Hollywood version of the kiss, the US occupation authorities in 1950 thoughtfully arranged a teach-in in a Tokyo restaurant where an American actress demonstrated her techniques for the benefit of the inquisitive Japanese profession. But this was another reform that did not stick. The Japanese do not even kiss much within the family. Only recently a provincial housewife, asked by her five-year-old daughter if she had ever kissed Daddy, replied: 'Me? Kiss Papa? Oh no! God forbid . . .' Japan's Kinsey, Professor Asayama, calculated that American eight-year-olds were kissed nine times more often than Japanese. The casual social kiss is simply un-Japanese.

The change in the Japanese attitude can be measured by the status of mistresses and prostitutes. A pre-Meiji mistress was not only unconcealed but enjoyed considerable status. In Chikamatsu's early eighteenth-century play *The Uprooted Pine*, when a wife allows her husband's mistress to see him in his hour of disgrace, the grateful mistress gushes: 'Forgive me, please, for having so often held your beloved husband in my arms and slept with him.'

Up to the end of the nineteenth century the common view remained, as before, that 'heroes are fond of women', and 'keeping a mistress is a badge of ability'. Newspapers wrote matter-of-factly about the political leaders' mistresses: did not Emperor Meiji himself have, according to the Yokohama City Directory, as many as five concubines – including the mother of Crown Prince Taisho? (When an American resident of those days unwisely asked his local public library to lend him a published book in Japanese about the Imperial concubines, he was refused, however, with the remark that foreigners could be freely informed only about what was good, true and beautiful in Japan.)

Under Emperor Taisho, in the first quarter of the twentieth century, attitudes hardened. Men in public life are now expected, though not quite as seriously as in Europe, to be monogamous. Neither John Profumo nor Cecil Parkinson would have lost politically in Japan, where opponents and the media still observe a taboo against making capital out of the sexual peccadilloes of public figures. You do not profit from what is happening 'below the navel'. When Prime Minister Kakuei Tanaka was forced to resign in 1974, it was not because he had an acknowledged mistress living openly with their children in a fine house in a good district of Tokyo, but because he accepted a £1 million bribe from Lockheed to influence Japanese government aircraft procurement.

The modernists did at least abolish the brothel, in 1958 – and the last night's customers all over the country went into a shamelessly plangent rendering of Auld Lang Syne. The Japanese used to be quite open about these institutions: an American once called on a Japanese businessman at his office and was cheerfully told that he was at the brothel – and could be seen there if the visitor cared to call. Twenty years after these institutions had been suppressed, Professor Hayao Kawai of Kyoto University regretted their passing. In a learned article he doubted whether men were capable of integrating what had formerly been their two separate but complementary worlds – of stressful reality and harem fantasy. New rationales for the brothels began to be advanced – by men, of course.

Wives did sometimes encourage their husbands to seek pleasure from more experienced professionals in the early stages of a marriage; wives unable to produce heirs were similarly cavalier in sending the husband off to have a child by another woman (and where else to go?). For men whose work was so demanding that they needed sex relief immediately afterwards it was altogether more convenient to call at the brothel than to interfere with such domestic arrangements as cooking, eating and coping with children – all without privacy. Even snobbery was often enough to mollify a wife's feelings, since not every husband could afford a brothel's charges. One poet expressed the verdict of a fond mother on her grown-up son's devotion to the bordello in the lines:

> But you know
> It's better than gambling.

The abolition left the male love-on-the-side scene unstructured. There is always, of course, the wife next door, about whose voluntary involvement fewer tears are shed or blows struck than in, say, Latin societies. The millions of Japanese devotees of *Dallas* failed to understand why, when J. R. Ewing spent the night with a married woman, her husband came round to try to rape J.R.'s wife. It made no sense to them. Prostitutes, mistresses and bar hostesses are still in evidence (and the converse commercial arrangements for women clients have just begun to appear), though their services are more expensive and furtive than before.

Recently, a pretty young hostess pushed her way into the house of her patron, a middle-aged company president who had told her he was ending their arrangement. She stayed there a whole month negotiating a better golden handshake than he had originally offered. His wife served her meals until she departed. It was a classic example of the two worlds, one of free-wheeling fantasy, the other of punishing slog, momentarily overlapping to the consternation of the subject.

So now post-brothel Japan is flooded not merely with bars where hostesses congregate, but also with Turkish baths and Love Hotels – called *Abeku Hoteru*, from the French, since you always come *avec* partner. These have no single rooms and serve no food, but some of them are the last word in luxurious fantasy, technically equipped for erotic sojourn, and catering not merely for the middle-aged man on the loose, but also for young people trying to get away from omnipresent parents. In some cities Love Hotels must not be within 100 yards of a school or social welfare institution, and one censorious municipality undermined them by banning double beds. But across the country they are now said to gross £13 million a year.

The Turkish Bath is another outlet. The sign outside one in Kyoto tells the story:

. . . with sufficient sweet-smelling soap you are washed from head
to foot and refreshingly massaged your burning body. Concealing
clear shame in glamour figures Turks girls are waiting for you. Fee
Yen 1,200 one hour in private room including service charge.

The general idea is so clear that the Turkish government formally
complained of its country's name being defamed, and now these
establishments are officially re-labelled – as 'Soaplands'. A group of
woman politicians tried to get the private room service made illegal,
but the bathhouses were well enough connected with the more
numerous and powerful male politicians to frustrate them.

Dating clubs, sometimes called lovers' banks, pioneered by the
so-called *Yogorezoku* (twilight set) are the latest on the sex scene. The
police have investigated them, but free association by amateurs
is legal and above board, and so they can flourish if they are careful.
One 'Adam and Eve' lovers' bank with 250 girl students and
secretaries was found to have on its books more than fifty members of
parliament, some of whom, the madame volunteered, 'ask me to fill
in the registration form for fear that their handwriting may be
recognized. But I know who they are because I keep seeing them on
TV.'

Sex is alive and flourishing, therefore, as it always was in Japan,
and bogus Westernization has had only limited effect. The institutions alter their façades, but their substance continues as long as
people need them. The biggest threat to them now is the revolution in
women's lives and prospects. On the one hand this leads to host clubs
for women as part of Japanese women's liberation; on the other it
means there are fewer women prepared to invest serious effort into
giving men pleasure (though there is no shortage of women ready to
make money out of them). Hence the universal complaint among the
older men that Japanese women have lost their charm. Hence the
embarrassing daily migrations of elderly males via Haneda airport on
diplomatically disastrous sex tours to Bangkok, Manila, Taipei and
Hongkong. 'Japanese men,' a travel agent elucidates, 'like to feel
superior to women. These ladies abroad can be very attentive.
Japanese women used to be that way, but maybe they're getting
spoiled, and Japanese bar hostesses are too expensive.'

Few Japanese today are upset by the idea of sexual permissiveness,
and parents are more worried about the risk of their student offspring
going 'red' (Communist) than 'pink' (promiscuous). The conformity
required of brain and heart is not expected of wayward organs 'below
the navel', provided the nonconformity is not flaunted in public.

Homosexuality provides confirmation of these complex trends, with a pedigree extending back into Japan's steamy antiquity. A twelfth-century romance retails the astonishing sexual adventures of a brother and sister at the lax imperial court who chose to live as members of the opposite sex, something echoed in the present century at Niwaka where every September men and women exchanged dress as part of an antique festival. The handsome Prince Genji, whose tenth-century amours filled a very long contemporaneous novel, when rebuffed by one scorcher despite the intercessions of her young brother, went to bed with the lad instead and found him 'no bad substitute for his ungracious sister'.

The *kabuki* theatre enjoyed today by Westerners as well as Japanese was founded by a sixteenth-century woman who wore Portuguese trousers and a crucifix in drag stage skits: when patrons started openly brawling for the favours of her pretty successors, the government (in 1629) banned them, so young men played the parts instead – leading to equally violent quarrelling by the *samurai* over their male favourites. Finally the government restricted the parts to mature men. The *noh* drama, where masks are used, is also linked with the homosexual world, having been inaugurated by a *shogun*'s boyfriend, and the first *geisha* were actually men. Today's *onnagata* who take female roles in *kabuki* are not necessarily gay: there is a *trousers* faction which acts male off-stage, in opposition to the *kimono* faction which goes on wearing women's dress even at home after the final curtain.

Unhappy *samurai* used to go in for double suicides with their boyfriends, a tradition resurrected in the *harakiri* of the writer Yukio Mishima and his friend in 1970. One of the *samurai* ideals, after all, was to avoid sex with women, who were thought distracting and impure. (It is only a couple of centuries since some families in southern Japan would not hang women's washing on the same clothes-line as men's.)

Unlike the West, Japan never outlawed the practice of homosexuality. A European missionary in Japan in the sixteenth century was surprised to find it treated so lightly. 'Both the boys and the men who consort with them brag . . . about it openly,' while the Japanese priests regard it as 'something quite natural and virtuous'. 'Sodomy', a Jesuit, Juan Fernandez, reported, 'was not a sin'. Contemporary Europeans confirm this. 'In Japan the word vice is neither uttered nor hinted at,' says Charles Grosbois, the French art critic, 'sodomy is a sexual pleasure like others.'

A Japanese psychologist corroborates this disparity with Western sexual inhibitions: 'It seems that homosexual desires are given abundant opportunity for satisfaction in Japan.' So open is the atmosphere that the Japanese themselves can misread it, as an encounter between two psychiatrists, Miyaki of Tokyo University and Magnus Hirschfeld, indicates:

'Tell me, my dear Hirschfeld, how is it that one hears so much about homosexuality in Germany, Italy and England and nothing of it among us?'

'That, my dear colleague,' Hirschfeld replied, 'is because it is permitted by you and forbidden by us.'

In another film of Nagisa Oshima called *Merry Christmas Mr Lawrence*, David Bowie and the late Ryuichi Sakamoto (in real life two very popular singers), kiss on the parade ground of a Japanese prisoner-of-war camp. Asked the inevitable question afterwards, Sakamoto told the press: 'I myself could be homosexual in certain situations. If there is a person, male or female, that I can really respect, I love that person. It's not an unnatural thing.'

It is a decade now since an innovating artist introduced Japanese newspaper readers to their first gay strip-cartoon hero. In 1980 an election candidate used his statutory time on TV to boast, in female *kimono* and lipstick, about his affair with one of the producers of that station (which was, he added, 'riddled with homosexuals'). He lost the seat: while private behaviour is not criticized, public conformity is still required. The lesbian lover of a popular woman singer once told all on a TV programme, whereupon the stations barred the singer until the whole incident had been forgotten by the fickle public mind. It was the public unsteadying of the boat of propriety, not any intrinsic wickedness in sleeping with another woman, which caused the trouble. Japan treats sexual deviation not as a neurosis but as a question of taste.

Lesbianism as a social phenomenon is newer than male homosexuality: it was a more direct beneficiary of the sex equality and personal liberation movements of the 1950s. Tanizaki's 1930 novel *Manji* had celebrated lesbian love, apparently influenced by his reading *The Well of Loneliness* in English. Today inquisitive foreigners go to the all-female Takurazuka Theatre in Tokyo to see all-female audiences enthuse over their favourite girls taking the boy's parts, while some sociologists theorize that young wives are left alone at home so long by their workaholic husbands that mutual sexual comforting may be widespread. But Japan's penchant for homosociability is usually innocent and does not necessarily lead to sex.

In any case, the pressures of modernization and Westernization have injected some prudery into this theoretically permissive gay scene, ironically beginning with the young. A recent survey showed that, among people in their late 'teens and early twenties, only one in ten is actually sympathetic to homosexuality, while three-quarters express repugnance. Those same young people, and their younger brothers and sisters, probably find in the lurid comics which purvey, for instance, the gay frolics of blond English boys, a harmless release from the calculating conformism into which their society is thrusting them. Soft pornography supplies an outlet for their fantasies, appealing to their inner natures which deplore the passing of the old Japanese freedoms. The apparent increase in superficial sexuality which we witness today, especially in the entertainment world, may thus disguise the opposite, a slow painful trend towards repressed conformity. What we see now may actually be the dying kicks of the old sexuality.

See how children's budding sexuality is warped by modernization. When everyone stripped off, regardless of sex or age, in the public bathhouses, children's curiosity about sexual differences was easily and naturally satisfied. Today people can afford their own bathrooms at home, and there is more prudishness about nudity, so the bathhouses are disappearing. Boys no longer automatically find out about girls, and in consequence there is increasing curiosity leading to sexual delinquency in the primary schools (one seven-year-old boy killed a girl who threatened to tell her mother he had tried to molest her).

Surveys show that young Japan does not have the courage of all its permissive convictions. Girls who 'sleep around' encounter prejudice when it comes to marriage, and doctors profit from their need of operations to 'restore' virginity. Only one secondary school student out of ten admits to experiencing full intercourse, while only half have masturbated, according to an official Tokyo poll. The key word in this plethora of opinion surveys is 'admit': in Japan you traditionally tend to admit to what you believe the other person wants you to. Nevertheless, these figures do indicate a broad social restraint about sex which stands in strong contrast both with aggressive American sexual attitudes and with the highly visible permissiveness of a small minority of Japanese who centre on the Ginza, Shinjuku, Akasuka, Gion and similar entertainment quarters of the big cities.

Thoughtful Japanese have already concluded, like Shuji Terayama in his book *Making the Rounds of America's Hells*, that the Americans altogether overrate sex. Perhaps, he suggests, Americans are driven by their growing personal isolation into a desperate reaching out for human contact: 'free sex is the search mounted by lonely bodies . . .' Japanese bodies are never strictly as lonely as western ones, though they may in various ways be frustrated, suppressed, unsatisfied – and the social cushion catches most of the individual misery which in a Western society falls out to breed neurosis and crime.

The only genuine Westernization going on in Japanese sex life is, oddly enough, as aesthetic one. The traditional qualities for which a red-blooded Japanese male would look in a woman were white skin and good skin texture, rather than shape or measurements. But the younger generation seems to have been gulled by Hollywood propaganda into placing structural criteria before textural ones – boobs and the hourglass figure before complexion.

The Japanese entered their modern period a century ago, permissive in sexual activity but restrained in the social circumstances in which they would pursue it. Today they have become slightly more prudish, having absorbed a few artificial attitudes from the West. For all the 1950s cult of Sartre and Left Bank individualism, Japan has not lost its basically sober attitudes. Sex is mainly to be enjoyed in limited, mapped-out situations like marriage or the modern substitutes for prostitution, and should remain a passing enjoyment – not something to dictate one's social life or get in the way of one's more important relationships. The naturalness and permissiveness come *after* the decision to open a sexual relation: before that, one agonizes over the social implications and consequences.

Sex can always be indulged with a person whose inferior social role may be considered as accommodating it – which means, for most men, a bar hostess, secretary, air stewardess or hotel receptionist. But men do not lightly tangle sexually with women who are their equals, or whose social status might be higher than their own. There are large areas of shyness in the average Japanese personality when it comes to sexual approach, but for social rather than sexual reasons.

Sex has its place and its time in Japan: once it happens, the naturalness with which it can be enjoyed, and the tolerance with which third parties may view it, would be envied by most Europeans. But the difficulty which the two persons concerned may experience in creating the opportunity in the first place would sometimes, to the contrary, surprise a Westerner. Not only the naturalness and the tolerance, but also the difficulty exceeds what might be expected in a Western society. Hence the mutual jealousy between Japan and the West, each suspecting the other gets the better sexual deal. Hence the falsely-labelled borrowing by Japan in the 1890s and early twentieth century when, in Tanizaki's claim, 'the greatest influence we received from Western literature was the liberation of love, and indeed even of sexual desire' – and again in the second wave of the 1950s and 1960s.

Actually, it was a dose of egotism, swallowed at the cost of numerous unwanted side-effects. Such old values as consideration for the feelings and expectations of others, of one's family, of the other person's family, of the unborn children and of the security of society itself, were weakened. It was ostentatious greed and short-sighted selfishness that Japan took from the West, a disliked import on which she is now seeking to clap quota restrictions – and which she would ideally like to return to sender.

5

The Loosening of the Group
Japan's Social Structure

'OLD JAPAN was like an oyster,' said Basil Chamberlain, the Briton who lived there a hundred years ago: 'To open it was to kill it.' Much that was distinctive about Japan then has indeed disappeared, and we see a new Japan that has its roots in tradition but its foliage formed by modern experience, by all the millions of changes since Chamberlain recorded the dying hours of the old *samurai* Japan.

To understand contemporary Japanese society, and the direction in which it is developing, the outsider needs to know first what the old tradition was – not in every detail but in broad spirit. He then needs to see what the social changes have been in the past century. And since the exact mixture varies with time, place and person, he must then test out his construct anew with each Japanese friend he meets, and each Japanese community he visits.

There has been so much theorizing about traditional Japanese society that a Westerner could be forgiven for assuming that the Japanese are too idiosyncratic, too different from anything in the West, too bizarre ever to be understood. But that is no more than a bundle of new myths superimposed by western anthropologists on the many equally extraordinary Japanese myths. The Japanese are not essentially different human beings in any major respect, it is just that they have built up a modern sophisticated society by a different route from the West's. Probably the most important distinction is that Japan never experienced the kind of monotheistic religion which has so marked the countries of the West. That makes for some differences in social relationships, in attitudes to other people and in the way in which morality is expressed in day-to-day life. It does not make the Japanese in any whit 'inferior' and, indeed, western scholars are now identifying ways in which that kind of system can produce socially superior results. The western reader of a book about Japan must resist the temptation to assume that, because something seems different from Western practice, it must therefore be worse.

Japanese traditional society was more a society of groups than of individuals. The family, the office or work-team, were the focus of life, within which individuals acted with only limited autonomy.

Because there was no universal ethic, an individual depended on, for example, the Confucianist categories of duty in his behaviour to others. He was kind to his son or supervisor, indifferent or even cruel to a total stranger. It was a label society: the label told what a person was, and that decided how he would be treated (which is one reason why name-cards are so important). Good and evil were relative terms, and morality sprang from a man's environment rather than welling up from within his own private conscience.

Instead of striking out to deal directly with a stranger, people preferred to use mutual friends or go-betweens. Obligation weakened the further a person went away from his community, and there was a saying that, 'a man travelling away from home need feel no shame'. Confronted by the human vivisection atrocities of his compatriots in wartime China, a Japanese writer commented: 'We do not act as individuals: Japanese can do any evil when they are in groups.' But this is not primarily a question of how to treat foreigners. Within traditional Japanese society native inferiors are treated with disdain rather than charity: there is no Japanese equivalent of the Salvation Army and its good works, nobody wants to adopt a Vietnamese refugee, and the common attitude to the blind and disabled is to hide them away.

Instead of the larger-than-life precepts of the New Testament, or the Koran, the Japanese followed a complex set of duties towards particular individuals or groups, in which mutual respect and consideration were the key factors – loosely conveyed in the word *giri*. It is as if the weak and infrequent urge of young English couples to pay that long-promised call on old Aunt Flo, which laziness and competing business have put off, were multiplied, intensified, codified, made more formal and taken far more seriously. Gifts played a central role in these scenarios. If a colleague called on your home with a basket of fruit, your wife would be at the greengrocer's next morning to find out how much it cost. That evening the two of you would discuss whether, when you next called on that colleague, it would be appropriate to take a bottle of liquor, and of what value. There is still an etiquette of relations with neighbours called *tsukiai* which extends to taking mutual advantage of services and contacts to buy opera tickets, for example, or get into golf clubs or enter children at good schools – all on a reciprocal basis, and not primarily to save money but rather to enrich the relationships.

The American sociologist Ruth Benedict argued in her classic *The Chrysanthemum and the Sword* that this system of piecemeal morality rested on the sanction of shame rather than guilt: it is what others might think of you ('face') that stopped you from beating your wife, not your inner conscience. The Japanese are the first to agree that they have no concept of sin or guilt in the Old Testament sense. The American scholar, George A. de Vos, detected an alternative source of Japanese guilt in the sense of failure to match the expectations of one's self-sacrificing parents (especially one's long-suffering, uncomplaining mother). This fuelled a strong drive to justify oneself through hard work, and so the Japanese emerged as 'oriental Calvinists'. The guilt stemming from intense family relationships was not as readily visible to the observer as shame, but was probably as important in the psychic mix as guilt of a different colour in Europe.

The most important small group to which a Japanese belonged was the family or household, followed by the people in immediate neighbouring households: your best friends, it used to be said, were in the three houses opposite yours and the two on either side of you. The real formality started at the next level, the *buraku*, originally a sub-unit of a village in which a dozen or two farming households systematically co-operated in agricultural work besides jointly running woods and pastureland on a profit-sharing basis – and often a shrine, cemetery, fire-engine and crop-processing unit as well. It was a kind of local self-government in miniature. Probably the germ of the Japanese group habit or collectivism had come from the need for prehistoric farmers to till hillsides by terracing and irrigation which could not be done by one family alone.

The solidarity was over-riding. Even after the war there was one village which ostracized a family, because its daughter had bravely exposed an election fraud and thus given the village a bad name with the politicians in power. The *buraku* is less important now, but its memory is cherished and its spirit may still inform the residents of a city street or the small industrial shopfloor when they need to undertake collective action.

In these small groups the traditional Japanese did not pick and choose his associates, membership being dictated by where he lived or worked: even his family was pre-selected. The only outlet for the volitional drive in human sociability was personal friendship, which the Japanese therefore cultivated tenaciously. Today friends are becoming ever more important in Japanese emotions as the family shrinks. Classmates, workmates and neighbourhood friends of one's own sex are the most popular people in whom to confide troubles.

The most intimate circle is called *shinyu*, friends between whom there is no barrier, no secret, no mistrust and no withholding – a kind of *Brüderschaft* bond which may be closer than ties within a family. A friend was someone about whom you would formerly tell a lie to help him get a job: today most Japanese claim (perhaps falsely) that they would report truthfully about any unreliability on a friend's part. So much at ease with one another, physically and emotionally, do such friends appear, so openly do they enjoy the comradeship of sharing pleasures, that Anglo-Saxon visitors can misinterpret. 'To western eyes', a Japanese psychologist surmises, 'Japan appears to be an unusually homosexual society' (he might better have used the adjective 'homosocial'). The emotional involvement can be intense, and Japanese seeking to build up some degree of independence, on a western model perhaps, can find it suffocating. 'One craves,' a Japanese ambassador complains, 'for those detached, half-tone friendships which are so frequent among Occidentals.'

One of the Japanese journalists whom I used to meet on my visits to Tokyo suddenly produced a little notebook at the lunch table in the 1960s and demanded to know my school, university and college. He had decided that such historical ties were important among Westerners, and that he could better analyse the views of his western friends by zealously logging their affiliations. Actually personal or ideological likes and dislikes often trump such institutional cards in Western reunions, but that kind of categorization is persuasive in Japan.

Groups were clearly defined and made many demands on their members. Even the Japanese themselves found it difficult to get inside a group: if a family moved to another town it might need to bring formal introductions to its new neighbours, and leave gifts at every door before being accepted. Once admitted, however, group members felt decidedly separate from those outside and were reluctant to socialize with them. Professor Chie Nakane laments how this caused many Japanese to miss 'the excitement or tension of coming to grips with people outside their own circle'.

The prize for a man's self-negation in belonging to a group was comradeship and security. As long as he obeyed the group consensus he would be protected, even to the extent of having excuses fabricated for some mistake he might have committed. But the price was not merely to suppress his personal desires when they differed from the others', but also to hide his own feelings by the use of flattery, insinuation and the smile – all to jolly the consensus along, safeguard the others' self-respect and avoid damaging confrontations. Belonging to a group in Japan was no formality. It took hard work over long hours, and was emotionally draining. Recently a drunken rugger player from Waseda University shocked public opinion by assaulting a taxi driver: his club not only expelled him but made collective penance by withdrawing the entire team from play for a whole season. Some fans accepted this as an expression of group responsibility, but the *Japan Times* condemned it as a feudalistic injustice. The group can be carried too far – and that is now recognized.

Individuals were brought round to supporting their group's decisions by consensus, which Lafcadio Hearn defined as the authoritarianism of the many over the one. Precedent, rules and principles did not stand in the way (as they can in England), so that rapid and wholesale changes were easy to effect when virtually everyone wanted them. On the other hand, decisions were excruciatingly slow if opinions strongly conflicted, for these could not (except in some rural areas under strong Buddhist influence) be resolved by majority. If you were on the losing side of the argument, you could try to exact some *quid pro quo* on another issue, but eventually you had to give in and join the majority if only to keep the wheels of life turning. You would then be expected to refrain from openly challenging the consensus, whatever your personal thoughts might be, and this led to the sophisticated system of formalized two-tier communication – *tatemae* (the group view, or the 'public' truth) and *honne* (one's private individual opinion). Friendship was measured by which of these double standards was applied to you. A Japanese scholar once told an American friend: 'We say only 60% of what we think. Other Japanese can guess another 30% that's left unsaid by the way the 60% is expressed. 10% remains an unknown quantity.' The strain of keeping up such pretence was considerable, and some younger Japanese are now voicing objections to the system as it survives.

The initiative would normally be taken by members in the middle of the group hierarchy. 'Superiors do not force their ideas on juniors,' as Professor Nakane puts it, 'instead juniors lay their opinions before their superiors and seek to have them adopted.' If there were many competing ideas and analyses, the field was saturated with them and then people waited for a consensus to emerge without a vote or a yes-or-no judgement on each one. Face was thereby saved and the necessary psycho-social unity for successful implementation assured.

The patron-client (*oyabun-kobun*) relationship was the model for the gradual transfer of skill and power from the successfully established to the promising newcomer – in return for other services rendered either now or in the future. It was based on the emotions of the family; the word *oyabun* means 'father person' – as in the British trade unions' 'father-of-chapel', but much more widely used (and there is no British equivalent of *kobun*, or 'child person'). One post-war Prime Minister, Hayato Ikeda, took his paternal role so seriously that he arranged the marriages of a hundred subordinates.

In the one-to-one relationship of *oyabun-kobun* a degree of authoritarianism was inevitable, but any leader trying to direct the affairs and collective action of a traditional group had to be subtle, because his followers expected him to accept and execute their views. Both sides needed to feel wanted. There was no dictatorship and, indeed, such groups were often plagued by factionalism.

The subordinate was careful to bolster his superior's outward authority, by calling on him and giving him presents, using especially respectful language and accepting favours. He always allowed the superior to win an argument, leaving him some escape route to save face if he had argued badly, letting it appear that the final solution was what the leader had suggested in the first instance. The way for a leader to get a subordinate to do what he wanted was not to give him orders but to make him feel guilty, and that was achieved by behaving as a parent towards his child, by being modest and self-sacrificing, willingly undertaking burdens and never complaining.

Leadership was therefore slow and ponderous. Another post-war Prime Minister, Masayoshi Ohira, defined it as not advocating what you think should be done but rather 'amalgamating everyone's desires and giving direction to those desires. That is the Japanese way. It takes time. But the Japanese think unanimity is best. To be able to say something was decided unanimously, and clap your hands in a display of approval, makes everyone feel good, even if it is a lie. To achieve an appearance of unanimity it takes many days of empty palaver during which we create a soup with no flavour . . .'

These leader-follower bonds had little to do with class. The Meiji government a century ago made a decisive break with the old semi-feudal class structure, but a modern adversary class system of the European kind did not emerge to replace it. It was the *samurai*, at the bottom end of the traditional upper class, who dominated public life then and whose descendants today still provide a disproportion- ate number of civil servants, businessmen, managers and professional leaders. There were no landed aristocrats to perpetuate an upper class, and none of those blatant distinctions of schooling and accent which survive in England. True, a hopeful ex-aristocracy of over a thousand sometime princes, marquises, counts, viscounts and barons survives, but unable since 1947 to make legal use of their titles (they have revived their Peers' Club, and succeed in casting a spell over the snobs in Japanese society).

Strong ties of kinship interconnect the classes, weakening the development of the working-class consciousness which industrializ- ation might have fathered. It was the younger sons of farming families who became the first recruits for industry: if they lost their job they could go back and live off the land with their family instead of forming a discontented force of urban radicals. There was also enough upward mobility to spike the idea of an unjustly treated proletariat. Most employers were in any case paternalistic, ready to maintain some of the traditional human relationships in the new industrial context. Then the post-war economic miracle assured workers of rapidly growing incomes. The upshot is that the class antagonism which the West takes for granted is largely absent from Japan. So much so that Professor Robert Scalapino of the University of California has hailed contemporary Japan as a post-Marxist society which can side-step the ideological battlefields of nineteenth- and twentieth-century European radicalism. The Marxists do not agree, pointing to continuing inequality and exploitation, with a well-paid 'labour aristocracy' helping managers to keep less lucky workers depressed. But the Marxist analysis of Japanese society is not as helpful as in the continent of Marx's birth: Japan is best viewed simply as a non-Marxist society.

It is generally believed that Japan's class structure differs markedly from the European in boasting a very large middle class, to which nine out of ten Japanese claim to belong. This is certainly the impression given in official surveys, and supported by a visible convergence in incomes, education, housing, speech, clothing and lifestyle. Wage and salary differentials are smaller than in Europe. But the figure was always suspect because very few of those nine-out-of-ten had assets to live off, and how could three-quarters of all Japan's farm and factory workers count as middle class? Such a middle class has no common tradition and does not act as an integrated political force on the European pattern. In the end, it turns out that the questionnaires on which this idea is based refer to living standards rather than class. When the Japanese are specifically asked about their 'social' class, about 70% put themselves in the 'working class', and only a quarter in the 'middle class'.

Economists report that the income gap is now widening again with the unrelenting prosperity of businessmen and landowners at one end of the scale, and the impact of the world recession on contract workers at the other. 'We are drifting towards a new age of class separation,' warns one commentator. This is seen by some as the latest wave of 'westernization'. But the relative quantities still differ: the pictogram of income groups in society comes out as a pyramid for most European countries, with few people at the top and many at the bottom, whereas in Japan it is more like a rugby football on its end – with few people at the top or bottom and most in the middle.

If class does not provide the Japanese with a high-level group identity, what do race, nation or state mean to them? Professor Gregory Clark of Sophia University in Tokyo regards Japan as an outstanding example, perhaps the only example, of a society which baulks at the final fence for nationhood, remaining stalled at the preceding stage – *The Japanese Tribe*, as he calls his book. (The Jews perhaps come nearest to this.) When Tsarist imperialism menaced Japan in the eighteenth century, a Japanese leader spoke of the threat 'not merely to a single clan but the entire body of the clans'. The Meiji Restoration of 1868 represented the victory of the Satsuma and Choshu clans of southwestern Japan over their rivals of the centre and northeast, and people remain aware of their several 'tribal' origins. The tribal image, though not literally intended, is suggestive.

If the Japanese were indeed a tribe, then the two million *eta* people fill the role of outcasts. One of the meanings of *eta* is 'somebody filled with dirt', and they used to be thrown together with beggars and prostitutes under a generic name meaning 'non-humans'. Today when this near-taboo subject is occasionally discussed, the more neutral name of *burakumin*, or 'special community people', is used. 'Many people do not regard us as human beings,' one of them pitiably complains. 'The prejudice is of unbelievable proportions.'

The particular fate of these people was to make their living from the slaughter of livestock. They are the only tanners in Japan (leather imports are still restricted for their welfare), and used to be the only meat-eaters. All that was anathema to Buddhist and Shintoist alike, so the *burakumin* had a hard time of it – and their suffering was cruelly formalized under the *shoguns*. The Meiji reformers began to dismantle this official discrimination, but in slow time. An official commission admitted in the 1960s that the *burakumin* community, 'owing to discrimination based on the class system formed in the process of the historical development of Japanese society, is placed in such an inferior position economically, socially and culturally that their fundamental rights are grossly violated even in present-day society . . .' The Prime Minister's office found it necessary to insist in 1977 that: 'The Japanese people are a single race and there is no legal discrimination among them because of sex, creed or other factors.'

The *burakumin* are physically indistinguishable from other Japanese. Though they can give themselves away through the language they use in this land of multiple choice of pronoun, many of them succeed in 'passing off' as ordinary Japanese, concealing their origins from employer and friends and even from wives and children. One changed his address twenty times in order to throw detectives off the scent, but ended as a suicide. 'We are consumed by fear every day,' says another. 'We are scared, terrified that someone will point a finger at us.' It is particularly dangerous for young men seeking marriage or jobs, whose background will be probed by matchmakers and employers. A book was circulated recently among big employers listing all the villages and hamlets exclusively occupied by the *burakumin*, making it possible, because of the thoroughness of family records, to identify many of those now pretending to be in the social mainstream.

These days the government doles out billions of *yen* a year in special aid to the *burakumin* communities, but with little visible effect on their progress towards social and cultural re-integration into Japanese society. It was encouraging, perhaps, that a *burakumin* girl recently won damages from her fiancé's parents, in compensation for his calling off the marriage after they withheld their approval for ten years because of her status.

The Japanese are proud of their ethnic connection with China. But of the two waves of prehistoric migration to form the Japanese race, it is the more mysterious southern strand about which their descendants wax poetic. Kunio Yanagita, who could be called Japan's first anthropologist, once found a coconut on a southern beach which might have been carried by the sea from Taiwan or the Philippines; he speculated that such currents might have borne his ancestors all those centuries ago. A poet friend, falling in with his mood, composed a famous song of nostalgia for the 'southern seas'. Definite echoes of Japanese music, design, dance and language can be sensed in Indonesia, the Philippines, Malaysia and the Pacific islands: mediaeval Japanese words for some parts of the body – eye, mouth, stomach – are the same as the Malay or Polynesian. Japanese intellectuals celebrate these affinities: 'In spite of our mantle of civilization, in the depths of the Japanese character there remains the naive generosity . . . characteristic of primitive southern tribal peoples.'

It is consistent with such nostalgia that Japan used to define itself as a collection of Japanese people, not as a slice of territory. The political status of under-inhabited Hokkaido to the north was ambiguous until quite modern times, and the public does not get worked up about territorial issues. The successful post-war campaigns for the restoration of the Ryukyu and Bonin Islands from American occupation were the creation of politicians, and the continuing disputes with China over the tiny Senkaku Islands and with Korea over even smaller Takeshima are not allowed to obstruct larger diplomatic goals. Japanese opinion, a few fishermen and fervent anti-Communists apart, is not even deeply stirred by Russian occupation of the four tiny northern islands of Shikotan, Habomai, Kunashiri and Etorofu.

'Tribe' does too little justice to Japan's modern millions: 'nation' may slightly exaggerate their degree of interconnectedness. But 'state' there certainly is, created by the *shoguns* out of clan chaos to form the ultimate political grouping for the Japanese, at about the time that the Tudors were making similar history in England. There were good foundations for the successful state which Japan eventually became: one race, one culture, one language, all under the protection of the sea. (No European state was so blessed.) Social unity is taken for granted, and the state has been described as the 'apex of morality'. So Japanese businessmen abroad ('in the front line,' they may write home) can identify with their country, confiding that in the fight for contracts 'it is the ambition of representing Japan that ultimately gives you support'. Conversely, a man who changes citizenship, as the Americanized son of Ambassador Ichiro Kawasaki did, is thought not just unpatriotic but contemptibly unfilial.

Japan is not a homogeneous society, all the same, and the search for its 'national character' is doomed to fail. The Japanese themselves are baffled: a group of scholars wants the government to set up a centre of Japanology to pin down once and for all just what the Japanese identity consists of. From the western point of view, it is the handling of emotion and relationships that appears most distinctive. It is not so much that the Japanese are more emotional than Europeans, or Europeans more rational than Japanese. It is more a difference over where to draw the frontiers between these two distinct human drives in daily life. Everyone, whether in Europe or Japan, has to don a mask of rationality from time to time in order to judge and analyze events, and this is particularly true of anybody in authority. When this mark is doffed, the internal mechanisms for holding the emotions in check sometimes run on, causing the emotions to dry up even when they may appropriately seek expression. This phenomenon of drying up after the mask is no longer needed is more common in Northern Europe, certainly, than in Japan. And this is perhaps due to the second major difference that most Westerners would identify: the multiplicity, warmth and yet intricate protocol of the relationships in the life of the Japanese. Northern Europeans are more self-sufficient, and they seem predisposed to cultivate just a few very close relationships, consigning the others to a lower priority. The temperature of Japanese relationships is several degrees higher than north European, but they are very particularly organized according to the status and role of the other person.

Many Japanese think of themselves, by comparison with Westerners, as more emotional, spontaneous and warm. A senior civil servant once observed that the Japanese in a political crisis go into an uproar for twenty days and then forget all about it. 'Japanese are not economic animals,' he went on. 'We are emotional animals. If we were economic animals, we would react more coolly but we are not so clever. We lose our ability to calculate.'

Specific sentient human relationships count more than such abstracts as truth, faith, rights of the individual, or transcendent good. A Japanese would rather feel intimately close to someone than know objective facts about him, would rather belong to a group than seek to lead it. Instead of relentlessly pursuing an egotistic goal he would concentrate on behaving appropriately, and in place of self-reliance he would cultivate dependable channels of trust.

Fatalism is thus a school in which most Japanese would confess enrolment. As Fosco Maraini colourfully put it, Japanese swim happily in the torrent of events, while Europeans fly above in their helicopters, detached and self-conscious observers. The life force is seen as something to be suffered passively, not manipulated or shaped. History is not under human control. Utopias, verdicts and punishment hardly exercise the Japanese mind, and Marxism in Japan lacks that dimension of universal perfectability which is half its appeal to Europe. When criticized at international conferences a stoical Japanese delegate will sit back, silently chain-smoking. Europeans would assume, from his offering no defence, that Japan accepted their charges. But to any Japanese observer, such impassivity would seem admirably dignified.

Among themselves the Japanese dwell morosely on their defeats, from Hiroshima to car import quotas, even deriving a melancholy satisfaction from them. The author Lin Yutang has said that the Japanese have no sense of humour. Since the Chinese are so well furnished with that commodity, he should know. Somebody once took the trouble of working out which words were most frequently used in Japanese pop songs, and 'crying' came top of the list – though that was a generation ago. Even the process of westernization itself becomes subject to mood change, a logical culture being absorbed emotionally. Japan 'took a culture in a major key', in the words of a Japanese music critic, 'and, in adopting it, transposed it into a minor key'.

But the heart of the Japanese personality is *amae*, variously translated as the need to be loved, pampered, or in another person's sympathetic control. In its literal physical dimension this might be experienced by anyone at the barber's or when having a massage or in the Turkish bath, as well as in some sexual circumstances: a Japanese will also search out situations of intangible *amae* throughout his circle of friends and relations. The ideal is to know people so well that you trust and confide in each other unstintingly, fully secure in knowing that your trust will not be taken advantage of, that you will never be laughed at or spurned and that you can always presume upon the other's indulgence in a totally accepting reciprocal relationship. With *amae* you can safely ignore the impersonally imposed expectations of society, and be accepted as just yourself.

In the colder world of the Nordic stand-off such impulses would be thought childish or impossible. Though real, they are repressed. In his book, *The Anatomy of Dependence*, Takeo Doi urged his compatriots to alter emotional course, substituting western individualism for their lattice-work of *amae*. The book became a best-seller, so the advice was presumably received with interest, but institutionalized *amae* is probably too much fun to give up. The experience of Japanese immigrants to North America suggest that the transition over the generations from *amae* to self-reliance is a painful one.

Doi is not the only Japanese to believe that cultural concessions are needed for survival. Niyozekan Hasegawa, for example, in his book *The Lost Japan* (1952), castigated the 'playful quality' of Japanese life, the perverse habit of not taking world politics or universal philosophies seriously, of treating mental satisfaction as an amusement. The classic example was Pearl Harbour in 1941 when, as Hasegawa puts it, Japan's 'characteristic reliance on intuition . . . blocked the objective cognition of the modern world', and plunged her into a contest she knew rationally she could not win. His moral was that Japanese culture needed root-and-branch reform.

Today, however, more and more Japanese are questioning this kind of advice, common during the 1950s in the aftermath of defeat. Enough concessions have already been made, they feel, and now, against the background of the economic miracle, the Japanese social tradition should take heart. 'The rebellion against western rationality and logic and in favour of emotions and feelings', the former Vice-Minister of MITI, Naohiro Amaya, warns, 'is becoming more intense.' He finds 'feminine' sentiment rising against 'masculine', to the detriment of many of those things which western influence had promoted in Japan – factual analysis, industrial competition, efficiency and fast economic growth, to name a few.

The Japanese never forget the shock of being press-ganged into the Anglo-Saxon-dominated world of the past century. Today the Anglo-Saxons are beginning to come to terms with their being a cultural minority in a world they had bullied into a modern sense of unity, and it is no longer so unthinkable for them to accommodate to some non-European modes. The Japanese are right to become less defensive about their own roots. Gregory Clark, having lived and worked in Japan for some twenty years, argues that it is Europe which is out of step, needing a restorative dose of instinct and emotion much more than Japan needs an injection of rationalism. To take a very basic activity, people work for emotional as much as for material incentives, and that is why European and American executives study the so-called Japanese management model. It is a question of mix, not of going over exclusively to one way or the other; the Japanese will not allow too many unfamiliar western ingredients to spoil the flavour of their lives.

Modernity and foreign influence are moving the Japanese, not out of his familiar social criss-cross but into a broader and more complex view of his situation. The younger generation may be edging towards a universal ethic modelled on the time-honoured structure of family relations, with the categories of mutual trust gradually widening at the expense of the 'outsider' category. This is one way in which Japanese society might evolve in a more modern, though not necessarily 'western' direction. The prototype for this kind of future Japanese might be Dr Hisao Shoga, who sacrificed his practice to volunteer for medical service in Vietnam at the height of the war there. Humanitarianism is not entirely unknown in Japan.

But there is a counter-current of selfish materialism which confuses the picture. 'There is this new wave of Japanese adults', a senior civil servant in the Ministry of Education, Atsuko Tayama, warns, 'lacking consideration for others, reflecting western individualism. They are very nice to their friends and the people they are close to, but they lack consideration for third parties, they lack the consciousness of being a member of a large society.' Ironically, the supposed example of western individualism, by encouraging the Japanese to stop suppressing their natural impulses, confirms many of them in their disdain for outsiders.

In the modern conditions of the 1980s, with greater mobility and the unprecedented opening up of Japanese society, one might have expected a certain relaxing of group ties. Job-changing became accepted during the economic miracle, and typically from factories, where groups form naturally, to offices and shops, where they do not. Groups are becoming more pragmatic and less emotionally intense. Some argue that it is no longer the group itself that is all-important but the consideration which individuals give to each other within the group – something defined as 'relationism', 'betweenism' or 'communitarianism' rather than 'groupism'. The group may simply be a defined area within which members relate to one another, striving for group goals which overlap with their own individual ambitions.

The individual does not necessarily stand, as a European might instinctively feel, in opposition to the group but may thankfully accept it as an effective agent of organizational activity, a unit in which he may submerge himself and gratefully shed the burden of making endless decisions on his own. The group is a device to share and delegate responsibility (and also to duck responsibility, as when a businessman tells a foreigner that his company prevents him from making a certain deal, using the group as a false front to buy time or exact more profit). Egalitarianism has certainly weakened the vertical lines of authority, but at the same time it has strengthened the horizontal links in a group. The group is revealed less as an authoritarian structure than as voluntarily composed by individuals to attain a common goal. It is adapting to modern conditions by developing and extending unique features of Japanese culture which owe nothing to the West.

The modernizing of Japan can thus appear sometimes to be bringing about contradictory social changes. People are now communicating with each other far more, for example, and making more complicated demands on one another. In the old days, you would typically have done this through your work group or family, utilizing its collective resources of personal relationships reaching into other groups. To ensure success your group's spokesman or envoy would have manipulated these personal relationships to put the other person or other group representative into a position where he must either meet your request or else lose self-respect or 'face'.

These days things are usually done in a brisker manner, through impersonal organizations like the Post Office, a trade union, a large corporation, government departments or even sometimes the courts, monitored by objective laws that apply to everyone regardless of circumstance. In that sense, life is more impersonal than before. Yet the person too will have changed, probably abandoning his former wholly passive acceptance of group representation to become a more conscious agent in life – thereby reducing the group's area for manoeuvre and making its consensus more elusive. That means a more individualized, more personalized way of life. Both sides of the modernization coin need to be seen together.

It was the egalitarian component of the social package offered by the West that most readily matched Japanese desires. Though lacking a universal ethic, a Japanese takes naturally to the idea of treating other people within his group (which is capable of enlargement) as equal human beings. Egalitarianism for a Japanese is, as Professor Nakane has said, 'an emotional aspiration rather than a rational belief'. You know very well that Sato is abler than Kato, but to acknowledge it would legitimize putting your own ability (or lack of it) on the agenda for discussion by Sato, Kato and everyone else. To avoid getting your ego hurt in any genuine competition, why not close your eyes to the qualities of others and refrain from evaluating them? A literary critic wonders if his countrymen even 'fear the advent of a society truly based on the principle of merit'.

The concern for horizontal relations also means a preoccupation with rank. If one man is singled out for promotion, the others in the group brood on why they were not considered worthy. Post-war egalitarianism makes for more competition, yet renders the results of the competition less palatable.

One school recently offered easier textbooks for night classes where average ability was low, but the students refused them. They wanted the same textbooks as their daytime counterparts regardless of whether they understood them. A commentator concluded from such 'incomprehensible egalitarian thinking' that equality was perceived with 'the half-hearted, sentimental, self-pitying and easily injured sensitivity peculiar to the Japanese'.

So the group reigns triumphant, but in a new horizontal dimension and in egalitarian rather than hierarchical robes. Collectivism is preserved, at the price of the father's (or father-figure's) losing authority. The Japanese are moving towards equality before becoming individually autonomous: they will probably go on adapting their group system to suit modern times without drifting into the solitariness of western-style individualism, without risking the breakdown of their society from the more destructive forces of human egotism.

People *are* becoming sufficiently individualistic to detach themselves a little from the groups, to keep a certain distance from them. They identify with them still, but on a more rational, sophisticated and less intensely emotional basis. While taking more and more responsibility for their lives fully into their own individual hands, they still treasure the comradeship and the insurance policy of their big and little collectives. The group remains an integral part of Japanese life, as it always has been, and no amount of foreseeable westernization will alter that.

6

Children of the Sun
Japanese Youth and Education

IT IS the young Japanese who will determine his country's social future. He stands somewhat alienated from the safe but obsolete world of his parents. Yet he is obliged to navigate the same labyrinth of social etiquette, the same obstacle course of classroom competition. In the result he may emerge numb and passive, conforming without commitment or effort. The consumerist inheritance of the Japanese economic miracle adds a dash of hedonism to his disengagement. Though conditioned still to put the group first, the young have become self-centred within a context of group life, using the group as a constant reinforcement of their individual self-image. Post-war youth feels an unfamiliar ego growing inside itself like an alien consciousness, while the furniture of the old Japan – the large family household, the unquestioned authority of teachers and political leaders – has been thrown on the rubbish heap. Uncomfortable with the new ways, naked without the old, many experience despair.

The educational reforms of the US Occupation that began in 1945 represented the strongest wave of westernization ever undertaken in Japan. Starry-eyed Americans hoped to make a clean sweep of feudalistic morality and substitute wholesome democratic ideas. The men put in charge were mostly Midwesterners full of the educational philosophy of John Dewey – 'a kind of child worship', the amazed Japanese elders called it. With this child-centred approach the older Japanese saw discipline, academic learning and the training of high-flyers go out of the window. Since the Americans had fought for freedom, those Japanese Communists who had been shut up by the militarist regime before 1945 now came into their own as heroes. Within a few years the cold war persuaded the Americans to suppress them again, but the teachers' trade union has remained Communist-dominated and many teachers still regard class struggle as more important than training young character. They welcomed the Deweyite reforms as offering the best climate for their own propaganda in schools. Japanese education swivelled in 1945 from a regimented extreme to a permissive one, and then in the 1950s swung back a little into demoralized confusion. 'People and teachers,' Akio

Morita, Chairman of Sony, concluded, 'have mixed up freedom and democracy, with the result that discipline has been lost in family life. That is why I sent my two boys to school in England . . .'

One must have a certain sympathy with the teachers, who lost face (and their credit with the young) twice in five years. In 1945 they had to switch overnight from the dogma of imperial divinity, the infallibility of the militarist powerholders and the fight to save Asia from Anglo-Saxon imperialism – to the contrary ideals of democracy, pacifism, the legitimacy of Communism and the break-up of the former business empires of the *zaibatsu*. Within five years they had to veer back again, under MacArthur's later Occupation policies, towards anti-Communism, re-armament, the restriction of trade unions and the legitimation of right-wing politicians and business cartels. The children of that generation left school with their heads reeling. Not surprisingly a big wave of juvenile crime broke in 1951.

Since then the conservative politicians have gradually built up a case for ousting Dewey and putting some good old traditional virtues back into the classroom. The ruling Liberal-Democratic Party's Education Committee insists that 'just because respecting one's parents and getting on with one's brothers and sisters were important values in the pre-war era does not mean they are bad now.' Government sniping at American policy is intensifying. 'It was Occupation policy,' said a former Education Minister accusingly in 1983, 'to destroy Japanese morality, traditions, customs and habits. There is not a single book nowadays that teaches children to revere their parents, because the Occupation policies ruled that it was wrong to do so.'

Is it so bad to teach children to serve others, the rightists demanded? Leftists argued that such a system would make people subservient to politicians and big business, as before the war. Middle-of-the-roaders noted that, by taking Confucianism out of the school with no Christianity or other kind of moral system to replace it, Japan risked turning its young people into unprincipled egocentrics. The debate goes on, with the conservative voice gaining strength. In 1985 the government ordered schools to fly the national flag and sing the national anthem at entrance and graduation ceremonies, and meanwhile fundamental reforms in the education system are under official discussion.

'The purpose of education should be switched,' wrote Yasuhiro Nakasone a few years before becoming Prime Minister, 'to gaining virtue, a sound body and knowledge – in that order.' What has not changed is the rat-race for entry in the schools and universities most likely – because of their social and academic prestige – to equip a young person for success in life. No responsible parent would have a second thought about making his offspring cram at whatever cost to body or mind in order to leap the successive examination hurdles that lead to the best jobs. There are even exams for places in the good kindergartens, and it is not thought unusual for a young child to be away from home chasing education (including perhaps two separate private crammers before and after school, each an hour or two's bus journey away) from 4.30 in the morning to 11.00 at night.

Many school-leavers never give up trying to enter the magic campus of the university. One in ten of the successful recruits to Tokyo University, Japan's premier campus, makes it only at the fourth try at the examination. Some hotels offer a package for the university entrance season – $75, in a recent example, for accommodation in Tokyo for a student and his mother with easily digestible meals, a graffiti wallboard to relieve tension, midnight study snacks, train or bus timetables to all the campuses and a doctor, dentist and counsellor on call. There were thousands of takers. Failure is not to be contemplated: there can be 800 school-age suicides a year, mostly connected with examination failure.

The group system provides some relief: once you have got into the institution by passing the exams, a solidarity forms in each class or year to inhibit open competitiveness. The university is thus derided by some outsiders as a placid non-competitive playground for revolution and sex. The concern for face usually rules out streaming in schools, or even the singling out of one or two individuals for prizes. Man, it is conceded, does not live by intellect alone: he has feelings to be considered. A third or a half of the class may get prizes, or none at all, and intelligence tests are not liked.

But school is a hard slog for the Japanese even between examinations. Their own language itself takes longer to learn than phonetic scripts such as English, and they are made to assimilate more knowledge than the average Western pupil. The mathematical terms *sine* and *cosine*, for example, are learnt two years earlier than in American schools. Saturday mornings are worked, and the days of the year spent at school are 30% more than in the US. 'We would have to send a British labour force back to school for ten years to compete,' an EEC official calculates. But some of this extra effort in Japan is at the expense of creativeness and individuality.

One of the big controversies is over school textbooks. Since seven teachers in ten are either socialist or Communist, publishers have tended to commission left-wing authors, and many of the textbooks are totally negative about capitalism – or about Japan's postwar achievements under conservative governments, from public order and high living standards to new technology. In practice teachers have room for manoeuvre in the way they elaborate on the texts in class, but right-wing politicians have grown increasingly restive. In the 1960s the government started to subsidize textbooks for free issue if they were approved by the Education Ministry, and this helped to turn the tide.

The university is for many Westerners a theatre where the young person can throw away the script he had to learn at school and start improvising. A Japanese undergraduate's first priority is to get his degree, so that he can count on a good job and social approval, and only the deeply alienated do not bother. A degree, another former Education Minister observed reproachfully, had become 'more valuable than the individual who holds it'. Some mock the 'degree-ocracy' that rules Japan. One university was found to have accepted twenty-two times as many students as it was equipped for, in its eagerness to meet the demand for degrees. Unfortunately the curriculum and teaching methods are often antiquated. Dewey may have swept some cobwebs out of the schoolroom but he did not make much impact on the lecture hall.

The professors, a student complains, 'impart knowledge without stimulating us to think'. Lectures are 'far removed from actual problems . . . There is something in the atmosphere . . . that discourages discussion with our professors, who give us lectures as though they were disregarding our presence'. Most universities recruit lecturers from their own best graduates, and there is little mobility after that, so the professors are commonly narrow in their horizons. They are promoted by seniority rather than merit and very few foreigners have been invited to join their ranks. The first American undergraduate to win a place at Tokyo University was aghast. 'The study is totally inhuman,' he reported. 'I learned self-discipline, but my eyesight deteriorated . . . Students are homogeneous in manner and thinking . . . They have no identity.' It was said at one time that almost one student in six on that campus was in need of psychiatric treatment.

When the job-hunting season opens, a degree is only the first weapon that is needed. Social climbing can be equally important. Each university alumnus favours his own, and every prospective recruit to a company or organization seeks a fellow-alumnus already ensconced who can help him get in. Company recruitment becomes a festive round of string-pulling, cliquism, patronage and nepotism (which is not as contemptible as it sounds if the nephews are as well-qualified as the others: companies prefer to have an inside patron who can lean on the new recruit and take a certain responsibility for him). This is why university friendships are more important than in the West. One of Japan's most successful receivers owes his enviable circle of business friends to the fact that he took his Keio University final five times, thus getting to know five times as many year-mates as those who sailed through first time.

But many Japanese students have been ready to jeopardize their degrees in the interests of political demonstration, especially in the 1960s when undergraduates, it was said, were pursuing 'revolution by day, and sex by night'. There were complex reasons behind the bloody riots in which police and students joined ritual battle with tear gas, batons and paramilitary equipment. It was left versus right, or anti-American versus pro-American, or even, in the end, left versus left. Sometimes personal frustrations lurked behind the politics. The demonstrations offered an arena of self-discovery which a student could not find in his more conventional activities, a means of asserting himself against the social uniformity which fettered his movements.

One ardent demonstrator was Ryuichi Sakamoto, who went on to become an internationally famous pop singer. 'I fought against capitalism by denying the bourgeois in myself,' he later recalled of his schooldays in the 1960s. 'I swept out my own racial prejudices such as the Korean problem, and recognized my class-consciousness.'

When the student fighters of the *Zengakuren* or Red Thunder Tribe attacked American targets on Japanese soil in the 1960s, they were labelled as 'hedonistic revolutionaries' out for ego trips rather than the realization of a well-thought-out blueprint for political change. This was the period of Shintaro Ishihara's novel *Season of the Sun* whose hero, at the funeral of the girl he had made pregnant, shouts to all and sundry: 'You people don't understand anything.' That launched the *Taiyozoku*, or Sun Tribe, borrowing something from the James Dean cult in the West. Ishihara followed with *Punishment Room* where a young man puts sleeping pills in a girl's beer, rapes her, rejects her when he finds that he has made her fall in love with him, and is finally beaten up in the student 'torture room'.

At the end of the 1960s came the last round of student violence, at least until now. Like the Chinese Red Guards (and partly in imitation of them), these demonstrators were primarily engaged in fighting each other, left wing against left wing. Each faction had its own distinctive colours, masks and headgear. The political issues about returning Okinawa to Japanese control and extending the Security Treaty with the US were mingled with more parochial questions about fees and university maladministration. One twenty-year-old died after being beaten up at Waseda University for spying on behalf of a rival group. The Dean of Literature at Tokyo University was held in his office for over a week, leaving exhausted on a stretcher. Konosuke Matsushita, the industrialist, angrily called for Tokyo University to be abolished and razed to the ground for redevelopment.

In the 1970s, especially after the oil price shock and the world recession, students' minds turned back to bread-and-butter issues. 'The company has more to offer than revolution does,' many of them admitted. Violence was canalized in the less frightening *Bosozoku* (Wild Tribe), teenage gangs in fast cars or motorcycles, calling themselves the White Herons, Lizards, Scorpions, Vipers, Black Angels or White Knuckles. There were eventually some 40,000 of these group speed freaks, self-consciously tattooed. Commentators had a field day explaining this phenomenon. Over-protective mothers had made their brood submissive and bored. 'All we have is Saturday night,' one of them complained. They had never brushed with evil: most of the hot rodders were from well-off homes where parents were too timid or busy to scold them, and they enjoyed their first experience of a reprimand at the hands of the law. They took their belated rebellion to the street, or waged it in the form of crime. One student in three said violence at home was unavoidable, and almost a half said they *wanted* to be violent there.

In 1980 the vogue novel was *Call Us Crystal*, by a Hitotsubashi undergraduate, whose young heroes and heroines, disillusioned with all the -isms, live only for the fashionable brand names – Vuitton, Courrèges, Ellesse. Sex and fashion exhaust the preoccupations of this shallow best-seller. 'We don't read many books or pursue things singlemindedly like some mad professor,' one of the characters explains. 'But we're not empty-headed or absent-minded. We're not stand-offish, but we don't cling to people either. And we aren't simpletons who swallow others' opinions . . .' Like crystal, these youngsters are reflections of other things, reacting rather than initiating.

Then the *Takenokozoku* (Bamboo Shoot Tribe), punk teenager with bizarre make-up and clothes, hit the streets. And the early 1980s also witnessed the third and most shocking post-war wave of juvenile crime. A schoolteacher who told a boy off for tampering with fire extinguishers had internal organs ruptured for his trouble. At a Tokyo middle school a physical education teacher was made to kneel and apologize to a student gang leader for reprimanding one of his gang members. It was said that this 'changed the balance of power' in the school. A few weeks later another member of the same gang was playing loud music, against the rules, in the classroom. A teacher unplugged his cassette-player, upon which the same gang leader not only punched and kicked him but marched into the staffroom to attack other teachers. Eight boys, some from good conventional homes, were arrested.

In another incident that pricked the nation's conscience, school-boys killed three tramps in a Yokohama park – 'for fun'. Two fifteen-year-olds killed a classmate for bullying them, and another killed a teacher while drunk. Six children out of ten report violence at school, four out of ten vandalism and bullying, one in ten attacks on teachers. The media play up such violence, and in 1985 an Asahi TV station director even paid a gang of motorcycle youths to kick and beat five schoolgirls in front of his camera, for an afternoon show entitled *Violent Shots: Total Confessions of Sexual Torture*. (He was fired.)

There was a national beating of breasts over what a *Japan Times* leader-writer called the 'general decline in morality, manners and mental vigour among the young'. Parents were again blamed for being slow to punish their children for fear of the social stigma they might incur. Diffident parents hoped that teachers would tell little Kazuo what to do and what not to do; teachers assumed the reverse. Since fighting was suppressed, and the study drive left children with little time for sport, they were insulated from the violence of real life. (The sex, violence, war, revolution, lust and cruelty of videos and *gekiga*, or strong comics, was largely ignored as an isolated subculture which children did not connect with their own lives.) The spread of egalitarianism made children feel expected to match their most gifted contemporaries, leading in practice to a sensation of inferiority and frustration. All this and more flooded the media.

What has fascinated Japan's social commentators is that the average delinquent appears to be more perceptive, more anxious to learn, more prepared for rapid change than the 'goody'. It seems that a broken home and a political riot provide just the kind of challenge a young Japanese needs to become independent. Can society find less drastic means to develop the questing individual personality which the country's future requires? Most children grow up in a comfortable hothouse of affluent, liberal, classfree adults incapable of implanting ambition or purpose in their young. So the children, cheated of maturity, are liable to reject social values in favour of violence and in extreme cases may even take revenge on their parents. The media talks of the Peter Pan generation, because there is a sense of not wanting to grow up. There are grown men who read comics, and businessmen who still take pocket money from their parents ('Parents are happy to think that there is still something they can do for you,' one explains. 'In a way I am doing them a favour.').

Young mothers find that what their own mothers taught them

about childhood is of little use today, yet they have no means of knowing any better, so they become over-anxious and over-protective. Their children never learn to be independent, but are guided at every turn and crammed for every test, so that a tutor warned one ambitious Mum: 'For the next two years, you will have to be prepared to have your husband go to bed with a *sake* barrel.' In that particular case the son passed his exam (though at what psychological cost is not stated) while the father divorced the mother.

Young people feel powerless in a society where there is no tradition of strong autonomous individuals, and in a world which seems always to gang up against Japan. What can you achieve on your own against giant corporations, mammoth trade unions, almighty governments and overbearing foreign powers? There is much pessimism because of all this. A distinguished Tokyo University economics professor has warned that creative scholarship in his field is doomed because of falling standards (which he attributes largely to the 'vile influence of TV and comics'). Some foreign teachers echo his despondency. 'Japanese students,' James Kirkup concludes, 'are the most charming, delightful, obedient but the least hardworking. . . They don't want to go to the library. They sit and take it in. But never . . . do they contest your point of view.'

While students in the 1960s and 1970s were unpleasant in manner, a Keio University professor comments, one could at least understand them. In the 1980s they have become pleasingly polite and attentive, but also apathetic and cheerless, disillusioned with ideology and apparently suffocated by society. Opinion polls confirm this judgement. Whereas a third of one student sample said their main goal was to look after themselves, only 4% were ready to work for world peace and only 1% to serve Japan. With the authority pyramid crumbling, and group discipline relaxing, teenagers' considerations are basically selfish. In politics students are veering to the right, not hawkishly but out of calculated self-interest or passive submission to parental guidance. Recent polls of new entrants at Tokyo University suggest almost half are Liberal-Democratic Party supporters, only about 3% Communist followers.

Yet the truth is not quite as severe as the Japanese themselves pretend in their commentaries and opinion surveys. Most teenagers in Japan do not ride fast motorbikes, dress up as punks, beat their teachers, torment their parents or kill themselves for failing exams – and this healthy majority rarely makes either the newspaper head-lines or the sociologist's notebook. Another western resident paints a happier picture of today's teenagers enjoying their high standard of living and their newly-won *puraibashii* (privacy) with their own room at home (and half with part-time jobs to give them some financial independence), a head taller than their parents, internationalist, not suspicious or afraid of the outside world, proud of Japan's belonging loosely to the western club (a pride reinforced whenever they set foot in any neighbouring Asian country, all with greatly lower standards). A certain rot may have started at the surface, but the main body of the social apple remains sound.

Although Japan's youth has cut down the palisade surrounding the group, it has not fully exploited its new freedom to go out in the world. Not psychologically prepared for individual autonomy, it prefers to relax in the newly democratized fellowship of the group. But this twilight zone, in which the authority of the group is broken before the autonomy of the individual flowers, is uncomfortable, and it is hardly surprising to find its inhabitants truly listless, unadventurous and conservative compared with their parents.

If the reformers of education have their way, we may see in the next century a new breed of Japanese adults with the moral base (restored from indigenous not imported strength) to travel farther and more successfully into the *terra incognita* of individualism. Until then it is an interim modern Japanese who takes the stage, one whose adult life is likely to be more tentative and less dynamic than that of some of his ancestors – or successors.

7

A Spoonful of Shinto
Japanese Religion

THE JAPANESE are eclectic when it comes to religion – 'atheists at college, Shintoist for their weddings, Christian every Christmas and Buddhist at funerals'. Foreigner observers trot out this old truism in a somewhat reproachful tone, but the Japanese too will repeat it of themselves, and without the least apology.

Shinto ('the way of the gods') is the oldest set of beliefs, rooted in the primeval worship of nature and ancestors in Japanese pre-history. Lacking any theology, moral code or sacred book of teachings, Shinto is not, strictly speaking, a religion at all. As more refined ideas began to be imported from China, India and Europe, however, the Shinto priests borrowed heavily from them to produce the hotchpotch which is Shinto today. It retains its following because it is the only indigenous religion, the only one to tell the story of the origin of Japan and the Japanese race, the only official state religion before 1945 and the only one still observed at the Imperial Court. Recent Prime Ministers – even the Christian Masayoshi Ohira – have bent to the nationalist wind by attending the annual Shinto memorial service for the war dead at the Yasukuni shrine in Tokyo.

Confucianism arrived from China in the third-century AD, by which time it had degenerated from the civilizing moral philosophy and individual ethic of its founder to a politicized ideology exalting state power. It is even less a religion, properly speaking, than Shinto – more a narrow code of obligations relating to one's family and government.

Buddhism followed, from India by way of China and Korea, in the eighth century. By then it too was a decadent version of the original, indulgently taking Shinto gods into its pantheon to gain converts (though Buddhism had begun as an atheistic system), and gladly helping the Imperial Court to justify its political authority. Finally St Francis Xavier brought Christianity in the sixteenth century. Though suppressed for 200 years, it flourished again from the mid-nineteenth century.

Each of these imports boosted the Japanese sense of morality, but not for long and not across the board. A vein of scepticism seems to run through the Japanese personality, which prefers to govern its conduct by personal relationships rather than by rules, and is thus more in tune with human agnosticism or atheism than religion. Indeed, Japan seems to have attained that freethinking attitude of healthy secularism which characterizes much of modern western society. But it did so without having first undergone the rigours of faith to create the moral backbone which could withstand the debilitating side-effects of such secularism.

'Religion is like tea,' Yukichi Fukuzawa, the nineteenth-century reformer, used to say, seeing it as serving merely aesthetic or sociable ends. His contemporary, Marquis Ito, declared: 'I regard religion itself as quite unnecessary for a nation's life . . . What is religion . . . but superstition . . . ?'

Powerful corroboration of the Japanese aversion to creeds comes from the many foreign missionaries who have conceded defeat. After eight years with the Ahmaddiya Missionary Movement trying to spread Islam among the Japanese, Ataul Mujid Rashed described them recently as 'a nation of irreligious people' and gross materialists. An American historian goes further, calling the Japanese 'irreligious in a manner almost incomprehensible to the Westerner.' It could thus be said that the Japanese took to Buddhism not for itself, but because it seemed a key to the Chinese-style modernity for which they hankered then, and because it served the ruling élite's purposes. Buddhist monks were originally state-appointed on an official salary, and religious teaching was bent to inculcate obedience. Buddhism means rather less to the Japanese, therefore, than to the Burmese or Thais.

Buddhists of today include the Abbess Kumien Okada of Kyoto who, fired by the commercial success of her chain of vegetarian restaurants, opened a nightclub in the Gion entertainment district; and the Reverend Endo, a physics graduate now in charge of a Buddhist temple in Yokohama, who has all his parishioners' family death anniversaries on computer and gives lectures to his less well-organized brothers on 'The Management of Parishioners and Tax Control by Computer'. One of the sources of income of such priests is the sale, for anything between US $600 and $2,500, of posthumous Buddhist names for the dead to bear in their final rest: Japanese kinsmen will fork out so that their dear departed can keep up with the heavenly Joneses, but might take no further thought of the religion until the next funeral in the family.

The Shinto thread in the Japanese fabric makes gods of everything. Even the Buddhists absorb the intoxicating message: 'A spirit lives here', a notice in a Buddhist temple bathroom warns, 'so do not speak or laugh while you are bathing, lest you offend it.' Man, being a part of nature, can also become a god or spirit under Shinto: 'Not only the Emperor, not only the Japanese, but all human beings are . . . gods in varying degrees,' a Japanese scholar concludes. Legend has it that two gods gave birth to the islands of Japan in the misty past, and to other gods, one of whose descendants in the sixth generation, a seventh-century BC coeval of Nebuchadnezzar, was Emperor Jimmu, the first *mikado* or emperor of Japan, direct ancestor of Hirohito – whom school-children only forty years ago were being taught to worship 'as God'.

There is no dichotomy of good and evil in Shintoism, so that an apologist can declare: 'Evil is often only the manifestation of a strong personality.' One can see here both the good and bad faces of tolerance.

None of the three traditional systems as practised in Japan is religious in the western sense. But with Japanese values and aesthetics broadly rooted in Buddhism, ethics in Confucianism, and Shinto playing a semi-political role, there is an urge to synthesize the three to make them stronger. A thirteenth-century thinker described Shinto as the root of the tree of Japan's way of life, Confucianism as its trunk and branches, Buddhism as its flowers and fruits. A successor in the last century prescribed as the ideal teaching a spoonful of Shinto, half a spoonful of Buddhism and half a spoonful of Confucianism – what might be called the Mary Poppins approach.

Because the 'old' religions lend themselves to such wishy-washy treatment, some contemporary Japanese openly regret that one of the 'new' ones – ideally, Victorian Christianity – never conquered Japan. But these have fared little better. Actually Christianity seems to draw out a nationalist streak in its Japanese converts. Xavier must have known what he was up against when the Japanese very reasonably asked him: 'If Christianity is universal, why has it not already appeared in Japan?' Masahisa Uemura, the outstanding Protestant evangelist of the Meiji and Taisho periods, wanted Japanese Christianity 'to surpass that of the West'; having received Christianity from the West, Japan should renovate it before offering it back in repayment of the debt.

Another pioneer Christian, Kanzo Uchimura, went further in insisting that the good word was received by the Japanese 'directly from God without any intermediary' – and he accused western missionaries, because they despised the Japanese language, of not truly loving Japanese souls. When Father Petitjean had built his new Catholic church in Nagasaki a century ago, after the 200 years of official suppression, a shabby peasant walked in off the street and began singing the Ave Maria before the Blessed Virgin's image as if nothing had happened. But when a journalist went in the 1960s to see the 'secret' Christian villages which had survived that suppression, he found the practices had evolved almost beyond recognition.

Some Japanese have actually appropriated Christ himself. There is an ancient tomb-mound at Aomori, on the northern tip of Honshu, which is claimed by legend as that of Jesus. The story goes that Christ came to Japan as a young man to study Shinto, leaving his look-alike brother to make the supreme sacrifice on Golgotha. Japan was the site of the birth of the world's first language (a fact which drew not only Jesus but also Moses, Buddha, Mohammed and Confucius to Japan). The study of graves at Aomori is said to suggest a Hebrew migration to Japan, and Moses supposedly married in Japan – to father Romulus! The climax of it all would be the future reunification of the Jewish race in Japan after its diaspora. This amazing story was learnedly expounded, with the aid of original documents, by the Third Civilization Society, meeting in a Ginza restaurant before the war. One cannot accuse the Japanese of unimaginativeness, nor of being bashful in their open love affair with the Jews.

There have been outstanding Japanese Christians. As well as Prime Minister Ohira, they include many leftwing political leaders, Shoichi Saba (President of Toshiba) and Akira Kurosawa, the film-maker. Christianity has especially appealed to intellectuals and businessmen because, in contrast with Buddhism or Shinto, it takes a practical interest in social uplift, especially education and medicine, and progress. The autobiography of Dr Toyohiko Kagawa, the outstanding Christian of the 1920s, who gave fifteen years of his life to the homeless and vagrants, sold 300 editions. The man who became Japan's first Marxist (and inspired the youthful Zhou Enlai when studying in Kyoto) was drawn to Christianity as a teenager by the passage in St Matthew about turning the other cheek.

In these shallower post-war days, it is the Christian wedding ceremony that has most appeal, down to the last sartorial detail of white tie and tails: one in ten couples observes it, which means many who are not formally enrolled in the church. (Shinto predictably pirated it to enhance its own ceremonies.) Otherwise, Christianity in Japan seems more a victory for Santa Claus than for Christ and one Tokyo department store actually put Santa, in its Christmas display, on the cross!

Some have left Christianity for a more conscientious style of Buddhism or Shinto. One of these advocated a merger between Christianity and Shinto – that would, he said, make 'a grand religion'. The 'old' religions lose no chance to persuade the Christians to join them. Shinto and Buddhist dignitaries now make a point of calling on the Pope in Rome, and nobody missed the fact that Prince Akihito, who stands next in line for the imperial throne, married a girl with a thoroughly Catholic education. Japanized Christianity is vulnerable to the synthesizing instinct of this society.

The other 'new' religions are the Buddhist sects which have sprung up since the war to cater for the spiritual needs of those at the lower end of Japanese society. Organizations like the *Soka Gakkai*, which now boasts ten million members, help small traders and artisans to counter-act their isolation vis-à-vis the giant unions and corporations and give them something to look forward to. Instead of the systematic self-denial of Zen Buddhism, potential converts to the *Soka Gakkai* are offered a happy life and the security of knowing that there will be no need to experience any 'inconvenience' in their next life, since they would be able to 'live in a house at least as big as this hall; possessing everything from piano to jewellery; your mother being a beauty; you being born with intelligence, fortune and excellent health'. Who could resist such a scenario from what the sceptics were soon calling '*Yen* Buddhism'?

These were sects which put cheerful electric lights into gloomy old temples, emphasizing how *this* life could be improved as well as the next. Women take positions of leadership, and in some ways these sects play the role which political parties and social organizations play in the West for newly liberated segments of society. That helps perhaps to explain *Soka Gakkai*'s launching of the *Komeito* (Clean Government) Party which is now the third biggest political party in the Diet.

When the *Komeito* was accused of seeking to have Buddhism established, contrary to the Constitution, as the state religion, the *Soka Gakkai* leaders over-reacted and tried to suppress the book setting out these criticisms. Documents were allegedly forged and prosecutors pressurized in an extraordinary outburst of strong-arm tactics by Daisaku Ikeda, the late *Soka Gakkai* President. Ikeda went completely across religious lines in the 1970s by masterminding a political pact with the Communist Party. It displeased many Buddhists and came to nothing, but the sect remains popular. Some of the new sects seek international influence, like the *Nippozan Myohoji* which has built seventy Peace Pagodas in Asia, America and now Europe (the latest examples being at Milton Keynes and Battersea).

What stands out in the Japanese attitude to religion is its ambiguity. There are men like Ansei Yamazaki in the fifteenth century who progressed from Buddhism to Confucianism, and thence to Shinto, without apparent discomfort, and Prince Shotoku, the mediaeval statesman, who professed Buddhism and Confucianism at one and the same time. Fukuzawa, who had likened religion to tea, later advocated that Japan take up Christianity in order to gain western goodwill, while reserving an intention to go back to Buddhism afterwards because that would suit Japan's evolution better. A seventeenth-century priest hit on the brilliant idea of taking all the gods of good luck in the various pantheons – Shinto, Buddhist, Taoist, even Hindu – and offering them to be worshipped in a group, as an irresistible package. Basil Chamberlain found them being so worshipped when he compiled his *Things Japanese* a century ago, and it is a good bet that some of them are still around.

Every year the Prime Minister's office collects information on religious affiliations, and the most recent count shows 104 million people adhering to Shintoism, 87 million to Buddhism, 1½ million to Christianity and 16 million to other religions, to make a grand total of 209 million in a population of only 118 million persons. In other words, 91 million Japanese double-count themselves. Some religions are simply too good to be left out of.

If you have to drive to work or take exams on an inauspicious day, a temple can help ward off misfortune. The Narita Fudo temple specializes in blessing cars (which at new registration periods drive slowly through the temple compound in a continuous stream like a motorized communion), whereas the Kameido Tenjin temple is the place to go if you have exams on the horizon. For would-be parents a phallic shrine promises 'either fertility, a happy conjugal life or' (presumably for speeding to the maternity hospital) 'protection from traffic accidents'. The little good luck inscriptions are tucked into silk brocade packets that hang prettily on your windscreen or dressing-table.

Prime Minister Tanaka once surprised the Soviet leaders in Moscow by producing one from his pocket and describing it as 'a spirit' (he must have left it at home on the day the Lockheed scandal broke). Another interesting overseas exhibition of the quest for a better run of luck was when the American factory of TDK, the electronic tape maker, suffered in rapid succession a truck hi-jacking, a robbery, death and divorces in workers' families, car accidents and a 30% drop in profits. The company brought in a Japanese Buddhist priest to bless and purify the enterprise, after which things started to look up. Superstition is so deeply entrenched that the first Japanese psychoanalyst always took care never to step on his own analyst's shadow.

Every European culture reveals paganism beneath the skin, but the sheer weight of the non-spiritual content of Japanese religion suggests that the Christian solution – or stage, as Fukuzawa saw it – is too alien for Japan. 'A yellow man like me,' says a character in a Shusaku Endo novel, 'has absolutely no experience of anything so profound and extreme as the consciousness of sin you white men have.'

True Christianity calls for suffering which leads to power; true Buddhism required a supermundane calm which kills desire – two quite different ways of manipulating and conquering reality. Neither really appeals to the Japanese mind. The only truth to the traditional Japanese is nature, of which man is a part, and interpenetration with nature is the only goal worth pursuing. It is an attractive philosophy, but some Japanese question whether it is adequate for Japan's modern international role. This is what the novelist-turned-politician Shintaro Ishihara has to say:

> There is a spiritual void at the core of the Japanese nation, a moral degeneration that characterizes everything that happens in this society . . . Japan offers a glaring example of a highly developed level of cultural achievement . . . supported by a pitifully mediocre . . . moral philosophy . . . Postwar Japanese have been so alienated that they have been unable to realize their responsibility and sense of duty as individuals and unable to conceive a moral code.

Since the postwar economic bubble burst in 1973, more Japanese have taken up Buddhism or Shinto. There is now a Buddhist Information Service which you can telephone in Tokyo around the clock, with thirty priests to answer queries and give advice. The temples have never been so busy. The Japanese are rediscovering their indigenous religions, but as much in search of better luck or cultural nostalgia as improved moral attitudes.

8

Tongue-Tied Muse
Japanese Arts and Language

THE STORY of Japanese art and letters over the past century gives the measure of Japan's running deficit in the trade of culture. Vitally affected by western civilization, Japan herself has only marginally influenced the West in return.

True, from Van Gogh's hailing Japanese art as the 'true religion', to Greta Garbo's confession that seeing the celebrated *kabuki* actor Utaemon perform on the New York stage was the greatest theatrical experience of her life, the capacity of Japanese art to stun western practitioners has never been in doubt. That impact has led to a visible influence on western art, from the entire Impressionist movement in painting to Yeats' later plays, the poems of Ezra Pound and the pottery of Bernard Leach. An unacknowledged transfer of technology was the revolving stage, invented for the *kabuki* theatre, and exported to Europe in the mid-nineteenth century. Japanese architecture has always been ahead of Europe in the prefabrication of standardized modular components such as *tatami* rush mat floor sections and *shoji* paper screens.

But these loans to the West are small by comparison with what Japan has absorbed from Europe and America. The Japanese lionize western artists: Beethoven's Ninth Symphony is played live over an average Christmas season at least seventy times, and *Messiah* is probably sung more often now in Japan than in England. The conductor Seiji Ozawa, the pianist Mitsuko Uchida and scores of other soloists testify to the enthusiasm with which Japan has taken up European classical music in spite of the cultural gap.

Yukio Mishima admitted that his novels are westernized to the extent they lack the *yohaku* or empty 'white space' so valued in traditional Japanese art. To fill a canvas with paint, to spell out every detail of a story is easy, but what pleases a Japanese better is to be left to guess a little, to call on his own imagination, to feel involved in the work instead of remaining a dumb spectator. Hence the unfilled spaces in Utamaro's *ukiyoe*, the things left unsaid in novels (in Junichiro Tanizaki's *Some Prefer Nettles*, for example, we are never told whether the hero ultimately makes up with his wife, steals his father-in-law's mistress or goes back to his own Eurasian *geisha*).

Yoshisaburo Okakura put it in another way when he first entered western drawing-rooms at the beginning of this century with all their porcelain, pictures and *objets d'art* on show. His hosts knew how to display their possessions, he observed, but still had much to learn from Japan about 'how to hide'. This is not just a contrast in aesthetic taste but a chasm between different ways of communicating. Many a European who sighs with pleasure over a Sharaku print for all its 'white space' may be numbed by its cinematic equivalent of long static scenes where the camera never moves and art yields to raw reality.

In this sense Akira Kurosawa, whose films are almost better known in the West than in Japan, is as un-traditional, as 'internationalized' as Mishima. His debut in the West was with *Rashomon*, where four participants tell their different versions of a robbery and rape. In Ryunosuke Akutagawa's austere original story we are left to wonder who was right and what will happen afterwards to the people involved. Kurosawa cannot resist adding an upbeat final scene where the innocent woodcutter witness compassionately adopts the abandoned child, allowing love its triumph. By filling in one of Akutagawa's 'white spaces' he betrays himself as a westernized director. Where Yasujiro Ozu, another master of the cinematic art, understates with sparingness highly appreciated by Japanese, Kurosawa wants his films to be 'like a steak spread with butter and topped with good, rich, broiled eels'. That is not a bad Japanese definition of western art as a whole. It raises the question of how far a higher standard of living in Japan will erode the old spartan values: is Kurosawa a rebel or is he merely coming to terms, a little ahead of his time, with the bigger dinners now commonplace in Japan – bigger dinners, bigger canvases, fewer 'white spaces'?

Many artists have sought to combine western with traditional Japanese elements in their work, like Kumi Sugai, the Paris-based painter, who adopted the strict rules of composition of the West but drew his sensitivity of design from Japanese springs. Kenzo Tange similarly inserted an uniquely Japanese spirit into the modern buildings he designed for the industrial or commercial needs of today.

Another kind of borrowing was sartorial. When the Emperor Meiji commanded that western clothes be worn for certain occasions, they were lifted wholesale off the western shelf. The spirit of that injunction survives – shoelaces and trouser creases are religiously maintained by older Japanese who are forever taking their shoes off to enter a traditional house and folding their legs underneath them for hours on the *tatami* inside.

Clothes, once borrowed, can be discarded, and artistic styles can arbitrarily change. But language is omnipresent, used by all persons at all times, and the westernization of speech is the most significant area of unwitting cultural imperialism to be suffered by Japan. Often there was no obviously suitable Japanese word for the new concepts coming in from the West, and Japan has been spared that kind of cultural chauvinism that wants always to invent a new and entirely artificial one from indigenous roots. So a strike is *sutoraiku*, bread is *pan*, beer is *biru*, work is *arubaito* and gram is *guramu*, to take five typical loan words borrowed from five different foreign languages (English, Spanish, Dutch, German and French) – each spelt to meet the characteristics of Japanese pronunciation. The way in which such words or names are romanized in Japan can be unintelligible to those not familiar with Japanese speech. A Swiss, for instance, may not recognize his Zürich rendered as Churihhi. There is a well-known British biscuit manufacturer with a joint venture in Japan called Meiji Macubiti, which makes that European delicacy, the *daijesutibu bisuketto*.

A recent estimate puts the number of loan words now at 25,000, and the borrowing goes on unabated. Slowly, some Japanese purists fear, their language may be reduced to a few core concepts, participles, prefixes and suffices acting merely as a framework for this profusion of foreign words. Will the cuckoo take over the nest?

There are a few reverse borrowings, like 'hunky-dory' which is said to come from Honcho-dori, the red-light district or main road of Yokohama. Foreign sailors were supposed to utter the word to their rickshaw pullers, and then it acquired a generalized meaning of anything that was desirable and exciting. But the derivation sounds doubtful, and linguistic exchanges must be adjudged as heavily one-way.

Not only words but artistic valuations were borrowed. The temporary ascendancy of western taste and values led the Japanese to 'discover' some of their own achievements through western eyes. This began a century ago with the American art critic Fenollosa who rescued the *ukiyoe* from the low regard in which it had hitherto been held. It was western art-lovers who 'discovered' Utamaro and Hokusai at a time when the Japanese believed them to have been working in an ephemeral and inferior medium. Then in the 1920s Frank Lloyd Wright built the original Imperial Hotel in Tokyo incorporating in modern guise many Japanese architectural traditions and using the native *oya* stone, while Bruno Taut in the 1930s wrote *The Re-Discovery of the Japanese Aesthetic* advocating the use of wood in traditional fixed-dimension units for new buildings.

Meanwhile contemporary Japanese artists were flocking to Paris, Rome, London and New York for recognition. Teiji Takai, Hisao Domoto and other painters first 'arrived' in the West before gaining reputations in Japan. This psychology is not dead, despite the greater maturity of the Japanese artistic climate.

The strength of Japanese art before Western influence was its inarticulate emotiveness. 'My poetry comes from my bowels,' Kotaro Takamura, the twentieth-century poet insists. *Haragei* – variously translated as belly play, stomach talk, visceral art or communication without words – is one of the keys to the Japanese personality.* It 'elevates silence above art', a law professor explains: the Japanese 'are not a talkative people'. Let the eyes do the talking, they often say. Words have core-meanings that are well understood, but their peripheral meanings are vague and various. Japanese like to use expansive, ambiguous words, full of visual (because of the written characters) and stylistic overtones but not in the least exact. The ideal in life is to live out your emotions, not cerebrate or verbalize them.

Inarticulacy can be quite literal. A postwar survey found a farmer's wife in northeastern Japan who uttered, on average, no more than two or three words a day. 'They say very little about themselves, or anything else,' a German businessman in Japan complains: 'Personal meetings are often awkward.' At lunch with colleagues, a foreigner will blurt out his preoccupations and goals, while a traditional Japanese in the same situation would quietly fish for clues to what the others are seeking (he would in any case regard talking over food as both impolite and bad for the digestion). Foreigners recall the embarrassment caused to Japanese viewers by a TV commercial in which Orson Welles actually recommended a particular brand of liquor and listed its good properties in support. The Japanese found him too explicit: something more subtly inferential would have drawn them better to the product.

The Japanese used to believe that silence is golden – especially in the male of the species. 'A talkative man,' they would say, 'is just like a girl,' while an articulate man arouses suspicion. Robert Ozaki, the American Japanese, puts it this way: 'In Japan, someone who speaks well and colourfully is regarded as belonging to the entertainment world, not to the realm of sublime human relations. A man who heavily relies on verbal communications as a means of expressing his feelings is said to prove his abruptness, immaturity and possibly

---

* Since the *hara* (literally the stomach) was believed to be the organ of thought, to cut it open (*harakiri*) was to bare your thoughts, revealing your pure motives and good faith.

dishonesty.' But Ozaki goes on to concede that it is hard to conduct business effectively 'when every party speaks in the language of suggestion'. It means that no Japanese likes to advocate, persuade or debate with others: open confrontation, even if only verbal, is disturbing. He prefers to stick to the group consensus, whatever that is, and not issue his own statements or judgments or go into the 'how' or 'why' of a matter. 'The mouth', it used to be warned, 'can be a source of trouble.'

Deep within him the Japanese has, as Yukio Mishima put it, 'the *samurai*'s disdain for self-justification'. In international terms this is disastrous. Japanese who do not need to explain themselves verbally to each other are abysmally weak in public relations with foreigners. At the United Nations successive Japanese delegations have won a reputation for practising the 'three S's' – smiling, sleeping and silence. Japanese can become quickly bored by the sustained conceptual argument that European intellectuals have conducted since Greek times, and yet this is now the model for international debates in the UN and elsewhere. At a Japanese-owned factory in Britain the monthly staff meeting can leave both sides irritated. The Britons find the discussion 'all one way', so they are left to wonder what the Japanese are thinking and why they don't come 'out with it'. That makes them feel aggressive – whereupon the Japanese in their turn wonder why such heat is being generated over nothing.

When words are *de trop*, the other indicators of feeling gain significance. Japanese distinguishes between five kinds of laughter, for example:

Ahaha means merry laughter,

Ihihi is vulgar,

Uhuhu is derisive,

Ehehe is the sycophantic outburst of a silly fool, and

Ohoho is the modest, reserved laugh of a gentleman.

Dreams also come into their own in an inarticulate society. A European girl had a shy Japanese boy friend who played footsy with her under the *kotatsu**for almost half a year before telling her that he had dreamed of making love to her on a deserted beach, then cutting off her head and swimming with it out to sea where he had drowned. 'You know,' the girl remarked afterwards to an English friend, 'that's the first time I realized he was interested in me.'

The former Foreign Minister Kiichi Miyazawa, a strong candidate

---

* A hole in the *tatami* (rush matting) floor allowing you to sit on the *tatami* edge and dangle your stockinged feet over a heated grid, the hole covered by a low table on which you can eat meals, play cards, etc.

for Prime Minister in the future, once admitted that his outspoken-ness was a handicap in domestic politics:

> I tend to express myself too articulately. This is a disadvantage and I realize that my critics may be right: human life and human relations are so uncertain and, at least in Japan, are so flexible and sometimes vague that to try and articulate them sometimes misses the point and frequently antagonises people. It is not so much bluntness as an articulate tendency to analyse. Amid life's uncertainties, it is dangerous to be too articulate, too precise.

Like other parts of the Japanese tradition, *haragei* (tummy talk) is now under criticism. The growth of individualism threatens it, as does the growing modern need to settle some conflicts by rational debate instead of slow silent consensus. The younger film director, Nagisa Oshima, feels that his challenge differs from that of the veteran Kurosawa because, 'our generation cannot rely on the congeniality of our all being Japanese in order to communicate'. The cosy ring of silence is now broken by alien incursions from a loud-mouthed world outside. Radio and television are congenital enemies of the soft voice, the understatement, the sustained pause, and Japanese life is thereby coarsened.

Some hope that this implacable world stream can be tamed, that the world can be persuaded to listen to the traditional Japanese voice. But even those who adopt the noisier manifestations of western culture find they are not necessarily helped to a readier communication with Westerners. Masanori Sera, who leads a rock band called Twist, speculated to an English visitor:

> I can talk to you intellectually in English, but emotionally I must do so in Japanese . . . In future Japanese artistes may be able to communicate emotionally – spiritually – with foreigners . . . I hope so . . . but we must work to cut the intellectual bonds and aim straight at the heart where the spirit lives.

Sera's meaning is clear: he wants to relate to his Western heroes not in arid words but through emotions expressed by the language of the eyes and the body as well as sound.

When Japanese live intimately with foreigners abroad they may feel deprived of some of the pleasure of non-verbal relating, and even suffer some loss of communication. A Japanese translator with an English wife describes his family life in London as bothersome: 'I have to speak all my thinking,' he complains.

The reverse of this is the difficulty which Westerners find in communicating with Japanese, beginning with the language itself, which even the most accomplished modern western Japanologist, Edwin Reischauer, a former US Ambassador to Japan, terms a 'barrier of monumental size' to outsiders. Because it expresses moods rather than precise judgments, lacking the tight grammatical structure which Aristotle taught to Europe, the Japanese language effectively isolates Japan in intellectual terms. Only a handful of Westerners can speak it truly as natives, and they are not always clasped with delight to the local bosom (as would happen in China or India), but may be stared at in disbelief and horror as if constituting an actual threat to Japanese culture – or as if the Japanese at bottom do not want to be understood, perhaps because that would mean their absorption into the outside world.

Translation, which usually saves some of the day in such cultural encounters, lets us down in Japan. Arthur Waley, that master translator from the Japanese, used to say that it was he, rather than the original writer, who had to do the talking: he needed two lines of English to convey one original line of that classic, *The Tale of Genji*. Such doubling of wordage is characteristic, and gives a measure of just how much the Japanese leaves to be filled in by the reader's imagination. So translation becomes a more creative exercise than it is between, say, English and Italian, involving much re-writing. Indeed, the translator of an English book into Japanese is normally paid a larger royalty than the English author himself.

These bars to Western understanding serve to protect the Japanese: they mean that Japan never developed a westernized cultural élite so at home with Shakespeare and Graham Greene, Sartre and Tennessee Williams, that it became alienated from its own origins, as happened in India and Africa in this century. Luckily for Japan, educational standards were always good enough to satisfy her own intellectuals without the need to go abroad. India and China were less fortunate.

But some aspects of the indigenous culture have undoubtedly held up Japan's progress, not the least of them being the ideograms inherited from China but supplemented over the centuries by later Japanese phonetic inventions. The ideographic characters, expressing meaning rather than sounds, are more beautiful than the roman alphabet: you can frame a piece of calligraphy and hang it on your wall to give you simultaneous visual-aesthetic and literal-intellectual pleasure, which nobody can manage to do with a page from, say, the English Bible. They also unlocked doors to the outside world, meaning for most of Japanese history the world of China. When a Chinese and a Japanese meet they cannot understand a word of each other's speech, but what they write down on paper was originally identical and is still largely similar. They can even 'write' their characters with a finger in the air, and the other person can understand just by watching the movement of that one finger. (The resulting invisible ideogram is so vivid that the 'writer' may unconsciously go through the motion of 'erasing' one phrase before 'writing' the next one on the same 'ground'.)

Shintaro Ishiharo wrote a tense story called *Ambush* where a journalist in Vietnam, waiting on a dark night for an enemy attack and under orders to keep silent, communicates his anxiety to a colleague by 'writing' on the skin of his back, so his friend could literally feel his meaning. Ideograms are compact and economical (saving time and space) as well as handsome. But the investment in their mastery is excessive. Whereas a European child need learn only 26 letters for a lifetime of erudition, his Japanese counterpart has to memorize 1,850 different characters at school and would need about 5,000 to graduate*: that usually represents a peak from which he will slowly slip back as he gets older. The Japanese student spends about two years more than a European simply to acquire the same linguistic access to knowledge, so that in terms of time the Westerner has a decisive built-in advantage.

When the scholars of Japan first appreciated this discrepancy they were appalled. 'What a nuisance, a waste of effort and a bother,' one wrote about the ideographs. They lamented the loss of energy involved in memorizing characters: it was like moving goods around without the wheel. Modern thinkers agree that the ideograms put a brake on Japanese intellectual development. Reischauer calls them 'perhaps the greatest single misfortune' in Japanese history, and some Japanese argue that if they had only changed their written language they might even have won the war in 1945. A distinguished line of scholars has pleaded for reform. The twentieth-century novelist Noaya Shiga wanted his countrymen to switch to French, 'the most beautiful language in the world'. Arinori Mori, the Meiji intellectual, had proposed English instead. But for most intellectual leaders it was a question of finding an easier script in which to express the same enduring spoken language. The new Korean script was advocated by some,† but the majority of would-be reformers chose *romaji* – the roman alphabet of Europe.

Like their counterparts in China, they had to fight against the

---

* China invented some 50,000 characters in all: Japanese encyclopaedias usually run to 10,000.

† Of the two other countries which had used Chinese ideograms, Vietnam changed to the roman alphabet but Korea invented a new phonetic alphabet of its own.

vested interests of those who had already devoted themselves to learning the ideograms, as well as the aesthetes who could not bear to think of losing those attractive artefacts of East Asian civilization. MacArthur wanted to use his occupation of Japan to decree the linguistic change which the country needed to become modern but was too conservative to effect by itself. Political leaders headed by Shigeru Yoshida, the great postwar Prime Minister, opposed him, however, and the American initiative foundered.

Even romanization would leave many problems unsolved. What do you do with a word like *senko*, for instance, which can mean remote antiquity, eternity, one's deceased, a dyer, a ship's carpenter, an incense-stick, a flash, military merit, special research, travelling in disguise, scarlet, ore washing, concentration, choice, submarine voyage, pig iron or preceding – according to the context or (in speaking) subtleties of intonation. There are in any case two rival systems of romanization, Hepburn which is based on English pronunciations, and Kunrei which is more catholic. The latter is apparently meant to be the official medium, but the former is used much more widely, including in this book. (China faces precisely the same problem of competition between the rival Wade-Giles and *pinyin* systems of romanization.)

The invention of the word processor, which can now handle all the ideograms with ease, enabling a Japanese to type his own language as painlessly as a European types his, may give the characters another lease of life. They are also displacing *romaji* on some road signs.

An ungenerous American critic has said that 'nowhere do disparate ideologies rest more comfortably side by side than in the head of a Japanese', and in this he spoke for many Westerners irritated by such blatant inconsistencies as professing to be at one and the same time conservative and socialist, or Protestant and Catholic, or Buddhist and Shinto. The Teutonic either-or mentality is not, of course, the only strand in European thought. It was Scott Fitzgerald who said that 'the test of a first-rate intelligence is the ability to hold two opposed ideas in the mind at the same time, and still retain the ability to function'. Consistency may be a good way of thinking, inconsistency a better way of living. Japan goes for the practical, thereby losing in such areas as abstract thought and pure research.

Today, faced with the alarming invasion of westernism, some Japanese are reviving tradition. The *kimono*, for instance, is worn a little more often by men or women of the older generation despite the outdoor prevalence of the western suit and dress. Men delight, after being trousered for a time, to feel a gentle breeze around their calves as they walk outdoors in a *kimono* (or in summer a cotton *yukata*). It became the practice in this century for men to wear a suit to work and change into a *kimono* at home afterwards. For women it was the other way round – *kimono* outdoors, western dress at home. But the female *kimono* was difficult to move about in: women appeared hobbled in it and could take only short steps. In the 1950s more practical *kimonos* were designed which were easier to wear, and now there are fewer women who slavishly follow the latest Parisian fashions, more who wear what their grandfathers would recognize as Japanese dress. There is also a generation factor: young women who flirt with Dior as young brides often settle down in later life to more traditional-looking clothes.

'You look better in foreign clothes . . .' a character in Tanizaki's novel *The Makioka Sisters* tells a woman friend, 'a *kimono* makes you look fat.' Above the waist women have the reverse problem: their bosoms have filled out with better diet and in response to westernized aesthetics. Flat chests are no longer the norm as they were before the war, and special undergarments now have to be worn to 'erase the curves' and allow Miss Yoko to wear the loose-hanging *kimono* gracefully.

As for men, nostalgia for past comfort has sent some of them back to the *fundoshi*, the traditional undergarment referred to in some haberdashers as the 'classic pant', which does not come in a fixed shape to hug the haunches as European underpants do, but ties more loosely and givingly in the manner of a small loincloth.

To move back to higher realms, the traditions of Japanese pictorial art – warm lyricism, muted colours, composition from a single high point and the placing of abstract shapes in a pattern – seemed to be going under when western art first flooded in a century ago. But in the 1950s Japanese artists stopped behaving as passive disciples of France and began to assert an equality of creativity. Leonard Foujita pioneered a blending of Japanese and European techniques, succeeding only in a purely decorative sense but blazing a path for others to follow. In architecture Kishio Kurokawa retrieved Buddhist precepts to restore the quality of ambiguity in modern buildings, freeing Japanese structural technology from its thraldom to western rationalism. Many modern Japanese buildings do not make a bold sweeping statement, defying nature like a Beethoven symphony, but rather cut a more modest, human, individually eccentric line that defers to nature and its surroundings in an amenable aesthetic.

The imitation of western composers crumbled beneath the genius of Toshiro Mayazumi, who brought traditional sounds back into the concert hall, and Toru Takemitsu, who put traditional Japanese instruments into the concert orchestra. Takemitsu spearheaded the cultural revolt against western purposiveness, against the mathematical relentlessness of European classical music. 'The worst thing you can do with sounds,' he observes, 'is to drive them around like a car.' He places sounds without developing them into ideas: 'Like a river . . . I have the very oriental idea of no beginning and no end.'

Japan is thus a battleground between a long-held tradition and a western army of cultural invaders – some easily cut down because they lack allure; others taking the palm because they have universal, enduring appeal; but many in between that exert a short-term attraction. The spectator might infer, from seeing so many dead men on the defenders' side, that the cultural war is over. But some of those casualties are only stunned, and likely to defeat the invader when they rise again. A great deal of the old Japanese culture, temporarily downed by Beethoven and Rousseau, is struggling to its feet as the Japanese people recover a little self-confidence in their ordeal of being individual battlefields in this war of arts.

9

The Cut Flowers of Democracy
Japan's Government, Politics, Media and Law

JAPAN'S POLITICAL institutions were hi-jacked by General Douglas MacArthur during the American Occupation of 1945–52, and firmly piloted towards the Westminster-Washington model. Practices born from the need to protect individuals were thrust into a society which placed the group before the individual, prizing harmony and consensus more than civil liberty. The resulting distortion was never accepted by most Japanese. For forty years they have paid lip service to western democracy, but the underlying discomfort is coming more into the open. The gap between the alien outward form which governs Japanese politics and the indigenous reality beneath is slowly widening. Young people are particularly disillusioned, even though their cynicism about the political process may be disguised by the surviving traditional habit of deferring to authority.

What happened in 1945 was a bargain struck by the Americans with the civilian Japanese politicians who came forward to deal with them. Japan could keep her Emperor if she renounced militarism. This was a perfectly acceptable deal: in any case the defeated Japanese had no alternative. When it came to putting it down on paper, however, all they could produce was a new draft constitution which broadly reaffirmed the old hierarchical view of the state. The Americans had expected something more sympathetic to their own democratic views, and so they introduced a counter-draft which the nervous Japanese Cabinet accepted, even though its wording made no concessions to establishing continuity with the Japanese past.

'We, the Japanese people', it began – a Jeffersonian flourish quite lost on most Japanese. The first article inferred the Emperor's new role 'from the will of the people with whom resides sovereign power'. Phrases like this were simply not understood by most Japanese, and the few whose foreign learning enabled them to appreciate such language did not for a moment believe it. So Yasuhiro Nakasone was right to complain, long before he became Prime Minister in 1982, that this Constitution of 1946 did not spring from Japanese free will, but was imposed, virtually without consultation, as a *fait accompli*. The democracy practised in Japan, he said, is 'an artificial flower, a cut flower' severed from national roots.

One Cabinet Minister described the Constitution as 'ridiculous' because it turned Japan into a 'mistress' of the USA. Another conservative legislator found it 'unforgivable' that the Constitution had been adopted 'almost without the hands of the Japanese touching it'. By the 1980s, right-wingers could carry intellectual resentment to the point of wanting to indict the Constitution as a breach of international law because its pacifist clauses placed an unbearable fetter on Japanese sovereignty. Others reject it as culturally uncongenial. Some day, a young woman law professor born after 1945 predicts, 'the ugliness of the spirit that permeates the Constitution will begin to gnaw at people's hearts'.

And yet opinion polls do not confirm a general desire for revision, and there is a sizeable body of opinion which settles for the proposition that the Constitution, despite its questionable origins, has over the years become assimilated or 'Japanized'. The issue has apparently polarized along party lines, with many in the ruling Liberal-Democratic Party favouring revision in order to reinstate more traditional Japanese beliefs and values, while the largely Marxist Opposition parties see in the American text a valuable protection of their minority rights (especially the vulnerable interests of trade unions) as well as a guarantee against military leaders' ever sharing in political decision-making.

Nakasone demanded amendments as early as 1947, though he later proposed the safeguard of a national referendum to confirm each one. He was the first Prime Minister to break the taboo on mentioning the matter in the Diet or Parliament. But revising the Constitution requires a two-thirds majority in the Diet and that is now beyond the Liberal-Democrats' grasp, so the *status quo* is likely to endure.

When Nakasone argues that the Japanese want more 'Asian-style democracy', he means first of all that the position of the Emperor should not be forced into a modern European mould as a constitutional monarch, but be allowed to retain some ambiguity as a quasi-father of the nation and embodiment of its history and culture. The disagreement is no longer over his divinity. The American de-deification of Hirohito (the right-wing novelist-politician Shintaro Ishihara called it deicide) has been readily accepted. Indeed, since 1945 Hirohito has adroitly cultivated an ungodlike image, taking walk-abouts among his subjects and making genuine contributions to the scholarship of marine biology. Crown Prince Akihito was permitted to bring up his own children and punish them personally, his commoner wife actually nursed them at the breast and his elder son,

Prince Hiro, who will eventually succeed to the throne, went to Oxford – all striking departures from imperial precedent.

There is, in fact, a stain on Hirohito's infallibility which he cannot wipe away, namely his share of responsibility for the war, an issue which is also now polarized along left-right lines. It is this question which has prompted suggestions that the Emperor should abdicate. Hirohito is said to have been ready to give up the throne earlier if, after four daughters in succession, he and his Empress did not produce a male heir – but then Akihito was born.

Most Japanese would still go along with the view expressed seventy years ago by that Japanese prophet of Asian nationalism, Ikki Kita: 'The system whereby the head of state has to struggle for election by a long-winded self-advertisement and by exposing himself to ridicule like a low-class actor seems a very strange custom to the Japanese.' It is bad enough, most of them inwardly think, to put the head of government through such a regular charade without debasing the head of state as well.

But the other side of the bargain, the price which Japan pays for maintaining its imperial link with the past, is much more controversial. In Article 9 of the Constitution:

> The Japanese people forever renounce war as a sovereign right of the nation and the threat or use of force as a means of settling international disputes . . . Land, sea and air forces . . . will never be maintained.

This goes far beyond earlier precedents (in France and Italy, for example, or in Burma) to render Japan uniquely hobbled in the international community. No credible defence force can be built up, and the entire burden of Japan's security against overseas attack is made to fall on another country, the United States. That was appropriate for the 1950s, but seems unsuitable for the 1990s. So the second plank in Nakasone's Asian-democracy platform is constitutional change. If Article 9 were amended, different pressure groups would want to alter other clauses in the Constitution, and a Pandora's box might be opened. Why tempt Providence by introducing the prospect of revived military respectability? It is a very common self-image for the Japanese to see themselves as reformed alcoholics, so to speak, to whom even small doses of that old militaristic drug are best denied.

Nakasone is nevertheless supported by many on constitutional change, for three reasons. The first is resentment at the derogatory status to which Japan seems indefinitely condemned. A more positive dissatisfaction is that the Constitution does not sufficiently reflect

Japanese values, particularly because it emphasizes individual rights at the expense of duty to one's group or state. This is not merely a right-wing complaint, but one which Marxists echo. Since socialism seeks to control civil rights in the interest of public welfare, a socialist politician once explained, the Constitution must be judged a 'period piece' – both 'pre-socialist and anachronistic'. A third kind of criticism comes from embarrassment over the phraseology of the Constitution, so hastily translated from an evangelical American text. Its sentences are 'not written by Japanese', the wording is 'funny' and 'awkward', 'full of expressions that are quaintly alien', a 'counterfeit Constitution' respected only by 'addicts of western civilization, schoolteachers and newspapermen' – to take comments at random over the past twenty-five years. The Constitution survives largely because people know that even worse things might replace it.

To observe the tension between MacArthur's western and Nakasone's 'Asian-style' political practices, one need go no further than the business of the Diet. Each of the two Houses (the House of Councillors or Upper House, and House of Representatives or Lower House) decides by majority vote, something which is second nature to anyone in the western tradition. Yet when the ruling Liberal-Democratic Party passed the Security Treaty with the US in 1960 against clamorous opposition from left-wing and neutral critics, that opposition could fulminate against 'the dictatorship of the majority'. Some Japanese thinkers analyse the idea of deciding the policy of a group or the nation solely on the basis of 'half the votes plus one' as a regrettable aberration of western societies, a patently impractical concept not worthy of imitation by people who have mastered the art of consensus (wherein the majority first convinces the minority, or makes a bargain with it, before they proceed together in an outwardly unanimous front).

It follows that the public slanging match of an election contest is distressing to most Japanese. The winner can get over his wounds, but the loser suffers a damaging loss of face from the extravagantly publicized fact that so many thousands of people in the neighbourhood have spurned him. Defeat is wounding in any society, but doubly so where public respect is the cornerstone of an individual's existence. The conservative scholar Shinkichi Eto has commented that transplanting western liberalism would induce a painful struggle within each Japanese person to transform his entire personality. This is what is underestimated by superficial western critics of Japan.

The sense of individual participation in politics is weak. Democracy means something that is done 'for' rather than 'by' the people. The ancestors of the modern Japanese had never fought for parliamentary power in the manner of King John's barons, and had never questioned their feudal duty to pay tax on land (the spark which kindled representative government in Europe). There are fewer voters than in the West who conscientiously weigh alternative policy platforms to decide privately which would be best for their country. More people vote in Japan as a favour to themselves or their friends to help achieve some personal or group aim – out of a sense of duty rather than of right. They also vote for the man rather than his programme, preferring to avoid the embarrassment of open debate on the issues. Once the candidate is elected, voters will fatalistically leave matters to his professional judgement and not regard him as accountable to them, at least until the next election.

A Japanese feels more at home with face-to-face decisions of the kind that he makes in small arenas like a city ward, or in humble organizations like the Parent-Teacher Association. The impersonal secrecy of the ballot-box as a means of deciding who shall represent 200,000 voters who cannot begin to know one another, runs counter to the Japanese instinct for placing visible human relationships above everything else: it is now a fact of life, but slightly uncomfortable for older citizens.

When the former Prime Minister Kakuei Tanaka described democracy as 'the politics of numbers', he was not taking his hat off to a system which counts every adult opinion as being of equal worth, but rather underlining the importance of his own speciality, which is the buying of a majority with favours, promises and gifts. Elections to the Diet are contests of social clout more than political wisdom. The one who wins is the fixer who can get more bridges built in your county, find more suitable brides for his supporters, secure more jobs and university entrances for constituents' sons – not the man who puts forward convincing arguments about reflation or national security. Tanaka's constituency of Niigata in central Japan was famous for getting a good 60% more than its fair share of national budget funds.

The electors made their views on corruption embarrassingly clear in 1976 when they returned six Liberal-Democrats to the Diet with resounding majorities despite their being prosecuted for bribery in the Lockheed case, where the American company had paid money to Japanese politicians to secure an important contract to supply aircraft. One of the six was Tanaka, of whom his satisfied constituents said: 'He did not steal our taxes, he merely took money from the Americans.' Even a socialist postman in Niigata commented: 'All politicians take money, that is how they got to the top. Tanaka got all the way without family, without any education. He was not ashamed of *kinken**. He did not try to hide it as hard as most do,' and was, indeed, 'too open, too honest.'

It was the intellectuals who professed shame that the highest Japanese leaders could be bought so furtively by an American company, which could then leak the matter so casually to provide evidence for the Japanese court. When Tanaka was convicted in 1983, the court rebuked Japanese politicians for giving 'precedence to partiality, greed and selfishness'. But the Minister for Justice parried that to look for purity in politics was like 'asking for fish at a greengrocer's', and a Harvard-trained critic dismissed the Lockheed bribe of over $2 million as the moral equivalent of shoplifting tisues in a supermarket: politicians were 'born dirty'. Japan found that the price for democracy was more corruption.

It is common practice for companies to finance candidates from whom they expect special favours afterwards, and to press their employees (and their subcontractors' employees) to vote for them. The sense of personal obligation fatally overrides whatever scruples a voter may have about more theoretical considerations of morality. A candidate may thrust bottles of *sake* into the hands of every voter as he canvasses at their doors, and the next time say to them: 'You accepted my gift, now you must vote for me.'

The salary of a Dietman is only about a third of what he needs, which opens up big possibilities of persuasion within the Parliament. When Tanaka contested the Liberal-Democratic Party presidency, which automatically carried with it the post of Prime Minister, he reputedly spent more than $30 million on persuading his fellow Liberal-Democrats to support him. Nakasone was the first Prime Minister to make his Cabinet declare their assets, but when the press found out that the Justice Minister had merely changed the ownership of property into his wife's name, he blandly apologized as if there were nothing seriously wrong. Many would echo today the rumination of a character in a novel by Soseki Natsume at the beginning of the century: 'If one can make as much money as father has by serving the nation, I wouldn't mind serving it myself.'

As for the Opposition parties, their role is a difficult one. To oppose somebody in Japanese society is to seek to reduce their public respect, and most people feel uncomfortable about that. Opposition therefore tends to polarize into a predictable routine on the one hand or unreasoning emotional violence (typified by the young radicals of the 1960s) on the other. But the Japanese tradition does give the small and mainly left-wing Opposition parties in the Diet a power out of all

* 'money politics'.

proportion to their size. To a western eye they may seem puny – 'like dogs barking in the distance', in one of Nakasone's stirring Asian-style phrases. But in fact the potency of consensus over Japanese minds gives them a weapon which no Opposition in a western parliament could wield, almost amounting to a right of veto.

To a Japanese legislator, passing a bill by 350 votes to nil in a 600-man chamber is no kind of victory. By boycotting Diet business, the Opposition can paint the ruling party as ruthless and dictatorial, and in nine cases out of ten, the government prefers to coax it back into the chamber with concessions reflecting its criticisms of the bill. One-sided Diet sessions feel uncomfortable, and go down badly in the media. Only occasionally was the Opposition bluff called, for such important measures as the Security Treaty of 1960, although these days the government can more easily 'railroad' its bills through without the Opposition because the latter is so fragmented.

Prime Minister Masayoshi Ohira in 1978 brought a new style of managing government business, consulting the Opposition parties, briefing them and giving them 'face'. It meant conducting, in his own phrase, 'the politics of waiting', and sometimes he had to work all through the night to achieve the unanimity for which ancient custom called. This is the leadership style which an American once described after working as an assistant to a member of the Diet:

> The leader is not the one with the booming voice, but rather the person most skilled in balancing various opinions and guiding the energies from below. He must be able to integrate the various ideas and energies coming up to him, and implement them in a way so that everyone down the line feels that their input was vital to the outcome . . .

To be able to persuade others to compromise is a gift prized more than the knack of knowing the right decision to make. The ideal leader in Japan consults everybody and gains unanimity, albeit for a watered-down version of what the majority wanted in the first place.

This contrast between western and Japanese parliamentary procedure can be expressed mathematically. In a western democracy a government with 51% of the votes or seats ('half plus one' as many Japanese derisively call it) may feel morally entitled to put its entire election platform through during its term of office, if it can. In Japan the expectation would be to compromise some of the programme, so that 60% of the popular vote might be regarded as permitting a government to carry out roughly 60% of its promises. The tension between the two approaches to decision-making appears everywhere, for example in the controversial Council on Education

Reform whose Chairman favoured decision by a two-thirds majority but from which the Prime Minister wanted consensus – or unanimity.

Even the political parties themselves are different from such bodies as the Republican Party of the US or the Labour Party of Britain. Group loyalty means that a Japanese party is less a convention of individuals united by a shared policy platform, more a tactical federation of closed and exclusive factions based on personal loyalty. Japan thus presents, as two political scientists, Robert Scalapino and Junnosuke Masumi, concluded, the 'paradox of an open society made up of closed components'. Japan imported the idea of modern political parties from the West, but the way in which they are built and work in the Japanese environment revolves around the traditional hierarchical leader-follower group or faction which is the old way of doing things in Japan.

Loyalty to a superior or to colleagues is the supreme virtue in Japan, and it goes against the grain to be always saying, 'Yes, I agree with you about this policy', but, 'No, I cannot support you on that one.' The construction of a genuine policy platform capable of commanding the support of all members of the group is the product of skilfully instinctive leadership rather than of open debate within the group. So politics are pursued as much on the basis of factional manoeuvre or personal loyalty as on policy choices: young voters are heavily influenced, for example, by the views of their parents and schoolfriends. (A quarter of the Lower House Liberal-Democrats have fathers or grandfathers who were in the Diet.)

The internal legality of parties may be blatantly side-stepped. Only a minority of the Presidents of the Liberal-Democratic Party (who automatically become Prime Ministers) have been properly elected according to party rules. Most of them won by extra-legal processes including the old-fashioned *hanashiai*, or power-broking behind the scenes. This is perhaps the most direct evidence for the proposition that western-style legalistic procedures for political matters do not work well in Japan. When an elder statesman arbitrarily engineered the appointment of one of his colleagues to the Liberal-Democratic Party presidency in order to protect party unity from a divisive contest between two others, his manoeuvre was hailed as 'the height of political artistry', though it was in clear violation of party statutes. Since then we have seen the Japan Socialist Party convention illegally 'frozen' to allow more time for the left and right wings to mediate their differences, which also threatened to tear the party in half.

The old instinct which has survived in the modern clothes of parliamentary democracy is something like the Churchillian view that it is better to talk than fight. Japan has carried out profound political changes without substantial violence or loss of life, through the process of monumental negotiation. This was the case, for example, with the so-called Meiji Restoration of 1868 which carried Japan out of feudalism into democratic capitalism. When two sides fought in Japan, and one had clearly won, it was customary for the losing leader to withdraw, whereupon the winning leader would affirm both his opponent's honour and the safety of his opponent's men. This would clear the ground for reconciliation and a new unity, symbolized by the ritual clapping of hands by all – *teuchi*. One can see the same psychology at work in the political parties of today.

The Liberal-Democratic Party has ruled for all thirty years of its existence, and there has been only one period of a few months in 1947–8 when the conservative half of the political spectrum has been out of power in post-war Japan. Its success rested on its first presiding over the economic post-war miracle, and then milking the new incomes of the urban masses for the benefit of farmers. In the 1960s its fortunes seemed to be sinking, but now the Liberal-Democratic Party usually wins a steady 45% or so of the popular vote in the Lower House, enough for it to hang on to power in the Diet.*

It was saved by the unexpected conservatism of some younger Japanese, whose sense of nationalism is inflated by Japan's vulnerability to external forces, and who have turned away from the left partly because of the revelation of Soviet imperfections in China, Hungary, Afghanistan and Cambodia. The taste of domestic affluence first makes young people more appreciative of the *status quo*, and then their insecurity about its continuing renders them more acquiescent in the social controls which have been handed down by tradition. Finally, the world recession following the oil price shocks of the 1970s benefits the Liberal-Democrats. Rather than toy with untried parties, voters stay with the seasoned helmsmen who have kept the economic miracle going through all the storms and stresses of the past fifteen years.

Now that the Liberal-Democratic Party has virtually lost its majority in the Lower House, it depends on incorporating enough Independents (many of whom are actually Liberal-Democrats who

* Results of the 1983 general election for the Lower House:

	Liberal-Democratic Party	Japan Socialist Party	Komeito	Democratic Socialist Party	Japan Communist Party	New Liberal Club
Popular vote	46%	19%	10%	7%	9%	2%
Seats won	49%	22%	11%	7%	5%	2%

won without constituency party backing), or going into coalition with one of the smaller Opposition parties – currently the New Liberal Club of disaffected ex-Liberal Democrats. If they were not enough after a future election, a coalition could be engineered with the Democratic Socialist Party or the *Komeito* (one Liberal-Democrat leader, Susumu Nikaido, has already sounded them out) and by these means the ruling party is likely to hold on to the reins of government well into the 1990s.

The obstacle could be the divisions within itself. The large factions within the party are in the process of changing leaders, and there must be a questionmark over their cohesiveness. Tanaka is still formally heading the largest faction (of 115 in both Houses), and is unwilling to pass it on to his heir, Noboru Takeshita, the present Finance Minister, whom he once dismissed as 'too young to polish floors'. The Takeo Fukuda faction (67 members) is similarly led by a former Prime Minister who is not ready to pass the baton to his successor, Shintaro Abe, the present Foreign Minister. Kiichi Miyazawa, the most intellectual of them all, has only just taken over the leadership of his faction of 78 members. Prime Minister Yasuhiro Nakasone and Toshio Komoto lead other factions of 65 and 35 members respectively. It is an unwieldy party.

Recent Prime Ministers have mostly been trained in the Civil Service and were relatively skilled, therefore, in handling the legalities of doing business under a western Constitution. The exception was the innovative and controversial Tanaka. Alone among post-war leaders, he never completed his school career or went to university. Instead of joining the Civil Service, he became a self-made businessman. Earthy and cunning in manner, he impressed everybody with his prodigious memory, his skill at fixing, his nonchalant handling of the seamy side of party finance and his open establishment of a mistress. The ordinary Japanese readily identified with him as a non-establishment contender for supreme power. But then, soon after becoming Prime Minister at the young age of fifty-four, Tanaka had to resign before a torrent of corruption scandals: a few years later he was convicted of receiving a huge bribe from Lockheed, the American aircraft manufacturer. Yet he remained in the Diet unrepentant, head of his faction and still the supreme king-maker with whom every candidate for the premiership must ingratiate himself. When criticized for this, he replied: 'Why should not a large shareholder sometimes name the president?'

Factional indifference to policy questions is such that, when a big policy issue does arise, the divisions run across each faction. This is why there are always a number of cross-faction groups pushing particular platforms. One of these a few years ago called itself the Centre for Refreshing the Popular Mind, and in the 1970s the hawkish novelist Ishihara and thirty of his Liberal-Democratic colleagues in various factions formed the Young Storm Association – *Seirankai* – to protest against the 'weaklings' in the government who had 'ditched' Taiwan in order to recognize China's Communist government. Most recently, Miyazawa has launched, with the backing of the industrialist Akio Morita, his own Research Group for a Free Society. Factions are to do with power, cross-faction groups with ideology and the party itself with government.

On the right of the Liberal-Democrats stand a small number of semi-fascist extremists who would like Japan to re-arm, stand up more strongly to the Soviet Union, give the Emperor more power and scrap the Constitution. A lurid example was the late Yoshio Kodama, who made a fortune from war supplies on the China front in the 1930s and then used it to finance the party which later became the Liberal-Democratic Party. Though never elected to the Diet, he organized Japan's gangsters into a National Congress of Patriotic Organizations, and boasted of having two million followers. Kodama, a Liberal-Democrat king-maker long before Tanaka, was also involved in the Lockheed scandal.

Another leading figure on the right wing is Ryoichi Sasakawa, organizer of the World Anti-Communist League and President of the World Union of Karate-do Organizations, who enjoys the lucrative monopoly on speedboat race gambling. These men and their successors are the confidants and financial backers of Prime Ministers, though their names rarely grace a newspaper. Ministers are guests at their sons' weddings and no social embarrassment is caused.

Yet the Liberal-Democrats should not be judged entirely unprogressive. Their record on economic growth, employment and technology show the good results of well-conceived intervention in the interests of change – whereas on many matters their socialist and Communist opponents have lamely backed the *status quo*. The Japan Socialist Party, for example, purchased a plot of land at Narita to try to thwart the construction of the new conservationist-embattled Tokyo airport there. Even on welfare policy, where the left-wing might be expected to have an advantage, Liberal-Democratic governments used to spend heavily to further party electoral strategy – and were criticized from a quite different quarter, by the financial bureaucracy and business world, for overdoing it.

The Opposition parties will never unite. In the late 1970s there were Opposition policy groupings that cut across party lines, like the

Society to Consider a New Japan which proclaimed a 'civic socialism' based upon free democracy, decentralized power and a regulated market – but rejecting Marx. The Communists and radical socialists would have no truck with this, but it looked as if the *Komeito* (Clean Government Party), the Democratic Socialist Party and the New Liberal Club might be forging a significant Opposition front. Then Nakasone deftly seduced the New Liberal Club (which mostly comprised former members of his own Liberal-Democratic Party faction well known to him) into a government coalition.

Recently, the left-wing has moderated its language. The Democratic Socialist Party, always the more moderate of the two socialist parties, has dropped the word 'socialism' from its programme altogether, and the Japan Communist Party (influenced by Euro-communism) speaks of workers' power instead of 'dictatorship of the proletariat'. Even so, Communists working in industry make no secret of their ambition to get on in their capitalist corporations, and in opinion polls they often put their own happiness before the success of their party.

The socialists and Communists are disadvantaged to some extent by being based on foreign models, but the *Komeito* is fully home-grown. When it began in 1964, it was hailed as filling a spiritual void in Japanese politics, not just because it is Buddhist, but because it alone courts those outside the mainstream in Japanese society. It attracts the small people who are not enveloped in giant corporations or trade unions – especially shopkeepers, the self-employed and women. Yet its leaders have been as arbitrary and undemocratic as those of other parties, and just as perfidious in seeking opportunist electoral pacts with them.

Ministers come and go, but the civil servants have permanent tenure, and the Japanese bureaucracy is able to exemplify some of the old Confucian ideals. Its prestige, ability and continuity in office, often enable it to thwart the schemes of politicians. A newspaper columnist recently claimed that: 'In no other advanced nation will you find the head of a government whose pledge is as worthless as that of a Japanese Prime Minister.' Foreign heads of government who have negotiated with Japan would fervently endorse the comment. In western constitutional theory, it is the Prime Minister who rules Japan, and yet that ruler can on occasion appear paradoxically powerless – and it is the civil servants whom he usually blames. The best wisdom about the locus of power is that it lies in a loose tripartite consensus between the Liberal-Democratic Party, bureaucrats and business leaders: each group can veto what the others propose, so that only schemes broadly acceptable to all three are implemented.

(In pre-war days one would have added the military leaders, but not now.)

The civil service used to attract the best-qualified job-seekers. Yukio Mishima spent the best part of a year in the Ministry of Finance before settling for a more bohemian life as an *avant-garde* writer, and three-quarters of today's top bureaucrats are products of Tokyo University. In the earlier post-war years many of the abler civil servants went into politics, some to become Prime Ministers. Almost one Liberal-Democrat Dietman in three is a former civil servant, typically from the Finance Ministry. Bureau Directors and Directors-General in the various Ministries openly boast about manipulating their political Ministers. 'The Minister of Finance', one of them told a foreigner, 'is our puppet. He can only operate with the opinions that we supply him.' The permanent Vice-Ministers who head their departments of government form a 'little Cabinet', which meets weekly to resolve inter-departmental friction and prepare the ground for an eventual Cabinet decision. It is extremely powerful.

Yet the Japanese bureaucracy is small, only half the size of Britain's (proportionate to the population) and with only two-thirds of the British budget to spend (again proportionately) – mainly because of the small scale of state welfare. It faces further slimming in the years ahead, as successive Cabinets try to implement past promises to trim spending and taxes and bring about smaller government.

While the politicians lost their *samurai* image in the war, the bureaucrats held onto theirs longer. Their dedication to work is legendary. One Ministry of International Trade and Industry (MITI) man, who was involved in the annual budget hassle with the Finance Ministry, when senior officials have to work so late on figures that they sleep and eat in the office for several nights in a row, refused to go home even though his wife was dying of pneumonia. But the other side of the coin is a fixation about rank which damages Civil Service efficiency. Appointments and promotions are made almost exclusively on the basis of seniority, so that weak officials will be given key jobs even if there are better candidates available.

The crowning achievement for any bureaucrat is to be made Vice-Minister and head the permanent officials in his Department. When that happens, all of his classmates sharing his seniority would normally resign in order to spare themselves and him the embarrassment of serving under him. Usually these wasted talents are fielded by private corporations who know how to use the connections and experience of such men. The loser is the state, which forfeits their services just when they attain their highest value. One Minister of Finance, a mere politician, tried to keep out the civil servant who was next in line to be his Vice-Minister, but the whole of his Department came together to frustrate him.

These days you see long faces behind the Ministry desks. Civil servants are disillusioned. 'We are mere office clerks,' one complains, 'it is annoying that we should be called upon to be far-sighted.' Politicians now draw up their own parliamentary bills, and the trend towards economic liberalization, spearheaded by the Liberal-Democratic Party and big business, means that there are fewer of those bureaucratic controls which used to be the civil servants' bread-and-butter. What they share with the politicians is a fuming anger against the system of Diet interpellation, which means that a Minister and a score of Department advisers may have to sit in the Chamber for hours, even late into the night, waiting to answer members' questions.

This is a matter on which criticism of the western-style parliamentary system is unanimous. 'The present Constitution,' a former Minister of Justice once told his constituents, 'requires that a budget should be sent to Parliament for formality's sake . . . Our Liberal-Democrats have no questions, no faults to find – because they have produced the budget themselves. They feel bored, they doze . . . We attend Parliament because it cannot debate without a quorum. Cabinet Ministers must attend a meeting of the budget committee every day whether or not there is business. It is the height of boredom. We only wait for time to pass, like a patient with measles.' He lost his Cabinet seat for his indiscretion, but there is general sympathy for such complaints.

In a western society a vital watchdog role over such things would be played by the press. In Japan the function of the media is fatally impaired by the customs and taboos which surround the journalistic profession. To criticize in public does not come easily; reviewers proverbially pull their punches so as not to 'discourage' readers or theatre goers. The leading newspapers do take most of their reporting very seriously. The *Yomiuri Shimbun*, Japan's largest-selling newspaper, has no fewer than thirty-six full-time foreign correspondents stationed around the world, and domestic events are followed with equal thoroughness. But the results are muted by the group spirit which informs the media.

Each paper allocates a specialist correspondent to cover each Ministry, and these correspondents band together to form what are called *kisha* clubs. Here they are led into an intimacy, not only with each other, but with their subject, which makes for collusion and news management. Foreign correspondents complain about this 'impenetrable guild system', and recently some openings have been made for them to join. But the fact remains that the media tend to work together, even on occasion producing a joint editorial on some important development, and investigative journalists work in packs rather than singly – so that the exposé must wait for a consensus to emerge in that particular *kisha* club, where one or two doubters can veto or delay the project.

A damning insight into how this can work was offered a few years ago when the Education Ministry gave its *kisha* club advance copies of revised school textbooks on modern history. To meet their deadline, the correspondents divided the books up, each taking responsibility for reporting on a particular one. The journalist who was given the book about the war with China beginning in 1937 reported, quite wrongly and irresponsibly, that the original text had been watered down. Words like 'invade', he claimed, had been replaced by such euphemisms as 'advance'. His colleagues took him at his word without independently verifying, and so the unanimous story went out. Japanese liberals were shocked, China lodged an official protest, the government promised to amend the book – and only a month later did the truth come out. The Ministry itself had been too busy and confused to correct the reports at the time!

There are many inhibitions which make the work of a journalist difficult. Nothing bad about the Emperor is normally published, no news about the *burakumin* (outcasts) or *yakuza* (gangsters), no reports 'below the navel' on the sex life of politicians. When Prime Minister Tanaka was comprehensively exposed in the monthly magazine *Bungei Shunju* as a dishonest wheeler-dealer mixing business and extra-marital sex with high political office, no newspaper touched the story for a fortnight. Foreign governments may benefit from this self-restraint: the Japanese newspaper-reader was never told of Chiang Kaishek's funeral, or Lin Biao's death, because editors believed that such items would offend Peking and spoil Japan's new friendship with the People's Republic of China. Distinguished exceptions apart, it is hard to treat the Japanese press seriously as a full part of the political process.

A more dramatic arena than politics for the clash between Japanese and western values is the law. The native tradition is for settling disputes on the basis of the personal relations involved, rather than on impersonal rules found in a book. A Japanese adjudicator tries to balance the considerations in the dispute before him, not for eternity in a fixed rubric, but just for that one case, creating a piecemeal justice which is warmly personal and neither distant nor detached. Instead of the western rule of law, a Japanese would invoke a 'rule of persons', preferring flexible face-to-face human judgement to written predictability. Instead of separation of powers, he would opt for a more traditional integration of authority under one reassuring Emperor.

Conciliation has thus become a formal part of the legal process, compulsory in family disputes, optional in others. Litigants are pressed heavily to settle out of court. 'In a quarrel,' the saying goes, 'both are to blame.' Justice is only one, and not always the highest goal, compared with the interest of the community and the avoidance of social friction.

An enlightening instance of this difference in approach came in 1982 after the European Economic Community took Japan to a tribunal of the General Agreement on Tariffs and Trade (GATT) for restricting European access to the Japanese market. Once this action had been put in train in Geneva, the EEC envoys in Tokyo boycotted a business discussion on the matter with Japanese economic officials which had been planned much earlier. The Japanese took that as a damaging lack of seriousness in resolving the dispute, whereas the Europeans felt that negotiating while the issue was *sub judice* would jeopardize their case. In the same way, an airline president in Japan will ceremonially apologize to the victims of an accident without worrying, as his European counterpart might, whether his gesture might be taken as a costly admission of legal liability for compensation.

'Disputes,' a Japanese publication explains, 'are expected to be settled by compromise without the strain of identifying the one wronged and the wrongdoer.' Litigation is not lightly resorted to, because it means publicly exposing who is wrong, and doing so by criteria and means not under the control of the two parties. When a company is sued for negligence because of the use of toxic materials, as in the famous mercury poisoning cases, a typical comment would welcome the liability of a corporation to compensate as a business risk for injuries arising from such industrial operations, while regretting the necessity to burden it with publicly-adjudicated moral fault as well.

The interest in the person rather than the crime means that repentance can become an overriding factor in a lawsuit: it is better to treat the offender than remedy the offence. Law and order must sometimes give way. Nowadays, Japan is trying to tackle hi-jackers and terrorists with the same toughness as other governments, but when these problems first arose a few years ago, the Japanese instinct was to concede to outrageous demands instead of risking innocent lives. 'Thinking of the lives of the 142 passengers and 14 crew, one cannot just speak of law and order,' said the Chief

Cabinet Secretary during a hi-jacking drama by Japanese Red Army terrorists.

Human beings, not principles, come first. Emotions were aroused recently when a couple left their small son of three in the care of a neighbour while they went shopping, only to find on returning that he had been allowed to drown in a nearby pond. The distraught parents sued the careless neighbour and the court awarded them $25,000 damages. But the two plaintiffs were then showered with angry letters and abusive telephone calls, and the father, an electrician, was dismissed by his company because of the storm of protest. The local community felt that it was inhuman to take a tragic issue between neighbours for exhibition before people who had nothing to do with it, and to be decided by a judge who had no obligation to involve the parties in his decision or reconcile them to live again as neighbours after the accident. In the end, the parents withdrew from the suit and forfeited the damages.

Personal self-respect prevails over generalized justice. The Minister for Justice publicly expressed the hope that ex-Premier Tanaka and his fellow defendants would get off their Lockheed bribery charges 'because they are my close friends'. The inspectors in the food and drug licensing administration cannot always bring themselves to make stipulated tests where they might publicly expose a fellow-pharmacist with qualifications similar to their own – possibly an alumnus of the same college. Honour among professionals can assume larger proportions, as a more palpable goal, than the safety of the public. Even perjury is socially excusable where the reason for it is more important than academic truth. You can lie in the witness box and feel no pang of conscience, if it is for loyalty to a friend or obligation to your company.

The commonest collision between western and Japanese legal traditions is over the interpretation of contracts. In Europe a contract has become a sacrosanct mutual obligation which the state will enforce on behalf of a disappointed party. The Japanese, on the contrary, rank it as secondary to the underlying human relations which prompted it in the first place. Take a case which stirred Japanese opinion in the late 1970s.

The big baseball clubs had agreed that they would draw lots for the best new recruits coming out of school or university, in order to damp down the competition for them. If a player chose not to join the club that drew him, he would have to stay out of the league for the rest of the season. Suguru Egawa, a champion varsity pitcher, wanted to play for the Yomiuri Giants but was drawn by a different club, whose offer he refused. The Giants found a loophole in the rules, however, which allowed them to put Egawa on contract the day before the next year's draw. The baseball commissioner ruled that Egawa should still go through the formality of joining the club which had drawn him, although the two clubs would then be free to negotiate a transfer, so that the Giants and Egawa got their way in the end. The affair demonstrated how a Japanese will unblushingly interpret a contract in such a way as to allow himself the greatest latitude, even against the prevailing general mood. A contract is not seriously thought of as a restriction on one's choice of action.

At about the same time as the Egawa case, Japanese sugar importers, having earlier signed long-term contracts with Australian growers, found that the world market price was falling a long way below the figure originally agreed with them. So they refused to pay the contract price and, in the end, the Foreign Minister was drawn into the quarrel. 'Japan would like to live up to its contracts,' he explained apologetically. 'We are that kind of people. But this involves the question of – if the contract is honoured, the companies will go out of business.' The gut instinct in Japan is to share that kind of risk by continual informal variation of the agreement, instead of sticking inflexibly to something which was not actually intended at the time by the two parties to apply to new circumstances they could not envisage.

So Japanese do not instinctively reach for the protection of a contract, in the way that Europeans would. Sony sent 100,000 radios to its first agent in Canada on nothing firmer than a handshake, and older workers in Japan find it hard to live with the cold, impersonal, contractual relation which they have with a modern corporation: they are used to man-to-man treatment of such matters, and the standardization of the contract makes them feel at arm's length and unappreciated.

A modern Japanese can choose between two ways of making a joint endeavour with another person. If the two agree to rely on the traditional relationship of trust, then mutual consideration and mutual benefit will be required. There will be a fierce give-and-take at every unexpected turn, and the two will treat each other as of equal validity and worth, not hiding behind the technicality, for example, that certain things were not originally specified and therefore remain outside the context of the agreement. If, on the other hand, the same two people make a contract, they both know that they are free to pursue their self-interest unrelentingly to the point where the precise letter of the contract stops them. In the West, we pride ourselves on the high status of contract, but in Japan the contractual obligation is lighter than the old-fashioned informal agreement and is sometimes treated almost as a game, a contest of wits. A western contract is fixed, safe from alteration by untrusting parties: a Japanese agreement is organic, responsive to the changing needs of mutually familiar men to whom litigation is a last resort.

Any Westerner entering a contract with a Japanese should know that, whatever the small print may say, the Japanese in his heart is committing himself to performing in the circumstances prevailing, and not if there is a drastic change of the kind that would give one side or the other a windfall advantage, like a lottery.

Fewer contracts, less litigation, fewer lawyers (hardly a tenth of America's) and more obedience to officials. This is the Japanese pattern, although the obedience springs more from prudence than from morality. Understating income for tax purposes is rampant, for example: one of many peccadilloes which become crimes only if you are caught.

Yet the judiciary has a fine record. No judge has been bribed for a hundred years – though Kakuei Tanaka thoughtfully sent copies of articles criticizing his conviction for bribery to several judges, with a note saying: 'We took the liberty of sending these publications to you. Please have a look at them.' Civil liberties are considered to be better protected than in France, Germany or Italy, and the American monitoring organization, Freedom At Issue, places Japan in the first rank of 'free' states, along with the Anglo-Saxons, Scandinavians and Swiss. It is true that, when the police carry out residents' surveys or organize neighbourhood crime prevention associations, they may act in a way which Anglo-Saxons might see as an invasion of privacy (not a well-developed concept in the group society of Japan). The police also use physical coercion to obtain confessions, though the recent exposure of abuses has lessened this practice.

But the equality of treatment and the good intentions disarm most critics. Paul McCartney, held for nine days for importing marijuana to Tokyo, was roped, handcuffed and led about 'like a dog', but had no complaint to make at the end. The popular image of the bobby on the beat is a good one. When Kakuei Tanaka returned to his home village for the first time after becoming Prime Minister, his mother made him give up the seat of honour at the table for its usual occupant, the local copper.

Nakasone is right to call the democracy practised in Japan an 'artificial flower'. It has not led large numbers of Japanese to feel individually involved in political decision-making. People vote from duty, as spectators, forming an inarticulate majority which waits to acknowledge in silence (and after the event) what the professional politicians decide or do in their name. This is a society where independent thinking and action are not the norm, and are not even admired, a society where people are not expected to air their differences of opinion in public – and may be ostracized if they try. If electors do feel any sense of participation, it is in a vast and complex exchange of material favours between pressure groups. They cynically send their candidate to bag the most spoils from the 'budget wars' of the bureaucrats, to win more infrastructure, projects and funds than the next community.

Democracy has won its place in Japan as a technical means of conducting state affairs by public decision, but the attitudes which people bring to the practising of democracy remain inappropriate and socially unconstructive. 'We don't go through the process of balancing pros and cons before making a decision,' a writer complains: 'We are emotional.' Decisions are made by mood, where consistency suffers and demagogues flourish. Yet a balance-sheet of the electorate's voting record since the war discloses a remarkable amount of collective wisdom. When the Liberal-Democrats were in firm control, the public gradually swelled the vote of the left-wing Opposition, preventing the Liberal-Democrats from swinging to the extreme right. In the last decade, by contrast, when the Communists and Socialists were growing over-confident and the Liberal-Democrats faced loss of office, people switched to vote Liberal-Democrat again.

It is the height of sophistication for an electorate to see to it that the parliament is not dominated by any one party. And whatever else one may say about the Japanese political system, almost all commentators agree that, after forty years, Japan will not go back to earlier forms of more restricted democracy or to autocratic government, however slowly democratic attitudes form.

Democracy is a front door into politics, which a Japanese may choose to use, but there are also back doors which accord more comfortably with social tradition. It is like the western suit which the older Japanese typically wears to work during the day, to discard for a *kimono* as soon as he is home again in the evening. Japan has accepted the basic idea of parliamentary representative government and the rule of law. But to understand how these borrowed institutions are being employed, what conventions have been hung upon them, and what motivations drive the people who use them, a western observer needs to investigate the Japanese past.

Pitched battles between students and police in full riot gear do not mean anarchy; a legislation denuded of its Opposition members does not signify abandonment of the parliamentary system, nor does regular Party collusion in the Chamber mean the abandonment of ideology; power-broking behind the scenes is not necessarily a bid for autocracy; reluctance to debate issues openly does not mean apathy about them; and the acceptance of 'money politics' does not indicate outright disillusion with the system. The worst misunderstanding would be to take the cut flower for a plant growing spontaneously even from that rich volcanic soil.

10

Naked Under Article Nine
Japan's Defences

JAPAN IS the only important country in the world that cannot try to defend itself. Its intellectuals despise their democracy as designed to survive only as long as another nation does the protecting. No other state finds itself so disadvantaged in world affairs.

Article 9 of the US-drafted Constitution renounces the right of war and the use of armed force in international disputes. But what began as an American desire to suppress Japanese militarism once and for all was soon modified, when the Korean War of 1950 created a new American need for Japanese military support against Communist aggression. A modest growth of what began as police reserves, but were later called Self-Defence Forces, was then permitted for Japan. When the American Occupation ended in 1952, it might theoretically have been possible to amend the Constitution and transform the Self-Defence Forces into an open, regular and conventional army, navy and airforce. But the earlier bargain was honoured, and American responsibility for the defence of Japan was enshrined in a Security Treaty which remains in force indefinitely.

During all the subsequent thirty years of independence, ambiguity has surrounded the purpose of Article 9. Was it meant primarily to acknowledge the nation's defeated status at the end of the war? If so, then amendment in a democratic spirit would surely be honourable so many years later. If, on the other hand, it was intended to pledge a positive Japanese desire for world peace, what *The Times* calls Japan's redemptive role of forestalling by example nuclear war between the two superpowers, then it should remain in force as a constant stimulus to others.

In that sense most Japanese today see Article 9 as long on idealism but short on practicality in a world where other nations retain – even augment – their armament. Yet over the years it has acquired a political value in thwarting the ambitions of those who would like to revive the political power of the military to its pre-war heights. It sustains civilian authority in Japan, and therefore stabilizes the complex geo-politics of East Asia, since neighbouring countries can for the time being relax their guard against the threat of resumed

Japanese expansionism. In these circumstances a change would be irresponsible.

So the Self-Defence Forces survive, boasting almost a quarter of a million volunteers – but highly restricted in movement, low in morale as well as in profile, embodying Japan's uncomfortable compromise in defence preparedness between total nudity and the conventional clothing which a comparable capitalist nation in the West wears. They are an undervest army in a world of overdressed powers. The real defenders of Japan are the 45,000 US forces stationed under the bilateral Security Treaty in Okinawa and other bases in Japan, with their offshore naval and air backup. Many Americans, including former President Nixon, now regret their imposition of Article 9. The Japanese are pragmatic: no one would dream of introducing such a self-restriction today, but, since it has been inherited from the American Occupation, it is best to keep it as long as possible in order to delay the revival of Japanese militarism and the possible entanglements abroad which that would bring. Besides, it secures Japan's place within the post-war western system, with the Americans paying most of the bill.

'True independence is impossible,' Premier Nakasone used to argue, 'as long as a nation chooses to depend in large measure on the military power of another country for its own territorial security. I have long contended that a Constitution that leaves room for doubt of one's own self-defence capability must be revised.' Liberal-Democrat hawks insist that constitutional revision is needed in order to legitimize the Self-Defence Forces, but most Japanese would rather co-exist with ambiguity than risk a sudden glorification of the military whose leaders had plunged them into the horrifying defeat of 1945.

On the opposite side of the spectrum from Nakasone, there used to be an idealistic dream that Article 9 had transformed Japan into a higher species of nation, a country without power, a literal practitioner of the goal of universal disarmament in the new era of the United Nations. General MacArthur himself talked of Japan's becoming the 'Switzerland of the Far East', and Robert Guillain was ready to admire, on behalf of European intellectuals, *'la grandeur sans la bombe'*. But one hears little of those hopes nowadays. Our planet has become a proliferating system of armed states, and Japan's unorthodoxy is seen for what it is, a particular case stemming from unique circumstances which others do not have to follow.

The latest opinion polls reveal that two out of every three college students would like to phase out or weaken the Security Treaty with the US. Older citizens are much more tolerant of it in the light of recent Russian provocation, and the trend in the nation as a whole favours the Treaty. The Soviet Union, by militarizing the northern islands which it illegally occupies off Hokkaido, by intruding MiG fighters and warships into Japanese airspace and coastal waters, and by building up aggressive power in Vietnam and the western Pacific, has alarmed Japanese neutrals and crystallized their feeling of gratitude for the US defence umbrella.

In 1978, after the Russian invasion of Afghanistan, the Japanese government felt emboldened to refer bluntly to the 'Soviet threat' in its annual *Defence White Paper*. Not long afterwards, the newspapers began to speculate, in that melancholic vein so dear to the Japanese imagination, what might happen if the Russians were to occupy Japan (a not entirely hysterical proposition, given the possibility that in a crisis the American fleet might sail off to protect western Europe or the Middle East, leaving Japan helplessly exposed). How to deal with that Soviet threat is something which is now debated. Some experts feel that, since Japan has no effective defence against a Soviet missile attack, pacifism is still justified. Others argue that, since the USSR has the capability, even if it lacks a present intention, to attack Japan, it might be tempted to use that power if Japan were to dismantle its defence apparatus altogether.

Most Japanese defence experts agree that a Russian missile attack is extremely unlikely. It would bring no benefit to the Soviet Union except in the context of World War Three, which would flatten Japan in any case. The more likely temptation for the Russians in any future crisis would be to harass Japan indirectly by interfering with shipping on the sealanes which bring vital foodstuffs, industrial supplies and oil to the Japanese market. The defence of the sealanes has therefore become a fashionable slogan in Tokyo. The 'new' military leadership that is emerging in Japan argues that the best national option is to concentrate on excluding Soviet submarines from the three strategic straits – Soya, Tsugaru and Tsushima – which lead out of the Sea of Japan into the Pacific Ocean, while deploying anti-submarine recon-naissance aircraft to patrol one thousand miles of the sealanes leading southwards towards Taiwan, Southeast Asia and Middle East oil. But even that is too radical a departure from post-war pacifism to be politically acceptable.

The awkward reliance on the US Treaty leads to many distortions. Japanese defence debates focus on whether or not to do what the Americans are asking, rather than trying to identify Japan's real interests. And, increasingly, there are questions about whether the power holding the defence umbrella over Japan understands the nation it is protecting, and is truly reliable. In some opinion polls, almost 60% of Japanese say they do not believe that the Americans would seriously protect Japan against an attack. Why should they shed blood for an ally which lacks the will to defend itself? Yet the cruel logic of the Cold War dictates that, if there are no American forces in Japan, there is little to deter a Russian attack: what holds the Soviets back from striking against Japanese targets is the certainty of American retaliation for the loss of US servicemen.

Even if the Americans pulled their troops out of neighbouring South Korea alone, as President Jimmy Carter once proposed, this would dangerously destabilize Japan. Japanese doubts about the strength of the American commitment would be reinforced, and Japan would become humiliatingly indebted to her former colonial protégé, Korea, for continuing defence support of the kind now provided by the US. The Koreans lose no opportunity to remind everybody that, in contrast with Japan's 'free ride' on defence, they allot some 6% of their GNP to military spending. Korea would enjoy trading further on Japanese guilt, and there would be nothing more calculated to spur the Japanese into a competitive military spending of their own.

But Japanese pacifism should not be entirely written off as a temporary post-war over-reaction. It has roots in history. Japan has never been invaded as European countries were. The Manchurians tried in the eleventh century AD, and the Mongolians made two bids at the end of the thirteenth century, but none was successful. Save for a few insignificant nineteenth-century incidents, no foreign armed soldier ever trod on Japanese soil until the Americans in 1945. The Japanese do not have the habit of thinking in terms of maintaining an army to defend their homeland. Few Japanese can take the idea of a foreign invasion seriously, and this is part of the reason why so many intellectuals accept the pacifist argument that Japan is strictly indefensible: her enormous population and industries, concentrated on a narrow strip of coastal land, could be 'taken out' by just a few modern bombs in minutes.

Contrary to the western stereotype, the Japanese are not a martial race at all. There are no walled cities, as there are in Europe, and when Commodore Perry arrived offshore in 1853, they meekly gave in to his demands on behalf of the American government to open up their country, even though he had only 600 men. Their famous victories over China in 1895 and Russian in 1905 were as much the result of luck and the weakness of the other side as of Japanese prowess.

All these earlier sources of pacifist feeling were shatteringly re-inforced by the Pacific War – that is to say, Japan's China War, which opened with the Marco Polo Bridge incident in 1937, merging into what Prime Minister Nakasone calls the 'Greater East Asia War', and assimilating with the Second World War after Japan's 1941 attack on Pearl Harbor. That continuous eight-year experience has killed Japan's appetite for warfare. Many Japanese are still bitter against their militarist leaders' adventurism. 'What was it,' said a former President of Tokyo University, 'if not a sin and an outrage, a crime against their fellows and against humanity?'

Former Prime Minister Kakuei Tanaka has a very common-sense view which is widely shared. There were good reasons, he says, to justify Japan's steps to protect her interests in East Asia in the 1920s and early 1930s when the Anglo-Saxon powers were blatantly discriminating against Japan on matters of trade and immigration. But, after the Marco Polo Bridge incident, Japan went 'too far' and it became 'aggression'. The Japanese had to live with the fact that three million of their young men died for no good reason.

Premier Nakasone stands for a different idea about the war. Japan's soldiers sincerely wanted Asia to become independent of Euro-American domination. Their idealism might have been frustrated, but perhaps history would eventually find merit in the war. (As one professor has recently put it, 'It was necessary to wage war to preserve our identity'.) The racial character of the war memory is articulated by Nakasone's having contested one election on the platform of representing the generation to have 'fought the white man'. He did serve briefly in the Japanese Navy, had a brother killed in action – and has been consistently returned to the Diet since. Japanese conservatives also ask why, if Japan were guilty of invading China, the same criteria should not objectively apply to the saga of western expansionism, from Columbus to Clive, and Raffles to Rhodes. Why should Japan be picked out?

Most Japanese soldiers were ignorant of the geo-political significance of their wartime sacrifice, though the surrender by Hirohito still hurts their pride. Westerners look back to VJ Day with little emotion, perhaps a subdued feeling of pride and gratitude. But for Japanese the same anniversary brings a twinge of terror at the memory of the A-bombs and, for the older generation, a sometimes passionate regret for the sudden loss on that day of all the excitement of taking on the Anglo-Saxons who had humbled Japan in her struggle for parity. Such nationalist emotions were fanned by the charade of the War Crimes Tribunal, hastily rigged up in post-war Tokyo, to try Japan's militarist leaders in a manner which convinced only some of the victors and none of the vanquished. Many of the 'criminals' were subsequently honoured by the Japanese government, and a taboo-breaking film, called *The Japanese Emperor*, recently showed the wartime Prime Minister Tojo exonerating the Emperor from guilt.

The famous soldiers who held out in the Philippines and small Pacific islands for years after the surrender, returning to an astonished homeland in the 1970s, were briefly saluted. But the glamour quickly wore off. One of them, Lieutenant Hiroo Onoda, was so disappointed at his reception that he emigrated to Brazil (he comes back now and again to teach youngsters self-reliance).

The defeat of 1945 strikes contradictory chords. For intellectuals dismayed by the militarists' conduct of power, it was liberating. But for those who had tried to make the best of the official decisions during the war, seeing themselves as honest implementers of valid goals, the defeat was humiliating. Both reactions reinforce post-war pacifism. The former group would like to see that the wartime experience is never repeated, while the latter wish to turn the page firmly because the memory of misdirected loyalty is too painful.

The cinema and TV screens, novels and comic strips are full of war themes, but they mostly indulge a harmless nostalgia without political significance. Those who suffered in the war and then had to swallow its moral questionability remain silent, nursing their wounds. This applies not only to those over fifty who actually experienced surrender, but also to their children, who came to sense through those parents the same deep, largely unspoken feelings of guilt and despair. Herman Kahn, the late American futurologist, used to predict that this emotional luggage would be jettisoned by 1980. He was premature: it is still on board for most of the older half of the Japanese population.

So when the socialist leader, Masashi Ishibashi, wrote a book called *On Unarmed Neutrality*, it went into the list of best-sellers. His right-wing critic, Shintaro Ishihara, compared him mockingly with a bejewelled woman going naked into the street. Yet a recent poll of students' opinion showed more than half opting either to 'run away' in the event of a foreign attack, or else to conduct non-violent resistance: only 29% voted for active resistance through the use of the Self-Defence Forces. These students largely reflect mainstream left-wing opinion, which has always been either pro-Soviet or pro-Chinese. When a victim of the Hiroshima bomb, speaking at a peace rally, even-handedly called for the abolition of Soviet as well as American nuclear weapons, she was dragged bodily from the platform by indignant Communist organizers. Yet when Mao Zedong in the 1970s counselled a degree of limited rearmament for Japan, calling its constitutional pacifism a kind of 'mental derangement', Japanese leftists feigned deafness.

The strong emotional streak of pacifism often makes defence debates unreal. It was only in 1978 that public discussion rose to a serious level, with the famous 'Red or Dead' exchange between Professor Yoshihiko Seki, who proposed that Japan should try to hold any conventional attack at bay for at least a fortnight, and Professor Michio Morishima of the London School of Economics, who claimed that the Americans would not fight for Japan, so Japan should surrender to Russia in the event of an attack – if only to keep militarists from assuming national leadership. Morishima argued rather persuasively that the integrity of Japanese culture would not be jeopardized because Russia would not, after all, be able to transform Japanese society. This head-on clash between two respected scholars brought many hitherto hidden opinions out into the open. Was it really militarism, one journalist asked, to want to defend oneself?

A measure of the change is the growing acceptance by Opposition parties of the Self-Defence Forces whose creation in 1950 they had so bitterly denounced. These days, opinion polls usually show more than three-quarters of the general public as accepting the Self-Defence Forces, with a small number even wanting to strengthen them. The *Komeito* acknowledged the Self-Defence Forces in 1978, and the right-wing faction of the Japan Socialist Party began to move in that direction soon afterwards: Ishibashi himself began to make the fine distinction that the Self-Defence Forces were at least legal, if not constitutional.

So the tiny band of Self-Defence Force volunteers still waits for recognition, hoping for the aura of illegitimacy to be torn away, for a sensible and coherent defence role to be decided, with the requisite equipment put in their hands to carry it out. It was recently calculated that the average soldier has only sixteen bullets, and the weakness of the organization may be guessed from the fact that the Cabinet post of Director-General of the Self-Defence Agency – equivalent to Defence Minister – changes hands roughly every eight or nine months. Whenever one of the Commanders complains in public about these matters, he is reprimanded and thereby silenced. These men are not like their wartime predecessors. They are apolitical, and well aware of public apprehension. Every now and again, however, some officers inflame these suspicions by short-sighted plots, and their reputation was not helped by military acquiescence in Yukio Mishima's eccentric, if harmless, band of *Tatenokai* (right-wing volunteers doing part-time training with the Self-Defence Forces).

For all these reasons many patriotic Japanese urge their western friends not to press Japan to increase its armaments, as many unthinking Americans do. 'We might go at it just as obsessively as we used to strive for economic excellence,' a senior bureaucrat puts it, 'and then the military could reassert its domination of Japanese politics.' As the defence industries, so far denied profitable outlets, grow in the future, the development of a belated military-industrial complex seems inevitable. It is interesting that General Tojo's son has become a leading figure in the Mitsubishi business empire.

One watershed will be the deployment of Self-Defence Forces personnel abroad. This is not specifically prohibited by the Constitution, but is denied under the law by which the Diet set them up in the first place. Voices have recently been raised to send contingents to serve in United Nations peace-keeping operations, for example in the Middle East, Africa and Latin America. What could be more respectable? But the nettle remains ungrasped. A few security experts have begun to work overseas, but as temporary secondees to the Foreign Ministry and not in uniform, so the question of principle remains to be challenged.

If all these hang-ups persist over conventional defence, one can well imagine the agonizing over nuclear weapons in the country where 'Little Boy' and 'Fat Man', the first atomic bombs to be dropped on human targets, were decanted. In theory the Japanese accept the atomic bombs as saviours, knowing that, without such a terrifying demonstration of destructive power, their militarist leaders would almost certainly have fought to the bitter end, subjecting the population out of sheer fanaticism and pride to mass starvation. Some have calculated that several million Japanese could have died in a last-ditch resistance with bows and spears. The atomic bombs on Hiroshima and Nagasaki in 1945 also allowed the Japanese right wing at home to see themselves as innocent victims of war, and to gloss over the atrocities for which their men at the front had been responsible.

Yet former Prime Minister Shigeru Yoshida recommended as long ago as 1962 that Japan be ready to take up nuclear weapons when the need arose, and since the 1970s there have been elected politicians like Shintaro Ishihara to advocate such rearming (for an unexpected reason, however, arguing that a few nuclear bombs would strengthen Japanese diplomacy in its economic disputes with the United States!). Professor Morishima also concedes the logic of nuclear armament, which another scholar, Professor Tetsuya Kataoka, describes as the 'logical capstone of autonomy and self-reliance'.

But all these various considerations of logic and national interest have failed to stir Japanese opinion. Japan simply does not live up to Herman Kahn's definition of a virile, healthy nation as one that must want to 'go nuclear'. More than 70% of Japanese oppose the idea, according to the opinion polls. The so-called 'nuclear allergy' endures through all the beguiling arguments. It is pointless, most intellectuals insist, to prepare for nuclear suicide. That kind of thing should be 'left to the superpowers'. If Soviet nuclear warheads are a threat, then better organize a non-nuclear zone in Asia.

Only in 1980 did a full-scale debate on nuclearization take place. The hero of the pacifist movements of the early 1960s, Ikutaro Shimizu, recanted his 'wishful thinking' of that time and amazed his compatriots by launching a realistic discussion of Japan's security options (a fellow demonstrator of those days has also turned full circle to become the Defence Minister – Koichi Kato). By then, successive governments had developed a national policy of Three Non-Nuclear Principles, renouncing the manufacture or possession of nuclear weapons by Japan, as well as their introduction from abroad. When the Americans casually revealed that their nuclear ships had been taking nuclear weapons into Japanese ports as part of their normal armament, there was consternation. The Japanese government had turned a blind eye to this infraction of its own rule for many years.

The debate was nevertheless won by the anti-nuclearists. Masamichi Inoki, the country's leading strategist, said that for Japan to become nuclearized would be to step straight from utopian pacifism to utopian militarism. It would undermine the US Security Treaty. Professor Yatsuhiro Nakagawa agreed, recommending that it would be better to revise the Treaty in order to allow American nuclear weapons into, say, Hokkaido, or else to finance the provision of nuclear warheads to US Forces – while simultaneously building up Japan's own conventional guerrilla forces. Many others noted that a second strike capacity is impossible along Japan's narrow land strip, so that nuclearization would be of no deterrent effect whatever.

The question of how much more defence capability to have, and of what kind, comes down in the end to a question of money. The government already pays over US $1 billion a year towards the cost of American forces, and is under pressure to contribute more, indirectly, through financial aid to less rich countries which are also hosting American troops. On her own Self-Defence Forces Japan spends more than $13 billion, an allocation which has for the last decade been held to a level within 1% of the Gross National Product – though if the NATO definitions of defence spending were to be used, to include pensions, rents and similar indirect costs, then the Japanese proportion would be nearer to 1½%. Even so, it is much below the level in western countries.

In the mid-1980s, however, the ratio has inched up, defence being one of the few heads of spending given immunity from Prime Minister Nakasone's budget cuts. Japan stands about eighth among the world's defence spenders, and only twenty-fifth in defence spending per head of population, so there is no reason as yet to fear Japan's throwing her weight about in military terms.

Some US Congressmen, angry with Japan's 'free ride' on defence and her ballooning trade surplus, have called for Japan to pay a 'tax' of 2% of her GNP for American security, and Japanese leaders are busy preparing the ground for their public opinion to accept a larger outlay on defence. Inoki has proposed that the defence spending be doubled to 2% of GNP over the next ten years. Political leaders also talk nowadays about an enlarged concept of 'comprehensive security' in which economic and political aspects of defence (foreign aid, and stockpiles of food and energy) are brought in as domestically non-controversial supplements to the defence effort. Nakasone has suggested that this larger basket of activities, including defence narrowly defined, should take as much as 3% of GNP.

But that is for the future. In the meantime, Japan, with all the qualifications to be a superpower, hobbles about the world stage like a disabled person. That is how Ikutaro Shimizu, the turncoat pacifist, sees it. Japan's neighbours would not agree. Lee Kuan Yew of Singapore accepts that some degree of Japanese rearmament is inevitable: most other governments in East Asia would privately agree – and might actually welcome an alternative flexer of non-Communist muscle in a region where American force is reducing while Russian armament conspicuously increases. China certainly believes a measure of Japanese rearmament is to the good in a region otherwise vulnerable to Soviet might. But the Japanese know that millions of Asians have not forgotten what the Japanese Army did fifty years ago, and they will be cautious.

In the 1983 *Defence White Paper*, it was argued for the first time that Japan should contribute to 'Free World' security, with the defence of 1,000 miles of sealane as a first goal. Japan should make a bigger contribution to her own defence, freeing the Americans to do more vital work elsewhere in the world. The trouble is that even the Japanese see themselves as a potentially dangerous country, capable of irrational enthusiasms not always healthy for neighbours or allies. When Americans start pressurizing Japan to rearm, they are seeing the world in theoretical moral terms: Japan has such-and-such capability, and therefore ought to do so-and-so. But Japan has its weaknesses, and is better left to find its own way in defence.

After all the theories have been expounded, Japan's choice comes down to a starkly simple proposition: deter Soviet attack by hosting

American forces, but prepare within reason for any limited conventional engagement that may occur in or immediately around Japan. Only if the Americans were to leave Japan would an entirely new strategy become necessary, and that is precisely why the Americans should remain in Japan until the Soviet threat is finally extinguished. This is the cornerstone of Japan's defence policy for the foreseeable future, regardless of the humiliation of depending so publicly on the protection of another power.

The Company is Eternal
Japan's Economic Structure

JAPAN'S ECONOMIC miracle makes it hard to credit today how devastated the country was when the curtain fell on the Second World War. Dr Saburo Okita, Japan's leading economist, tells the story in his own career. He was one of a group of experts in the early post-war months who predicted that the Japanese people might have to revert to an 'Eskimo' way of life, with neither raw materials nor manufacturing industry. The Americans, asked how Japan might earn a living in the world, suggested the export of eggs. No one guessed then how Korean War procurement, the invention of the transistor radio and the latent social energies available for consumer manufacturing would transform Japan – so that Dr Okita went on to mastermind the government's seminal income-doubling plan in the early 1960s and now devotes himself to warning his fellow-countrymen not to become too rich, but rather to spend more of their wealth in the world.

Today, one-tenth of the world's Gross National Product is created in Japan, by only 3% of the world's population living on 0.3% of the world's land. Every Japanese person is roughly three times more productive than others in the world, each Japanese acre roughly thirty times more fruitful. This is a relatively recent phenomenon, and Japan still lags behind western countries in terms of accumulated wealth. Measured by the current flow of real income, however, the average Japanese is just better off than the average European and has climbed to about 80% of the American level.

Having high income but low wealth means inadequate sewerage, poor roads and spotty public amenities and welfare. Only half of Japanese houses have flush toilets, and only one in five are connected with the public drain – in most western countries it would be nearer 90% on both counts. Arriving home from a party in her Paris gown, Mrs Kato may have to step over the open running sewer of her house to reach her front door. Public welfare in the widest sense is only now beginning to compare with Europe or America.

Premier Kakuei Tanaka in the mid-1970s won votes with his novel blue-print for a high-welfare society in a beautiful environment throbbing with human warmth and happiness. But OPEC and the technocrats sabotaged him. While the Ministry of International Trade & Industry (MITI), along with most of the country's political leaders, is eager to stoke the fires of economic growth, even at the risk of a little overheating, the financial establishment is not. The powerful trio of the Ministry of Finance, Bank of Japan and the Keidanren, representing private business, is pretty conservative, wanting the budget to be balanced and economic growth to be steady. The post-miracle phase of building national infrastructure and social welfare therefore proceeds slowly.

Why was Japan so successful economically? Opinion in the West seizes on a handful of pat explanations, all faintly reprehensible – skilful government direction of business, cosily interlocking industrial ownership, paternalistic management practices and low wages. Yet none of these holds the key. True, the Japanese economy is not as free as the British or German, but it is not planned in the Soviet sense either. The best description of what the government does to businessmen is – guide. *The Economist* describes Japan as the most intelligently *dirigiste* system in the world, and several western economists feel that Japan has come nearer than other countries to the ideal balance between intervening or not intervening in the economy. That is not the product of ideology, however, but of good sense and custom.

Government officials are not experts in industry or commerce, and they freely admit that their plans usually turn out differently from what was intended. Appalling mistakes have been made, for example not at first allowing the upstart Sony corporation to spend precious dollars on the American transistor patent which was to prove its salvation, and not approving American investment in Japan for production of the first Integrated Circuits – decisions which seriously delayed the progress of Japan's electronics and computer industries.

The administrative guidance (*gyosei shido*), which the West believes to be one of the keys to the Japanese miracle, is not intrinsically different from what happens in France or Britain, even though they have no special term for it. It is a fact of life everywhere that, if a government controls the issue of licences, planning permission, development subsidies and export or import quotas, it finds itself in a position to require adherence to various official goals in return. Administrative guidance is something which all governments would like to practise, but only those governments with a battery of restrictive controls on industry are actually able to practise. Such opportunities were at their height in Japan in the 1960s, but are now diminishing with the liberalizing of the economy.

Guidance comes mainly from MITI. Where shipments to overseas markets are being 'voluntarily' restrained, MITI is responsible for allocating export quotas to Japanese manufacturers. That gives it exceptional power over those companies. But things can go wrong. When MITI told the car-makers that the unpopular export quotas for the US market would definitely not be renewed after 1984, one of the smaller companies invested billions of *yen* in a new factory to serve the American market when it re-opened. But MITI, having mis-judged the American mood, changed its mind at the last moment, and the company lost a packet.

Another failure of which MITI does not like to be reminded was the expensive but useless programme to build an electric car. Indeed, the cases where private manufacturers have made themselves inter-nationally competitive by their own efforts, as in steel, electronics, and cars, are more numerous than the cases where MITI has helped them succeed by 'tidying' them up into suitably sized groups, en-couraging new entrants or pressing the firms already in the field to merge. In the case of oil refining and distribution MITI's nurse-maiding in the 1960s proved disastrous, as evidenced by the weakness of Japan's petrochemicals today.

In one respect MITI's judgement has been universally admired and envied, and that is its instinct for protecting the industries of the future while helping sunset industries to leave the scene quietly and with dignity. Western governments usually do the opposite, caving in to pressure from workers to protect textiles and shipbuilding, in which Third World countries are already more competitive, while not doing enough to help the infant high-technology and information industries which are not large employers. MITI has funded five leading com-panies to collaborate in making Very Large Integrated Circuits (VLIC), while the textile firms and shipyards have been helped either to make orderly moves up-market, leaving the lower-cost end of the business to Third World manufacturers, or else to diversify into new fields.

The contrast with the West is not total: textile manufacturers can make a big noise in Japan as well as in Europe, and on occasion they have successfully twisted the arms of weak politicians to win a degree of import protection. Japan invokes the GATT Multi-Fibre Arrange-ment in order to restrict textile and clothing imports, though not on the same scale as the Americans or Europeans, and stiff quotas are fixed for Chinese and Korean silk products.

But the sparkle is beginning to vanish from the eyes of the MITI mandarins. To diffident manufacturers twenty or thirty years ago, MITI offered inspiration and optimism. Starting in the 1960s, how-

ever, its self-appointed mission to protect industry from the worst
blows of foreign competition began to be questioned by politicians
and businessmen alike. Industrial bosses increasingly prefer to pursue their own fortunes and take whatever risks attend. MITI, its
authority undermined, has drawn back to sulk. Companies can no
longer be counted on to obey its orders, not since the famous day
when the Sumitomo steel mills rejected MITI's administrative
guidance over production cuts.

The Fair Trade Commission, a legacy from the American Occupation, increasingly – and more loudly – exhorts MITI to leave
adjustments and cutback decisions for the market and the managers
to decide. Naohiro Amaya, the most brilliant of MITI's mandarins,
warns that Japanese industry cannot be allowed to run a happy-go-
lucky course, relying on invisible hands to solve its problems. But the
Ministers in charge of MITI, seasoned LDP politicians all, play a
different tune, promoting private industry to the lead part and
confessing that MITI now lacks the coercive power necessary to be a
great conductor of Japan's industrial orchestra.

What tilted the balance for the private sector against MITI was the
success of the business lobby in rolling back one of the most important
American Occupation reforms. MacArthur had systematically
broken up those giant pre-war business empires, the *zaibatsu*. But he
could not prevent the managers of the individual Mitsubishi or Mitsui
companies from informally collaborating in spite of their new-found
independence. By the 1960s the old empires were more or less
re-established, though on a much looser basis than pre-war, and a
huge chunk of Japan's industry became strong enough to do without
MITI's molly-coddling. They were not stopped by the American-
style anti-monopoly law, which the business lobby claimed did not fit
Japan's case: cartels should be permitted, it argued, unless they hurt
the general welfare. Competition is different, after all, in Japan,
where a loser cannot simply start again after forfeiting his self-
respect. The Japanese, it is explained, are not hard-boiled like the
Americans, not cold seekers after profit alone, but get satisfaction
also from earning prestige, serving public goals and retaining a
respectable market share.

Another unfair aspect of Japanese government policy, in western
eyes, is the neglect of social welfare at home, which allowed manufacturers to escape with a lower tax burden than their European or
American competitors. Only one-third of what a person or company
earns goes towards tax and social security, whereas the proportion
in Europe and America is nearer to half: the Japanese individual
keeps more of his own income to spend as he wishes, encouraging

industrial re-investment (via his High Street bank) as well as personal consumption.

But this is not deliberate. The family system provides a cushion for almost everybody in need, and so the Japanese do not need a state substitute. To introduce the kind of state welfare society found in Sweden, a typical magazine article runs, would 'lead to the people's losing their will to work, for not only will they have to bear the burden of excessive taxes, they will also start to take such wholesale welfare for granted. The young people brought up under these conditions will also lose their self-reliance and the will to work . . . bringing on a kind of psychological demoralization. For the Japanese, who always like to tell the state to do things for them, this danger is particularly strong.' So a 1950 proposal for a 'Beveridge'-style programme was shelved by the government, and the general opinion persisted that, to bring in national welfare provisions would not only impede the growth of individualism (by encouraging dependence), but would also lead, as the *Yomiuri Shimbun* once put it, to 'rampant idleness, drunkenness and sex crimes'.

In the 1970s, when the cohorts of the aged first began to mass, government welfare spending, mainly on pensions but also on medical care, rose much faster than tax revenues. Towns like Musashino offered to look after old people who would bequeath their property to the town after death – and one can imagine the feelings which that stirred up among children and grandchildren. Medical costs are probably going to quadruple by the end of the century. A controversial new law requiring patients to pay a larger proportion of their medical bills, 20% instead of only 10%, hardly solves the problem. Pension handouts will escalate relentlessly as the population gradually greys.

But the financial consideration is not the only one. Many Japanese concede that the quality of life in their country would make any other great economic power blush, and question why Japan's stock of social capital per head should remain at only a quarter of the German level. They are outnumbered, however, by those who see traditional family relations and loyalties, already under stress in the modern industrial age, as being vulnerable to a system of state welfare. Prime Minister Nakasone for one wants more welfare only if it will encourage what he calls the software of the home (nourishing emotional links and the sense of mutual obligation) rather than its hardware (the material structure and equipment of the building). The upshot is that the government will have to spend more money in future years on welfare, especially the care of the elderly, but it is doubtful that it will ever match European or western levels.

So the average Japanese pays fewer taxes, and his government spends less per head of population than western counterparts. Yet the budget deficit is bigger than in America or Europe, more than twice the British. Billions of *yen* go every year to subsidize rice farmers, to no discernible national economic advantage, and another huge amount goes to pay for the losses of the nationalized railway, Japan National Railways, which the government is making belated efforts to privatize. Medical care is the third major outlay in the budget. The government also has to service a big debt, representing some 40% of GNP.

Prime Minister Tanaka was an unashamed spender, in government as in personal life: he declared roundly that there was nothing wrong with owing money, and that a distribution of costs between generations was a very good thing. But when the unusually austere businessman Toshiwo Doko, appointed to head a public finance reform commission in 1981, reminded the public that every baby came into the world with a one-million-*yen* debt tag around its neck, people began to take notice. His monetarist message, to stop borrowing and cut spending, has not been fully implemented even by the political leader most sympathetic to it, Prime Minister Nakasone. But at least huge new increases in spending are being avoided.

Taxes can be low, and industry prosper, because the Japanese wage-earner is thrifty. He saves about a fifth of his income, which is more than three times what an American does, and puts it in the bank, which lends it out to industry until he actually needs to draw on it. The government is not, in sum, the key factor in Japan's economic success, if only because people work hard and save money of their own accord, driven by social compulsions far stronger than any conceivable political pressure. Government intervention has not always achieved the result hoped for, and the opportunities for it are narrowing. It is in the industrial corporation that the real reasons for Japan's success lie.

There are companies in the West which see themselves as temporary alliances of men and chequebooks for a particular purpose which could be short-lived. At the other extreme are Japanese companies like the one whose executive committed suicide after becoming implicated in the Lockheed scandal a few years ago. 'Our employment may last for only twenty or thirty years,' his farewell message ran, 'but the life of the company is eternal. I must be brave and act as a man to protect that eternal life.' You go into a traditional Japanese company as into a marriage, you live in it as in a family, and you all share the risks of adversity together. The Chairman of Sony, Akio Morita, defined his company as 'a fate-sharing body'. A good traditional employer reckoned not just to hire a man's labour in a petty commercial transaction, but to take responsibility for the man as a whole – *marugakae*, meaning to embrace and support him completely.

Businessmen in Japan regard a company not as a mere asset base, but as a team of human beings – and to sell or take over human beings is immoral. A contested bid for a company is thus almost unthinkable – the first significant case was over a precision machinery maker in 1985. So high are the human beings ranked that there was said to be a manager of the Sumitomo Bank who knew the names and personal details of all of the many thousand employees, staying up late at night to pore over the records and keep his knowledge up-to-date. To some extent the corporation in Japan plays an intermediate role between the family and the state, for which there is no equivalent in the individualistic West.

The apogee of this philosophy is the policy of the YKK zip-fastener company whose employees deposit a tenth of their wages in return for shares. They draw dividends, of course, but, more importantly, by contributing to the future development of the company, they ensure the success of their later life and future generations in what their president grandly calls a 'Cycle of Goodness'. Yet if you ask a Japanese what he thinks of capitalism, only one in six would enthuse, and half would fudge their answer. A Mitsubishi executive calls the Japanese system an economy of enterprise, but not of capitalism. It is certainly enterprising, but not fully private and only partly free.

Where the different goals can be separated, a Japanese executive would rate the corporation's social obligations higher than profits. A survey shows that only one businessman in four believes in profit as an absolute goal. The others would see the maximizing of profits as a pre-condition for pursuing other goals – keeping products in the market, meeting social requirements, safeguarding the welfare of workers and offering a fair return to shareholders. Even the stock market is so hedged with restrictions that it has been called an 'administered market', an example of 'managed capitalism'. (Prime Minister Nakasone's bold proposal to de-regulate Japan's financial markets and make Tokyo the unchallenged financial centre of the Pacific hemisphere by 1989 will take some doing.) Edwin Reischauer described the whole system as post-capitalist, and he may be right.

The Japanese corporations are in fact a marvellous blend of Japanese tradition and American reform. Amaya describes them as having 'inherited the physique of their western father and the mind of their Japanese mother'. From the Japanese side they took their built-in deference to authority, their discipline, their mutual support. MacArthur's reforms removed the heavy hand of the shareholder, minimizing the role of ownership and making it open for a corporation to see itself as a community of workers and managers. Many companies, especially the new post-war ones, transfer shares to their employees instead of putting them on the market for speculators to buy. Four in every five companies listed on the stock exchange have some kind of stock ownership plan for their workers.

The company is not considered to be private property, as in Europe. It is regarded much more as a group of people associating for a work purpose (like a European co-operative) than as an object of property. A 'united body of employees' is one business writer's definition. In crowded Japan, with an undeveloped sense of individualism, private property acquires a public character and becomes something to be used for the best interests of the community. The European concept of three separate kinds of actor – owners, managers and workers – linking themselves together by contract, with three separate pairs of hands on three different steering wheels, has no place in Japan. In his younger days the Liberal-Democrat leader, Kiichi Miyazawa, actually suggested that private ownership of land be abolished. That did not earn him a radical label, because it matches the inner sentiments of most Japanese.

It is this separation of ownership from management, intended by MacArthur to humble the *zaibatsu* barons, that enabled conscientious managers to take control of their enterprise, virtually ignoring the shareholders, and to take decisions on the basis of long-term strategy rather than quick dividends. This is the single most important factor in Japanese industry's post-war vitality. It follows that, when managers need finance, they borrow from the banks (primed by personal savings) rather than put new stock on the share market. Something like three-quarters of the financing of Japan's industries takes the form of bank loans, and that in turn gives the banks a very strong incentive to keep the companies in business and tide them over their crises.

Japanese managers also plough back a larger proportion of their profits into the enterprise than their western counterparts. Where a British company might pay about 70% of its profit out in wages, leaving 30% for re-investment, a Japanese company would more likely split the amount 50:50. The government's tax cut is rather small, about half of what it would be in the West. The dividend paid to that interested outsider, the shareholder, is also small, figuring as a capital cost comparable with the interest payments on a bank loan. Dividends over the last decade have averaged only 1½%, well under half the handouts in New York or Düsseldorf.

Shareholdings in Japan tend to be small and scattered: only one company in thirty has any individual shareholders holding more than 10% of the equity. Even the newer companies formed by pioneering individuals and their families do not act much differently: Matsushita and Honda each hold less than 5% of their company shares. So the typical annual report in Tokyo will talk about 'our company', rather than follow the American style of 'your company'. The boardroom role of accountants and financiers, whose thirst for rapid returns has de-humanized the management style of many a European company and led it to disaster, is reduced.

When Sony allowed a recent Annual General Meeting to last for a record thirteen hours, with managers trying to answer all the share-holders' questions, this was thought an astonishing departure. The AGM is usually a boring formality, to be got through in the quickest possible time. A system has grown up in all companies of hiring professional 'AGM-minders' in the form of the *sokaiya*, men who buy a share in order to qualify for the meeting and then attend it in order to help the management keep obstreperous or difficult shareholders in order. They will shout in unison for the 'next business' to be taken up, or even browbeat and scuffle with the 'rebels' challenging man-agement decisions. Recent legislation has made it more difficult for the *sokaiya*, but they have not given up. It all goes to show that the manager and worker, not the shareholder, is king.

Japanese companies perform the basic ritual of capitalism by competing with each other, but in their own distinctive style. The kind of competition which a Briton or American sees as necessary and legitimate for the economy does not commend itself in Japan. Amaya of MITI puts this well: 'The cold detached attitude that responsibility for oneself, survival of the fittest and elimination of the weak constitute the ultimate in rationalism, will not work in Japanese society.' Here people crave for emotional relationships of mutual dependence, and there is an age-old instinct to temper conflict by talking with the other party over a drink.

To compete openly against another person is an un-Japanese kind of behaviour, and when one of the first economics textbooks was being translated, there was no word for 'competition'. Yukichi Fukuzawa, who was doing the translation, invented *kyoso*, which literally means 'race-fight'. But a colleague thought it too aggressive, so Fukuzawa dropped the 'fight' part of his new word and left it merely as 'race'. Today, a century later, every Japanese knows what competition means, but it is a much circumscribed definition compared with the western.

When a company is successful it always seeks to control the damage which others can do to it, but not usually to destroy them. It will check a competitor but not push him out of business. It will feel inhibited from going all out in a fight with a rival, preferring to leave that rival with some self-respect. It was not the big boys in the car industry who innovated with the Wankel rotary engine or the stratified charge engine. That was left to Toyo Kogyo and Honda, then two small companies, for whom such innovations, had they been successful, would have brought them up into the first rank. If Nissan or Toyota had done it, they would have been seen as seeking morally excessive market dominance, and they would have lost prestige even if they had been commercially successful.

Another example can be taken from the Japanese newspaper world. Rival journals will collaborate, sometimes writing joint editorials or jointly boycotting some issue of the day, rather than hunt for the spectacular scoops which set Fleet Street a-buzz – yet they chase each other's circulation figures in all other ways. In any one industry, all companies can be said to share the goal of maintaining approximate parity among themselves. It is rare for them to feel impelled to try to improve their own relative position very substantially and very quickly.

Competition for supplies of materials on the market also works a little differently from Europe. The Japanese economy is a maze of inter-corporate deals, where private arrangement often replaces the market mechanism. The car-makers, for example, agree with the major steel manufacturers, acting through the *sogo shosha* (trading corporations), on how their annual steel requirement will be shared between the steelmakers, and the price to be paid for it. Competitors trying to get in on the act are fended off by lavish entertainment, by invoking the interlocking directorates of the companies involved, and by the fact that finance often comes from within the group or from a bank closely involved with it. 'Once the partners in a group are firmly tied together by such techniques,' an economist explains, 'not even other Japanese firms can gain entry . . . much less foreign firms.'

Manufacturers, in any case, like to deal reciprocally with each other. A steelmaker will sell its products to firms that can provide a supply of raw materials in return, meaning in this case one of the *sogo shosha*. Since that trading corporation will then depend for its sales of raw materials on its purchase and turnover of finished steel products, it is little wonder that cheaper steel from abroad, for example from South Korea, finds difficulty getting into the market. Most of the former *zaibatsu* groups have their own network of manufacturing and distribution companies, where the production work is shared out among many member firms, and the sales are kept inside the group network – although rival groups will collaborate abroad or on very big contracts. The name often given to this kind of group dealing is *keiretsu**, and it is a major obstacle to Japan's having an open market economy of the kind Westerners would prefer. The *keiretsu* system is a conservative force in the economy, protecting the interests of those who have already gained their position on the market, and denying it to others (often more efficient) who seek to replace them. It is an expensive luxury, but one which the Japanese insist on having.

The *zaibatsu* are not, however, the force that they used to be. Mitsubishi, it is said, was once a monarchy, but is now a republic, the 'United Companies of Mitsubishi'. The individual companies have more autonomy in practice than they used to, and the famous Friday meetings of senior Mitsubishi executives are merely for the exchange of views and information, having no controlling authority over member companies. Mitsubishi is only one of some ten major groups each embracing companies in manufacturing, banking, distribution and other services, but its turnover as a group has been estimated at half as big again as Exxon, the world's largest single corporation.

What gives the key managers in these companies their power is the extent to which member companies own each other through interlocking shares, often to the extent of a quarter of the total. The Fair Trade Commission denounces it all as a useless and dangerous concentration of power, by which companies are forced to deal within their group even when they could buy cheaper outside. But the business establishment vigorously defends the *zaibatsu* and points to the stability of prices (at a very high level!) which they bring about.

The Mitsubishis and Mitsuis of Japan are bureaucratic in nature, with great importance attached to the circulation of documents and the stamping of seals. They are slow to make decisions, reluctant to delegate. The paternalism which Westerners associate with Japan, and criticize so frequently, is to be found in the middle-sized and smaller enterprises.

A man positively enjoys having a close relationship with his supervisor rather than keeping him at arm's length, quite unlike his British brothers. He joins a company not just to work in it, but to live some of his non-working life within its frame as well. A traditional company will arrange marriages, housing, holidays and even funerals for its workers, in some cases buying plots in the cemetery so that their unity will not be disturbed even after death.

A sociologist likened a new employee to a daughter-in-law entering a household, and having to cut her links with former relatives and friends outside her husband's family in which she is now adopted. On

* Literally: interlocking shareholdings.

the shopfloor workers will use informal language between themselves, just as they would in a family, regardless of age differences.
The social pressures that build up can be measured by the fact that
some senior men ask for their names to be kept on the company roster
after their retirement, at least until their daughters have married, so
that they can use their affiliation to attract the best possible sons-in-
law.

All this is now beginning to change because the younger generation
is falling out of step. They consider it feudalistic for a supervisor to
interfere in a worker's personal life, in his use of leisure time, in his
marriage plans. Their life outside the factory or office is richer than
their fathers' was, and they will not surrender it so easily. The
situation in any given workplace today is a mixture between the old
tradition and this new rebellion against it.

Westerners who speak of the group spirit in Japanese industry as a
marvellously enviable affair, often overlook its human costs. There
are countless cases of chronic overwork leading to physical and
mental illness, particularly among managers or supervisors, and the
traditional psychology prevents such a man from asserting his 'rights'
by demanding decent working hours. 'Inhibited by his concept of the
company as a family,' a Japanese psychiatrist reports of a patient in
this position, 'he was unable to make forthright demands regarding
his rights and duties.' He treated the company as if it were a family,
but found the family atmosphere was only a superficial covering for
the cold-hearted rational corporate enterprise beneath. That is how
the giant enterprises seem to Japanese who remember the old
traditions.

It is not uncommon for people to surrender themselves Faust-like
to a company in their early years, giving up their personal life and
working late day after day, but then, perhaps after some disappoint-
ment in mid-career promotion, to become more sparing to the
company, building up a private life of their own outside. The stresses
and strains of playing a good father, a good son or daughter in a
paternalistic system are heavy.

Even the new enterprises formed since the war, adopting a more
western-style individualistic character in contrast with the old business establishment, cannot break away entirely from the group
concept. It is romantic to look back to when Akio Morita, now Sony's
Chairman, had to drive the truck carrying the first products to the
market, because he was the only one with a driving licence – or when
Konosuke Matsushita, founder of another famous electronics company, on his first trip to the United States, could not write his name in
Roman letters and had to get somebody else to sign the immigration

form for him (and when ushered into a hotel room, he was found next morning sleeping on top of the blankets instead of underneath them, never having met a western-style bed before). Such companies start out with a highly personal management, often full of fresh egalitarian ideas, but they also take full advantage of the group feelings which their recruits bring to the company.

Groupism, after all, does not necessarily mean something very bureaucratic and all-embracing. The Japanese prefer where possible to de-centralize activities like industry, farming out responsibility and targets to small teams, even to small firms undertaking sub-contracting. The President of Sanyo, the electronics firm, likes to think of his company not as a big business but as an assembly of small ones. Maekawa Manufacturing has pushed this to its limits, organizing its work programme among a hundred autonomous work groups, each of which can take quite different decisions about how to get the job done. Actually, the giant corporations are not as important in Japan as might appear from the media. Almost three workers in four are in companies with fewer than a hundred employees. There are only ten corporations employing more than 40,000, against a hundred in America and almost forty in Britain. Small is beautiful in Japan.

The underlying structure of business and industry is different in Japan from Europe or America, since it reaches back to another tradition and other social values. Both government and the corporation play a bigger role, being more paternalistic and supportive of the companies or workers under their charge. There is no question of industry or commerce swinging over to a Western model and thus becoming more easily intelligible to Westerners. The institutions are built on social values deeply rooted in Japanese psychology, and their evolution will necessarily match whatever slow fermentation goes on within that national psychology – not so much towards the West or away from the Japanese tradition as towards a richer interaction of both under the stimulus of the new material challenges of techno-economic advance and internationalization.

The reliance on group feeling and the family model can reduce efficiency at work as much as it improves motivation. Japan benefits less than the West from the fresh, if unsettling winds of competition. Where Japan does score over the West is in the way she operates her basic economic structure – in other words in the work ethic of her labour force and the skill of her managers.

12

Bottom-Up Workaholics
Japan's Management, Labour and Science

JAPANESE WORKERS traditionally approached their managers with the kind of deference owed to a father, head of household or elder brother, and the West therefore stereotypes them as malleable and subservient. This is not necessarily so, as anyone who has lived in a family should know, but the habit of outward deference at least survives.

Full employment ought to have made a big dent in this traditional attitude. The supply of young men and women from the farmhouses to city factory gates was about to dry up in the early 1970s. But then the oil crisis broke and industry went into recession, laying off workers instead of taking on new ones, and Japan's unemployment picture is now hardly better than that of western countries. The official figures are rather low, based on narrow definitions*, but the best estimate of the number of Japanese actually out of work is about four million. If one adds the under-employed (the 'seat-warmers' or 'window-gazers' who are kept on a company pay-roll just to sit idly in an office all day) the jobless rate could probably be put at 9%, comparable with most western countries – and it may well double over the next ten years, respected Japanese economists predict.

So Japan has never truly experienced full employment, one sign of that being the absence of foreign labour in her factories. Japanese workers have never been able to approach the labour market with the collective bargaining power enjoyed by their American and European comrades over the past thirty years.

But those who know Japanese life at first-hand find it comical that anyone should think the Japanese too hard-working. As James Kirkup, who taught English in several places in Japan, reports: 'In private and government offices, as in factories and other concerns, much time is spent in holding staff meetings, gossiping, playing *mah-jong* and drinking green tea and spending expense account

---

* Excluding, for example, those still waiting for their first job. In mid-1985, 1½ million jobless, or 2.6% of the labour force, were officially reported.

money (tax free) at . . . restaurants and bars.' One tradition in Japan sees the office as a glorified social centre, offering an escape route to a more exciting private life. Surveys show that most Japanese would ideally prefer to live in idleness, off interest or dividends, than work. What they enjoy about an industrial or commercial job is not so much the work as the companionship.

A Japanese writer accepts that 'Americans are superior in the degree to which they can concentrate their labour during a given period of time . . . The Japanese, in contrast, prefer a more leisurely manner of working, as if they were engaged in gardening.' That is an interesting metaphor, because a Japanese college once asked students to weed the campus during the summer vacation, and everyone was much taken by the fact that the German students in residence weeded a smaller area than the Japanese or anyone else: they were thought lazy. A week or two later, however, when it was seen that only their weeds had been uprooted and did not come back, their thoroughness was appreciated.

The 'silly illusion that Japan's prosperity will continue for ever', says Professor Tsuneo Iida, 'comes from the equally silly illusion that the Japanese people are diligent . . . by nature.' There *is* a cultural difference here between Japan and the West, but it is about the way of behaving to others at work, not about the actual effort the individual puts into work. 'The Japanese do not work harder than us,' a Briton observes, 'but they work together better than we do.' An American manager who employs Japanese workers in a subsidiary in Japan reports that they do not work particularly hard, although they are co-operative and flexible (i.e. they at least do not work *against* one another or the enterprise).

Actually, productivity throughout Japan – especially in agriculture and services – is lower than in America or Europe. Morita of Sony concedes that in the sectors where American productivity is weak, it is not inherent labour attitudes but poor management that is to blame: the American sense of duty, once harnessed, is stronger than Japan's. Japan has had to sacrifice and struggle for the productivity gains she has made in industry, and will have an uphill task to retain them in the future.

What group feeling and emotional motivation on the Japanese factory floor can produce is not just a good industrial atmosphere but more effective procedures. Take the question of flexibility and mobility of labour. As a late developer, Japan was able to avoid some of the dated ideas developed in Britain, such as craft apprenticeship, which compartmentalizes skills – and job specification, which unnecessarily complicates production. Workers move around a

Japanese plant, getting a variety of experience which makes them versatile. Specialists and technicians may bounce out of the office area to circulate on the factory floor, encouraging the development of new products and ideas. All these things can be done without suspicion or resentment of the kind that would occur in some western factories.

In psychological terms a Japanese, in a factory as in any other social situation, has a well-developed set of antennae for sensing what other people expect of him, and his energy is directed into meeting these social expectations more than to realizing his own individual goals. Indeed, a western psychologist finds that Japanese workers, with their concern about achievement, come nearer to western middle-class than western working-class values. Some students of Japanese social psychology conclude that the motivation to work hard comes from the sense of needing to repay parents for their loving care, or even to make things hard for yourself as a penance, in some way matching their sacrifice for you. This works for some Europeans, too, but in Japan it is more widespread. Your parents worked hard for you, you must work hard in recompense. That is the non-Protestant work ethic of Japan.

But what may start as an atonement can become a habit with pleasurable aspects. The 'subservient' Japanese worker not only bows and scrapes to his employer, in the western stereotype, but works abnormally long hours. The reason why people do not always like to leave their workplace is the fellowship, however, not the drudgery. 'When one goes off duty,' David Plath concludes in a study of the relation between Japanese work and leisure, 'there is a sense in which one becomes socially dead.' In some offices men are prepared to pay fines in order to stay on after the permitted maximum time. There is also a conscientiousness about hours that is not strictly work-oriented. No one is greatly surprised at the old-fashioned older employee who arrives half-an-hour late in the morning, works the rest of the day, but designates that day as part of his leave – in order to safeguard his reputation for not cheating on the hours.

There are more reports now of illness caused by the stress of work. Sexual impotence is spreading among workers in their thirties, and seven out of ten workers complain of mental or physical fatigue. In a particularly bad case which was well-publicized in the West, workers in an all-male Toyota plant, sleeping in a company dormitory, were refused the opportunity of socializing with the staff at an all-female textile mill nearby, and after a period of time there were breakdowns. But the real stress came from the noise and speed of the production line, the hazards of accident and inadequate safety precautions. In this respect, as in many others, Japan is still a certain way behind Europe.

Is there a biological angle to the Japanese success? Are they unusually dextrous? Much has been written about how sensitive they are to details, how adept at miniaturization, how good at the fine tuning of a machine or the maximum satisfaction of small, fiddly consumer demands – catering, a Japanese writer suggests (indulging the national taste for sexual imagery), 'for the female world, while the Americans go for the male'. The craze for *pachinko* – pinball machines – slumped recently when their mechanization made them easier to play. It seemed that the demonstration of manual skill, including table-tipping, was part of the attraction.

There is something in the physical delicacy. Sony reports that the tolerances on its San Diego TV set production line have to be 15% higher than at home, because Americans are not so alert to detailed accuracy. They tighten their screws too softly – or too hard. But the manual dexterity which was admired earlier in the century in Japan's textile mills, for example, may be going. Now elders complain that young adults cannot use chopsticks properly any more, or that children cannot peel fruit as well as their parents used to.

Not only physical dexterity but also conscientiousness at work is changing with new circumstances. The shortening of working hours goes on steadily, with a five-day week now the norm in offices, five-and-a-half days in many other work-places. Older workers may regret such change, but younger ones, who know what they want to do with their leisure, welcome it. The Saturday holiday sinks a big nail in the coffin of the work ethic. Saturday workers become heavily job-centred, often using Sunday merely to get rested for Monday. With two consecutive days off, an employee begins to use at least one of them for recreation and camaraderie, developing positive leisure interests which then compete with work throughout the week.

Another former incentive for working hard is on the way out. As long as welfare benefits were ungenerous, and a Japanese could not expect to see his full medical and pension needs met by the government, he had a reason to exert himself, to get them covered by a company. But two things are about to alter that. Firstly, official spending on welfare is going to rise steadily, so that a man's dependence on working hard for a company in order to have his health and his future looked after will correspondingly diminish. Secondly, the ageing population will progressively overload his pension contributions at work in the years to come, and the patent unfairness of that is expected to undermine his will to work.

Even more important than these is the advent of *my-home-ism*, which is one of those phrases invented by the Japanese using English words to convey a Western import, in this case, the idea of individual home-ownership and all the enjoyment that can bring. It is a philosophy in which younger workers put wedding anniversaries before work deadlines, and go home on time every day in order to socialize with friends, take wives out to dinner or play with children. They are no longer moved by pleas from senior supervisors about the importance of the work that remains to be done after hours. The small beginnings of *my-home-ism* came in the 1950s when TV and electronic gadgets first made evenings at home more tempting: at one time the Cabinet debated whether to launch a campaign against it. Japanese often say now that they will take a job only if it does not cut into their private life. One survey even suggests that, by 1984, Americans had become more loyal to their company than Japanese, and that most Japanese below the age of thirty had a low work motivation, which only means that the intense hothouse pressure of the 1950–75 period is easing, and the enduring human characteristics of Japan are once more visible.

Instead of bringing their personal problems to their foremen, young workers take them home to discuss with family or friends. They are not at all rebellious, indeed they seem passive, but they 'do what they are told and not one iota more'. They do not dodge hard work on the factory floor or the office desk, but they do now go to some lengths to avoid those tedious and time-consuming 'shop talk' sessions in the local bars after work.

The British may think the Japanese unkind to refer to these quite natural developments as catching the 'British disease'. But whatever the label, the Japanese are seriously worried by the failure of the younger generation to inherit the qualities which have taken Japan almost to the top. Most young workers today do not show the responsibility and initiative of their fathers and, although they retain vestigial feelings of guilt about putting leisure first, that too is in the process of evaporating. The 'British disease' is not much more, after all, than a yen for a better quality of life. As the 21-year-old carpenter Masakatsu Hayashi (who fell in love with England on a visit, sold up at home and came to live in Wigan) says blissfully: 'Life in Japan is all work, while England is wonderful, a place of happiness.'

Some slackness is already apparent. Westerners suffering nightmares about purposive and efficient Japanese workers should take a look at Japan National Railways (JNR). This is an enterprise where an oil drum can stand for several days while two workers wait for a third one to join them to make the required minimum of three set by the trade union to move it. Politicians once made a surprise visit to a railway station to find all kinds of irregularities: the stationmaster did not know how many of his 192 staff were on hand, and they frequently took surprise leave, it was explained, making it necessary for supervisors to substitute. Managers were frightened to tell the trade union to stick to the rules in case it disrupted the train schedules, and it was not unknown for them to be physically attacked if they took a strong stance. JNR is far from typical: the private railways are much more efficient. But the example shows that Japanese workers are not superhuman. It was only by a considerable effort that the Japanese were able to keep up the standards of work by which the West has now come to judge them, and there are many cases where that kind of effort is no longer made.

The European might sympathize with such incipient post-industrial behaviour, but go on to ask why the Japanese trade unions do not also endorse it. Why instead do they collaborate so closely with management? Actually, the group feeling in factories, the remarkable sense of community of interest between workers and managers, casts the unions in a quite different role from what they play in the West. As a result of an accident of American Occupation policy, they are vertical enterprise unions rather than horizontal craft unions, and that in itself helps them identify goals in common with company management. This is eased by the management habit of promoting people from within an enterprise, often by a process of evaluation not only from above but from below as well, through the channels of consensus, instead of bringing an outsider in from above – as typically happens in a western corporation. It also explains why only three workers in ten are unionized.

Some companies virtually run the unions as a part of management, sending their promising junior managers to the union office for a spell to gain experience in negotiation and personnel affairs. One textile industrialist initiated a union in his plant in the hope that it would get new recruits for him in a difficult labour market. The pay-off for both sides is when former union officers join the senior management: at a recent count there were seven directors of Nissan Motors who had at one time served in the union.

When it goes too far, especially in very large companies, workers begin to feel that the trade union is 'working for the management'. Its leaders may find it difficult to squash minority opinions or dissident groups, and in the case of Toshiba and some motor companies this has led to harassment and violence. Unions may also collaborate with management to support company candidates in local and general elections, to ensure that their common interests are looked after at the political level.

However, the Japanese unions are not by any means creatures of management, nor are they backward in serving their members. They can be extremely tough on wage claims, and on access to information about the enterprise. Some of them hire well-qualified professionals to conduct economic analysis on their behalf. Japanese wages and hours of work are already at the European level. But unions do not price their members out of the world market, taking wage increases in the last five recessionary years that averaged less than 1% a year in real terms. Unions and workers are still willing to sacrifice for the future prosperity of the firm, an attitude unrivalled in the West. It is partly a product of rational calculation about the enterprise's need to invest for higher profits, partly a habit of meek deference to authority scooped out from the feudal past. Neither factor owes anything to the West.

To strike is to hurt yourself as well as your employer, and the Japanese union does not need to be told to look for an action which will hurt the employer without hurting workers. 'If the management loses money', a Nissan union leader explains, 'so do we'. Strikes in Japan receive little publicity but, during the 1970s, Japan ranked fourteenth among the industrial countries in terms of the number of days lost per thousand workers from industrial disputes – a rather worse record than Holland's or Germany's. When there is a strike it can be bitter: some owners and managers are very old-fashioned indeed.

Instead of downing tools and interrupting corporate revenues, Japanese union members in dispute usually stay at work, but wear armbands denouncing the management or assemble during the lunch break in order to shout abuse at the managers. Public service strikes and working-to-rule, by railwaymen, for instance, are made short and the public given good notice so that inconvenience is minimized and goodwill retained. The strategy is to engineer the most shame, humiliation and inconvenience for management executives (for example by failing to provide figures or information not needed for immediate production purposes). Factionalization within unions, often along party political lines, can, however, spoil these good intentions.

The conclusion is that there is nothing extra-terrestrial about Japanese workers. Their race has always had to work hard to snatch a living from an inhospitable terrain, but they have never been fanatical about work and as little as a hundred years ago were thought to be rather indolent. Then all the favourable conditions came together in the post-war years for their crowning industrial achievement. But now they are affected by individualization and changing values in their own family structure. Succumbing to the attractions of the consumer life, they find themselves entering a downward curve of diligence, their sun at noon. Can their managers cope with an inexorable decline in the work ethic?

The Japanese know how important it is to have high-quality managers. More than 80,000 engineering graduates are employed in industry, almost ten times as many as in Britain, and the director who does not know how to strip a machine down and assemble it again is a rarity. Graduates go for employment in private industry or commerce much more than in Europe. Hitachi employs 600 doctors of engineering, and the President of Teijin, a big diversified manufacturing firm, resigned because he could not, he said, keep up with the technical reading. The West thinks of a manager as someone who counts the money or looks after the men: in Japan he is seen primarily as production manager, a product manager, a machine manager. The 'technical people' have the power to run the show.

Another quality admired in a manager is unpretentiousness, of the kind which Konosuke Matsushita displayed in the 1920s when touring his little factory to inspect the New Year cleaning. He came to a dirty bathroom. Nobody sprang into action to clean it: the trade unions had just begun to organize, and there was a certain tension in the air. Matsushita found a bucket, filled it with water, splashed it on the floor and started mopping. He sensed that he should set an example, and his action relieved the strain. 'I learned to cultivate humility,' he recollected afterwards, 'for often management by example works best.'

There is a moral climate surrounding Japanese management which has consequences for industrial relations. It is expressed in the emotional closeness which managers expect to form not only with equals but with subordinates as well. A Japanese manager had this to say about the role of the office secretary, so beloved in Hollywood dramas:

> You Americans overload the boss-secretary relationship with all the caring and mutual help that is denied in your boss-to-subordinate and peer relationships. In Japan the reverse is true. We meet our emotional needs and develop our strongest ties with colleagues within the professional ranks. We don't need to burden the clerical people with that.

Workspace arrangements are informal – no internal walls or partitions, but an open office plan instead with standard furniture and equipment at each workplace. A Japanese manager will usually see a subordinate immediately, whereas in Europe or America that all-powerful secretary will probably 'try' to fit you in to see him sometime next week.

If an employee makes a mistake, he will not necessarily be dismissed. Two American economists once compared Matsushita with another famous manager, Harold Geneen of International Telephone and Telegraph. They found that a Geneen executive who did something wrong was humiliated and possibly fired. Matsushita would merely re-assign such a man, possibly to a lower rank, allowing him the opportunity to learn from his mistake and become more valuable to the company later. That reinforces the idea of workers and subordinates having self-respect, enabling them to identify with the enterprise and redouble their contribution to it. Personal prestige is a major motivation. More than four million Japanese bear the title of company President, twice as many as in America with its much larger population. Everyone who works for YKK, the zip-fastener maker, is called a *member* of the company.

All this makes for a good atmosphere in the factory, but somebody has to take decisions, possibly unpopular decisions. How is the consensus so prized by the Japanese arrived at? In large enterprises the world over, company decisions sometimes originate in the middle ranks rather than at the top. But nowhere is this more systematic than in Japan, under the tradition of *ringisei*. Whether in industry, commerce or government, it is accepted that the ones who know most about a problem in the first instance are the people who do the substantive work or are in touch with the shopfloor, however low they may stand in the hierarchy. It is they who, by discussing among themselves, often initiate a suggestion which may then be cleared with even lower levels, and presented to the next higher level for transmission to the top.

At each stage of this bottom-up system new snags may be discovered, new factors brought out, and modifications made. But when the final decision has been approved, it is seen as the will of the whole body of people, and everyone will back it fully (in contrast with the more autocratic procedure common in Europe whereby decisions are seen to come from the top and to be imposed on the lower levels with relatively little discussion or consultation).

In practice there is a mixture of bottom-up and top-down decision-making in both Japan and the West, but there is more of the former in Japan and it is more formalized, with numerous rules, conventions, and persuasive devices of its own. Twenty years ago, when Japanese companies were falling over each other to copy American management methods, some of them abandoned *ringi*, but most have since gone back to it to some extent.

One of the astonishing sights of Tokyo is a large new building being landscaped: full-grown trees of great size are brought in by lorry on a Sunday with their roots lovingly wrapped in straw. *Nemawashi* is the word used to describe the work of preparing the roots of these trees for such a challenging transplant. The largest roots are first cut short and sealed, and the tree is given time to adapt to drawing nourishment from the smaller roots. Later in the year the small roots are cut, the tree is moved to its new place and there the big roots are uncovered and placed in the soil. *Nemawashi* is also the accepted metaphor for the laborious task of persuading people in an organization to accept a new policy, helping them to adjust to it in advance so that when the time comes they will support it wholeheartedly. As with almost everything Japanese, there is nothing unique here, but in no other country is this kind of preparation for organizational policy change so painstakingly thorough.

Senior managers do not always sit back and wait for their juniors to act: they develop the complementary skill of making sure as far as possible that the decisions which come up are the 'correct' ones. 'To be truthful,' says a Sony executive, 'probably 60% of the decisions I make are mine. But I keep my intentions secret. In discussions with my subordinates, I ask questions, pursue facts and try to nudge them in my direction . . .' Instead of telling your juniors what to do, you put your own ideas into their minds and convince them afterwards that they were theirs. That way the implementation is willing.

This is a system in which workers are trusted. In Toyota, any assembly operator may stop the production line if he judges it necessary. One manager, Koichi Tsukamoto of Wacoal, carried trust to a remarkable extreme. He decided to accept automatically all the official demands of the company union. Even if it wanted a pay-out of ten million *yen* per head, followed by dissolution of the company, it would be done. The horrified directors said the enterprise would go bankrupt, but Tsukamoto replied that, if a majority of workers were ready to drive the company to bankruptcy, the management must already have provoked them and there was no hope of stopping them. So he threw away the time clocks, and everyone suddenly became very punctual.

But the trade union leaders already had a strike planned, and wanted Tsukamoto to pressurize them – just for form's sake. They could accept a reasonable compromise only if it were seen that they had pressed the original pay claim strongly in the first instance. Tsukamoto would have no hypocrisy, however. He accepted the high wage demand without even looking at it. His only comment was that performance at work should be improved if the union wanted the company to prosper. The union passed on the message, the atmosphere cleared because the demands had been met, future claims became much more reasonable, and within six years a mutual trust had developed which enabled the company to forge ahead without any labour trouble whatsoever. But Tsukamoto's example was not generally followed in managerial circles.

Not everybody admires the consensual model. It lands mediocre people in the top jobs, an American observer complains, and never copes with unpleasant decisions. If workers must suffer because of developments outside the factory gate, it is too much to hope that they will agree to it. Consensus is good for deciding tactics, not so good for strategy. Some enterprises, like banks, find consensus inappropriate, and they adopt something nearer to the western system. It is certainly time-consuming: everybody has a story to tell about contracts lost because of the delays of consensus.

Some foreign critics see *ringi* as a cloak behind which Japanese executives can dodge responsibility for big decisions – 'a system of common irresponsibility'. If the mandate proves wrong, no one can be blamed (everyone must be blamed – and everyone cannot be punished). These days, consensus appears to have more critics than defenders, but then the Japanese are notoriously inarticulate, and it is foreigners and westernized Japanese who are the principal fault-finders. Beneath the surface, the old consensual habits persist and very few organizations have abandoned them.

Rather the same can be said of another famous constituent of industrial management in Japan, *shushin koyo* or lifetime employment. This grows out of the important fact that it is hard to take a person's job away from him in Japan. 'Firing a man creates a serious social problem,' explains Soichiro Honda, the motorcycle and car maker. 'Dismissal is possible only when someone causes serious damage and loss to the company, or in the case of a very serious moral wrong.'

Lifetime employment as such was not traditional in Japan, being invented by the cotton spinners at the end of the nineteenth century as a device to restrict labour mobility when they became short of hands. At that time, corporations in other industries were as cavalier with their labour as companies in the West; only in the Great Depression of the 1920s did they come to see it as a worthwhile goal not to deplete the human capital of an enterprise. And there were always exceptions to the idea. Fewer than one in five of Japan's workers actually benefit today from the lifetime employment system, and there are frequent cases at the executive level where able managers and specialists move from one company to another in mid-career. There are many head-hunting firms to cater for such itchy feet. Labour turnover in big companies is about 13% a year.

But where lifetime employment does exist, it can be fiercely defended. One company kidnapped a disloyal worker back from his new workplace, like a piece of stolen property. Most employees are gratified not to be made to feel 'disposable like toilet paper'. The practice so limits the power of managers that Morita, the Chairman of Sony, offers another definition of the Japanese company – as a 'kind of social security organization, not a business'. It means that workers will not be laid off, even in recession, and that represents the ideal to which all companies aspire. In one recent year Hitachi, which employs more than 85,000 people, dismissed only 57 of them. Even if work becomes unavailable, special measures are taken. When Teijin had to lay off 400 men, they spent six months at a corporate residence on full pay doing no work. A rich corporation will maintain the payroll, though none could do it for ever without new orders coming in. Meanwhile, managers redouble their efforts to diversify production, from ships to aircraft or oilrigs, from motor cars to space equipment. A successful employer in the Japanese book does not send his men home but finds them something else to do.

Lifetime employment reinforces the longer-term thinking of a company, removing, for example, the temptation for a manager to get quick profits before he moves to another firm a few years later. Morita points out that a man is more willing to take responsibility for decisions if he knows he will not be fired for making wrong ones. On the other hand, it is wasteful to have trained manpower permanently tied up and not fully exploited by the employer, and the motivation of young people is doubtful with such slow-moving ladders of promotion before them. These problems are also faced by many workers in large western corporations like Exxon, and in western bureaucracies, armies and police forces, all of whom enjoy a form of lifetime employment. Linked with life employment is the system of paying wages by seniority rather than performance. Seniority is psychologically important in Japan: when Konosuke Matsushita chose the man who ranked twenty-third in his corporation as the new president to succeed him, he created quite a stir.

It is the young who lose out with lifetime employment and seniority wages. They have to be very patient to win the eventual rewards. And since the system fails to provide incentives for unusual effort, it is usually supplemented by schemes that do. Japanese factories today present a mixed picture of wage criteria: Nissan has four distinct categories of workers – permanent, probationary, provisional and seasonal – all treated differently and with different wage scales.

nly the first is never laid off. There are numerous exceptions to the
eniority wage system, including the employees of subcontractors
who furnish most of the parts and components for Japanese industry.
Their workers have been described as down-and-out cheap labour,
drawn from the underworld to work in sweatshops for very little
reward – passengers numbering 70% of the workforce who have
to travel steerage to allow the 30% who are unionized lifetime
employees to luxuriate in the first-class.

This is the part of industrial Japan that foreigners find easy to
despise. Yet these people are more often gainfully employed than
their European counterparts, and the subcontracting relationship
need not be as bad as it is painted in the left-wing western press. The
patron corporation often protects the subcontractor, for example,
making payments when there is no work available, rehousing him
when the plant has to be relocated, or helping him to get cheap credit
for new equipment.

There is not too much for serious European and American corporations to copy in all this. Yet managers have gone crazy in the past
decades, trying to follow the Japanese model, in the hope of emulat-
ing Japan's industrial success. The way the Japanese manage their
factories has two distinct ingredients, one spilling out of the native
tradition which western societies cannot hope to replicate, the other
judiciously imported from America and Europe at an earlier stage –
and that, having first appeared in the West, does not need to be
recopied from Japan. The particular amalgam in Japanese enterprises, of Japanese social groupism with western systems of organizing industrial production, is too varied to constitute a general mode
for other countries to mimic.

The whole scenario is unreal. First, diffident Japanese companies
in the 1950s and 1960s copied western management practices in order
to catch up with the Americans and Europeans. Then, after tasting
success, they returned to many traditional Japanese practices which
are   more   comfortable.   Whereupon   demoralized   American
companies copied Japanese management practices in the 1970s and
1980s in the hope of recovering lost ground. Such mutual lack of
self-confidence recalls the day in Fleet Street when the *Daily Mail*,
seeing its rival, the *Daily Express*, leading the first edition with a
different news story from its own, switched to that lead story for the
second edition – while the *Express* changed to the *Mail*'s original lead
story!

What could profitably be applied by western managers is not
Japan's imaginary magic formula for industrial success, but such
time-worn universals as the practice of a little more care and

thoroughness, a lifting of sights to the slightly longer term, a greater consideration for the self-esteem of employees. Some of the new American union agreements with Ford include guaranteed employment and the institution of discussion circles to head off industrial trouble, in conscious imitation of Japan.

But Western managers do not really need to go to Japan for these improvements, the ingredients of which are nearer at hand: more likely they have reached an impasse in their own affairs where the changes that have to be made for survival need to be presented to the workforce not as yet another whim of distrusted indigenous manage-ment but as a foreign medicine from the country they 'have to beat'. What is missing from all the prescriptions is the formula for reconcil-ing individualistic western workers to the self-effacing patterns of Japanese-style co-operation. If those vital family-style relationships, that in-built acceptance of authority, do not exist on the shopfloor, how can any Japanese-style edifice be built on top of them?

One illustration of the problem is the acceptability of mechaniza-tion. Workers in large Japanese enterprises see new automated equipment or robots as a key to expanding production, turning out better products at cheaper prices, making more profits and thus earning more pay (about which they may feel more secure than western counterparts because of lifetime employment). The Nissan union boss says that his members 'love their robots. They take the drudgery out of work.'

Quality control circles provide another classic illustration. While European and American companies struggled with the legacy of an earlier generation of industrial theory driving home the virtues of specialization, the Japanese with their participative tradition and high level of training were natural candidates for QC circles. At a recent count there were more than 135,000 of them operating in Japan, taken up from the ideas of the American theorist W. Edwards Demming – just as other Japanese drew from the earlier experience of Sears Roebuck to create *kanban*, the tightly controlled system of components supply designed to minimize waste, storage and over-heads. Yet western trade unions are suspicious of QC circles because they fear they will lead to redundancy, the downgrading of shop stewards and a squeezing out of the union role.

The same problem of mediating different work attitudes is encoun-tered from the other side by Japanese companies setting up in the West. It is difficult, for cultural reasons, for most Japanese managers to be effective abroad. Many observers say flatly that a Japanese company can never become truly internationalized. A Japanese writer thinks of 'those Japanese silently working in the forefront of internationalization' as 'today's equivalent of front-line soldiers or even as hostages sent to foreign lands'. Many Japanese executives in the West plough their lonely furrow, eating their heart out for home and never understanding why local employees do not respond to their ideas in the way their Japanese workers do. Yet there are now some 12,000 Japanese executives and technicians guiding the work of some 100,000 Americans in more than a thousand Japanese companies in the United States – though only a part of that is manufacturing. Europe stands host to a smaller Japanese presence.

On both sides of the Atlantic fewer than half of the Japanese firms are unionized, and the role of the trade union is one of the chief points of discussion. Toshiba has a closed shop at its British TV plant in Plymouth, but it also has elected staff sitting on an advisory board with access to company information. Honda began by rejecting American union approaches, only giving in after threats of boycott. Indeed, many Japanese manufacturers go to areas like the American South precisely in order to avoid union domination. Nissan's executives at their Tennessee factory remarked that having a trade union would be like 'living with mother-in-law': who needed a third party in a good marriage? The Sony TV plant in San Diego circulated anti-union T-shirts, but there are *samurai*-like stories, such as that of the Sanyo executive who once slept the night on the trade union office floor in a successful effort to establish rapport.

With or without a union, the Japanese have been chastened by their western workers striking. When YKK dismissed a man at its Cheshire zip-fastener factory who smashed some furniture, more than 250 workers went on unofficial strike – and they struck again for a month a few years later over pay. The same firm was taken to court by a trade union in Italy because its executives were thought to have exceeded the proper limits in labour questions. It is not easy to launch the Cycle of Goodness in western orbit. But Toshiba, Sanyo and Hitachi in their British enterprises have no-strike agreements with the Electrical, Electronic, Telecommunication and Plumbing Union, which seem to satisfy both sides.

Some of the Japanese firms in America have deliberately set out to recruit workers of East Asian origin, knowing they would work conscientiously and perhaps hoping that they would have some familiarity with Japanese methods. This is one reason for the Japanese concentration in Southern California, where Hitachi was sued for discrimination and had to promise to take on more black and Hispanic labour. Sumitomo was also sued in New York, but for sexual discrimination in recruitment. The general complaint is that Japanese firms do not employ enough women or blacks and do not promote enough local people to senior positions. Working for a Japanese firm is, they say, like joining the Navy: you know you'll 'never make Admiral'. To which the Japanese retort that, if only the people concerned would learn Japanese, they would get all the promotion they wanted.

C. Itoh, the trading corporation, was sued by some of its white American employees for discrimination because the key managerial meetings were restricted to Japanese personnel. One of the senior British employees with a big trading corporation describes how the British staff are always outsiders, and how the Japanese always avoid becoming subordinate to Europeans. These are not good advertisements for Japanese management in non-Japanese conditions, and do not provide the preconditions of internationalization. But there are bright spots, too. When the Sony plant in San Diego ran into the oil recession in the 1970s, it kept its workers on for training instead of laying them off, as a result of which their loyalty and attendance rates much improved. Sumitomo Electric cleverly delegated its welfare programme to the self-management of its American workers.

But Japanese executives do complain that American and European labour is not as good as Japanese. British workers, say Hitachi managers, are only 80% as productive as Japanese – and how to deal with the British 'cuppa tea ceremony'? Other firms say they are satisfied with European labour, finding it not as inflexible as had been expected, although they commonly add the proviso that, while Europeans work well individually, they are not as strong working as a team (the reverse of the Japanese situation).

The Japanese have become the ambassadors of egalitarianism, especially on European shopfloors. None of that 'English pin-stripe nonsense' in Sony's South Wales plant, and a British engineer at the NSK ball-bearings factory near Durham tingles with the rare excitement of being allowed, even encouraged, to work on the shopfloor itself. 'They take over your machine if you are sick,' a YKK worker in Britain comments about the lack of aloofness on the part of Japanese executives. And information is fed to workers more seriously than they have usually experienced before: 'I force the staff to know how the company is doing,' says one Japanese manager in Europe.

The Japanese are now accepted. Andy Imura, pioneer of the Matsushita TV plant in Britain, was appointed to the National Economic Development Council for the Electronics Industry, and in that capacity had to give honest counsel to the British about how to defend themselves against competition from, among other countries, Japan. His opposite number at Sony, in the same Welsh valley, won not only an Order of the British Empire, but a Queen's Award for

Exports – and when he went to Buckingham Palace to collect it, most of his delegation were proud shopfloor workers. Little wonder that Margaret Thatcher asks her people to emulate Japan instead of criticizing it.

Because Japan has mastered the mass-production engineering of a limited range of electronic and mechanical consumer equipment, some excitable Westerners assume it has a lead in all of science and technology. Yet Japanese management remains weak in basic science. True, Japan discovered ferrite and invented the electronic microscope, the Yagi antenna and the magnetron vacuum tube (all before the war). True, there have been six Japanese winners of the Nobel Prize for sciences (though they were all educated before the war, and hardly compare with Britain's seventy-seven). True, mathematics is a particular strength in Japanese education. *The Economist* calls Japan's civil service the 'most mathematically-minded' bureaucracy in the world, and there is even a National Statistics Day.

But in any comparison of mathematical and scientific capability, Westerners usually get the highest individual scores, while the Japanese as a group get the best average. There are few geniuses, perhaps because of the cultural pressures for conformity, but many capable practitioners. When Dr Reona Esaki won his Nobel Prize for physics in 1973, a Japanese newspaper commented: 'Like some other exceptional Japanese scientists, he has found it necessary to work abroad in order to stimulate and satisfy his creative bent . . . We suffer a brain-drain, not for any lack of funds, equipment or high standards in individual fields, but for a system that holds down adventurous spirits.' A national science that does not encourage people to show their ability at the highest level is not one that assures technical progress. For Japan to achieve creative breakthroughs in scientific research, it would have to endure mavericks, and that goes against the social grain.

Western critics who fear the Japanese for their scientific potential also profess to scorn them, with scant regard for consistency, for being cheap copyists. Japan has, indeed, copied very well throughout its history, composing mediaeval Chinese poems which discerning Chinese critics hailed as quite 'free of Japanese feeling', and baking sixteenth-century bread which the Portuguese missionaries rated tastier than anything in Europe. The whole burden of Japan's modern century since 1868 is a steady accumulation of imitations from the West.

Soichiro Honda came to Britain in the 1950s a keen motorcycle buff. Refused permission to go round a British carburettor plant, he returned home with suitcases full of engine parts bought in English shops for him to copy. Now he is one of the most famous car and motorcycle manufacturers in the world: Britons queue for his products. The Japanese even copy themselves. Sony in particular is plagued by Walkman and Watchman imitations.

Since the Japanese do not admire originality as much as Europeans, they are less troubled by the whole question of copying. Today as a nation they pay more than a billion dollars a year for foreign technology. It is surprising how many western inventors have had to wait for years and years before seeing their ideas realized on any production floor – and then a Japanese one. The classic example was the Bell transistor, which Sony first used in a radio in the 1950s, but there is also the chromatron system of colour TV which Sony bought from Paramount in the early 1960s, the thyrister semiconductor and many more.

The Chinese can be rather rude about Japanese imitation, too. Noting that Japan absorbed many of the arts and spiritual values of China in earlier centuries, one of them says that the only item not successfully transferring to Japanese soil was 'originality . . . For lack of this one element Japan remained a dwarf tree'. That is as may be, but no one can gainsay Japan's superb achievements of production engineering and industrial management, and as long as new patents can be bought from elsewhere, it is not a bad way of achieving wealth. The only thing is that Japan may be coming to the end of the road as a borrower. Western corporations and governments are not as keen as they were to release their know-how under licence, and most Japanese companies do not do enough research of their own to make cross-licensing deals.

Despite her late start, Japan has surpassed the West in several high-technology areas, including optical fibres, robots and microprocessors. But in computer software, aerospace, chemical and energy technology, and biochemistry, the Japanese fall behind. Japan's industrial future does not look so rosy when one considers her relatively small base of knowledge and research on the Josephson Junction for computers, for example, or three-dimensional circuits or genetic engineering. Where the best American talents have gone into those seedbeds for the future, defence and space technology, Japan's have gone into consumer technology.

The much-publicized programmes mounted by Japanese industry under government co-ordination, for example to build a fifth generation computer, are somewhat artificial. One of the scientists involved describes his team as 'like people who are trying desperately to fly with the aid of artificial birds' wings even though they have no previous knowledge of aero-dynamics'. The first results have actually been impressive, and some admirers see Japan as standing on the threshold of new developments in science. But if the past is anything to go by, it would be wise to wait and see.

At the humbler level of working technology, the Japanese are rich in invention and creative modification. They imported laser scalpel technology from the West, refined it, and then made money by exporting it back. They were very successful with the lithium battery and circuit diagrams, and the Germans could not believe it when a Japanese licensee developed one of their machines to the point where it could automatically sew trousers. It was the Japanese who made television sets work so well that the British public was persuaded to start buying TV sets again instead of renting them. And one can go back to before the war, when Platt Brothers bought the technology of the Toyoda loom, and Japanese engineers went to Oldham to teach the British all about it.

The Japanese are good at filling the gaps between western achievements, particularly where conservatism holds Europeans back. Seiko made its famous quartz watch fifteen years ago by dividing the motor into separate parts and fitting them into the tiny spaces between the watch gears, to save space. In European countries the motor is usually made by a separate specialist company, which would have been squeezed out of business by such a development. In a similar way, Japanese engineers were able to take the corpus of mechanical and electrical achievement of western science and weld the two together in a highly imaginative yet practical way to create mechatronics.

But companies tend to be too busy, placing too many immediate demands on their technological staff, to allow much long-term creativity. 'It slows things down,' a philistine Nissan executive comments, 'when every individual is free to spout his own ideas.' Curiously enough, whereas the Japanese are long-term in their management, production, marketing and financial thinking, they work on a shorter time-span than their western rivals in the laboratories.

Both in science and in economic management, therefore, Japan tends to be over-estimated in the West. The marvellous cars, radios, ships and television sets which the world eagerly buys from Japan for their high quality and value for money, have to be set against the indifferent or over-expensive products of Japan's agriculture, and of her chemicals, cement, aluminium or foodstuffs industries. Very few foreigners would buy a packet of Japanese rice (seven times dearer than Californian) or fertilizer, unless they were highly subsidized. In

all these resource-based industries, as well as in aerospace, pharmaceuticals, defence and most of the service sector, Japan has not
offered outstandingly good products to the world.

It is because of these troughs of efficiency that the productivity of
Japanese workers as a whole is lower than European or American, in
spite of the small areas like motor cars and electronics where it is
higher. Edward de Bono goes so far as to suggest that 'the Japanese
are possibly among the most inefficient people in the world'. Many
examples can be found of bungling, for instance in the four consecutive failures to launch a satellite. The breaking in half of two
Japan-made ships at sea was an early blot on the record of the
shipyards, and there are cases where even the wizard car industry
went wrong, for example sending replacements to France calculated
for left-hand driving instead of right. Such mistakes may happen
more frequently in future as the standard of conscientiousness on the
shopfloor falls.

Everything is now under change in Japan. The companies which
created the economic miracle, together with their élite workforce,
will in future have to share more of the rewards with others, through
taxation, through more national welfare, through more investment
against pollution and environmental hazards, in more safety and in
accommodating more aspirations of the second and third ranking
sectors of the industry below them. The ageing of her population will
push costs up and make the workforce less motivated as well as less
adaptable to technological innovation.

Japan's factory workers are getting old and expensive, and in those
respects the advantages for manufacturing have already shifted to
South Korea and are in the process of moving further afield to
Taiwan, some Southeast Asian countries and China. And when that
happens, Japan will find herself less well placed than the US or
Britain to take up the slack by developing the service industries. The
wholesale and retail trades are already over-manned and will have to
slim down with supermarkets to make High Street prices more
reasonable. Other services are not geared to make money abroad.

There is no invincibility in the Japanese economy, merely some
good possibilities which were intelligently taken up in the past
thirty-five years and exploited to the full, while leaving large areas of
the economy in no better position than their counterparts in Europe
or America (some of them far worse). It will take a sustained world
boom, continued good industrial judgement and better political
leadership over the coming decades to ensure that Japan's appropriate place in the world system is consolidated. That applies to every
branch of the economy except trade, which is something else.

13

Capturing the Regimental Colours
Japan's Foreign Trade

ON A rare foray east of India Rudyard Kipling reported that the Japanese had 'no business savvy . . . A little huckster who can't see beyond his nose'. It seems hard to believe today, but this was a common opinion among Westerners until relatively recently. There is little in the Japanese tradition, after all, to suggest a national aptitude for commerce. It has always been bad form to ask for the price of anything (because that would betray a laughable degree of stinginess in your nature) or to check the specifications of what you are buying.

The Japanese are so shy in social encounters that it is a wonder they ever sell an egg, let alone an encephalograph. Money used to be wrapped up in white paper before being handed to another person, because it was thought dirty and indelicate, even into the 1950s. 'They used to think about money the way we thought about sex,' a foreign resident explains.

Against this background one may sympathize with Akio Morita of Sony, on his first visit to America and Europe for his fledgling company Sony in 1953. 'I was overwhelmed,' he recollected, 'by the size and history of western industry. I therefore felt almost hopeless expecting to export something using our own technology. At that time, the term 'Made in Japan' had the image of something cheap and of poor quality.' Yet today, hardly thirty years later, Japan has not only vanquished all competitors in world markets, but has developed such a high standard of domestic after-sales service and customer satisfaction that foreign competitors in the Japanese market complain about not getting a chance.

Precisely because they were not naturally gifted at commerce, the Japanese had to work very hard to master it. Their perseverance has delighted consumers all over the world, but is now meeting its match in the vested trading interests of other countries. The trade frictions which Japan has encountered in the past twenty years are complex, but they mostly come down to western unwillingness to treat newly-arrived Japan on a par with other established western suppliers in the world market-place. Western arguments usually start from factual ignorance, feed on cultural misunderstanding and distend with racial prejudice in a process qualitatively different from intra-western exchanges.

Things have fallen to a low point in international relations when a congressman in Washington can refer to 'little yellow people' and a Japanese newspaper commentary can attribute American restrictions on Japanese goods to 'the racial prejudice of the white people who regard Japanese as "yellow-faced upstarts"'. When John B. Connally was campaigning for the US presidential nomination in 1980, he told the Japanese rhetorically: 'You had better be prepared to sit on the docks of Yokohama in your little Datsuns while you stare at your little TV sets and eat your mandarin oranges, because we've had all we're going to take!' And Morita of Sony, who had found the American market so daunting, but then went on to flood it with electronic gadgetry, found by the 1980s that the Americans were 'trying to impose their own laws and their own ways of life on the rest of the world . . . Things seem to have gotten as bad as they were on the eve of World War Two. I myself am repulsed by it.'

The Europeans are not backward in insults. Within the past few years a senior French official has defended restrictions on Japanese goods with the insolent comment: 'In a card game, you can't accept it if one of the players cheats all the time.' The last British ambassador in Tokyo called the Japanese 'arrogant' for advising would-be European exporters to work harder. A French Minister has told Japanese visitors that if their country were to 'disappear from the face of the earth, we would be able to live happily', and the Dutch newspaper *Handelsblad* echoed French bitterness: 'If one day Japan should suddenly vanish under the sea, no country except Australia would shed tears.'

One of the biggest storms was released by an EEC report of 1978, drafted by Sir Roy Denman, a very senior official. It referred to the Japanese as workaholics living in rabbit hutches. Many Japanese took the substance of the criticism as valid, and some did not feel at all insulted. 'Beehives would be more appropriate,' said one. But a *Nihon Keizai Shimbun* correspondent saw in it 'the naked racist tendency Europeans have towards the Japanese'.

Surprisingly eminent Westerners began to complain that Japan demeaned the West by turning it into a hewer of wood and drawer of water. George Ball, the former Under-Secretary of State, was one of the first in the 1970s to describe the situation where most American exports to Japan are raw materials (whereas most American imports from Japan are manufactures) as a 'pattern for an under-developed country, not for the world's most powerful economy'. An influential Washington report warned in 1980 that the Americans were becoming 'Japan's plantation: haulers of wood and growers of crops in exchange for high technology, value-added products . . . This relationship is not acceptable.' Fritz Mondale was elected to be Vice-President after a campaign in which he asked: 'What are our kids going to do? Sweep up around the Japanese computers?' On the other side of the Atlantic a British scholar said in 1981 that his country, by inducing Japanese investment, was 'accepting the position of a second-ranking country in technological terms'. To place remarks like these together is to see through their mischievous absurdity.

The Japanese usually bow their heads before such onslaughts and retreat an inch or two in pained silence. But occasionally they reveal their anger. For the Americans to attack Japan's industrial policy, said one writer, is like warning Japan not to try to become Number One, but settle for Number Two or Number Three, just as in the naval agreement which had caused so much resentment in the 1920s. The EEC market, a Mitsubishi executive drily commented in 1976, was not absolutely vital for Japan. 'If it comes to the worst, we can envisage the possibility of entering into a total economic war against Europe.' And a Japanese diplomat in Paris asks: 'Why should we be nice to them when they walked all over us in the nineteenth century in the name of free trade?'

Japanese businessmen often tell Europe to repatriate its immigrant workers before complaining about Japan-induced unemployment, and to 'work harder' before complaining about trade deficits. When Japanese do speak, they are blunt about the pervasive flabbiness in western industry. Workers in Europe, said Naohiro Amaya of MITI in a revealing metaphor in 1977, 'are like undisciplined troops. They have stopped marching and go to bed . . .'

Western unreadiness to understand another culture operating in the international trading system is quite transparent. The American Under-Secretary of Commerce, Lionel Olmer, does not beat about the bush: 'We are asking for fundamental changes . . . in part of the Japanese way of life.' One German official actually wanted Japan to change its language because it constituted a non-tariff barrier. And a professor diagnosed in 1982 a 'war of cultures' between Japan and the West, for whom the whole of Japanese society functioned as a trade barrier.

The Japanese social structure does not fit into western categories, being neither regimented in the totalitarian sense, nor free and loose in the libertarian sense. Western rules for international trade are rooted in European values and categories: it is not easy to squeeze Japan into them without much discomfort and furious argument. For western economic interests on the decline, unable to retain their international competitiveness or victims of technological change, Japan is an ideal scapegoat upon which to vent their frustration, blaming it for their own failures. Westerners know from experience that the Japanese do not normally hit back, and the pressure of western opinion has made the Japanese feel guilty about their exports – not enough to stop them, but enough to feel politically and morally defensive about them. This is in spite of the fact that the proportion of the West's international trade in which Japan participates is not much more than one-eighth. Japan has not for the past twenty years been a low-wage country, and millions of consumers on both sides of the Atlantic have voted with their wallets for the enrichment that Japan brings to their lives.

A few perceptive Japanese recognize the trap sprung by special interests in the West. Anti-Japanese feelings, a Japanese writer concludes, 'have never been spontaneous in the US and Europe . . . They were deliberately created and nurtured in uninformed people by a minority of politicians, bureaucrats and industrialists to serve their own interests.' Each dispute, alas, requires a mobilization of public opinion which is never allowed to return to 'normal' even when that particular squabble is ended. The scene is then set for the next round (and they come in quick succession) with less mutual trust than ever – and so the animosity snowballs.

To be fair, there are leaders of opinion in the West who manage to keep their minds clear of cultural or racial prejudice when dealing with Japanese trade competition. Enoch Powell falls into this honourable category, but France or America have fewer such public figures. Nor are there many publications like *The Economist* to say that, 'Japan should export more of its industry, and faster, so as to spread its efficiency and to curb the spread of populist protectionism in the West . . . *Vive le défi japonais.*'

Leaving the rhetoric, the prejudice and the bad manners behind, the actual problems in Japan's trade with the West are threefold. The first is the imbalance of trade, the second is the concentration of Japanese exports in specific sectors (cars, TV sets) where particular harm is therefore caused to employment, and finally western difficulty in selling to the Japanese market. Each of the three problems is complicated, and de-mythologizing them is not easy.

Japan's imbalance of trade is huge. In 1984 she ran a surplus with the rest of the world of $34 billion*: with the United States alone her surplus was $33 billion and with the EEC $10 billion. The surpluses are big because Japan's world trade is big; and Japan imports about a quarter less than she exports. As Enoch Powell often reminds us, there is no requirement in either economics or morality for trade to balance, either between two countries or between one country and the rest of the world. It is not natural for the exchange of goods between countries to be so neatly symmetrical. Bilateral imbalances are without significance in the multi-lateral trading system of today's world and cannot by definition be 'obscene' – as some western writers profess to find Japan's.

Closer examination further reduces the significance of the Japanese surplus with the West. Most of Japan's imports are of energy and raw materials to feed her industries, and those come mainly from the Middle East, Southeast Asia and other regions of the Third World. Those countries in turn buy most of their imports (which are finished consumer goods and capital equipment) from America and Europe – and if this trade, of Atlantic manufactures to the Third World, could be boosted, then the problems of imbalance would be solved: world trade would go round in a satisfying circle. But bilateral balances are not easily achieved, because one side does not necessarily find the other's goods as attractive as its own or a third country's. The Japanese complain, for example, that Europe has little to sell them that they want. They have also suggested many times that, if the Americans believed in their much-vaunted free trade, they would allow Japan to buy Alaskan oil to reduce the trade imbalance, but that has been forbidden by the US government.

If trade reciprocity were to be insisted upon, it would mean the fragmentation of the world into barter blocs. The Chairman of a French car manufacturing firm describes the situation where Japan exports a hundred times more cars than it imports as 'completely incompatible with the harmonious development of the motor industry world-wide'. This is not, of course, something which was ever

---

* Based on goods physically clearing customs: if payments through the banking system are taken as the basis, the surplus reaches $44 billion. But if the money changing hands is the criterion, should we not include in the equation goods bought from local affiliates? It is calculated that American-owned factories in Japan sold $44 billion worth of goods to Japanese purchasers in 1984, Japanese in America $13 billion to American purchasers. That Japanese deficit of $30 billion would reduce the trade surplus to a far more manageable $14 billion. Alternatively, why not take the relative populations into account (should Monaco and France balance their trade)? Even with their big surplus, the Japanese are still buying more from America per head than the other way round. And if the money gap is what hurts, what about the capital accounts?

mentioned by western industrialists some decades ago when they were in the position of exporting more cars than they imported.

Actually, western arguments against Japan's trade imbalance may often be punctured by asking about the surpluses of other partners. When British opinion first began to be exercised in the 1970s about Japan's large surplus with Britain, it turned out that there were half-a-dozen other countries, including the US, West Germany, Holland, Canada and Saudi Arabia, which had even larger surpluses with the UK. If there was something wrong in running up a trade surplus of that size, why were these other countries not being criticized also? It became so clear that the whole thing was an exercise in uninformed racial prejudice that this particular argument lost a great deal of its force in the relatively fair mind of the British public.

It is still possible, however, to play upon the ignorance of people who have not thought much about economic matters, by talking about the 'unfairness' of Japan's buying less from Britain than Britain buys from Japan, as if this kind of exchange could have any moral meaning. British consumers ask for those Japanese goods (including cars) and pay good money for them: if any hidden additional price is being paid by way of lost British motorcar manufacturing jobs, then it has to be asked whether those jobs would really have been saved merely by excluding the Japanese competition, whether other jobs have become available to replace them, whether excluding Japanese consumer goods from the British market would allow Japan to continue importing goods from Britain, and so forth.

Trade and manufacturing are extremely complex operations, producing questions to which there is no simple answer and to which any one answer poses further consequential questions. But the climate of opinion in which this is discussed in the West is so murky that, when the President of the EEC Commission, Roy Jenkins, was asked at the end of the 1970s about Japan's trade surplus with the EEC, he revealed himself sublimely unaware that Austria, for example, ran an even bigger one with the Community. If a man of Jenkins' experience and stature could be so unbusinesslike, so ready to brand Japan before examining the context, one can forgive the Japanese for throwing up their hands. This is what is meant by saying that Japan is an easy target.

A recent report of the US Congress conceded that in strict economics a trade deficit may not be important, but added the qualification that 'this economic truth is a political falsity'. The French let the cat out of the bag by admitting that they tolerated larger trade deficits with the United States and Germany than with Japan, but they defended these as excusable for political reasons (America providing

NATO defence cover, and Germany being a major EEC partner), whereas Japan had no such political sweetener to throw in. Can we blame Japanese officials for referring to the EEC's trade deficit with America as 'a white man's deficit'?

Several of Japan's traditional industries were destroyed in the nineteenth century by the sudden influx of better goods from Europe. The Western powers insisted upon free trade then, when it suited their commercial interests, but in the 1930s, when Japan began to be competitive, it was suddenly no longer sacrosanct – and Japan was prevented from penetrating western markets as freely as the West had invaded hers. Japan also had a persistent trade deficit with the West for the first half-century of her Meiji modernization, but did not then complain publicly about these difficulties imposed on her development. All this history is now forgotten in the West.

So when, today, the West complains to the Japanese that they are working too hard, they hear it like the class dunce 'tearfully begging a bright student deliberately to do poorly in an examination'. Any artificial balancing of these bilateral trade exchanges would, of course, depress the Japanese standard of living. A MITI official has spelt out the way some Japanese would react to that. 'If the US and Europe do not trade with Japan, politics here would change. There would be no benefit to Japan to remain a member of the free world. If that happens, we would probably join the Communist bloc.' The *Yomiuri Shimbun* had suggested many years earlier that, if the West shut out Japanese goods, the government should cultivate 'firm economic ties with China'. It is all rhetoric, but it gives a measure of Japan's anger.

Yet another problem with the imbalance debate is defining the surplus: should it include the services trade, involving the so-called 'invisible' account? Japan is a very large net importer of services, especially in banking, investment income, insurance, royalties, tourism and all kinds of transportation, particularly from Britain and the United States. But no one can satisfactorily measure these transactions. They are not material goods which have to pass a physical frontier and be seen by customs officials. Statistics for the invisible account depend on voluntary declarations by those who provide and enjoy the services, and there is little incentive for them to be accurate, let alone honest. The City of London in particular is known to guard such figures most closely, to avoid its true income becoming widely known.

The Japanese invoke the invisible account to show that their surplus in the exchange of goods and services taken together is not as big as that on goods alone. But their measurement of the invisible figures turns out to be larger than the West's, because companies are better attuned to obeying government requests for information.

When the British argue about this, they say that most of the money coming from Japan on the invisible account is for immediate onward remittance to third countries, for investment or freight, only a tiny proportion being retained as a profit in the UK. That is true, but how else can the service trade between two countries be measured except by money 'crossing the frontier' into the other banking system? For the purposes of bilateral accounts between two countries, this catchment of gross receipts (not profits) is all that can matter, while what happens to the money immediately afterwards (or where it came from before leaving the remitting country) is irrelevant, something to be taken up in other sets of bilateral accounts and thus eventually in Britain's global multilateral account.

The ingenious Japanese rider to this is that, if all that money on invisible account is to be denied, then the same reasoning should apply to goods. When a Japanese car arrives at Southampton, instead of its being counted as a full £5,000 worth from Japan, a certain proportion should be attributed to Australia, where the iron ore came from, another amount to Malaysia for the rubber content, yet another for the plastic materials to Taiwan or Mexico, and so forth. Merely to say all that is to demonstrate the illogicality of the western arguments on this score. But the City of London is powerful, and has many friends.

The most extraordinary tangle into which Japanese and western officials have tumbled is the latter's charge that the ratio of manufactured goods in total Japanese imports, being only about half of the European or American ratio, is unacceptable. The EEC even lodged a formal complaint about this to the GATT in 1982. As the Japanese point out, the difference comes from Japan's lack of native raw materials and energy, and also because there is no interlocking system of industrialized countries immediately surrounding Japan comparable to the countries of Europe or to the economy of North America. Japan has formed the habit of manufacturing most items for herself. Nevertheless, European officials thankfully seize upon a complaint which sounds good for their home opinion. The low manufactures import ratio of Japan, they say, is 'unacceptable', 'abnormal', 'incomprehensible'.

The real cause of a trade surplus lies within each of the two economies, reflecting changes in relative competitiveness because of different wage levels, inflation, the state of the work ethic, management strategies, exchange rates and a host of other factors. Whether Japan is overloading the western free trade system by accumulating such large surpluses is a matter of opinion: little concern was expressed when similar things happened in the past with other leading economies, like America and Britain in their time. Japan must use the foreign exchange she accumulates, if not in imports then in the form of either aid or investment – some of it financing the US government's budget deficit! At worst, a little more of our planet will become Japanese-owned (starting from practically nothing), but it hardly lies in an Anglo-Saxon mouth to complain of that.

A typical Japanese-western argument would now turn to Japan's allegedly 'unfair' exporting practices. If goods are sold in a western market at less than a fair price, so that they appear subsidized, aggrieved domestic competitors can, of course, take action through the anti-dumping legislation enshrined in the GATT. It is difficult to succeed in this because it means establishing before a western tribunal what the Japanese domestic retail price is. Although a few cases of dumping have been established against Japanese manufacturers (electronic typewriters and hydraulic excavators in the EEC recently), there are many more that were not proved.

The real complaint is that Japan concentrates on a small number of products and floods western markets with them, instead of sending a wide variety of goods which would not have such disastrous effects on particular sectors of western manufacturers and workers. The overall trade balance may worry statisticians, but the so-called 'laser attack' exports in selected sectors arouse immediate fears in the particular industry concerned, typically in an electrical or engineering sector like television sets or motorcars.

When Sir Michael Edwardes was British Leyland Chairman, he spoke of Japan's exporting in such a way as to destroy entire industries in Europe, and many other western politicians, ambassadors and business leaders have deplored the 'torrential rains' of Japanese exports in what a British Chancellor once called a 'not acceptable pattern'. Japan's export revenues are indeed derived heavily (and unwisely) from a narrow range of politically vulnerable products like cars and ships and TV sets. We see at work here the 'bandwagon' factor which leads Japanese companies to emulate the first one to be successful in exporting a product to a foreign market, rather than find something different. Laser attacks in the West are thus part of a domestic war between Japanese competitors.

'We have a right to some industry too,' an American union leader cries. He is wrong, of course: a western community has a right to compete, but there is no God-given right to any particular way of earning a living in the world. So the affected industries issue alarmist figures of lost jobs. Ford told European politicians that the free inflow of Japanese cars would destroy 133,000 jobs in Europe in the first half of the 1980s. An American investigation in 1983 found half a million jobs – about 6% of the labour force – sacrificed to Japanese competition. British business leaders calculated that each Japanese car arriving in Europe lost a European worker three months' work, and the French said that every car imported from Japan put five Frenchmen out of work.

Dr Saburo Okita mildly points out that foreign trade represents about one-fifth of the GNP of the EEC, and Japan accounts for roughly 2% of that foreign trade, so that Japanese sales to the European market must equal less than half of one per cent of European GNP. It is hard to imagine that so small a factor could be an important source of unemployment. The real reason for job losses is the declining competitiveness of European industries, and that makes Europe vulnerable to all imports, not only from Japan – and can be remedied only by the Europeans reforming their industries and working harder.

The Europeans suggested at one point that a ceiling be put on Japan's share of their market in consumer durables – 10%, it was proposed, and that in fact was the level ultimately agreed for motorcars in the UK. But how would such a decision be fitted in with other trade relationships? There are many American, French and German products which take more than one-tenth of the British market: should they be restricted? And there are European products, such as whisky, which take more than one-tenth of the Japanese market. Do the Europeans expect Japan to restrict those, thus reducing the trade levels both ways?

The Japanese are not commercial fanatics, and they recognize a political current when they see one: indeed, they usually over-react. From the very beginning they have responded to western complaints by offering voluntarily to restrain their exports of the goods concerned, and they continued to do this even after gaining parity with the western nations in the GATT. These so-called Voluntary Export Restraints now cover a considerable proportion of Japan's overseas trade and, although at first sight they appear to meet the complaint by the importing country, they are still controversial. They satisfy the western producer by stabilizing the competition he faces from Japan, but they inconvenience the western consumer who has less choice and pays more.

As *The Economist* concluded, 'Trade restrictions against Japan have proved mainly to be a way of enabling the Japanese to charge more for their exports than they could otherwise have done.' Milton Friedman spelt it out to his fellow-Americans that, to restrict steel imports from Japan might save American steel jobs, but it would also make the car industry less competitive because it would have to pay more for its steel. Jobs saved in steel might well be lost in cars and other steel-using industries.

There are ample provisions under the GATT for a western country to restrict its imports against all comers if it has problems with balance of payments: even if a western government sought to justify a measure of that kind on some other ground such as loss of jobs, it would be understandable to the Japanese. But the key words are 'against all comers'. When western governments ask Japan to restrict sales, they discriminate by not asking other foreign suppliers to do the same.

Japan has had a long history of discrimination in the GATT. Many western countries refused to accord Japan equal treatment in the GATT in the 1950s, and even in the 1960s, when Britain finally signed a Treaty of Commerce with Japan, it was riddled with reservations based on Japan's image as a low-cost producer. The British dropped these discriminatory safeguards only on the understanding that they would be replaced by voluntary restraint on the part of Japan on many lines of product. But the insistence of some European countries on retaining the right to restrict Japanese goods unilaterally was the sticking point that prevented a trade treaty being negotiated between Japan and the EEC as late as the 1970s. The whole saga, a leading Japanese businessman told Europeans in 1982, was 'psychologically offensive to the Japanese, since it made Japan a second-class citizen in the world of international trade'.

The high point of the 'laser attack' dispute was the French restriction on video-tape recorders (of which Japan was the only supplier) in 1982. Rather than risk international censure by a formal exclusion, the French declared as an administrative 'convenience' that every video-recorder would have to be cleared by the customs at Poitiers, far inland from any port, unequipped to deal with large number of products, and full of emotional significance to the French. 'We are not the Saracens,' Hitachi was reduced to saying in a French media advertizing campaign.

The Japanese were newcomers to the world market in the 1950s, outsiders wanting to succeed at all costs. Few of them thought they would ever be able to sell a car in Britain or a television set in the United States, competing against what seemed then to be unassailable superiors. Once they did succeed, however, they were not inhibited from pushing their advantage for all it was worth, rather than invest in spreading their industrial capability across a wider base. This was understandable in the circumstances in which Japan found herself, and did not infringe any of the trade rules which the western powers had written (without consulting Japan) to govern the international exchange of goods. And the products which the Japanese found they could make competitively were precisely those which were beginning to slip from the grasp of western manufacturers, because of rising costs, structural changes and altered work habits at home.

The gripes about trade imbalance and laser attack exports might have been relegated to the business pages of the western press if a third and even less tractable problem had not been posed about the 'closed' nature of the Japanese market. For your main competitor to flood your market with his goods, and to cap that by refusing to buy even your best lines himself, was wounding to the most dispassionate western manufacturer.

The EEC representative in Japan has described her as 'import impervious', suffering from a 'self-sufficiency syndrome'. An important American enquiry concluded in 1981 that there was a 'societal' or 'cultural' indifference to imports. The notion that 'export is a virtue and import a vice' was dinned in so hard in Meiji Japan, and again in the early post-war years, that those who actually man the customs posts and small provincial offices still believe it. Even new Japanese manufacturers find it difficult to break into the charmed circle of established suppliers in the Japanese market.

People in the West think of Japan as a very large exporter, but then Japan is also a country with twice the population of Britain or France, and with a very large domestic economy where goods are made efficiently on a large scale and at relatively low cost for 120 million consumers. It surprises some western critics to learn that only 14% of Japan's GNP depends on her exports, whereas for most European countries the proportion would be in the 35% to 50% bracket. In terms of getting raw materials Japan must export or die, but in terms of money there is no such urgency.

Japan was heavily protected by import tariffs and quotas in the decades when her economy was developing in the nineteenth century and in the early part of this century. Protection continued into the post-war period but, under the pressure of her western partners, the tariff levels have gradually been reduced since 1973 to an average level of only 3%, hardly an impediment to trade and slightly lower than in Europe or America. It is no longer the import duty that stops western exports to Japan.

So the limelight shifts to the non-tariff barriers which the West finds scandalously prevalent in Japan. Customs officers have rigorous, rather literal habits of work dating from long ago which militate against imports; they used to reject pineapples whose labels bore no hyphen. The requirement of certificates and the myriad regulations applying to imports (mostly in Japanese, which to Westerners means an added cost) multiply the difficulties. The American Chamber of Commerce has produced an extended catalogue of complaints about all kinds of regulations covering health, hygiene, dimensions, ingredients, labelling and packaging – and even postal and visa red tape, all seeming to add unnecessarily to the burdens of bringing goods in.

The Ministry of Health found that an ingredient used in biscuits was dangerous. It banned it, but importers and agents of foreign suppliers were not told until the last minute. Inefficiency, or bias against imports? How long should foreign tenderers have to prepare to bid for projects in Japan, given the time consumed in translation? Should health certificates be required for directors of firms importing medical equipment into Japan (a Japanese journalist found it 'outrageous' when he discovered this 'barrier created by bureaucrats')? Should Perrier water be boiled before entering Japan? Which pharmaceuticals should be newly tested on Japanese humans, which ones should be brought in on proof of testing on Westerners, given the slight differences in metabolism? And should pharmaceuticals that are tested on guinea pigs be re-tested on Japanese guinea pigs, or should the western certification be accepted? These are some of the questions that have weighed down international officials in recent years (some of them now resolved in foreign suppliers' favour).

Some official Japanese specifications are unbelievably meticulous, reflecting the Confucian tradition of government looking after subjects in minute detail. There was an angry summer in 1982 when American baseball bats piled up on the Japanese docks because of requirements that the alloy would have to be changed, rubber plugs used and each shipment separately tested – which seemed a clear indication that no foreign bats would be permitted that season. An American shipping line was furious because its 9' 6" cube containers were not allowed on Japanese roads, the police having ruled that they were a foot too high for safety. Japan claimed that other countries in Europe made the same specification, and that the density of traffic on Japanese roads justified it. The Americans saw it as a charter for excluding imports, and Tokyo has now given in to them.

But some of the complaints merely lift a curtain on the soft life which many successful western exporters have lived for so long, like the British woolly manufacturer who indignantly reported his Japanese importer's request to cut two centimetres off the sleeve, something that had never happened to his firm before in any other market! How anyone could expect to sell to Japanese customers except by catering for their physical measurements is beyond belief.

The Japanese bristle at the idea that their own high standards of safety and hygiene should be diluted merely to accommodate foreigners, whether it be the high anti-pollution requirements for cars or the semi-perfectionist hygienic regulations for a nation of notoriously fault-finding consumers (shoppers are shy in specifying their requirements in the shops, but quick to complain after delivery). The Transport Ministry in Tokyo says reproachfully that it translated its car type approval regulations into English several years ago, but this was never reciprocated (a polite reminder that Japanese manufacturers won their way into European markets without such mollycoddling). All these regulation arguments usually have a cultural issue buried inside them. Americans familiar with the Japanese market will confirm that success in importing depends on how you deal with Japanese officials about these regulations and requirements, how you ask – and answer – questions; unnecessary difficulty can be created by cultural ignorance.

The same thing applies to the trade ombudsman appointed by Japan in response to repeated requests from the West, whose role is fatally impaired because companies in Japan do not like to make complaints against each other. Any foreign company with a future in Japan understands that complaining to such a third party would, like the use of a western-style legal institution, bring out the argument into the public eye and prejudice its future relationship with its partners in Japan.

The Japanese consumer would certainly like to buy foreign goods: most western products used to have star quality in the Japanese market, fetching a premium above local makes. 'We Japanese admire anything that belongs to foreign countries,' a Japanese *sake* brewer complains. 'It is not fashionable to like Japanese products.' Only in the past five years has disenchantment with western wares set in, mainly because of difficulty in getting spare parts. Perhaps a certain chauvinism takes advantage. When the Labour Minister bought a Chrysler Fifth Avenue limousine in compliance with recent Cabinet guidance about Ministers' buying imported cars for their official fleets, his comment after riding in it was: 'It's rather like meeting a bride chosen by your own parents. I prefer a Japanese wife, and the same goes for cars.'

These days potential buyers are put off by the high prices of imports, and by the fact that they are often difficult or unsuitable to use (because of their specifications, standards, sizes or inadequate after-sales service). Like consumers everywhere, the Japanese buy for quality, and also seek value for money, without particular reference to the country of origin. But standards are very high, encouraged by the exceptional competition between Japanese suppliers, so that a housewife would not buy a refrigerator with a paint scratch on it, even at the back. A beer fancier has 120 different variations of brand, size and type of container to choose from.

But if Japanese household consumers still look hopefully for the competitive western product in their High Street, the buyer of industrial equipment cannot afford such cosmopolitanism. Many of them buy their replacements from reliable and trusted local suppliers, sometimes within the same corporate group, from whom they can expect the very highest standard of service, and behaviour of the expected Japanese type. To go to a western supplier instead would invite all the hazards of fluctuating exchange rates, uncertainty about allocating the risk of loss at sea, additional insurance costs, doubtful after-sales service arrangements, doubtful readiness to re-supply immediately in the event of any found defect (even a slight one), and the likelihood of quarrels over the contract, translation snags and linguistic misunderstandings.

There is a general climate of opinion among business groups that it is unpatriotic to buy foreign machinery when Japanese is available, something going back to earlier days when protection was necessary. So western leaders call for Japan to abolish such cultural loyalty. National self-sufficiency is a deeply-rooted cultural habit, however; it was entirely appropriate to a stage of development which has passed only within living memory, and it may take a long time to respond to new circumstances (one could say the same of Luddism and class antagonism in British society).

For Japanese firms to buy habitually from sister companies strikes western competitors as unfair, but such intra-group deals are hard to expose or combat. Trading corporations often give special terms to wholesalers linked with them, and, other things being equal, one would obviously rather buy from a company in which one has an equity stake. Western officials talk darkly about 23,000 business associations which allegedly restrict imports, but actual proof is hard to come by and Japanese economists say that only about 10% of what the big companies buy in Japan is intra-group.

What really counts is that Japanese corporations, like Japanese consumers, are choosy and have become accustomed to very good terms. They like to buy equipment on a steady, secure and long-term basis, not changing suppliers every time in order to save a few dollars. Given the standards of Japanese factory organization, it is very important for them to minimize stock and thus have prompt deliveries, especially in emergencies – and that would almost rule out a foreign supplier unless he were ready to risk a large inventory on Japan's very expensive storage space.

For all these reasons, even Japanese businessmen concede that their market is not as open as Japanese think, because it is a closed society, in which human relations are stressed as well as intimate government links with business. Nevertheless, the government has done much in the past few years to disarm the criticisms. Many regulations have been rewritten, abolished, waived, translated or made easier to obey. Many testing, hygiene and safety requirements have been modified. In 1985, in response to American demands and consequent upon the Market-Oriented Sector-Selective (MOSS) talks, Prime Minister Nakasone in fact proposed over 250 changes in regulations to bring Japanese import procedures closer to western practice. The sectors affected included telecommunications, electronics, medical and pharmaceutical equipment, and wood products.

So the formal tariff and non-tariff barriers have largely gone, leaving western businessmen to contemplate a market which is tough and competitive for everybody, including the Japanese themselves, and where the real barriers are now commercial and cultural. MITI has called for a 'spiritual revolution' in importing manufactures, which is a pretty bare admission of how deep-rooted the conservatism has been until now. Foreigners have been appointed to some advisory committees to ensure that a degree of international input goes into decisions affecting Japan's trade, and that is a very big concession. In his 1985 Action Programme, Mr Nakasone even went so far as to propose cuts in tariffs in manufactured goods that would, by 1989, give Japan the most liberal tariff system in the world. Yielding to American pressure, his revealing comment on Japan's trade imbalance was, 'It's like winning every time you play a game of *mah-jong*. In the end no one will play with you.'

With many more wholesale and retail layers than are found in Europe, and goods being bought and sold about four times before reaching the shop, the complex distribution system has been compared to a ritual mating dance. Manufacturers woo their wholesalers like lovers, bringing gifts, doing favours, giving parties – and foreigners find all that difficult to emulate. Packaging has to be much more thorough than in the West and the result is a mark-up on goods which is quite unheard-of in most western countries. A bottle of Scotch whisky imported for *Yen* 400 is retailed in the High Street at *Yen* 3,000. Half of that mark-up goes to tax and special excise duty, the other half to distributors on the long journey from the port, via the sole agent, the general distributor, the appointed wholesaler, the secondary wholesaler and the retailer. The use of a sole agent increases these costs, but the whisky exporters apparently prefer a secure limited up-market trade to the risks of a mass market where their label would lose its prestige value.

In 1974 a young American, Steven Rempell, started import-ing foreign liquor and underselling the big established importers. Nothing illegal in that, but a few years later he was convicted of fraud and tax evasion and given a heavy fine and suspended prison sent-ence. The case revolved around the method of arriving at the 'real' price of the liquor. Rempell said he could get cheap supplies of brandy and whisky from abroad by obtaining rebates and exploiting foreign exchange rate fluctuations, but the court disbelieved him. The case was taken in the foreign business community as another sign that Japan was not going to open up seriously to western business prac-tices, and that anyone pioneering new cost-cutting methods would be felled by the power of the big companies out to perpetuate the *status quo*.

Many western companies do succeed in breaking into the Japanese market, some by linking themselves with a successful established Japanese firm, as Maxwell House has with Ajinomoto. Others started early in the post-war period, enduring years of preparation and hard slog, making friends, learning the language and absorbing the ways of the market. But for cars, for example, it is an almost impossible task to duplicate the sales networks, which each Japanese company already has, without investing more than any western motorcar manufacturer can afford.

The success stories include Rotaprint and Dale Electric of Britain, or Schick, Nescafé, Coca-Cola and Wella of the United States. In the motorcar market, BMW has done well, and Gadelius of Sweden sells many robots. But these companies make little contribution to the policy debate about Japanese trade. They have succeeded in getting through the maze of obstacles and regulations by their own unaided efforts; why should they help others to come in freely to share the pickings without having made the investment? It is the unsuccessful who complain.

Some compare the antiquated distribution network to that of France but, like France, Japan is slowly rationalizing, and there are more and more supermarkets to be seen. Political and adminis-trative pressure has slowed this process down, however, because of job losses in the small corner-shop which the supermarket replaces. Those little shops are a part of the Japanese welfare state in disguise, employing armies of the elderly. So there is a mixed distribution system which both Japanese and western manufacturers have to use, and which is not in itself anti-foreign.

It is left to western manufacturers to promote their sales to Japan more effectively and vigorously by the best means of their devising. Japan's very first encounter with the British was an eye-opener into inept European salesmanship. Will Adams*, the first Englishman in Japan, was saved from the shipwreck of a Dutch trader just off the Japanese coast in 1600. The ship was intended to take its cargo of woollens to Indonesia, the owners being unaware that the hot climate made them unsuitable. Market research is still a weak point in Europe.

Most western manufacturers have dozens of other markets nearer to hand than Japan, easier to serve and with stronger cultural and administrative connections. Britain, for example, is able to sell in Commonwealth and European countries with hardly any special preparation, and indeed Daimler has refused the urgent pleas of its Japanese agent for more supplies by explaining that it had to serve its home dealers first.

The Japanese market cannot be stormed on the cheap. The product itself must be right for the Japanese market, and Japanese officials are fond of pointing out that not a single American car has ever been sent to the Japanese market with the steering wheel on the right (a few Japanese motorists are ready for prestige reasons to buy a car with the steering wheel on the wrong side, but it is never going to make the mass market). For every western exporter's office in Japan, Japanese companies have six abroad, and for every western employee trying to sell goods to Japan, there are a dozen Japanese doing it abroad. Japan makes a bigger effort.

In any case, half the Westerners trying to sell in Japan have no Japanese language training, and 90% of them rely on English language newspapers. Distillers, the British liquor manufacturer, maintains no full-time representative in Japan, in spite of enjoying a £40 million-a-year turnover there. To make a comparison specifically with the United States, there are only a few hundred American businessmen living in Tokyo (a handful of whom speak passable Japanese), whereas there are several thousand Japanese businessmen in New York, and most of those speak reasonably good English. Of course, it costs at least £100,000 a year to maintain a representative in Tokyo, more than almost anywhere else.

There are two particular sectors of the Japanese market where western producers have encountered inordinate difficulty, though for quite different reasons. Japan's farmers are so inefficient that the

---

* Model for the hero in James Clavell's novel and television serial *Shogun*.

government has to protect them heavily. And in the case of motorcars there is the opposite problem that the Japanese product is too competitive. Both of these areas have generated lively controversy.

The farms in Japan are now worked by women, children and grandparents, the men of working age having long ago succumbed to the temptations of higher wages in the factories and towns. This is one reason for the poor productivity of Japanese agriculture: another is the hilly terrain which does not lend itself to either large-scale working or mechanization. So the government cushions the farmers, particularly the rice-farmers, by a system of purchasing their crops at a subsidized price, as well as restricting imports – rather as the United States and Europe do.

It is the Japanese consumer who pays, with food bills some 25% more than they need be. An urban family might save more than $2,500 a year if the import of beef and oranges were liberalized – better than a 7% wage increase. Beef is a story in itself, with an extraordinary system of scarcely-veiled monopoly and restrictive business practice ensuring that meat sells in a butcher's shop for five times its original price. That scandal has been exposed but never reformed. Whenever the consumer lobby beats the drum for import liberalization, the farmers shout back. Organized into a powerful union, they recently boycotted Sony products because that corporation came out strongly against agricultural protection.

The farmers can be confident because Japan, despite the Supreme Court's ruling it illegal, is still living with political constituencies drawn up in the early post-war period, before the spectacular development of industry and cities, so that rural residents have disproportionate voting power. Some experts believe that as many as 200 seats in the Diet are vulnerable to the 'agricultural vote'. A more conservative figure is 80, still enough to sway the legislature. Individual leaders can even be at risk on particular commodities, the constituencies of Foreign Minister Shintaro Abe and former Foreign Minister Kiichi Miyazawa being heavy citrus-growing areas, for example.

But would the farmer actually vote against the Liberal-Democrats if they were to back down on agricultural protection? Most farmers are firmly opposed to socialism or Communism and would probably go on voting Liberal-Democrat on other matters, even if they opposed it on the agricultural protection issue. If the featherbedding of farmers stopped, the result would probably be more Independents in the Diet inclined to vote Liberal-Democrat on the majority of issues. And the ruling party would gain urban votes by bringing the prices of food down.

But allowing free imports of foodstuffs rouses deep passions in Japan. 'The American farmers won't take their clothes off, yet they want us to go naked,' is a typical comment. Actually, the experience with apples and cherries, whose imports have already been liberalized, suggests that Japanese farmers are not as helpless as they paint themselves. The apple-growers switched to a species of better quality when foreign apples started coming in, and kept a place in the market.

But emotional arguments are used to preserve the *status quo*. People still remember the food shortages of the 1940s, and the idea of not having domestic production in the event of a future emergency frightens them. As recently as the 1970s, the Americans embargoed their soya bean exports (on which Japan depends), as well as grain exports to other markets, so that people in Japan do not feel fully secure about foreign supplies. The country is only one-third self-sufficient in grains, and about 70% in farm products as a whole. To allow western foodstuffs in freely would make Japan a colony of the United States, says one prefectural governor, neatly reversing the US paranoia on the same subject. Meanwhile, the arguments with American citrus and cattle farmers have been temporarily stifled by a Japanese commitment to double imports of beef and citrus fruits over the four years ending 1988.

But the really emotive issue is that symbol of virility, the motorcar. It took a long time for the Japanese manufacturers to get a foothold in western markets. Their first dealers in Sweden twenty years ago went bankrupt, but then in some countries like Britain they had the good luck to inherit dealer networks made available by the merger of domestic manufacturers. Once in, it was plain sailing, since these were cars that cost less to make than European or American cars – initially because of lower wages, among other things, but increasingly because of more efficient production on a larger and larger scale.

As wage costs have risen in Japan over the European level, robots and automation have enabled the labour content of the price to be brought down to perhaps a quarter of the American level. In any case, Japanese makers have always gone all out to seduce customers on those small matters of accessory and comfort which mean so much to a motorist. Western consumers have found Japanese cars on the whole to be more economical, more reliable and more fun than their competitors. Yet it could hardly be said at the height of Japan's success that the Japanese runabout was nosing its rivals off the road. True, Japan's production soared from less than 10% of the cars made by the 'big six' (US, Britain, Germany, France, Italy and Japan) in 1965 to almost 40% in 1980. Japan was also responsible for one in five

cars exported by the end of the 1970s, but that was roughly comparable to the West German performance, and only half the level of the
EEC as a whole. Toyota is still only the world's third biggest car
maker, Nissan the fifth.

The American and European makers began to scream when Japan
established parity in motorcar exports in such a short space of time. In
France a car dealer was expelled from his Rotary Club because he
took a Japanese agency, so he dropped it. Detroit came out in a rash
of 'No Japanese' signs in car parks, and Japanese cars were systematically damaged for a time – some of them with baseball bats of the kind
turned away from Japanese ports for infringing the Japanese requirements. In 1980 there was a 'Real Americans Buy American Cars'
movement. Because of the rate of increase in Japanese exports, the
western manufacturers, all of them in trouble for one reason or
another, felt threatened and actively lobbied for government help.

Britain in the mid-1970s and the US in 1981 opted for voluntary
Japanese restraint, which the Japanese offered in spite of the fact, in
the American case, that the International Trade Commission formally judged the decline of American car-making as not in fact due to
import competition. The Japanese manufacturers slated this decision
by their government, branding the official responsible, Naohiro
Amaya, as a 'concubine' of the United States, but Amaya warned
them that the motorcar was the regimental colour bearer of American
industry and needed special sympathy. Besides, he reminded Nissan
and the others, Uncle Sam had given the Japanese industry a valuable
ten year respite after Japan joined the GATT in the 1950s by not
objecting to Japanese protection of their own car industry. That was a
debt that had to be paid. Japanese cars once had a handicap, so they
should be generous now that they were in the top league – it was
only fair! In this mood was the car trade problem discussed.

Again, it was the consumer – in this case the western consumer –
who paid. The first year of restraint in the US market added $1 billion
to the prices paid on Japanese cars, which now attracted a scarcity
premium. With Japanese cars less cheap, American models could sell
for more and, if those price increases are included, the cost of
restraint could be quadrupled. In terms of the expense of getting each
American car worker back into his job again, it did seem exorbitant.
An editorial in the *Los Angeles Times* in 1984 declared that Japanese
car quotas had proved 'a sham and an economic rip-off of consumers'.

Japanese restraint cannot stop Westerners from buying cars, it just
makes them buy other cars. French, German and other continental
European makers were the beneficiaries of Japanese restraint in the
British and American markets. The British Trade Secretary eventu-

ally conceded that the Japanese restraint was pointless when British carmakers could not supply enough cars to fill the gap. And there were vexed questions about alleged evasion of the restraint through third countries, for example Australian-made Mitsubishi cars coming in to Britain over and above the quotas from Japan. A British manufacturer said of this possibility: 'We cannot allow our market to lie back and be raped' (the metaphor was naughty since no one is forced to buy Japanese cars: he would do better to put time into improving his own product's attractiveness and technique).

The metaphors of regimental colours and raped women become more intelligible when one looks at the other side of the problem, the failure of western motorcars to sell in the Japanese market. Japan has tougher anti-pollution requirements than western countries, and no western factory has ever made a car specifically designed for Japan, with the steering wheel on the right side and the anti-pollution measures all in place.

Adapting cars after they arrive in Japan is expensive. It is not economical to make fully adapted cars for a distant market where the volume is small, and yet the volume will never get bigger until those adaptations become cheap. And so we have the same sad tale as the joint of beef and the bottle of Scotch: a western car landing in Japan with a price-tag of $4,000 sells in the High Street showroom for $15,000 after adding sometimes extensive remodelling and adaptation costs, and dealer's margins. Yet foreign cars are liked and wanted in Japan: the gangster bosses (*yakuza*) insist on them.

The British ought to make a killing in Japan because their steering wheel is already on the right side, but British Motors and its predecessors never undertook the very large investment needed for sustained and systematic promotion in Japan. It used to have a Chinese agent in Tokyo, following the semi-colonial pattern of pre-war trade, which was hardly a tactful approach, and it has never been able to guarantee the regularity of supply needed in the Japanese market. The attitude of many western manufacturers is that they are doing their agent a favour by sending him a few cars. When Mitsui gallantly agreed to import 200,000 British Leyland cars to help narrow the trade gap, they could not at first be shipped because of strikes in the UK, and Mitsui eventually pulled out because of inadequate supplies of both cars and spare parts.

The prejudice and racism of the car trade arguments both ways was disturbing. The serious press tried to hammer the important points home. Free trade, said the *Financial Times*, was 'consistent with an unstoppable trend towards inter-dependence between the economies of the world. It allows the European consumer to be the judge of what he wants to buy. It makes European manufacturers face up today to changes which will still be necessary, but more painful, tomorrow.' An economist tells the British public that it should import cars in the same way that it imports food, on the basis of comparative advantage: if it restricted them, 'we will simply be importing high-priced cars where we could import low-priced cars'.

The Japanese car industry itself knows it is unlikely to retain its competitiveness as new materials, new electronic developments and the lower-wage newly industrializing countries take over. Indeed, some Japanese were surprised that, at a time when their own car-makers were actively planning diversification into aviation and space, Mrs Margaret Thatcher so conspicuously sought their help in setting up a conventional car plant in northern England. It made them feel more forward-looking than the Europeans.

Gradually, the very high standards of Japanese products will settle down, first to high and then to average standards, as the Japanese industrial revolution passes its peak with the rising sun at noon. As the *yen* inexorably appreciates in value, Japan's exports will decline and her imports grow. By then, western manufacturers will have turned their attention to 'unfair' competition from Korea, Taiwan, Southeast Asia, Latin America – even India and China. At least the Japanese export restraints will have given western opinion time to analyse the dilemma more clearly.

14

Betting on the Anglo-Saxons
Japan and the West

THE LATE Prime Minister, Masayoshi Ohira, once remarked, 'We have points, but no broad surfaces of contact with the rest of the world.' Japan's insularity and cultural distancing have slowed down her engagement with foreign powers, making it appear sometimes tentative and ambiguous. So rich in potential misunderstanding are her international relations – and not only concerning trade in beef and cars – that Japanese intellectuals talk about Japan and the West as 'passing each other in opposite directions'. A Japanese abroad finds fewer echoes of his own cultural tradition in other people's life-styles than Europeans do. He travels the planet, like A. E. Housman:

> A stranger and afraid
> In a world I never made.

Even in the vast domain where Chinese civilization has touched, he senses himself as hailing from a peripheral provincial outpost.

It is easy for him to see his country as an orphan at the world's edge, perennially excluded from the inner circles of power. Japan may control one-tenth of the world's income, but is not one of the insiders in world economic management. Such systematic exclusion is as psychologically unsettling now as it was in the 1890s or 1920s. A Japanese anthropologist wonders morbidly whether all these failures to gain appropriate status should be attributed to 'a flaw in the national character', or perhaps a 'structural defect in Japanese civilization'.

Although it is 130 years since Japan came out of her centuries of seclusion, there is still a sense of being new to the outside world, an intense curiosity that resulted in enormous sales of books about the West and of translations from western literature. Now the novelty is wearing off. Some of the more romantic ideas about the West have collapsed on closer acquaintance. In any case the interest in the printed word or moving picture of the West was a kind of voyeurism which most Japanese were too shy to extend into personal encounters. Japanese tourists still comb the world at an average rate of 12,000 a day, but in self-contained groups which avoid personal contact with foreigners, and thus preclude experiences of genuine cultural interchange.

A poll in the 1970s showed that only 3 people in 100 had actually spoken to a foreigner, whether in Japan or while travelling abroad. Even the half a million businessmen and their families who live overseas have a reputation for keeping their own company, not mixing with natives. In the past five years or so far more Japanese students have gone for full training abroad, and more foreign students (and young foreign teachers) have gone to Japan, and that will herald a deeper mutual acquaintance in the longer run.

Meanwhile Japanese who go abroad, even intellectuals who ought to be receptive, can return home more chauvinistic than when they set out. 'The longer one stays abroad,' the Chairman of the Japan Socialist Party, Masashi Ishibashi, once reminisced about his own travels, 'the greater one's love of Japan grows until one begins to believe that Japan is the best country in the world . . . Sometimes I would become nostalgic for Japanese food like *sushi* or a bowl of rice with tea poured into it; at other times I would proudly recall Japan's landscape and climate, the kindness of the people and their high level of education.'

Would-be seekers after foreign truth are further deflected by the so-called 're-entry' problem. Going to school abroad may equip a child with a foreign language, but also punishes him by retarding his Japanese – which calls for special training, constant practice and long hours. The 50,000 Japanese children of school age who live outside Japan cannot progress in their own language in the informal way that Europeans or others can. Written Japanese is too difficult for parents to teach on an amateur basis. Prudent youngsters attend one of the extremely expensive special schools around the world that teach the Japanese language, even though it means, taken together with the other syllabus, that there is little time to mix socially with their contemporaries in their host country. The alternative is to return to Japan two or three years behind in Japanese language, to fail in university entrance and to 'say goodbye to Tokyo University', as parents tearfully put it.

Some unfortunate teenagers come home to find themselves 'bi-cultural outsiders'. One nineteen-year-old, mocked by his aunt for his poor Japanese after living abroad, became so enraged that he killed her. A desperate parent wrote to the press about her daughter, who had been raised mainly in England: 'We came back to Japan and, after two years of unhappiness for her, we sent her back to England to stay with friends. She didn't belong in Japanese society.'

It is not unusual for Westerners visiting a Japanese friend in Japan with a western degree to be asked anxiously beforehand not to go to his office, because the man would not want his colleagues to be reminded of his foreign links. Such a man might well be exceptionally careful in his own environment not to use foreign words or foreign dress (no coloured shirts or fancy ties) and not to talk about his happy days abroad. This is a standard re-assimilation strategy for returned students who would otherwise find it difficult to gain acceptance. People influenced by three years at Oxford or Berkeley are instantly recognized by their stay-at-home colleagues as pushy, talkative smart alecs, or restless weirdoes. A banker observed on returning home from several years abroad: 'To be popular with foreigners is the kiss of death in Japan.'

All Japanese are acutely afraid of becoming internationalized – unless they burn their boats and emigrate. A teacher at a New York school has noted how Japanese children arriving from Japan become, under the influence of their new American friends, more open, more self-aware and outspoken – qualities which will render them suspect after they return home. Even a Prime Minister will conceal his fluency in English in case he is branded with the general contempt which the Japanese majority shows for such linguists – reflecting the common belief that, if you learn English too well, you might lose your command of the Japanese language – and thus your identity as a Japanese.

It is said that the Japanese are poor at languages, particularly English because of its wayward spelling and grammar. An English dictionary is often found at the scene of a suicide, and grown men complain that trying to learn English makes them neurotic. Only three hours a week are normally allotted to English in the schools, and there are said to be only two Japanese alive who have completely mastered the language. But then one could equally well say that there are only a handful of foreigners who have mastered Japanese to the point of being indistinguishable from a native. Most Westerners stationed in Japan for a few years feel themselves discouraged from learning Japanese because of the near certainty that they will not be able to use it anywhere else afterwards. There are few languages less useful outside the country of origin. As Professor Joseph Yamagiwa defines it, Japanese is 'a minor language in a world dominated first by Chinese and then by English'.

With all these flaws in the lens, it is only to be expected that Japan's view of the West is distorted. The Japanese do, of course, admire many basic qualities of western life. That admiration began in the sixteenth century when mutual contact was first established, and reached exaggerated heights during the two centuries of seclusion.

The influential thinker Toshiaki Honda wrote this (at second hand) about London Bridge 200 years ago:

> The magnificence of the stone embankment along the river and of the construction of the bridge itself is such that one doubts if it were accomplished by mere human labour. When it comes to grand edifices, no country in the world can approach England. There is also no country comparable to England in the manufacture of very delicate things. [In London and Paris, he went on,] live people who are virtually without peers in the world, the handsomest of men. The houses in their towns and cities, even in the outskirts, are built of stone. They are from two to five storeys high and surpassingly beautiful.

There was much more in the same vein, so that when in the 1860s the Japanese began to go to see for themselves, they found Europe inspiring in its institutions, but not as physically attractive as had been painted. 'I have no liking for England,' the novelist Soseki Natsume confessed soon after the turn of the century. 'But I must be honest; whether I like the country or not, I do not think there is a place in the world so free or so orderly.' A Japanese builder recently came back from visiting the West full of enthusiasm: 'People talk about the British disease . . . but it clearly wasn't always like that. Look at the care that went into the building of those old Victorian houses in London, or the riveting of those big iron bridges they used to build in the US. Even in Japan we don't see craftsmanship like that.'

This experience of sudden exposure to the West, through long-distance binoculars, at the height of its technological advance, and finding that Japan needed a century of devoted imitation to catch up, has left the Japanese with a pronounced sense of inferiority. A Korean writer in Japan declares that what she least likes about the Japanese is their blind admiration for anything western, running to a kind of masochism.

Yet the Japanese are also alienated by western culture. 'They respect and envy western culture,' says Professor Eiichiro Ishida, the Vienna-trained anthropologist, 'for its indomitable will to live and its fierce affirmation of human existence, yet in the end the pace proves too much for them, or they react against the unrelentingness . . . of western culture and come to seek spiritual relief in an 'Oriental' tranquillity. In the European's frantic pursuit of life, on the other hand, one senses an almost terrifying thoroughness.' Japanese novelists have made much of the lonely shallowness of western life, especially American.

When the first official Japanese delegation went to the West in

1860, it described the Americans as big-hearted, honest and faithful. 'Englishmen, by contrast,' it reported, 'are jealous, ill-natured, perfidious and at times discourteous.' The British still attract waspish comments. A Japanese diplomat went into print a few years ago with the observation that, 'Once in a while the British can be brazenly selfish.'

Britain casts a hypnotic spell over Japan, however, being in so many respects the model she has tried to follow as a modern island nation with a distinctive culture, and that influence reached its zenith in the early years of this century when the two countries were in formal alliance. The feeling of inferiority towards Britain began to evaporate only when Japan's economic miracle brought the living standards of the two countries on a par in the 1970s. Now Britain is referred to as the original source of the dreaded 'British disease' of economic inefficiency and social irresponsibility – more graphically as *shayo*, the land of the setting sun.

The West was coloured in Japanese eyes by its open discrimination against the Japanese in the century following Perry's black ships. 'What Japan confronted as a late-comer on the stage of world history, at the height of the nineteenth century war for colonial acquisition, was a ruthless hazing like the breaking of a wild animal in a circus.' That is how Professor Keiichiro Kobori describes the scene a hundred years ago where Japan met mounting animosity in her attempt to raise herself to parity with the European countries. 'The hostility that was directed against Japan,' Kobori goes on, 'contained not the slightest respect, instead there were only contempt and hatred . . . The reason can be found in racism.'

The bitterness remains embedded in the insulated Japanese memory. A Japanese writer caustically explained only a couple of years ago how white people 'lay out the world with God on top, the chosen people next, then other sects, pagans, yellow-coloured peoples and livestock.' There is a predisposition to over-sensitivity. Eighty years ago, Arthur Diosy diagnosed in the Japanese a 'morbid hypersensitiveness, the consequence of centuries of insular seclusion, to such a degree that they resent honest foreign criticism, however gently administered, as an insult to their race.' A more recent observer, Professor G. C. Allen of London University, begged his Japanese colleagues not to take foreign criticisms, which were often the product of envy, at face value.

But what the West did to Japan in the early part of this century was no fancied slight. The Anglo-Saxons not only refused to admit Japan to their club of conquerors, they slammed the door against Japanese immigrants. Finally, after signing her alliance with Britain and faithfully helping the Anglo-Saxons in the First World War, Japan found her new friends relegating her in the 1920s to a diminished naval role in the world. These were the provocations that led to Pearl Harbor.

The Japanese had to endure showers of insults in the years of their emergence. Even Westerners today find the invective of their grand-fathers embarrassing, from Pierre Loti's 'little yellow monkeys' to the cruelly insensitive verse of Ogden Nash:

> How courteous is the Japanese!
> He always says, 'Excuse it, please.'
> He climbs into his neighbour's garden,
> And smiles, and says, 'I beg your pardon';
> He bows and grins a friendly grin,
> And calls his hungry family in;
> He grins, and bows a friendly bow;
> 'So sorry, this my garden now.'

To which one is tempted to respond:

> How odious is the Yankee bard,
> Blind to events in his own backyard . . .

There were counter-currents. A Japanese man of letters wrote back from the West excitedly in the 1870s to report that, far from being under the spell of profits and utility, western people were actually as passionate as Japanese. The way the Japanese translated English literature supported the point. There were two renditions into Japanese of *Romeo and Juliet* in the 1880s, for instance, one called *Spring Passion: Dream of the Floating World*, another, more down-to-earth entitled *Western Girl's Handbook*.

But we had to wait until the 1970s for the first fully realized western character in Japanese fiction, a lovable French teacher called Father Mockinpott, whose unwitting involvements with *pachinko* halls, striptease and women's panties were affectionately satirized in a best-seller by the popular novelist Hisashi Inoue.

Much of today's emotions are explained by the necessary status of Japan in most of modern history as a pupil of the West. This could be said to have begun one April day in 1771 when a Japanese doctor, who had read a Dutch anatomy manual, attended the dissection of an executed woman criminal, and found that the lungs, kidneys and intestines matched the Dutch descriptions rather than those of the traditional Chinese textbooks. 'We . . . came to realise what wrong ideas we had been fettered to for many long years in the past.'

One of the Japanese sages of the nineteenth century gracefully acknowledged the debt by saying that it was one of the five pleasures of a gentleman 'that he is born after the opening of the vistas of science by the Westerners, and can therefore understand principles not known to the sages and wise men of old'. Nor was the borrowing confined to the sciences. There were twenty-three impressions of one outstanding annotated translation of *Hamlet* in only sixteen years. The novelist Ogai Mori said of his student days in Germany at the end of the nineteenth century that he had reacted to everything around him 'with the sensibilities of a young virgin'. There was, indeed, an element of calf love in the youthful enthusiasm of young Japanese intellectuals for western modes – not always sustained in later life after return to Japan. One hero in Japanese fiction called his son Eeyore in honour of *Winnie the Pooh*.

During the Second World War, anti-western feelings became stridently orchestrated and a little of that persisted into the post-war era. Tadao Umesao argued savagely in a newspaper article in 1967 that Europe had become bankrupt, an exotic attraction for tourists, the hare which stopped for a nap while the Japanese tortoise overtook it – though a hare which could still grow fat on nourishment plundered from former colonies. Resentment is fortified by the knowledge that Japan did not depend upon the West for her modernization. Research shows that Japan actually pursued a parallel path to modernity, rather than following behind Europe at every step: that the prerequisites for modernity had been constructed before the Meiji Restoration of 1868.

Under the *shoguns* of the eighteenth and early nineteenth centuries, Japan was already goal-oriented, and the economy was open to competitive individual enterprise with little government intervention, benefiting from the diversity of feudal divisions as well as from a surprisingly good banking system. Economically, Japan at the time of Napoleon resembled Europe more than China or India. She had only to cast off the superficial garb of feudalism, to 'change her costume, not her soul', as John Randolph put it, and she was ready for modernity. Even the living standards of 1800 may have been higher than Europe's or America's. Japan owed nothing substantial to the West.

The event which overshadowed all earlier western influences was, of course, the American Occupation of 1945–52. There were many scholars ready to pronounce the judgement, once the Americans had gone home, that the experience had destroyed the Japanese soul and left behind only superficial reforms. The sense of national impotence was graphically caught by the film *Black Snow* in which a literally impotent Japanese, who brings a loaded gun into play when his own weapon fails in love-making, shoots some GI's.

Yet the Occupation was surprisingly free of trouble or resistance. Asked his estimation of MacArthur, a farmer told an American researcher that 'the Emperor could not have chosen a better man'. Indeed, the American commander was lionized as a 'blue-eyed *shogun*'. The somewhat left-wing Rooseveltian New-Dealers who ran Occupation policy intended to bury the vestiges of feudalism and unlock power for the common man. But it made no lasting impact to have American soldiers, for example, force Japanese men on the subway trains to give up their seats to women. The real impact of the American stewardship was to pre-empt socialist revolution through a land reform which, paradoxically, created a conservative rural stronghold from which the Liberal Democrats have ruled ever since. However the Japanese may argue over the merits and demerits of the US Occupation, they accept that it was humane and well-intentioned, and not merely a pursuit of short-term US interests.

That gave Japan in the subsequent years the confidence to deal with the US as a special ally. According to most post-war polls, America is the country that the Japanese like best. The problem is that the Americans have usually put Japan rather low down the list of countries which *they* like. This may be changing: a 1984 Gallup poll ranked Japan sixth in this regard, after the other Anglo-Saxon-Scandinavian countries traditionally favoured. In American terms, that is impressive, because it promotes Japan in front of Germany, France, Italy and China in American eyes. But Japan is still far from the number one place which the US has in Japanese hearts. It is, a Japanese analyst laments, a 'one-sided love affair'.

In one respect the balance is improving. The Japanese can indulge the luxury of feeling sorry for the Americans and trying to find ways of helping their former benefactors. One of Japan's veteran industrial managers, who had introduced quality control from the US very early on, recently formed an 'Association to Rescue the US', later tactfully re-named 'Association to Encourage the US'. A small manufacturer calls for an enquiry into why the high creativity and productivity of the West was lost. The same psychology informs Dr Saburo Okita's defence of Japan's new superiority on the grounds that it stimulates western industries to perform better and so helps to save western democracy from disaster. Japan is holding the front line in the world economy.

Yet Japan expects at the crunch to give in to the economic demands of her powerful yet unpredictable patron. It is still remembered how the 'junior partner' was given only ten minutes' warning by President Nixon of his measures to defend the dollar, and only three minutes' warning of his *volte-face* in China policy, in 1971 – because of the notorious inability of Japanese politicians to keep their mouths shut about such matters.

One way of claiming a voice in a club is to pay the dues. All through the 1960s and 1970s, Japan was belaboured for parsimony in paying her membership fee for the western 'club', defined by some founders as devoting roughly 4% of GNP to foreign aid and defence. Many Japanese agree that their country is 'outstandingly stingy' in giving only about a third of the ratio of GNP which other western countries allot to these international duties. Only in the last two or three years has Japan begun to increase its aid substantially to countries politically important to the western alliance. Only recently has the Japanese government shown serious signs of increasing the defence share of its budget.

Ironically, it was an American book, Ezra Vogel's *Japan As Number One*, that lowered the curtain on the teacher-pupil relationship, putting an analytical structure to the various ways in which enterprises, governments and individuals in America and Europe were beginning consciously to emulate Japanese models in order to improve their own societies.

During the post-war years the Japanese had to stand behind insensitive American policies towards China, Korea and Vietnam, often against their own instincts: their attitude to the US alliance has become more mature. There are only two policy areas where Japan dissents from American leadership, and both reflect Japan's different geopolitical needs. The first reservation concerns the Soviet Union with which Japan, like Europe, would prefer a stable to a combative relationship. The second unease arises from Japan's strong sense of interdependence with the Third World, cultural affinities and commercial ties outweighing the ideology which the Americans invoke.

A candid Japanese diplomat recently explained to the public that, 'for possibly the next thirty years we have no choice but to place our bets with the Anglo-Saxon world'. Nakasone has always agreed, but when he supported the NATO heads of government on security questions at the Williamsburg Summit in 1983, the *Asahi Shimbun* denounced his action as 'inexcusable'. Other newspapers supported him, however, and he did not suffer electorally for his forwardness.

Zbigniew Brzezinski pictured America as 'Japan's roof against rain and . . . window on the world.' It is unthinkable that the US-Japan alliance should break up in the foreseeable future. Japan has nowhere else to go and, whereas earlier the United States might conceivably have toyed with abandoning Japan, that country is now an essential link in America's plans for Pacific Basin development – so much so that the Japanese have more bargaining power than they perhaps realize. The two countries are beginning to know each other better, and their exchanges continue to grow. Only when the American taxpayer feels he can no longer afford to keep all those troops on Japanese soil will there be serious problems, and even those could be deflected by larger financial contributions from the Japanese side.

By no stretch of the imagination can it be said that Japan needs Europe in the way she needs the United States. She also respects Europe less. Dealing with Europe, a Japanese official once suggested, was 'like playing golf with a man whose handicap is twenty-five, but who does not realize he is so bad'. Western Europe's post-war policies of welfare and full employment, which weakened the will to work and reduced incentives for industrial investment, are seen as visibly bankrupt. Most Japanese see little more to learn from countries seeking defensively to preserve what they have, mistrustful of the wider global future.

What the Japanese still admire about Europe is its flexibility and sophistication, and also its skill in making the fullest use of historical assets. There are important common concerns with Europe, including security of oil supplies from the Middle East, the taming of the dollar, and giving minimal satisfaction to both the Third World and the Soviet Union in order to keep the world system running smoothly. The fascination of Europe for Japan is that it offers a lead in how to preserve the western system without constant kow-towing to Washington – and with the collaboration of Africa, the Middle East and Southeast Asia. In this respect at least, the European connection is still important for Japan.

In 1973 the Japanese saw one of their great wishes fulfilled in the launching of the Trilateral Commission where, for the first time, high-level figures from the US, Europe and Japan meet frequently for discussion of world affairs. It was the first recognition of Japan as a more or less equal partner in a triangular structure with America and Europe, but its impact on western opinion proved disappointing. The Japanese continue to feel that they are being left out of the 'inner core' of western leadership comprising the US, Britain, France and Germany. This was distressingly confirmed at Guadeloupe where senior Ministers of that 'white' American-European 'inner club' met to discuss world affairs, to the exclusion of Japan, in early 1979. Later that year, the same countries concerted their views on the Soviet invasion of Afghanistan, in Japan's absence, and rubbed salt into the wound by holding a breakfast discussion without Japan at the Tokyo Summit – on Japanese soil!

Australia and New Zealand are crucial for Japan, both as markets and as sources of supply for minerals and foodstuffs. There is a direct community of security interest, and Prime Minister Hayato Ikeda was the first non-Anglo-Saxon Prime Minister from another country to sit in on an Australian Cabinet meeting. Australia is Japan's third largest trading partner, and boasts the largest proportionate number of students learning the Japanese language per head of population. Yet both sides are uneasily aware that, if Japan had not voluntarily secluded herself for the two centuries of Pacific settlement, not only Australia and New Zealand, but also Malaysia and other areas might today be under the Rising Sun.

It was the Russians, not the West Europeans, who first disturbed Japan's self-quarantine from the world 200 years ago, and some would trace the present apprehension about the Soviet Union to that date. The relationship is a strange one in that Japan and Russia stand back to back with each other, the Soviet Union facing westwards from Moscow, Japan facing eastwards from Tokyo. Yet they are very close neighbours, by water, if not by land. From time to time, the big Japanese corporations have become involved in development schemes in Siberia, offering to provide knowhow and money for the unlocking of resources to which they could have access. But such proposals have usually foundered on political difficulties, the Japanese government not wishing to upset China and the Russians being reluctant in the end to throw Siberia open to international inspection.

And Japan's most important territorial dispute prevents any real improvement in relations with the Soviet Union. If you look through the telescope of the Nosappu Lighthouse on the most easterly point of Hokkaido, Japan's northernmost major island, you can actually see Russian soldiers at their monitoring post on one of the tiny islands to the north. When the Russians joined the war against Japan for the few days between Hiroshima and V-J Day, they seized the opportunity to occupy the four small islands of Shikotan, Habomai, Kunashiri and Etorofu, all of which had been under Japanese control. The tiny population of Japanese fishermen was shipped to Hokkaido, and there the matter has stood for forty years. The islands do not add up to more than 2,000 square miles, no larger then the Balearic Islands off Spain, but they control vital seaways into the Pacific Ocean.

Almost everybody agrees that the first two of the four islands could belong only to Japan, being so close to Hokkaido (only 2½ miles in one case) and forming an extension of small peninsulas on Hokkaido's coast. Khrushchev once hinted that they might be returned. But the other two islands are geographically a part of the

Kurile chain and there is a good natural argument for Soviet sovereignty were it not for earlier Russian recognitions of Japanese
possession going back as far as the 1850s. The Russians are unlikely to
give up because they need control of their submarine exit from the
Sea of Japan, while the theoretical validity of some of their European
expansion in the 1940s could be called in question by any concession
to Japan.

Japan seems fated to meet roadblocks in its pursuit of a just place in
the world. It was initially excluded from the United Nations by virtue
of being a wartime loser, but lately it has been trying to secure a status
matching its acknowledged rôle as the second biggest financial con-
tributor (after the United States) to the UN budget. No big power will
back Japan for a new permanent seat in the Security Council because
that would open up claims from such Third World states as India,
Brazil, Nigeria and Egypt. At one point, the Japanese unwisely
pressed their claim in tandem with West Germany, which particularly
incensed the Third World.

Japan is thus reduced to pleading with the UN membership every
few years for election to one of the rotating Security Council seats,
going cap in hand to beg the vote of small countries with insignificant
populations or GNP. Recently, Japan was defeated by Bangladesh
for the Security Council seat she sought. Even if she had won that
vote, she would have remained in an inferior position to countries like
Britain and France whose eminence was not disputed in 1945 but is
now doubtful. A permanent member of the Security Council enjoys
automatic privileges in other UN bodies like ECOSOC.

A Japanese Cabinet Minister ridiculed the UN in the 1970s as like
'a rural credit association in which a person can become a member for
only Yen 10,000 and gain a right to elect its directors'. He singled out
the very small countries for particular vituperation – 'the Maldives is a
terrible country – it is a kind of aborigines' nation. But it has one
vote.' In the uproar that followed, this Minister was dismissed, but he
had only voiced what was in the mind of almost all his countrymen. To
compound the difficulty, Japan does not provide its share of personnel to work in the United Nations Organization, taking up only a half
of its quota and only 1% of the senior positions. This is because of the
difficulty which Japanese have in resuming their careers after a period
of service outside, and also because of language handicaps.

Japan suffers from a general lack of articulacy in dealing with the
outside world. The Japanese do not like to talk about themselves,
least of all to foreigners. 'We must realize that silence is a virtue only
within Japanese society,' a professor warns his countrymen. A recent
Defence White Paper noted how America under-estimated Japan's

help in achieving international diplomatic goals, and put it down to Japan's 'innate modesty and shyness'. The Japanese are preoccupied introspectively with themselves, morbidly worrying about what others think of them.

That inhibits their getting to know strangers, especially foreigners. The novelist Kafu Nagai spent more than four years in America at the beginning of the century, but only one American character – a Washington prostitute – appeared with any vigour in his subsequent writings. Soseki Natsume was similarly unimpressed by the English in London, where his long stay was brightened by only one recorded tea party in Dulwich to meet natives. A novelist in the next generation, Saneatsu Mushakoji, declared flatly: 'I do not wish to be understood by foreigners. It is enough if the Japanese I so love understand me . . . I do not find foreigners unpleasant. But I am satisfied with myself.' His contemporary Roka Tokutomi told the Japanese in San Francisco that it was better for nations to keep to themselves: 'I am glad that the Americans first sought to expel the Chinese and now . . . the Japanese. I should like them to do the same with the Negroes. The Negroes should return to Africa . . . and in the same spirit I should like America to leave Japan . . .' That was soon after the First World War.

A few years ago, the municipal fathers of Düsseldorf, which boasts the largest assembly of Japanese residents anywhere outside Japan, suggested that the Japanese community provide a queen for their annual carnival. Flattered, the Japanese businessmen agreed. But when a local newspaper asked ill-humouredly why the town had to turn to Japan for pretty girls, the Japanese withdrew from the project. That is how excessive self-consciousness can harm Japan's international relationships. Where else in the world can one see such shelves of books about one's own country, its characteristics and place in the world? Some works by western scholars on Japanese literature, politics or economics, sell far more copies in Japan itself (in Japanese translation) than in their countries of origin. Vogel's book, telling Americans why they should copy Japan, sold twenty times as many Japanese translations as English originals, reaching more than 350,000 sales in Japan.

The Japanese appear to prefer to wear clothes modelled by Caucasians, patronize Japanese films which are praised in Hollywood or Cannes, trust only the reports of foreign correspondents and visibly lose heart if events like World Expositions in Japan and the Tokyo Summit of western political leaders fail to arouse the West's enthusiasm and praise. There were forty new books in one year recently on the question 'What is Japan?'.

The one-and-a-half million people of Japanese descent now living in America and Europe are potential intermediaries in the encounter between Japan and the West. Half of them live in North America, and those that were there during the Second World War suffered brutal detention after Pearl Harbor, regardless of their citizenship. The reverberations of that episode are still being felt, and a highly popular TV series in Japan was based on painful reminiscences from it. Japanese-Americans are now rising, of course, in their adopted society and there was a third-generation astronaut called Onizuka who still spoke a few Japanese words. In Brazil, after many setbacks, the half-million Japanese now control important banks and have provided members of the Cabinet.

Although those big waves of late nineteenth- and early twentieth-century emigration have finished, there are still new examples to show that one should not generalize too flatly about Japanese insularity. To take two recent examples in Britain, Tadayoshi Tazaki runs a profitable restaurant, employment, newspapers and foodstuffs business of his own after going through English boarding-school and Cambridge University, while Kiku Horinouchi emigrated with his family to England at thirty-six, and has settled down there as an engineer, also converting to Christianity.

But the bridge-building role of the overseas Japanese (*Nisei*) is limited. Their chief concern in their new host country is to gain acceptance, and for that a demonstrated independence from Japan itself is essential. But Japan has learnt that her overseas offspring do not always lend themselves to Japanese designs, as when Senator Daniel Inouye of Hawaii blocked Congressional funding for the United Nations University on the grounds that it was a 'Japanese project'.

Misunderstanding is fanned by the Japanese method of deciding foreign policy by consensus, which means slow reactions and a wait-and-see approach that suit Japan well enough in normal times but not always in a period of crisis. Consensual policy-making creates irritation and distrust among foreign allies not accustomed to it. The group society does not easily produce leaders who are continuously and individually conscious of a responsibility for decision-making. The men at the top are much concerned with their obligations to each other, with keeping their own interests upheld in the domestic game of interlocking dependency relationships. That means equivocation and the focusing of attention on allocating blame for things that go wrong. Professor Masao Maruyama found, after studying the militarist period, that pre-war and wartime leaders had often decided on the basis of panic, without serious or sustained thought, and it would not be difficult to find impulsive decisions in more modern times as well.

The Japanese do find it difficult to articulate foreign policy goals. Their ambiguous feelings create a deep uncertainty as to whether Japan belongs to Asia or the West. Other Asians despair of her support against the overwhelming flood of westernization, a reproach well put by a Korean who accused the Japanese of trying to become 'yellow Caucasians'. Yet Europeans and Americans do not accept Japan either, and so the Japanese feel lost in the gap between these conflicting goals.

The contemporary socio-economic problems of Europe and, to a lesser extent, the United States, encourage some Japanese to think of themselves, in Vogel's challenging phrase, as 'Number One'. In the most literal sense, this is untrue, Japan today being only the third wealthiest power (in terms of income) after the two super-powers, though there is a reasonable chance that she might overtake the Soviet Union at some point early in the next century.

The dreams of empire are not quite dissipated. The Japanese still remember how the Yamato race walked tall in the days of the First World War. But racial resentment at the loss of the Japanese empire in 1945 and at the victory of the Anglo-Saxons in dictating a world order was deeply buried in the years following 1945. Those who could attest to it with knowledge and passion were the militarists and right-wingers whose political judgement had become discredited. Professor W. G. Beasley of London University and others warn of the danger of further Japanese expansionism in the future, but the evidence for this is flimsy. 'The Japanese should stand up for themselves,' a rightist declared after Yukio Mishima's suicide, 'destroy the cloying atmosphere of modern materialistic Japan, and win *Lebensraum* overseas.' That was fifteen years ago, and there is no indication that it is anything more than the irresponsible prattling of extremists with no popular support.

Actually, by removing Japan's empire and helping to build up her consumer economy, the West has made sure that the Japanese can survive only within its ranks. Well over 40% of Japan's foreign trade is done with western countries, only 6% with Communist countries, and the balance of more than half is with the Third World. If you depend upon the Americans for atomic fuel and key foodstuffs, and on the Arabs for energy, your options are limited.

At the same time, pride and self-respect dictate a certain independence on secondary issues. Earlier post-war Prime Ministers adopted the slogans of equidistance between the Soviet Union and the United States, or a multi-directional foreign policy, in order to accommodate the pro-Soviet lobbies in Japan. The steam went out of all that with Afghanistan and Cambodia. But a former Foreign Minister, Toshio Kimura, recently urged that Japan should not give mindless support to the West on every matter; Britain, for example, could be left to deal with her Falklands problem on her own, while less than full backing need be given to the United States in Central America.

Kimura also urged that the Japanese Ministry of Foreign Affairs expand its staff by almost a half to bring it roughly to the level of Italy's Foreign Ministry. Japan currently endeavours to conduct foreign policy with only half the diplomats of France, one-third of Britain's and one-quarter of the United States'. Even the MITI is several times bigger than the Japanese Foreign Ministry: looking after the international aspects of Japan's industries and trade is thought to be more important than political diplomacy.

This helps to explain why Japan makes so many diplomatic mistakes, often to do with misinterpretation. Two little words which did much harm were uttered by Prime Minister Eisaku Sato to President Nixon on the contentious issue of textile exports in 1969. Nixon had returned Okinawa to Japan, a gesture of great importance to the Japanese, and he expected Sato's co-operation on textiles in return – so that Nixon could repay his debt to the Southern states which had helped vote him into the White House. '*Zensho itashimasu*', the Prime Minister declared, meaning 'I will do my best'. Nixon took that as a commitment, but it was not. The textile lobby in Japan was also important for the Liberal-Democratic Party.

Later summit meetings were equally rich in misunderstanding. In 1980 President Carter asked Prime Minister Masayoshi Ohira to build up Japan's defences, and the Japanese leader replied that he would seriously consider it, bearing in mind Japan's role as an American ally. The Americans took this as 'Yes', but, a few days later, Ohira told Japanese reporters: 'Just because President Carter made a request, that does not mean that I would be stupid enough to agree to do exactly as the President wishes. I understand his request, but it is only natural that I should insist on doing things my way.'

Within months, Ohira's successor, Zenko Suzuki, was also in trouble for subscribing to a joint communiqué with President Ronald Reagan which referred to 'the alliance between Japan and the United States'. Many people in Japan did not want to be bluntly labelled as allies of America, despite the US Security Treaty, and Suzuki had to water it down afterwards when talking to the Japanese media. A Tokyo University professor lectured him: 'In the United States the announcement of an official opinion is a commitment to act consistently with that opinion thereafter. It is not a statement intended

only to fit the circumstances at that particular moment.' No sarcasm
was intended, as would have been the case in a British context.

Another professor, Kinhide Mushakoji, attributes these misunderstandings to two distinct cultural premises of diplomacy. A
Westerner, he asserts, concentrates on using logic in order to make
the best choice (*erabi*) from two or more different outcomes, whereas
a Japanese rather aims at adjusting (*awase*) fine gradations of change.
When a Japanese and a western official misunderstand each other, it
is like the Japanese inviting the Westerner to an upstairs room and,
when he seems reluctant, urging him to come up anyway because at
least the view is better. But the Westerner may insist on knowing
what kind of view he can expect before agreeing to climb the stairs,
and so the negotiations collapse.

A western negotiator usually wants to define the issue first, whereas the Japanese priority is to get to know the other person first, so that
they can size each other up and get down to mutual adjustment
without preconditions to reach a settlement. In the Japanese way of
doing things, the result of such a negotiation may not embody the
final and irrevocable choice, but merely bring the parties into a close
relationship which can develop further in the future, so that if the deal
is successful, both sides may seek more concessions. The Westerner
might think that insincere, but to the Japanese it seems highly
practical as well as benefiting both sides.

It would be typical for Japanese negotiators at their first meeting
with American or European counterparts to start by thanking them
for previous gifts or favours, something which would encourage
Americans in particular to make bigger demands than originally
intended. The Japanese, on the other hand, would merely see
themselves as setting an emotional foundation for the negotiation.
Contrary to myth, high-pressure sales tactics do not appeal to the
Japanese. If a western negotiator makes a counter-argument against
what the Japanese are asking for, the Japanese may well refrain from
arguing back or pressing their position further, even if they know they
are right. They may lapse into silence, not being proficient in the art
of debate, not attaching importance to theoretical coherence.

Internationally-minded Japanese diplomats sometimes encourage
the Americans and other western powers to bring strong pressure on
Japan, as a means of accelerating the modernizatioin and internationalization of their country. Where their own arguments to
compatriots to open up Japan to foreign influence make little impact,
the firmly-stated demands of a US President can sometimes do the
trick.

Such shameless manipulation of Japanese inferiority feelings was no doubt justified in earlier decades. But it is no longer needed, and does damage on the American side, as witness an unguarded metaphor which the White House Chief of Staff, Donald Regan, once used of Japan: 'I have a sheepdog that is friendly but over-excitable and not very responsive. To get its attention, I have to roll up a newspaper and whack the dog over its head.' Too many senior officials on both sides of the Atlantic now believe that the best way to deal with the Japanese is to be twice as tough and crude as you would with any other country.

The combative type of western negotiator takes the failure of the Japanese side to refute his argument as a sign of guilt or weakness. The Japanese are notoriously bad at putting their case. Their leaders travel about the world without giving press conferences, and it so pains them to disagree with a host in public that they curl up in embarrassment rather than give their side of the picture. A classic example was when Nixon and Sato met again in 1972 and the Americans, who had braced themselves for the Japanese leader's criticism of their sudden change in China policy without consulting him, were astonished to find Sato saying nothing at all about China. (As his wife once touchingly said of him, he 'never reveals what troubles him'.) The upshot was that the Americans began to doubt his competence, because he did not take full advantage of the rare meeting.

A Japanese writer observes that Japanese operating in western society have to 'develop the strength of mind to argue one's viewpoint until the other party agrees, a characteristic that is abhorred in Japan as "pushiness"'. He must learn how to speak and act without worrying too much about other people's opinions, and without becoming fearful of the effect on his personal relations. Such men exist in the Japanese foreign service, and are usually successful in swaying western opinion, but invariably they turn out to have lost the respect and confidence of their less outgoing colleagues at home. Actually a Japanese negotiating team at an international conference will characteristically postpone deciding its own point of view until it knows what the others are thinking, thus ensuring that it is always one step behind the others in such negotiations.

There is no hope of a world order based on Japanese culture. For her unwilling engagement with the outside world (dictated by the need for raw materials to feed the new living standards her population has come to expect) Japan has to go more than halfway to meet western culture, and risks being submerged by it. It is instructive that the Japanese word for 'understand' carries a secondary meaning of 'accept'. The isolationist pressures created by this tension are misunderstood in the West, which must eventually realize that Japan needs only a modicum of applied pressure to consolidate her integration into the world system. Too much crude persuasion would be counter-productive and, if they want the western-founded world system to last, the western peoples must become more sensitive to the cultural deprivation which Japanese feel.

15

Half-Hearted Elder Brother
Japan and the Third World

LONG BEFORE Europe loomed menacingly over the southwestern horizon, Japan was a dedicated follower of Chinese fashion. Although the islands of Southeast Asia and Polynesia also gave cultural nourishment to the early settlements in Japan, it was China that was the author of most of the ideas which benefited their life. Indeed, the sword was so destructive on China's mainland that some expressions of Chinese art are better preserved in insular Japan, which was at least safe from invading armies, then in China itself. 'If you want to know something about the Tang civilization,' a Chinese writer advises, 'go to Japan', and Chinese visitors gasp with surprise to see examples of Chinese architecture no longer extant in China.

When controversy raged over the recent revision of textbooks about Japan's modern conquest of China and Korea, a Japanese newspaper declared of those two countries: 'We are profoundly indebted for their intellectual, technological and moral enrichment of our own culture.' Such public admissions are not common, but they are well justified. For their part, Japanese who visit China feel as if they are being welcomed to the very heart of their culture, so that they run the danger of almost forgetting their own nationality and being easily outwitted in negotiations.

The feeling approximates to what an Englishman may experience when he visits Greece, Italy or France. But it is more concentrated, because China served Japan in all three roles, as the respective models of classical antiquity, Renaissance and Enlightenment.

Japan owes the greater part of her writing, her art, her religion, her morality and her social structure to China. When it comes to Japanese cultural exports to China, only a handful of minor items like the rickshaw and cormorant fishing can be listed. The well-educated Japanese is sensible of his cultural inferiority. Economically, of course, Japan has brought herself up by her own efforts to the highest world rank, leaving China far behind and, on that score, the Japanese can look down on China. But it does still hurt them that China, unlike Japan, has such a clear concept of her own mission in the world and is so articulate about her own values – which is why the West respects

China but not Japan. This inner self-confidence gives the Chinese an advantage in dealing with their Japanese colleagues.

The Japanese soldiers fighting China in the 1930s were moved by a general feeling of contempt for a once-civilized country that had degenerated into chaos. But they felt guilty about those feelings. General Iwane Matsui, who commanded the expeditionary force to Shanghai, explained the conflict as 'a fight between brothers within the "Asian family" . . . We must regard the struggle as a method of making the Chinese undergo self-reflection . . . not because we hate them but, on the contrary, because we love them too much. It is just the same as in a family when an elder brother has taken all that he can stand from his ill-behaved younger brother and has to chastise him in order to make him behave properly.'

But most of the men serving under General Matsui had more disdain than brotherly love for the Chinese. Their well-disciplined fathers had gone into the first Sino-Japanese War of 1895 with the idea, as one of their war poems put it, that:

> China was wise of old,
> China is wise no more.

The backwardness of China had to be destroyed if Asia were to progress. This role of Japan in the first of the two wars was praised by Westerners: Sir Edwin Arnold spoke of Japan's 'guarding the civilized world'. But there was another soldiers' song about

> Chinka, Chinka, Chinka,
> So stupid and they stinka.

That kind of emotional contempt became general among General Matsui's conscripts. One soldier's wife told her children: 'Your father is at last going to beat up the cheeky Chinese.'

It was these men who went on to perpetrate the 1937 massacre of Chinese civilians in Nanking. The Emperor Hirohito's brother noted in his memoirs, à propos of his military posting in Nanking, that an officer and classmate had advised him that 'the best way to develop the mettle of the troops was to have them run their bayonets into living prisoners'. These atrocities were inexcusable, even against the background of disregard for human life which then prevailed in China, and the cruelty with which the Chinese behaved towards themselves.

Considering the scale and brutality of the killings at Nanking, not to mention the bacteriological warfare experiments on live Chinese (in company with Russian and Korean) prisoners, it is hardly surprising that the Chinese still feel bitter. A Chinese chauffeur in the 1950s objected to driving Japanese visitors, telling their official Chinese guide: 'My father was killed and my sister violated by Japanese troops, and I've never forgotten. Don't make me drive a car for the Japanese.' To which the Chinese official reasonably replied: 'But the Japanese who come to China nowadays are not militarists. You are not the only one who feels as you do about the Japanese troops during the war. But what should we do to get over the feeling? Fight the Japanese again? . . . We Chinese have just got to forget this kind of hatred, for the sake of peace. It gets me the same as you, but I'd like you to go on driving as before.' And he did.

There were many instances, of course, where Japanese behaved well, saving Chinese lives and showing compassion and solidarity with the soldiers and civilians they were supposed to be fighting. But the end of the war left an overwhelming balance of indictment against Japanese behaviour, and in due time the Japanese apologized. In the understatement of the century, Prime Minister Tanaka, when normalizing relations with the People's Republic of China in 1972, offered amends for the 'great deal of trouble' which his country had caused. The Emperor was equally mealy-mouthed, and it was left to Tanaka's counterpart, Zhou Enlai, to compare that apology with 'what you might say when you spill tea over a woman's dress'.

But this has not prevented China and Japan from developing relations vigorously in the years that followed. True, the Japanese know by now that China's regard for them is less than their regard for China. It is another classic case of unrequited love for Japan's collection. A Chinese writing unguardedly can label the Japanese as narrow-minded, bigoted, intolerant and inflexible. Yet today, against the backcloth of the Deng Xiaoping economic reforms, China is intensely and openly interested in Japan's economic success, and how it was achieved.

Nevertheless, when it comes to negotiating with Japan over the details of industrial projects or financial assistance, the Chinese can be baffled and frustrated. The idea that the two countries share a superior mutual understanding is a myth. Japan's guilt, compounded by enchantment with China's past and scorn for China's present, is not enough to transform what is now a largely businesslike relationship of partly complementary economic needs with only an occasional burst of emotional content. China for geopolitical reasons and Japan for economic must both play global roles in the world at large that leave little energy available for the bilateral link. The possibility of their becoming close partners in the future is remote unless the West excludes both of them from its international system.

China can thus merge, from some Japanese points of view, into something much larger, namely the undeveloped Third World, of whose members Japan is concerned chiefly with those in Asia. It is a strange feeling, not often considered by Westerners, to be the only country in your continent which has successfully modernized to western standards. This is an especially difficult role to play when your continental neighbours share the superior non-economic values of 'Asian civilization' with you.

Tenshin Okakura, the Meiji thinker, put this viewpoint in his classic *The Ideals of the East*. 'Love for the ultimate and universal . . . is the common thought-inheritance of every Asiatic race, enabling them to produce all the great religions of the world, and distinguishing them from the maritime peoples of the Mediterranean and the Baltic, who love to dwell on the particular, and to search out the means and not the end of life.' The language may be flowery, but a Japanese does have a gut sympathy with the Buddhist and Confucian practices which he observes in other Asian countries.

Ever since the Meiji Restoration, Japan has struggled with the opposing pulls of East and West. The far-sighted, unsentimental Yukichi Fukuzawa preached the doctrine of *datsu-a*, meaning that Japan should forsake stick-in-the-mud Asia and join the pioneering West. But there were plenty of others to plead the contrary case, that Japan should first lead Asia to a higher stage and then compete with the West. Tokichi Tarui, a contemporary of Fukuzawa, suggested in the 1890s an amalgamation of Japan, Korea and China into a 'grand federation of yellow people's nations in Asia'. As late as the 1970s, a Japanese scholar could describe the central debate in Japan as whether to turn away from Asia or stay with it.

If it were merely a question of measuring self-interest, it would be easier. But emotional factors cloud the judgement. 'I used to tense up when I met Caucasians,' a Japanese diplomat confessed years ago. 'But I did not feel any need to be on my guard when I met people in Southeast Asia.'* The Japanese usually feel not just at ease but actually superior in other Asian countries – but inferior in western.

Other Asians did not applaud Japan's decision to ape the West. 'True modernism,' Rabindranath Tagore lectured his Japanese friends severely, 'is independence of thought and action, not tutelage under European schoolmasters.' But then India is not truly admired in Japan either. Despite the Indian background to Yukio Mishima's

* The most common usage of 'Southeast Asia' in Japan is to mean South *and* East Asia, i.e. including China and the Indian subcontinent. The western habit is to use 'Southeast Asia' to mean only the smaller countries of ASEAN and Indochina, a difference which can lead to enormous confusion.

final masterpiece* on the theme of reincarnation, and the laudable Japanese Buddhist missions doing good work among the untouchables and lepers in India, most Japanese deplore the influence of caste in India in obstructing progress.

The beguiling idea that Japan should take the lead in a resurgent Asia to assert ancient values and link them with western technology has had a good innings in Japan over the past century. Heaven chose Japan, said Shumei Okawa, and groomed it for 3,000 years to fight Europe as Asia's champion. Even Tagore, before Japan started to bully other Asians, had given his blessing to Japan's custodial role: 'In your voice, Asia shall answer the questions that Europe has submitted to the Conference of Man.' Jawaharlal Nehru never forgot the inspiration he felt as a fourteen-year-old when Japan defeated Russia in 1905 in the first modern Asian victory over a European power.

The idea of a 'Hundred Years War' against the white world, which Japan has lost physically but won morally, never quite departs from the Japanese mind. It is accepted, reluctantly, that the Chinese, Koreans and Southeast Asians did not submit to Japanese rule any more readily than they did to European or American. But at least, the Japanese often argue, the Pacific War made a return to sustained western colonial power in Asia impossible.

This sophistry is seen through by some intellectuals. 'Asian people did not become independent through the power of Japan,' one professor writes, 'but they attained independence in resisting Japan. That was Japan's disgrace . . .' The real heroes of the entire episode of Japan's 1940 intervention in Asia were the genuine idealists like Colonel Suzuki in Burma and Major Fujiwara, who inspired the Indian National Army which went on to play a role in Indian independence. These two, and others like them, fully identified with the people to whom they were assigned, and are described as in the mould of T. E. Lawrence. A British colonel interrogating Fujiwara afterwards about his work with the Indians commented drily, 'I never loved them as you did!'

But they were the exceptions. The majority in Japan were people for whom the Navy made a cartoon film in 1945 showing Japan freeing the Asians from the western grasp: it represented the Asians as cuddly jungle animals from the Disney studio, waiting for a Japanese Tarzan to deliver them. Other writers have preferred an almost religious view of Japan's self-imposed mission ('like a martyr on the cross,' one correspondent wrote) to change the old Caucasian view of coloured people.

* The tetralogy entitled *The Sea of Fertility*.

Japan's growing power was, by the 1920s, undermining the hypnotic authority which white people had exercised till then in Asia. And in the years after 1945, it turned out that many leaders of Asian nationalism – Sukarno, Ne Win, Lee Kuan Yew, Park Chung Hee – had learned basic statecraft in the service of wartime Japan. That did not mean that their countries felt grateful to Japan. Lee Kuan Yew, for one, became in the 1960s and 1970s a waspish critic of the Japanese. But that was precisely because of Japan's readiness to play mindless stooge to America's maladroit moves in Asia. 'Japan,' said the Singapore Premier in 1979, 'will have to ask itself whether it is part of Asia or not.'

The Japanese colonial record in Asia inevitably influences Japan's answer to that question. In the first half of the twentieth century Japan ruled Korea, Manchuria and Taiwan in a tough, 'European' manner. To a great extent, especially at the beginning, Japanese administrators brought constructive change, reducing corruption, strengthening education and transport, building economic infrastructure. The Koreans, who rebelled most fiercely against Japanese rule, can sometimes be persuaded in retrospect to recognize its good points.

Emperor Hirohito told the Korean President when he made his historic visit of reconciliation in 1984 that it was 'regrettable that there was an unfortunate past between us for a period in this century, and I believe it should not be repeated' – the second understatement of the century! But the Japanese have emerged from their colonial experience with a deep dislike for the Koreans, avoiding intermarriage, ignoring the cultural debt of the past, and resenting Korea's greediness for aid.

It might have been expected that half a century of shared administration would lead to trade and economic collaboration of the kind which the British maintained with their Commonwealth. But when the idea of a customs union with Korea or Taiwan is floated, usually by Japanese managers anxious to bring in cheap labour or components, it is promptly torpedoed by the Japanese trade unions. The old colonial links have all but disappeared, and now Japan counts it an asset to be able to boast of 'clean hands' in colonialism outside East Asia – for example in the Middle East, where Japan is free of any anti-semitic record, and in Africa.

Again and again one comes back to the sense of Japan's having shaken off its Asian connections. In the course of mastering the western civilization, it lost its affection for the Asian. Japan, a scholar suggests, constitutes an exception to the Asian tradition and has little cultural resonance with other Asian countries. The Japanese must in any case communicate with the rest of Asia in the English or French languages, and even by the use of European concepts. Japanese schoolboys learn English, not Chinese, Korean or Malay, and Japan depends on the West for its protection against Communism.

It is western figures like Kennedy and Churchill who are admired, and the only Asian personalities as widely respected are Confucius himself and, to a lesser extent, Gandhi. In human terms, the Japanese are usually warmer towards Westerners than towards fellow-Asians. A recent poll showed that 90% of Japanese preferred western to Afro-Asian pen-pals. Corporation representatives stationed in Asia join the club of local western colleagues rather than 'go native' with their host nationality, and there are few applicants for the Asian youth ship voyages where Japanese students share quarters with Asian counterparts (whereas the Australasian voyages are over-booked).

But whenever Europe or America slights Japan, Asia is always there to provide solace. Kiichi Miyazawa, the former Foreign Minister, put this squarely in 1978:

> As we feel that we are not quite as welcome in the US or the European Common Market as we used to be, we are naturally inclined to turn our eyes towards our 'God-given' constituency . . . Closer feelings for our friends to the south will be a natural reaction over a longer period of time . . . The recognition in Japan is growing that our future literally lies in Southeast Asia.

What Asia now expects of Japan is economic leadership. In the contemporary conventions of economic summitry, Japan speaks for the Asian developing countries at the annual meeting of western heads-of-government. Japan, says *The Economist*, is a beacon for the poor two-thirds of the world to follow. But it is not a matter of simple imitation. The foundations for Japan's modernization reach back, not merely into the nineteenth century but beyond. The major lesson that the Meiji reformers did leave behind, that of encouraging thousands of small private businessmen to take risks free from government control, was not a particularly popular one in the socialist-leaning post-colonial states of South and Southeast Asia.

In the 1980s, however, Malaysia and Singapore have led a 'Learn from Japan' or 'Look East' movement, seeking a way to create modern industry without destroying indigenous social dynamics, to retain social interdependence instead of building relations of conflict. But further thought has shown that the Japanese model is not clearcut on these matters. The Singaporeans have realized that unless they are discriminating, they might be letting themselves in for an educational system that discourages individual achievement, employment policies which reduce job motivation and industrial automation which dehumanizes.

The Japanese themselves also like to point out that they paid cash for their early development through the export of silk and cotton goods (besides squeezing funds from weaker countries, as with the Chinese indemnity of 1890). There were no international handouts available on soft terms then. Moreover, the Japanese people had to suffer for their development, enduring horrific conditions of work and forgoing some of the luxuries that developing countries in Asia now take for granted. One Indian in twenty-five reckons to go to university today, but when Japan was at a similar development stage sixty years ago, only one Japanese in sixty-five was so privileged. Yet another difficulty about the Japanese model is that so many countries in Asia and Africa are already enmeshed in the western economic system.

What the Japanese have reassuringly demonstrated is that an Asian country can become modern and remain Buddhist or Confucian, without Christian ascendancy. Also, the Japanese example shows that the polarization of incomes, which has become such an ugly feature of progress in the Third World, is not inevitable if a high rate of savings can be encouraged.

In a way, this all boils down to the fact that, to develop, you have to take development seriously. When a Pakistani Premier referred to the Japanese as 'economic animals', he meant it in an admiring spirit, following the usage of Aristotle who had spoken of men as political animals. He wanted to draw attention, without meaning to denigrate, to the priority which the Japanese gave to economic activity. This kind of phrase, however, translates into Japanese without benefit of Aristotelian associations. It set off an orgy of self-abasement, in which the Japanese Prime Minister demanded to know why his people had been called *dobutsu* (animals). 'A nation,' explained Professor Tetsuya Kataoka, 'that knows no higher goal than 'doubling national income', and that is at a loss to know how to spend it, can justifiably be called animal-like.' Every Japanese took the reference literally. 'Japan is regarded as an economic giant,' said a former Ambassador, adding, 'and, in a less complimentary sense, some even call her an economic animal.' The image is reinforced, of course, by remarks such as that by the President of the Japanese Chamber of Commerce and Industry some years ago during the debate on what to do with the trade surplus: 'Maybe we could buy New Guinea . . .'

The next salvo from overseas was easier to take. The Southeast Asians began to talk of the Japanese as 'erotic animals', because of the group sex tours for well-off Japanese in search of coital conquest. The Japanese were angry at being relegated to the animal kingdom, but are not unduly bashful about sex. It ruffled no brows when a group of Philippine worthies complained to the Japanese Prime Minister that the friendly image of Japan was being 'destroyed by the Japanese male tourists who invade Asia in organized sex tours to degrade our women shamelessly'.

All these are variants of the 'ugly Japanese' who have been spotted all over the world, but particularly in Asia. 'All they want to do is to make money and say *sayonara*,' as a Singapore diplomat sourly puts it. These are the Japanese businessmen who flaunt their wealth in poor countries, fail to learn the local language, and avoid mixing socially with the natives. These are the men in responsible positions who say in public that it is the hot weather which prevents Thailand from producing a modern civilization – trailing a generation or two behind Westerners who have either grown out of such unscientific ideas or else keep quiet about them. The damage they do to Japan's image is only beginning to be offset by a smaller, younger and more sensitive wave of teachers, students, and aid volunteers.

A new locale for these confusing Japanese sentiments about being Asian or Western is the Pacific Basin, where Asia and America meet. The Pacific is not at all a Japanese lake, as some Europeans believe. In security terms it is a mainly American lake, with Soviet incursions, and in economic terms there is no dominant country. It is too big to be Japanese. But there is a movement to promote economic and possibly political collaboration among the forty or more littoral states, and Japan has been at the forefront of such ideas.

At the beginning of the 1970s there was a Japanese scheme for a United Community of Pacific Countries with headquarters in Hawaii, and Professor Kiyoshi Kojima has pioneered the idea of a Pacific Free Trade Area (PAFTA). Jiro Tokuyama, the leading advocate of Pacific Basin ideas, claims that its establishment would be 'both a historical imperative and a pragmatic policy option . . .' for Japan. The huge economic weight of Japan would have been balanced not only by the membership of the US, Canada and Australia, but also by the large number of developing countries which would take part. Many observers see it as an ideal framework within which Japan could develop her trade and investment with neighbouring countries without appearing to seek domination. But the political will among the developing countries is still too weak for the idea to take off.

The ambivalence which appears in Japan's relations with Asia is also apparent with the Third World as a whole. There are occasions, as during the Falklands dispute, when Japan places the Third World before a western ally. The Japanese are still capable of asserting their ethnic bond with the non-Caucasian world. As recently as 1971 a president of Mitsubishi declared that, since Europe had its Community, and the USA was self-sufficient, 'we coloured peoples must unite'. But in most Japanese homes that would be regarded today as very theoretical talk. The real links that tie Japan with Africa, Asia and Latin America are economic.

As Dr Saburo Okita, the former Foreign Minister, never tires of explaining, Japan cannot remain an island of prosperity in an ocean of depression – but the Japanese aid programme also helps prevent poor countries from turning to the Soviet bloc. The real give-away about Japanese thinking on aid came from the Prime Minister Takeo Fukuda, making a large aid pledge in 1978, when he commented: 'with this we may escape international censure'. Some of the weaknesses in the Japanese aid programme stem from the fact that it is seen domestically as a duty owed as much to the West as to the South.

That kind of pressure has nevertheless lifted Japanese aid to the level which should be expected from a country of its size and wealth, with appropriately generous interest rates and freedom to spend the money in Third World countries. In 1984 Japan's official aid ranked second in the world after the US, though as a percentage of GNP it ranked only eleventh, and the government has promised to double it by 1992. The amount spent by Japan on aid, investment and the import of manufactured goods from the Third World is around $100 million a year.

One of the outstanding successes is the Japan Overseas Cooperation Volunteers – Japan's version of the American Peace Corps. One volunteer was recently elected as a village chief in Ghana, after spending six busy months building, teaching and growing crops. Another who went to Bangladesh and became absorbed in that society wrote, 'I have stopped thinking of myself as a Japanese.' That is a government organization, but there are private counterparts too. The Reverend Ejo Takata from Kobe recently completed Buddhist missionary work in Mexico (against Catholic opposition), introducing the soya bean to the Indians there. Another private group worked with the Vietnamese refugees in Thailand, building toilets and sewers, and conducting technical education.

The Japanese are particularly good at down-at-earth industrial training, firmly telling Algerian oil refinery supervisors (élite graduates to a man) that they must get their hands dirty if they are to do their job. But the 50,000 trainees who arrive every year from the Third World have an unusual language problem. One of them calls it a 'humanly impossible' challenge to go through a university using the

Japanese language throughout. It is so difficult to learn to speak, read and write, and its mastery for university purposes takes so long, that it is impracticable for all but the most gifted linguists.

The trade between Japan and the Third World is the constant lubricant of the relationship, with Japan's never-ending thirst for raw material and energy, and the complementary Third World need for consumer and capital goods from Japan. Under pressure from Japanese manufacturers, the government protects textiles, plastics and some other goods from competing imports. But this is less a problem in Japan, where the contraction and upgrading of an industry like textiles can be supervised by the government over a period of years, than in other western countries.

On political matters, however, Japan is greatly handicapped by her short history of contact with the Third World, and by a certain insularity and 'groupism' which sometimes prevents an individual Japanese from making the most fruitful relationship with his African or Asian counterpart. Despite Japan's historical connections with China and Korea, and despite the 'favourite uncle' image which Japan seems to be acquiring in some Southeast Asian minds, Japan does very much convey the impression of having decided in her own collective psyche that she is neither Asian nor Third World, and perhaps not western either, but a *sui generis* country closely involved with all of those groups of nations but having to strike her own path independently of them all.

16

Conclusion
Finding the Staircase
Japan's Future

IT IS only a hundred years since the Japanese trainees helping to build the first railways amused their imported European supervisors by coming to work in *kimono*, complete with the obligatory two swords – one long and one short. Only when they discovered that their weapons interfered with the magnets of their compasses did these pioneers consent to leave them at home. Change has come so quickly and continuously since then that there has scarcely been time for the Japanese to think where they were going, or for their society to grow spontaneously – no time to consolidate each layer of cultural alluvium before the next wave of reform rolled in from over the seas.

Japanese often complain that their country has lost its essential character in the course of such traumatic modernization. From the inside, it was easy to feel drowned in the torrent. But outsiders can see things in a longer perspective, and a Chinese philosopher at the beginning of the century wondered aloud whether the changes in Japan were so swift and orchestrated that they must be superficial. This is the central conundrum: have the Japanese *really* changed, or have they kept their traditional characteristics in a modern guise? The question is made harder to answer because of Japan's cultural diffidence. These days, says Nagisa Oshima, the film director:

> The Japanese don't know what their culture is, what their inherit-ance is, or to what extent it has become mixed up with western culture – and, at the same time, a true world culture has not yet come into being . . . The Japanese should . . . ask themselves what their true inheritance is and identify the particular things which they might contribute to a future common culture . . . At the moment things are purely chaotic.

The discovery of the World War Two survivor Sergeant Yokoi, in the Pacific jungles in 1972, spotlighted both the rapidity of post-war change and Japan's uncertainty about her own values. Yokoi stood for earlier Japanese virtues which most of his compatriots had tried hard to forget. An *Asahi Shimbun* leader writer asked doubtfully: 'Are we correct to have changed as much as we have? Or is Yokoi correct not to have changed at all?' Commentators caught between guilt towards Yokoi and pride in Japan's new post-war affluence, were at a loss to know what to say about the embarrassing contrast between the values of 1942 and 1972. The modern Japan is the real Japan, but deep within it lie the shades of Yokoi and all the other *samurai* and their pre-Meiji culture, still active in a new body, for whose mastery they vie with the rational technocrats of the modern age.

It is almost as if there is something in Japanese genes that preserves the old traditions. The way in which Japanese emigrants to America have become westernized after two or three generations proves otherwise, of course, but it is suggestive that, when Japanese writers discuss how the Japanese tradition survives in its encounters with western individualism, they are sometimes reduced to a physical metaphor. The principles of group organization 'are carried virtually in the blood of the Japanese, including the younger generations, almost as a hereditary code,' say three Tokyo University professors. And a leading Japanese Jungian supposes that the centre of the Japanese ego is actually outside the individual personality, lodging somewhere in the group to which that individual belongs and shifting according to that group's demands – contrasting with the western personality whose ego finds its centre of balance within.

Japan imported change by first receiving abstract ideas from foreign countries and then realizing them in the quite different climate of Japanese life. The ideas were not first analyzed and then selectively synthesized with native concepts or beliefs, as happened for example in India or among the Chinese of Singapore and Malaysia: instead, western learning was left to coexist with Japanese Confucian ideas unharmonized. Japan's cultural history has therefore been a constant accretion of successive innovations living side by side. As one critic says of early architecture, 'The idea of a style becoming extinct was foreign to the Japanese . . . New styles were not born at the expense of the old.' We come back to the quality of the Japanese as having not an either-or but a both-and personality, where opposites combine. They were thus able to adapt successfully, and with remarkably little dislocation, to the modern world, by adopting western civilization, though only to a shallow level.

What do the Japanese see as their coming problems? A dull panel of economists point to internationalization, loss of economic vitality and the ageing of the population. Creative intellectuals are more colourful in their prognostications: what about materialism, that green snake, as Mishima glimpsed it, gnawing inside Japan's bosom? Or loss of dynamism?

Deep down, a university professor insists, the Japanese feel 'that excessive happiness and equality have engendered a kind of spiritual mediocrity or cultural decadence'. The novelist Soseki Natsume forecast eighty years ago a 'general psychic breakdown' following the meeting of East and West in Japan. The intellectuals of that day were described as becoming 'the disinherited souls of Japan and the adopted sons of the European world', and that stark fate still threatens the Japanese who cannot integrate the two sources of life within his own person. Even the Japanese race itself, some alarmists agonize, might vanish from the earth, smothered by the enveloping West.

This latter nightmare is never far below the consciousness of the Japanese intellectual: the architect Arata Isozaki, asked to explain the curious sunken plaza at the heart of his civic centre building at the new 'Science City' of Tsukuba, described it as a central void symboliz-ing Japan. 'Putting it in an extreme way, and choosing a wilful mode of expression,' he elaborated, 'the Japanese nation has been wiped out.'

Many Westerners also detect a firm trend toward this – which they call westernization. Arnold Toynbee, who had known the Japanese before the war, was impressed after the war by the fact that the 'living in two worlds' so typical of his pre-war friends had broken down, 'as if the Japanese people had gone entirely western'. It is economic change that goes the deepest. The American economist John W. Bennett once talked of the consumer revolution as carrying Japan on a 'landslide into westernization'.

When Japanese are asked to say where they think their society is going (something they are notoriously bad at doing), they commonly embroider the idea of a cultural mix without specifying its precise ingredients or their relative weights. A thoughtful example was provided by a Vice-President of the Keidanren, the premier private business organization, during a visit to America in 1981: with the consolidation of an advanced industrialized society in Japan, he predicted, 'the philosophy and the manner of corporate manage-ment, lifestyle (housing, clothing and dietary habits) and the way of thinking (the sense of values) will gradually . . . become similar to those in the United States and Europe. There are people in the West who regard . . . Japanese society as something of a different nature from their own, economically, socially and culturally. It is certainly true that old culture, tradition and lifestyle remain in some parts of Japan. However, the people's life, I should say, is mostly the same, be it Denver, Tokyo or Seoul.' The Keidanren, of course, like the Foreign Ministry, has a particular interest in eradicating the western myth that the Japanese people are different in kind.

Even intellectuals quite innocent of diplomatic ulterior motives may be so much in love with cosmopolitanism as to take the same line. Issey Miyake adores being called the 'Japanese-Parisian designer', because he believes that 'the cultural melting pot is the keynote of our times'. A political scientist, Professor Kazuo Kawai, puts it in the heavy language of his discipline: 'Although a considerable time lag is to be expected and although, because of historical differences, Japan can never exactly duplicate the West, there may eventually evolve a transformed Japanese cultural pattern in which political, social and spiritual values fairly comparable to those of the West will be truly more expressive of Japan's own new national life and the traditional standards of her fading past.'

Many, particularly among the young, would like to see the traditions weakened. 'We are losing our traditions,' says former Foreign Minister Kiichi Miyazawa, 'and most Japanese are not regretful. Not many tears are shed for the old Japan.' That is an over-simplification. No Japanese, for example, regrets the poverty of the old Japan, and few perhaps regret its stringent family discipline. Some other aspects of the tradition continue to appeal, however, and many Japanese would like to retain them if possible. Why not aim for an American standard of living, to be enjoyed by people who are considerate of each other's needs and feelings as in the old Japanese group system? The trouble is, as a German teacher in Japan puts it, 'A Japanese works downstairs in a business suit and comes upstairs in a *kimono* – but we Occidentals can never find the staircase.'

If Japanese groupism is something dictated by the socio-economic structure of society (including the peculiar needs of rice irrigation), then the drastic recent changes in that background will break it down in time. But, as Ronald Dore has pointed out, if groupism is a cultural pattern rooted in the structure of individual personalities, it will not change so readily or automatically. If the environment dictates groupism it will change, but if individuals choose it, it will stay. In point of fact, many of the young people who follow western fads and fashions mysteriously settle down to 'Japaneseness' again when middle-aged.

So the westernization which reached its peak under the American Occupation was mostly superficial. What was borrowed from western life was only partial and for the short term. Sensitive Japanese suspected all along that western social values were second-rate beside the best of their own. The son of the leading post-war Prime Minister once explained with delicate sarcasm how valuable the Occupation had been because it had once and for all demonstrated to the Japanese the 'enduring superiority' of their own way of life. Japan was like the hero in Tanizaki's novel *Some Prefer Nettles* who, after a long infatuation with a western 'goddess', goes back to Japanese women. The Emperor Hirohito himself appeared to predict what would happen when he wrote a poem in 1946 clearly referring to Japan's psychological suffering under the Occupation:

> The pine is brave
> That changes not its colour,
> Bearing the snow.
> People, too
> Like it should be.

What it means for ordinary people was well put by a young official and his wife, married in 1980 but without the elaborate traditional ceremonies. 'We tried to shake off the old ways,' he observed. 'But without us realising it, I suppose, deep down, we really are Japanese. We wear . . . jeans or we have western-style homes, yet our way of doing things is Japanese. We look Americanized, but it's just a superficial face.'

In a few instances, the return to Japanese values has already been accomplished by legislation or administrative order, as with the formalization in 1978 of the *gengo* system of numbering years by Imperial era rather than the Gregorian calendar, a move hailed by a former Chief Justice as restoring a 'precious cultural inheritance'. Another instance was the law of 1982 requiring candidates for the House of Councillors to stand for a party and not as individuals. At the mundane level, more ideographic road-signs are appearing in place of the romanized ones so helpful to foreigners and, after a brief honeymoon with metrics, the traditional units of measurement have been reinstated for house-building and clothing. Professor Yuji Aida comments:

> Though we tend to think that we have been unconditionally pursuing modernization, following single-mindedly in the footsteps of the West, and though we tend to believe that we have been divesting ourselves of the characteristic Japanese mentality, in fact this is not so. Superficially we have lost our Japanese quality, but essentially speaking there is, if anything, an ever-strengthening regression – for better or for worse – to Japaneseness.

Successive surveys commissioned recently by the Education Ministry show a gradual gaining of ground by traditional values, by

conformism over individualism. People are becoming more interested in religion, in morality, in family relationships. 'The
Japanese are at long last beginning to regain self-respect and view
their own culture and traditions with less prejudice,' a Japanese
journalist interprets. Japan no longer has to imitate the West, and
there is a noticeable access of self-confidence and self-assertiveness.

This does not mean a regression to outdated beliefs or to the
untenable conservatism of earlier decades. There is a new kind of
Japanese forming, different not only from his 1950s father, but also
from his 1930s grandfather and all his earlier ancestors. He does not
go consciously seeking the traditional descipline of which its victims
used to complain in earlier generations, but he may well accept a good
dose of it where he encounters it from his own contemporaries, his
school or work groups and his family. It is in this sense that a British
editor recently put the view after visiting Japan that westernization
was a camouflage for the Japanese reality retained behind the scenes
– he saw it as more an insult than a compliment to the West.

Fewer western books are now read, compared with the 1950s and
1960s, traditional instruments are back in vogue, and traditional
values are more commonly depicted in the cinema. In the past fifteen
years there has been something of a re-discovery, particularly by the
young, of traditional religion, including the modernized sects. Dr
Hideki Yukawa, a Nobel Prize winner for physics, has called for
Japanese science to break from the western idea of exploiting nature,
and reconcile itself instead with traditional Japanese ideas about
serving man in harmony with nature.

If one had to oversimplify what is going on in Japanese society, one
would say that the old-style Japanese family has gone, and the
new-style one replacing it is smaller, with more intense, more personal 'horizontal' relationships between husband and wife, or
between brother and sister – but looser 'vertical' parent-child links.
There is more equality, less authority, and the same goes for other
social groups at school or work which have become more tolerant of
individualism on their members' part. Individuals have more freedom than before, but most of them do not yet practise autonomy,
preferring to exercise their individuality within the security of their
groups. This process of group relaxation and individual freedom will
go further, but rather slowly and without threatening, in the foreseeable future, the existence or importance of Japan's characteristic
group structure.

In economics Japan now stresses uninhibitedly the trustee element
in ownership, the attenuated rights of shareholders, managers' and
workers' power, the cottonwooling of competition, administrative

guidance and group collaboration – all deriving from indigenous traditions.

In politics, the western allies may have thought they had 'given' Japan democracy after the war, but the Liberal-Democrats often seek consensus with Opposition parties because it is hurtful to cause another group to lose face. The Diet strove valiantly to replicate the adversary pantomimes of Capitol Hill or Westminster, but by the 1970s the emphasis was once again on compromise. Individual participation in politics, is, professionals apart, desultory. Prime Minister Nakasone believes that four-fifths of the agenda under the 'final settlement of accounts of post-war politics' has been achieved, through the restoration of national self-confidence and spiritual identity and the overhaul of the forty-year-old 'American' system of administration and education – but there is still more to be done.

In the field of law public opinion reacts angrily when citizens obtain damages from neighbours under the western system of justice, contract remains unpopular and individual treatment of wrongdoers is preferred to the rules of abstract justice. All these trends will surely continue and even intensify, within the confines of Japanese pragmatism, capacity for multi-level behaviour and instinct for deferring to overseas patrons.

In foreign policy the American tie seems inseverable whatever rendings it may suffer, since the claims of commerce and security combine to rule out alternatives. It took twenty years for Japan to begin to break ranks with the United States over the oil crisis and policy towards the Arabs but, since then, there has been a gradual increase in that inward-lookingness which could be taken for Japan's form of nationalism. 'Nothing international can be mainstream in Japan,' a Japanese banker explains. Everyone has noticed how the two Ministries which deal with the outside world, the Foreign Ministry and the Ministry of International Trade and Industry, both extremely powerful in earlier post-war years, are now losing influence to the numerous special-interest home Ministries, especially the Finance, Agriculture and Transport Ministries. It is one sign of lessening admiration for the West.

'There is no race called "Internationals",' Sohei Nakayama has warned. 'We have to look for something in our culture that can be accepted and admired internationally.' One recalls the famous outburst by Mishima about the distortion of values under westernization:

The temperament of the men who studied abroad during the Meiji period, who derived their pride from being agents and importers of western rationalism, still remains in the character of the Japanese intelligentsia. Those things which have never become westernized are to be hidden at the back of the closet as uncivilized things, as Asian things, as unenlightened things, as loathsome things, as disgraceful things, as contemptible things, and as things we don't want foreigners to see.

What are these things shut up in the closet? A leader of the Japanese Commune movement, with experience of the *kibbutz* as well as the London School of Economics, describes how neither capitalism nor Marxism is any good, both being centralist and unfree; Japan should cultivate instead 'the good, natural life . . . based on the best of original Shinto culture'. Many writers today see the young generation escaping from imported criteria of efficiency and rationalism, and rediscovering their own emotions and feelings (which, the older generation concludes sadly, will mean more seclusion and slower economic growth). Artists cite Oshima's film *Empire of the Senses* as an example of the free sensibility of the Japanese personality uncontaminated, not merely by the things learnt from the West, but by Buddhism and Confucianism as well. It is some kind of oriental Arcadia that Japanese really hanker after.

The jilting of a foreign culture has happened before. In the eighteenth century Japanese intellectuals systematically disowned their legacy from China, then seen as a model of misgovernment and fount of boring didactic verse, useless moral speculation, pompous archaic language and a time-wasting script for it. The earlier Japanese culture of Yamato, with its pulsating love poems and lyrical expressiveness was hailed as a kind of Japanese Arthurian legend – as far removed from Cathay as Donne from Pope in the English poetic treasury. Yet the traces of Sinification remain today, from ideographs to Confucianism.

Insularity is a key factor in it all. The Japanese, an author confessed recently, were 'sympathetic, sensitive, well-educated and show commonsense, but it only goes as far as the seashore . . . We tend to be quite insensitive to things that happen outside Japan, not because we are not sensitive, but because we just don't consider that there are people over there who cry and have the same feelings as we do.' The President of the McDonald's hamburger chain in Japan, Den Fujita, found this a very practical question: 'The Japanese have two psychologies. On the surface we have a great inferiority complex about foreign things. But on a deeper level, Japanese hate the foreigner – we don't like anybody.' For that reason he toned down the American image of McDonald's in order to win sales.

The Japanese endlessly discuss whether they can ever be internationally-minded, or whether that is a contradiction in terms. Anyone coming back from residence abroad needs to go through a process of 'de-internationalization' before he can slip back into Japanese society. If he has become truly 'international', he will have to project a superficial conventional image to fellow-Japanese at home, reserving the expression of his genuine international ideas for foreign company.

It may thus be doubted whether Japanese corporations can ever become truly international, not just because of language and communication problems, but because the Japanese do not feel themselves to be thorough-going participants in a world system. Toyota, one of the biggest 'multi-nationals' of Japan, has no foreigners on its board of directors, and the International University, where Japanese students can for the first time in their nation's history pursue knowledge on an equal basis with a large and varied group of foreign students, is still small and only in its third year.

So 'abroad' is a place where, if men stay long, they come back bald; a novel like *The Makioka Sisters* has conversations about the coarse looks of emigrants returning from America. Japan stands outside the world, and the ordinary Japanese does not see himself as being westernized, in the sense of becoming like the West, but only as making changes of his design and volition. He does not accept the necessity to co-operate with other countries, and is not convinced that the world outside needs Japan. He finds it difficult to lift himself above his country to see it and the world in an objective light. International conferences regularly lament Japanese unreadiness to interact and work with foreigners in non-Japanese settings, the limited instances of Japanese management in overseas manufacturing subsidiaries notwithstanding. In an editorial published in 1983, the *Yomiuri Shimbun* pronounced, 'Japan is in the process of becoming gradually isolated from the rest of the world.'

What can we most realistically guess about this insular, greying Japan's future? In the early 1970s, Japan's economic growth was so much faster than that of other industrialized countries, that economic futurologists almost all agreed that her standard of living or income per head would overtake first Europe's and then, sometime between now and the end of the century, North America's. The first part of the prediction has already happened, but the second is taking a little longer to accomplish.

Economic growth was hitting 10% a year for a long time before the oil shock, but has since settled to a much more modest rate, and the present working assumption is for a 4% real growth rate in the balance of this century. So the exhilarating prospects, dating from the 1960s and early 1970s, of Japan's overtaking the Soviet Union and the United States and becoming the richest country on earth, twice as rich per head of population as anyone else, by the end of the century, should be forgotten (in fact, it probably still colours some of our subconscious apprehensions about Japan). The rising sun has reached its zenith.

How will Japan use her unprecedented economic power? The former MITI Vice-Minister Naohiro Amaya once referred to five ways in which a country could influence the world – through man, culture, armies, money and commerce. 'In the case of Japan,' he went on, 'only commerce has a remarkable power of expression. Man does not speak, culture whispers, military strength is silent, money speaks a little but trade speaks a lot.'

The low profile suits Japan's psychology and, in any case, her options are few. A future Foreign Minister, asked whether Japan was embarking on a geopolitical role in Asia, replied: 'I don't think we Japanese understand geopolitics – and I'm not sure that we want to.' Except for very recent efforts in Indochina and Iran, the Japanese have avoided mediation in Asian disputes, notably in Korea and between Taiwan and China. Most Japanese have no idea what they would like to do in the world with their economic achievement, and the usual advice by politicians is, in one Prime Minister's phrase, to be 'a porcupine and not a roaring lion'. Japan sways with the tides like a sea-anemone, skilled at day-to-day survival but without a direction or strategy.

The Japanese do sometimes try to believe that they are a source of civilization. The socialists now proclaim that Japan should become a 'cultural power', promoting welfare and Third World development. There was at one time enough residue from the sense of competitiveness with the West to make a role. The Christian leader Kanzo Uchimura had said that Japan should not be satisfied merely with imitating the West, but should 'add to what the Europeans have created'. In this kind of vein Ezra Vogel's idea of *Japan As Number One* can stir Japanese hearts, and one academic in a 1980 book called *Japan: A Super-Developed Country* claimed that Japan's welfare system, independent judiciary, separation of church from state and decentralized government were the best in the world and others should learn from them.

Prime Minister Nakasone has offered Japan the prospect of bringing home the glittering prizes from every quarter of the cultural globe, in order to achieve 'fusion between Oriental and Occidental cultures' (he defines the latter as American culture since 'when we go to Europe, we feel the eclipse of European races'). Japan, he explains, should do this by assuming leadership of 'the culture of coloured races' to 'unite the wisdom of peoples in both cultures' (i.e. Occidental and coloured). But his scenario illuminates the continuing identity problem of Japanese intellectuals and their uncertain grasp of the world more than the realistic policy options of the 1990s. A more down-to-earth writer proposes that Japan should become a centre for international medical care, recreation and tourism, international cultural and aesthetic exchange, Third World technology research (based loosely on the existing United Nations University) and finally foreign aid and refugee relief. These are all concrete goals which are within Japan's resources and fit her circumstances. Whether enough energy can be mustered for them is another matter.

Meanwhile, powerful puritanical voices are shouting more and more loudly from outside Japan that, as an American Cabinet member put it, 'Japan now has the power, and thus the inescapable duty to help shape and execute tomorrow's agenda for the world economy.' In the same vein Prime Minister Margaret Thatcher declared: 'We want to know what Japan thinks', meaning that, if Japan disagrees with western policies, it should say why. In one of his books, former US Ambassador Edwin Reischauer wonders if the Japanese would ever 'overcome their sense of separateness and, to put it bluntly, show a greater readiness to join the human race'. The younger Japanese are receptive to such calls. One explains that the elders in his family had all fought the world – his grandfather for control of China, his father to create the economic miracle. But now he and his generation wanted international harmony so that Japan did not have to strive against other countries.

There are hints of Gaullism here. 'Regain spiritual nobility,' exhorts one intellectual – by seeking autonomy for Japan. The Japanese political system does not, however, throw up leaders of the calibre of de Gaulle or Churchill, even in wartime. The faction system entirely inhibits this and, when Mr Nakasone was looking for Japanese leaders to compare with Churchill and Roosevelt, in contrast to the passive power brokers who have ruled modern Japan, he had to go back to the thirteenth century. So a more complex role is now put forward by some, namely to join the West selectively, collaborating in its good works (like strengthening the international monetary and trade system), but not its self-seeking or racially chauvinist goals.

Mr Amaya addressed Japan's underlying dilemma with his usual colourfulness in a magazine article in 1980. What did the Japanese people want, he asked – to live as merchants or as warriors? To be a merchant meant begging for oil in the Middle East, and grovelling before the military powers. But if the *samurai* role were chosen, then force would have to be used to protect oil supplies: 'Japan must be prepared to run to the scene, sword in hand.' The merchant role remains the clear favourite.

A number of western thinkers have predicted that the twenty-first century will be Japan's, beginning with Spengler, who saw the torch of civilization moving across the globe from the Middle East to Europe and America, destined next to alight on East Asia. Toynbee also believed that, after eight centuries of European domination, the cultural initiative would now move to the Asian-Pacific region.

If earlier Atlantic sages merely pointed the finger of glory to a general area of the world (East Asia), post-war futurologists, from Herman Kahn in 1962 to James Abegglen in 1970, firmly awarded the role to Japan. Writing after the oil crisis, Kahn reaffirmed his position, though with new reservations over the transferability of Japanese culture. Even the Japanese themselves, who often reply with pessimism to international questionnaires, are ready to accept the fact that they are likely to become one of the two great nations of the twenty-first century, along with China. But what to do with the part?

The idea of being a model for others naturally appeals to the Japanese. A senior Nissan Motor executive eulogizes Japan as 'the model country, the best country in the world in terms of competitiveness, freedom, democracy, a low crime rate and a peaceful life . . . We are free of social envy. We don't pay our company president, chairman or directors huge amounts of money. Anyone can rise to the top . . .' Konosuke Matsushita, founder of one of the best-known of the new post-war corporations, believes that Japan could ultimately become a state governed by virtue rather than laws, a state without taxes, the centre of world civilization in the twenty-first century.

Less visionary thinkers stress the possibility of Japan's offering a lead to other countries in post-industrial structure, perhaps on the basis of the role of its bureaucracy. A gathering of intellectuals in the 1970s wondered if Japan might not be the forerunner of a new kind of utopian society where western permissiveness and individualism would be blended with Japanese 'stoical' harmony.

What could prove valuable to the contemporary world is Japan's experience of mass society. Old tradition and recent practice combine to create a sense of participation in a modern economy, greatly helped by the prevalence of employee stockholding in corporations. A literate banker, Kimindo Kusaka, defining civilization as the 'technique of communal life', gives his country full marks in this subject. He finds that Japanese excel in the 'culture industries' – the media, entertainment, publishing, restaurants and travel. Even in modern manufacturing industry the peculiar success of the Japanese has been to develop new ways of pleasing, serving and delighting the public and turning them into products for people to buy at low cost. Kusaka would dispute the thesis that Japan's strength is primarily industrial, believing that we should rather look at the attention given, before the manufacturing process begins, to the human needs which can be served.

Many western observers agree that Japan could be a model, not only of industrial relations as many European managers and trade unionists believe, but also of economic priorities. Chalmers Johnson makes the penetrating observation that, unlike Communist states (which direct industrialization for ideological goals) or western countries (where the state does not direct at all), Japan is a developmental state whose unashamed *raison d'être* is to implement industrialization solely for efficiency. If only, *The Economist* once lamented, other countries would emulate 'the mechanism of output-orientedness which Japan has created . . . there is no limit to what our children could achieve'. In a sense Russia, America and Europe all muddy their economic process with ideology, leaving Japan to run the only 'neutral' example. She manufactures, not for levelling or for licence but for livelihood.

However, it would be wrong to conclude that any of these cultural, political or economic models for the world are being actively and consciously promoted by Japan's leaders. The Japanese are frankly opportunist in their relationship to world trends, and are unlikely in the end to take leadership on such matters. Japan opted out of aggressive expansionist roles in the past. In the sixteenth century she could have chosen to develop maritime power, emigration to Malaysia and Australia and dominion in the Far East in competition with the Europeans or, alternatively, to become Christian, like Korea, and join the Euro-centred world civilization: instead she trimmed her sails. In the seventeenth century she could have become a centralized national state along the European model, losing some cultural distinctiveness in order to integrate into the world of that time. Instead, she chose seclusion. In the 1870s Australia begged Japan to send settlers, but they were denied.

The common thread in all these decisions was to stay free of entanglements, keep other powers out and maintain Japanese society in that loose form, falling well short of anarchy, yet also of individualism, which so suited its members. Westerners today chiefly remember Japan's choice in the 1930s to take military control of China and then challenge the United States for the Pacific. But the decisions before that were mostly cautious to the point of timidity. Little help is gained from history in trying to predict a physically expansive Japan in the 1990s and the twenty-first century.

It is not very constructive to tell the Japanese to their faces that they must stop being Japanese and become international citizens instead, as a New Zealand Prime Minister recently did. Despite occasional nightmares about their becoming culturally, even genetically absorbed into the world pool, the Japanese are going to remain Japanese (as we understand that term) for a century or two yet at the very least.

It used to be thought that the heat of western dissatisfaction would be taken off Japan as other East Asian countries followed along in her economic footsteps. Korea is standing now economically where Japan was some twenty years ago, Taiwan and Singapore are not far behind, and China will eventually join the club. Japan is only the first Asian country to challenge what had appeared as the monopoly of the West. But now that the cultural factor has been identified as the main obstacle to greater understanding of Japan by the West, it is seen that the newly industrializing East Asian states are all, in some way or another, more attuned than Japan to communicate with the West and its culture. Japan really is unique in having this particular insularity.

And that perhaps is why the Japanese remain fortified in the natural pessimism with which their fatalistic tradition endows them – fatalism meaning that the Japanese are optimistic about tomorrow, but pessimistic about the day after. Recent surveys seem to show that Japanese pessimism is growing. Two people in five are unhopeful about the future of their society, much more than in European countries, and this is the case even with the young. In one international survey only 6% of the Japanese polled looked forward to the twenty-first century with hope. The creative artists of Japan reek of pessimism. The fundamental flavour of modern Japanese poetry, and of much fiction too, is one of hoplessness.

A group of intellectuals, in the wake of the oil crisis of the 1970s, wrote an article under the title *The Suicide of Japan*, warning that the country faced inner disintegration on a Roman scale, becoming a paradise for the lazy as a result of the abuse of liberty from misunderstood democracy, together with the introduction of state welfare based on materialist utilitarianism. Yukio Mishima told an American friend that Japan had 'gone, vanished, disappeared . . . there is nothing more to save'. His friend, the Shakespeare critic Tsuneari Fukuda, elaborated: 'There is little left that is genuinely Japanese in our daily life.'

That is exaggerated, but the reality reinforcing this pessimism about the future is the conviction which Japanese form from an early age of their country's vulnerability. In kindergarten they are taught that their country is a poor island, lacking natural resources and at the mercy of world storms. They are told that their own unity, discipline and sacrifice are all that stand between Japan and disaster. They come to adult life believing that no one outside Japan can understand them or communicate effectively with them. Their language is not comprehended by foreigners and the Japanese do not have linguistic skills. In times of urgent crisis, such as the war, this pessimism could be harnessed to collective action harmful to the outside world. When left bobbing on the minor ups and downs of the post-war scene, it merely reinforces the instinct to disengage from the world.

The Japanese are no different from anybody else in basic human make-up. As with other peoples, the interior man is hard to know – even more so in the Japanese case, because of the length of cultural history empty of interchange with other societies. But the exterior man is visible to all, and when it comes to clothes, there is an interesting trait which marks out the Japanese. From about a hundred years ago, the Japanese began to adopt items and styles of western clothing to supplement their traditional garments. But whereas in India or China you will see today clothes in which both indigenous and foreign influences are evident, resulting in mixtures and blends of various kinds, the Japanese tend to project only two kinds of clothing, one which is wholly Japanese and another which is wholly western. Mutual influence is lacking, and this surprises many western observers.

It is as if the Japanese recognize the need to go along with the world, but at the same time insist on keeping their full distinctiveness, hoping to allow the two exteriors to coexist on the same body. Many of them are skilful and clever enough to do it, but the emotional effort is great and not much energy is left over for such other pursuits as genuine exploration of foreign cultures or even foreign friends. It means that some Westerners superficially suppose that they are dealing with a person who accepts western values, and that causes unnecessary misunderstanding. It would be equally wrong, of course, to conclude, from observing a Japanese in his *kimono* at home, that he is a pre-modern person not at all in tune with developments in the West.

The use of clothing could provide another metaphor for Japan's modernization. Japan is like a man who lost everything in 1945 but was given a marvellous, warm fur-lined rainproof coat by a generous American. The coat served its purpose, the man has never fallen ill from cold or wet, and under that coat he has gradually grown bigger and fatter and stronger. As his circumstances improved, he was able to introduce beneath the coat the kind of underclothing and middle clothes that he was used to, in that way losing his original feeling of discomfort when wearing only that alien coat.

But now, forty years on, the coat is holed, dirty and worn, seams have come apart and it is neither effective nor smart any more. A rational response would be to throw it away, and put on a new Japanese-style coat better tailored for the cultural habits of the man, his race, the climate and geography with which he lives. But he does not take this course. He has formed a sentimental attachment to the coat, perhaps even seeing it as a source of good luck. To change coats after so long might risk a change in his own personality, leading to changes in the way he behaves or, much more important, changes in the way other people, especially the original donor of the coat, see him. Will his friends recognize him?

So he hesitates, and is not too proud to go on wearing this strange mixture of clothes – the out-of-date foreign coat on the outside, and his clean, snug, comfortable Japanese clothes inside. When the coat does fall off of its own accord through sheer age, there will be virtually nothing that is American left about the man's outward appearance. It will be as if the coat had never existed, was never anything more than an outer shell, was never absorbed into his clothing system to modify his indigenous style.

And when that last remnant of MacArthurite cloth does fall away, Westerners may be shocked to see their reassuring picture of the Americanized Japanese shatter. The person underneath the clothes has, of course, altered, continuing a process of internal social change which has been going on for at least the last century and reflecting the enormous differences in everyday life – material changes, mechanical innovations, the quickening pace of life and all the other impositions of modernity which western people also experienced and absorbed in the light of their own cultural traditions and values.

The Japanese have become modern, but they remain Japanese and the borrowed clothes of westernization are about to be discarded. Westerners may then come to accept that there can be no more excuses for neglecting the homework of learning the history and cultural traditions of this island race, that has so much to teach the rest of the world about reconciling modernity with nature.

Acknowledgements

I thank Lewis Bush and Sally Backhouse for reading my draft several times and making many good suggestions, and also Kiyo Arafune, Sadao Oba, Ian Nish, J. A. A. Stockwin, Takashi Yuki and two very old friends whom I should not name for doing the same service for certain chapter drafts. My thanks to Adam Baillie and Diane Farquhar for feats of research and typing.

After thirty years' acquaintance with Japan, I owe so much enlightenment to so many people that it is impossible to make a full list of debts. I did, however, draw particularly in this book on conversations with Naohiro Amaya, Tatsuo Arima, Gregory Clark, Ronald Dore, Morihisa Emori, Shinkichi Eto, Kimirou Fujita, Takeo Iguchi, Matsujiro Ikeda, Shuichi Kato, Yoshiya Kato, Shunkichi Kisaka, Michihiko Kunihiro, William Lockwood, Shigeharu Matsumoto, Yohei Mimura, Wasuke Miyake, Shiro Miyamoto, Kenya Mizukami, Akio Morita, Moriyuki Motono, Ryo Nakanuma, Sadanobu Oda, Kaheita Okasaki, Saburo Okita, Jutaro Sakamoto, Yukio Satoh, Masaki Seo, Charles Smith, Henry Scott Stokes, Richard Storry, Noriko Takata, Hiroshi Takeuchi, Sadakazu Taniguchi, Koji Watanabe, Taizo Watanabe, Endymion Wilkinson and Toshio Yoshimura.

Notes

The notes that follow have been kept to a reasonable space by the use of abbreviations for the main periodicals and books cited, as follows:

1. Periodicals

Echo	Japan Echo (Tokyo, quarterly)
FEER	Far Eastern Economic Review (Hong Kong, weekly)
Fin Tim	Financial Times (London, daily)
Int Her Trib	International Herald Tribune (Paris, daily)
Interpreter	Japan Interpreter (Tokyo, quarterly)
JQ	Japan Quarterly (Tokyo, quarterly)
JT	Japan Times (Tokyo, daily)

NB *Bungei Shunju, Chuo Koron, Jiyu, Sekai, Shokun, Shukan Bunshun* and *Voice* are all magazines, mostly monthly, published in Tokyo. *Asahi Shimbun, Mainichi Shimbun, Nihon Keizai Shimbun* and *Yomiuri Shimbun* are daily newspapers published in Tokyo.

2. Books

Authority J. Victor Koschmann (ed) *Authority and the Individual in Japan* (Tokyo University 1978)

City Life Ronald Dore *City Life in Japan* (Routledge, London 1958)

Condon John C. Condon & Mitsuko Saito (eds) *Intercultural Encounters with Japan* (Simul, Tokyo 1974)

Daedalus Hiroshi Wagatsuma 'The Social Perception of Skin Colour in Japan' in *Daedalus* (Journal of American Academy of Arts & Sciences, Boston) Spring 1967

Discovery Donald Keene *The Japanese Discovery of Europe* (Routledge, London 1952)

Experience Ronald Bell (ed) *The Japan Experience* (Weatherhill, New York 1973)

Failure Tatsuo Arima *The Failure of Freedom, A Portrait of Modern Japanese Intellectuals* (Harvard UP, Cambridge 1969)

Fukuzawa, The Autobiography of Fukuzawa Yukichi (Hokuseido, Tokyo 1934)

Geisha Liza Crihfield Dalby *Geisha* (University of California Press, Berkeley 1983)

Hearn Lafcadio Hearn *Japan, An Interpretation* (Tuttle, Tokyo 1955)

Interlude Kazuo Kawai *Japan's American Interlude* (University of Chicago 1960)

Landscapes Donald Keene *Landscapes and Portraits, Appreciations of Japanese Culture* (Secker & Warburg, London 1972)

Letters Elisabeth Bisland (ed) *The Japanese Letters of Lafcadio Hearn* (Constable, London 1911)

Moloney Dr James Moloney *Understanding the Japanese Mind* (Tuttle, Tokyo 1954)

New Writing Yukio Mishima & Geoffrey Bownas (eds) *New Writing in Japan* (Penguin, Harmondsworth 1972)

Portrait Robert S. Ozaki *The Japanese, A Cultural Portrait* (Tuttle, Tokyo, 1978)

Socialization George A. de Vos (ed) *Socialization for Achievement, Essays on the Cultural Psychology of the Japanese* (University of California, Berkeley 1973)
Sources Wm Theodore de Bary (ed) *Sources of Japanese Tradition* (Vols I and II) (Columbia University Press, New York 1958)
They Came M. Cooper (ed) *They Came to Japan* (Thames & Hudson, London 1965)
Twelve Doors John W. Hall & Richard K. Beardsley (eds) *Twelve Doors to Japan* (McGraw-Hill New York 1965)

Introduction (pp. xiii–xxi)

Earthquakes see e.g. *Fin Tim* 30 Aug 1980 or *Int Her Trib* 8 Jul 1980; **bicycle** in *Echo* Vol 12 Special Issue 1985 p. 65; **madness** Prof Hiroshi Hazama in *JT* 3 Mar 1975; **Sasayama** in *JQ* Vol 16 1969 p. 410; **Kono** in *The Times* 20 May 1980; **enzymes** *JT* 29 Dec 1981; **Anzai** *New Writing* p. 205.

Chapter 1: Pale Shades of Yellow – The Japanese Race (pp. 1–17)

'**Average body**' 'Penetrating the Japanese Market, No 1, Product Marketability and Business Practices' (MIPRO Tokyo 1981); **Dalby** *Geisha* p. 133; **Terayama** *Amerika jigoku meguri* (Haga Shoten Tokyo 1969), see also *Interpreter* Vol 11 No 1 Spring 1976 p. 34; '**muscle-centred**' *Experience* p. 121; '**are white**' 16th century Portuguese missionary in *They Came* p. 37; **Ihara** *Koshoku Ichidai Onna* (*The Woman Who Spent Her Life At Love Making*) (Tokyo 1949) p. 215; **Mainichi** 2 Aug 1965; **male types** *Daedalus* p. 419; '**yellow indeed**' *ibid* p. 423; '**turn red**' *Interpreter* Vol 12 No 1 Winter 1978 p. 105; **Hearn** letter to Basil Chamberlain of 6 Mar 1894, *Letters* p. 269; **Giants** *Echo* Vol 6 Special Issue 1979 p. 37; **Ishida** *JQ* Vol 11 1964 p. 281; **Tel Aviv** see *Bungei Shunju* Sep 1972, also *JQ* Vol 19, 1972 p. 483; **Minami** 'Japanese Views of Foreigners' in *Ningen no Kagaku* (Tokyo) Vol 2 No 1 1964 p. 14; **prostitute** *Daedalus* p. 422; **Endo** *Up To Aden* (Tokyo 1964) p. 128; **goblins** *Discovery* p. 22; **Honda** *ibid*; **Alfred** *Fukuzawa* p. 218; **freckles** *Daedalus* p. 420; **hog** *ibid* p. 421; **scholar** Tomoko Inoue in *Chuo Koron* Dec 1981 p. 210, also *Echo* Vol 9 No 1 Spring 1982 p. 45; **Buchanan** *Daedalus* p. 415; **fat** *ibid* p. 420; **Endo** *Up To Aden* (Tokyo 1964) p. 128; '**white hearts**' in Douglas Sladen & Norma Lorimer *More Queer Things About Japan* (Treherne London 1905) p. xx; '**last border**' see *Daedalus* p. 424; '**discontinuity**' *Daedalus* p. 421; **Aida** in *Journal of Social & Political Ideas in Japan* Vol 2 No 2 Aug 1964 p. 32; **Manchuria** in *Daedalus* p. 426; **Tamura** *Jo Taku* (*A Folio of Women's Rubbed Copies*) (Tokyo 1964) p. 73; '**white slavery**' *FEER* 27 Sep 1984; **Sagawa** *FEER* 27 Jun 1985; **Spencer** letter to Baron Kentaro Kaneko in *The Times* 18 Jan 1904, quoted in *Hearn* p. 483; **mixed** Theodate Geoffrey *An Immigrant in Japan* (Laurie London) p. 189; '**full up**' Marion Jansen, a teacher, in *Experience* p. 193; **missionary** Peter Herzog *ibid* p. 67; **Hearn** *Letters* p. 208; **Dingell** *JT* 19 May 1982; **Natsume** quoted in *Socialization* p. 502; **Kiel** *Contemporary Japan* (Tokyo) Vol 28 1964–7 p. 797; **Jap** *JQ* Vol 15, 1968 p. 491; **motorbikes** *Guardian* 25 May 1981; **Jews** *Interpreter* Vol 11 No 4 Spring 1977 p. 493; **Ben-Dasan** *The Japanese and the Jews* (Weatherhill New York 1972), see *JQ* Vol 19, 1972 p. 208; **blacks** *Daedalus* p. 413 and Churyo Morishima *Chitchats with the Dutch* (Tokyo 1943); **Perry** *Narrative of the Expedition of an American Squadron* (Appleton New York 1856) p. 296; **Fujishima** *Bungei Shunju* Feb 1966 p. 308; **Oe** *New Writing* p. 84; **Sawada** *JT* 9 Jul 1978, also information from Lewis Bush; **porter** *An Immigrant in Japan* p. 281; **arms** Henry Champly *White Women, Coloured Men* (Long London 1936) p. 132; '**surface concern**' Edward Seidensticker in *JQ* Vol 15, 1968 p. 491; **black dates** see Ian Buruma in *FEER* 11 Jul 1985; **Koreans** 'The Racial Problem in Japan,' *JQ* Vol 15, 1968 p. 286;

Kim see *Interpreter* Vol 11 No 4 Spring 1977 p. 534; **dogged** in *JQ* Vol 19, 1972 p. 39; **'handful'** Japan-US Economic Relations Group First Report Tokyo 1981 p. 66; **sumo** see *FEER* 8 Nov 1984 and *Asian Wall St Journal* (Hongkong) 13 Mar 1985; **Nishio** *Chuo Koron* Dec 1982 p. 216, also *Echo* Vol 10 No 1 Spring 1983 p. 73; **Amaya** *Bungei Shunju* Mar 1980, also *Echo* Vol 7 No 2 Summer 1980 p. 58; **Oe** *JQ* Vol 12, 1965 p. 350; **Raffles** *Encyclopaedia Britannica* 7th ed Vol 12, 1842 p. 510; **Rudyard Kipling** *From Sea to Sea* (MacMillan London 1900) Vol I p. 332; **Uchimura** *Sources II* p. 349.

Chapter 2: Drive A Nail of Gold – The Japanese Individual (pp. 18–38)

Debate Toshio Azuma in *JT* 21 Jul 1985; **Okonogi** *Chuo Koron* Jun 1978, also *Echo* Vol 5 No 4 Winter 1978 p. 88; **'abnormally'** *Chuo Koron* Aug 1982 p. 226, also *Echo* Vol 9 No 4 Winter 1982 p. 107; **hijack** *Echo* Vol 5 No 4 Winter 1978 p. 95; **Kosawa** see *Moloney* p. 200; **Frenchman** Jacques Lacan in *Interpreter* Vol 8 No 3 Autumn 1973 p. 389; **Hearn** *Letters* p. 10; **'alienation'** *Asahi Shimbun* 4 Jan 1968; **'unwise'** Kanji Nishio in *Echo* Vol 6 No 2 Summer 1979 p. 65; **'weakness'** *Sources II* p. 94; **bandwagon** see Basil Chamberlain's list in *Things Japanese* (Kegan Paul London 1890) p. 115; **Okakura** *The Japanese Spirit* (Constable London 1905) p. 53; **Morris** *The Phoenix Cup* (Cresset London 1947) p. 95; **'Sixteen Ways'** *Condon* p. 185; **Fukuzawa** p. 20; **smile** Yoshihiko Masuhara in *Shokun* Dec 1980 p. 56, also *Echo* Vol 8 No 2 Summer 1981 p. 122; **Hearn** *The Japanese Smile* (Hokuseido Tokyo 1952) p. 5; **Ohtski** quoted in *Moloney* p. 191; **Tsuburaya** *Chuo Koron* Dec 1981 p. 210; **directive** *Authority* p. 48; **White Paper** quoted *JQ* Vol 16, 1969 p. 406; **'not creative'** *Sunday Times* 27 Jun 1982; **baseball** see *Echo* Vol 8 No 2 Summer 1981 p. 30; **Kirkup** *JQ* Vol 12, 1965 p. 120; **Seidensticker** quoted in *Echo* Vol 2 No 1 Spring 1975 p. 143; **honorifics retreat** Yasusuke Murakami, Seizaburo Sato & Shumpei Kumon, *Echo* Vol 2 No 3 Autumn 1975 p. 25; **Shiba** *Interpreter* Vol 11 No 2 Autumn 1976 p. 146; **Dore** *International House of Japan Bulletin* (Tokyo) Aug 1965 p. 44; **Suzuki** *JQ* Vol 9, 1962 p. 165; **Kirkup** *JQ* Vol 17, 1970 p. 272; **Oshio** *Echo* Vol 8 No 2 Summer 1981 p. 53; **conversion** in Magnus Hirschfeld *Women East and West* (Heinemann London 1935) p. 18; **Nakasone** *JT* 4 Nov 1982; **glue weakening** see also Masakazu Yamázaki 'Signs of a New Individualism' *Chuo Koron* Aug 1983 p. 62, also in *Echo* Vol 11 No 1 Spring 1984 p. 8; **Natsume** see *JQ* Vol 12, 1965 p. 506; **Arima** *Failure* p. 78; **Mushakoji** *ibid* pp. 113–4; **Akutagawa** *ibid* p. 161; **Sugai** *JQ* Vol 12, 1965 p. 190; **Mishima** *Echo* Vol 8 No 1 Spring 1981 p. 112; **suicide** Yamazaki, see Minami in *Annals of the Hitotsubashi Academy* (Tokyo) Vol 4 No 2 1954 p. 148; **Okonogi** *Echo* Vol 6 No 1 Spring 1979 p. 110; **Sogo** Culture Encounter Symposium, Tokyo 22 May 1982; **Okonogi** *Echo ibid* p. 106; **Thatcher** see *Echo* Vol 10 No 3 Autumn 1983 p. 74; **Hagiwara** *JQ* Vol 19, 1972 p. 173; **chocolates** see *Intersect* (PHP Tokyo) Feb 1985; **'outsider'** *Condon* p. 235; **Ilara** *Interpreter* Vol 11 No 1 Spring 1976 p. 58; **'choice'** Masako Shinkawa in *Interpreter* Vol 11 No 3 Winter 1977 p. 402; **'race values'** see Prof Michiko Hasegawa in *Chuo Koron* May 1984, and further discussion in *Echo* Vol 11 No 4 1984 p. 48; **rape** see *JT* 21 Jun 1985; **'shapely'** in *Makoto, British Teachers' Impressions of Japan* (ed Tames) (Japan Foundation London 1978) p. 36; **Hamaguchi** *Kikan Chuo Koron* Spring 1981 and *Echo* Vol 8 No 2 Summer 1981 p. 53; **Endo** *Echo* Vol 10 No 3 Autumn 1983 p. 88; **Doi** in *Aspects of Social Change* p. 334; **3%** see Sen Nishiyama in *JT* Aug 1985; **Doi** *The Anatomy of Dependence* (Kodansha Tokyo 1973); **Dore** Arthur Palmer MP quoted *New Society* 9 Jul 1981; **Hearn** *Editorials from the 'Kobe Chronicle'* (Hokuseido Tokyo 1960) p. 60; **Buchan** *FEER* 11 Nov 1977.

Chapter 3: Lions or Lambs? – The Japanese Family (pp. 39–51)

Tayama in *Failure* p. 119; **housewife** quoted in *New Straits Times* (Kuala Lumpur) 10 Nov 1980; **fathers** see *Tokyo Newsletter* Feb 1984; **touching** in *Condon* p. 76; **Akihito** see Vogel *Japan's New Middle Class* p. 182; **ironing** see *Interpreter* Vol 11 No 1 Spring 1976 p. 61; '**sleeping together**' in *City Life* p. 49; **sex frequency** *The Observer* 25 Aug 1985; **Ajase** Keigo Okonogi 'The Ajase Complex of the Japanese' *Chuo Koron* Jun 1978, also in *Echo* Vol 5 No 4 Winter 1978 p. 89 and Vol 6 No 1 Spring 1979 p. 104; **Rapoport** *Fin Tim* 14 Sept 1985 and subsequent letters from readers; **Kosawa** Okonogi *op. cit.*; **orgasm** see de Vos *Socialization* p. 58; **Sato** *The Times* 31 Dec 1968; **extra-marital** Welfare Ministry 1960 survey, see *Straits Times* (Singapore) 20 Jun 1970; **Mifune** *JT* 3 Dec 1974; **Sada** *Int Her Trib* 24 Sep 1979; **wife-swapping** see *JT* 21 Jul 1975; **Morita** *JT* 4 Dec 1978; **Diana** Tomoko Inoue in *Chuo Koron* Dec 1981 and *Echo* Vol 9 No 1 Spring 1982 p. 43; **Edwardian** Sladen *op. cit.* p. 11; **Mother House** *Guardian* 15 Aug 1981; **Levine** quoted in Harris *House of the 10,000 Pleasures* (Allen London 1962) p. 211; **aunt** see Don Oberdorfer of *Washington Post* in *New Nation* (Singapore) 8 Sep 1975; **hamsters** cited by Tomonori Ito in *JT* 25 Feb 1980; **potty-training** see especially Vogel *Japan's New Middle Class* pp. 235–52; '**today's parents**' *Japan Times* 6 Feb 1983; **Kubo** *JQ* Vol 9 1962 p. 262; **Hattori** *The Times* 14 Nov 1968; '**brothers**' Koji Nakamura in *FEER* 4 Mar 1972; **Iwai** *Voice* Nov 1981, also *Echo* Vol 9 Special Issue 1982 p. 51; **couples reacting** see *JT* 29 Sep 1985.

Chapter 4: Life Below the Navel – Sex in Japan (pp. 52–64)

Tanizaki the professor in *The Key*; **Portuguese** Jorge Alvares, quoted in *They Came* p. 238; **Smith** *Ten Weeks in Japan* (Longman London 1861) p. 104; '**device**' Junichiro Tanizaki *Some Prefer Nettles* (Tuttle Tokyo 1958) p. 194; **bath** housewife in Smith & Beardsley (eds) *Japanese Culture* (Methuen London 1963) p. 125 and Stanley Levine in Harris (ed) *House of the 10,000 Pleasures* (Allen London 1962) p. 211; **Sakura** quoted in R. H. Blyth *Oriental Humour* (Hokuseido Tokyo 1959) p. 445; **Ozu** *Good Morning (Ohayo)*, see *New Statesman* 12 Aug 1966; '**malodorous**' quoted in *Interpreter* Vol 12 No 1 Winter 1978 p. 66; **pee-ing** *FEER* 3 Sep 1982; **balls** see Louis Allen 'Death and Honour in Japan' *The Listener* 24 Jun 1976 p. 801; **examples** from Buruma *A Japanese Mirror* p. 110, *Fin Tim* 5 Jan 1984, Ryotaro Nohmura in *PHP* Jan 1982, and *JT* 11 Apr 1984 from *Elle Teen*; **Maraini** 'Westernization of Sin', *JQ* Vol 14, 1967 p. 220; **Mishima** Warburg's letter in *The Times Literary Supplement* 26 Mar 1971; '**the mouth**' Tsuya-giku in *House of the 10,000 Pleasures op. cit.* p. 107, see also James Cleugh *Oriental Orgies* (Blond London 1968) p. 190; '**Kiss Papa**' *JT* 30 Dec 1984; **Hollywood** *FEER* 24 Dec 1976; **Asayama** *Sex in the 20th Century* (Tokyo); **Chikamatsu** *Four Major Plays* (Columbia New York 1961) p. 156; **American** Sydney L. Gulick *Evolution of the Japanese* (Revell New York 1905) p. 151; **Kawai** *Chuo Koron* Feb 1976 and *Echo* Vol 3 No 2 Summer 1976 p. 129; '**gambling**' Blyth *Oriental Humour op. cit.* p. 378; **handshake** *JT* 14 Aug 1978; **lover's bank** see Robert Whymant in *Sunday Times* 8 Mar 1984; '**Japanese men**' *Int Her Trib* 22 Sep 1981; **12th century** see *JT* 18 Jun 1983; **Genji** Lady Murasaki *The Tale of Genji* (trans. Waley, Boston 1925) p. 80; **clothes-line** *City Life* p. 110; '**brag**' Alessandro Valignano quoted in *They Came* p. 46; **Fernandez** *ibid* p. 47; **Grosbois** *Shunga* (Nagel Geneva 1964) p. 54; **psychiatrist** Tadao Miyamoto 'The Japanese and Psychoanalysis' in *Tenbo* Jan 1983, also in *Interpreter* Vol 8 No 3 Autumn 1973 p. 388; **Hirschfeld** *Women East and West* (Heinemann London 1935) p. 30; **Sakamoto** in *JT* 20 Aug 1983; **candidate** *The Times* 21 Jun 1980; **lesbian** cited in Buruma *A Japanese Mirror* p. 45; **opinion survey** cited in *Echo* Vol 9 Special Issue 1982 p. 67; **Terayama** see *Interpreter* Vol 11 No 1

Spring 1976 p. 34; **measurements** *Daedalus* p. 440; **Tanizaki** *Renai Oyobi Shikijo* (Tokyo 1932), quoted in Buruma *A Japanese Mirror* p. 52.

Chapter 5: The Loosening of the Group – Japan's Social Structure (pp. 65–79)

Chamberlain *Things Japanese op. cit.* p. 268; **vivisection** in Seiichi Morimura *The Devil's Gluttony*, see Whymant in *Guardian* 14 Aug 1982; **de Vos** *Socialization* p. 9; **psychologist** Keigo Okonogi in *Chuo Koron* Jun 1978 and *Echo* Vol 6 No 1 Spring 1979 p. 105; **ambassador** Ichiro Kawasaki *Japan Unmasked* (Tuttle Tokyo 1969) p. 169; **Nakane** *Human Relations in Japan* (Foreign Ministry Tokyo 1972) p. 22; **rugger** *JT* 27 Feb 1977; **Buddhism** Yasunori Sone 'Stereotyping the Japanese' *Business Nippon* (Tokyo) 1982; **60%** Hillis Lory *Japan's Military Masters* (Viking New York 1943) p. 176; **Ohira** *JT* 26 Apr 1979; **post-Marxist** Rob Steven *Classes in Contemporary Japan* (Cambridge 1983) and Tadashi Fukutake *The Japanese Social Structure, Its Evolution in the Modern Century* (University of Tokyo Press 1982); **middle class** see especially Earl H. Kinmonth in *JT* 17 Mar 1985; **'drifting'** Shigeru Aoki 'Debunking the 90% Middle Class Myth' *Asahi Janaru* 9 Mar 1979, see also Masako Ozawa in *JT* 28 Nov 1984; **'clans'** Kokingo Ohara cited in *Failure* p. 17; **burakumin** 'Many people' *Int Her Trib* 9 Mar 1983, 'discrimination' Akio Imaizumi *Dowa Problem* (Foreign Ministry Tokyo 1977) p. 3, 'single race' *ibid* p. 1, 'consumed' Hideo Watanabe quoted in *The Times* 23 Dec 1977; **Yanagita** see *Echo* Vol 5 No 2 Summer 1978 p. 67; **word similarity** Susumu Ono in Smith & Beardsley (eds) *Japanese Culture op. cit.* p. 20; **'mantle'** Hyoe Murakami in *Mugendai* No 32, 1977 and *Echo* Vol 4 No 3 Autumn 1977 p. 132; **Kawasaki** *Japan Unmasked* (Tuttle Tokyo 1969) p. 152; **Japanology** *JT* 15 Aug 1985; **'emotional animals'** *Guardian* 1 Mar 1974; **Maraini** in *Experience* p. 16–7; **Lin** cited in *PHP* Sep 1980; **'crying'** *City Life* p. 448; **'minor key'** Toshiro Mayuzumi in *Voice* Jul 1978 p. 106, also in *Echo* Vol 5 No 4 Winter 1978 p. 112; **Doi** *The Anatomy of Dependence* (Kodansha Tokyo 1973), see also Keigo Okonogi in *Chuo Koron* Jun 1978 and *Echo* Vol 5 No 4 Winter 1978 p. 89; **Hasegawa** see *Sources II* p. 385; **Amaya** in *Shukan Toyo Keizai* 9 Apr 1977, also in *Echo* Vol 4 No 3 Autumn 1977 p. 26; **Clark** *JT* 14 Feb 1982; **Shoga** *JQ* Vol 14, 1967 p. 221; **'relationism'** see Study Group for Trans-border Policy and Administration *Beyond Economic Frictions* (Tokyo 1982) pp. 9–11 and Hamaguchi in *Echo* Vol 8 No 2 Summer 1981 p. 50; **Nakane** *Human Relations in Japan* (Foreign Ministry Tokyo 1972) p. 46; **'fear the advent'** Nishio Kanji 'Competition: Its Merits & Contradictions' *Chuo Koron* Mar 1979 p. 58, also *Echo* Vol 6 No 2 Summer 1979 p. 66; **textbooks** *ibid* p. 65.

Chapter 6: Children of the Sun – Japanese Youth and Education (pp. 80–88)

Morita *Japan Economic Journal* (Tokyo) 28 May 1974; **'respecting parents'** *JT* 3 Apr 1984; **'Occupation policy'** Mitsuo Setoyama in *Int Her Trib* 21 Mar 1983; **Nakasone** 'The Logic of New Conservatism' Oct 1978, cited in *JT* 12 Aug 1984; **EEC official** *Int Her Trib* 30 Mar 1981; **'more valuable'** Michio Nagai in *Los Angeles Times* and *New Nation* 16 May 1977; **22 times** *ibid*; **unstimulating professors** cited by Kazuko Tsurumi in *JQ* Vol 15, 1968 p. 443; **first American** Morley Robertson 1981 see *Int Her Trib* 16 May 1984; **psychiatric treatment** *Portrait* p. 285; **receiver** Tanezo Hayakawa see *Fin Tim* 5 Dec 1975; **Sakamoto** *Int Her Trib* 12 Mar 1985; **Matsushita** *Japan At The Brink* (Kodansha Tokyo 1975); **violence at home statistics** Iwai in *Voice* Nov 1981 also *Echo* Vol 9 Special Issue 1982 p. 47; **Call Us Crystal** by Yasuo Tanaka; **violence at school statistics** Yoshiya Soeda 'Changing Patterns of Juvenile Agression' *Echo* Vol 10 No 3 Autumn 1983 p. 12, also Akira Fukushima in *Echo* Vol 9 Special Issue 1982 p. 93; **'Japan Times'** 6 Nov 1983; **comics** Nobuko Hara *Fin Tim* 15 Jul 1985; **sake** *ibid*; **'vile influence'** Tsutomu Ouchi *JT* 16 Dec 1979; **Kirkup** *Int Her Trib* 28 Jun 1984;

248   *Notes*

Keio *Bunka Kaigi* Mar 1981 p. 40, also *Echo* Vol 8 No 3 Autumn 1981 p. 121; **selfishness poll** *Voice* Nov 1981, also *Echo* Vol 9 Special Issue 1982 p. 47; **Tokyo University politics** *Chuo Koron* Dec 1983 p. 62, also *Echo* Vol 11 No 1 Spring 1984 p. 28; **western resident** Binstock *Fin Tim* 23 Jul 1984.

Chapter 7: A Spoonful of Shinto – Japanese Religion (pp. 89–95)

Ahmaddiya *Guardian* 3 Jan 1984; **American** *ibid*; **Rev. Endo** *JT* 21 Aug 1984; **bathroom** *JQ* Vol 15, 1968 p. 496; **all gods** Kazuo Kawai *Interlude* p. 73; 'Evil' *Mugendai* No 32 1977, also *Echo* Vol 4 No 3 Autumn 1977 p. 133; **spoonfuls** Sontoku Ninomiya *Sources II* p. 80: **Uemura** *JQ* Vol 11, 1964 p. 226; **Uchimura** *Failure* p. 27; **Petitjean** *Echo* Vol 1 No 1 1974 p. 75; **journalist** Peter Robinson in *JQ* Vol 14, 1967 p. 490; **Christ's tomb** Rowland Gould in *This Is Japan 1969* (Asahi Shimbun Tokyo) and *JQ* Vol 16, 1969 p. 207; **Marxist** Hajime Kawakami *Sources II* p. 315; **Santa** *Fin Tim* 27 Dec 1984; **merger** Kanji Kato see *Authority* p. 105; **Soka Gakkai** Richard West *New Statesman* 12 Jun 1964; **cars** *JT* 3 Jan 1969; **phallic** *Shukan Bunshun* Aug 1974 and *JT* 5 Aug 1974; **TDK** *JT* 14 Nov 1983; **psychoanalyst** Heisaku Kosawa see *Moloney* p. 96; **Tanaka** *New Nation* 24 Jan 1974; **Endo** *Yellow Man*; **Ishihara** 'A Nation Without Morality' in *The Silent Power, Japan's Identity and World Role* (Simul Tokyo 1976) p. 75.

Chapter 8: Tongue-Tied Muse – Japanese Arts and Language (pp. 96–106)

Garbo *Unesco Courier* (Paris) Sep 1968 p. 45; **revolving stage** *JQ* Vol 11, 1964 p. 302; **Okakura** *The Japanese Spirit* (Constable London 1905) p. 127; **Kurosawa** *JQ* Vol 12, 1965 p. 64; **Takamura** 'My Poetry' in *Landscapes* p. 155; 'elevates silence' Takeyoshi Kawashima in *Sekai* Feb 1979, also in *Echo* Vol 6 No 3 Autumn 1979 p. 108; **farmer's wife** *Echo* Vol 4 No 4 Winter 1977 p. 131; **German** *Newsweek* 23 Mar 1981; **Ozaki** *Portrait* p. 228; **Mishima** *Interpreter* Vol 7 No 1 Winter 1971 p. 78; **the dream** told to Angela Carter in *Experience* p. 31; **Miyazawa** interview Derek Davies *FEER* 4 Nov 1977 p. 23; **Oshima** in *Voices from the Japanese Cinema* Joan Mellen (Liveright New York 1975); **Sera** in *FEER* 13 Jun 1980; **translator** Noriaki Suzuma in *Illustrated London News* Feb 1983; **Reischauer** *The Japanese* (Belknap Cambridge 1977); **Waley** see *JQ* Vol 18, 1971 p. 108; 'Ambush' see *New Writing* p. 143; **ideographs** 'nuisance' Kamo Mabuchi in *Sources II* p. 14, Reischauer in *Twelve Doors* p. 202, 'won the war' see Ikutaro Shimizu in *Chuo Koron* Nov 1974 and *Echo* Vol 2 No 1 Spring 1975 p. 107; **Shiga** see *JT* 12 Nov 1984; 'nowhere' Edward Seidensticker in *Encounter* Jun 1970; **Fitzgerald** in *National Geographic Magazine* Vol 149 No 1 1976 p. 59; **Makioka Sisters** (Tuttle Tokyo 1958) p. 478; **Takemitsu** in *The Listener* (London) 16 Feb 1984.

Chapter 9: The Cut Flowers of Democracy – Japan's Government, Politics, Media and Law (pp. 107–127)

Nakasone flower *FEER* 20 Oct 1978; 'unforgivable' Kingo Machimura *JT* 5 Dec 1980; 'ugliness' Michihiko Hasegawa in *Shokun* Dec 1984, also *Echo* Vol 12 No 2 Summer 1985; 'Asian-style' see Kenzo Uchida in *Chuo Koron* Jan 1983, also *Echo* Vol 10 No 1 Spring 1983 p. 22; **Kita** *Sources II* p. 272; 'period piece' quoted in *Authority* p. 285; **phraseology** see *Interlude* pp. 52 and 57, Gregory Clark in *FEER* 20 Jul 1970, and Sadanori Yamanaka in *JT* 26 Apr 1972; 'dictatorship' *Asahi Shimbun* 17 Jun 1960, see Saburo Matsukata's discussion in *JQ* Vol 7, 1960 p. 421; **Eto** *Bungei Shunju* Feb 1977 and *Interpreter* Vol 11 No 4 Spring 1977 p. 422; **Tanaka** *Nihon Keizai Shimbun* 25 Jan 1983; 'not steal' quoted in *The Economist* 10 Dec 1983; **postman** quoted in *The Economist* Oct 1976; 'fish' Akiro Hatano *Asahi Shimbun* 11 Nov 1983; 'shoplifting'

Naoki Komura *JT* 24 Jan 1983; **sake** *JT* 19 May 1972; **Justice Minister** Eisaku Sumi *JT* 5 Feb 1984; **Natsume** Daisuke in *Since Then*; '**dogs**' Uchida *op. cit.* (*Echo* Spring 1983) p. 21; **Ohira** *JT* 14 Jun 1979; '**The leader**' Timothy Langley *JT* 28 Aug 1983; Robert Scalapino and Junnosuke Masumi *Parties and Politics in Contemporary Japan* (Berkeley 1962); **teuchi** see illuminating discussion by *Yomiuri Shimbun*'s Hiroyuki Kawaguchi 'The Japanese Method of Settling Disputes' in *Chuo Koron* Dec 1982 and *Echo* Vol 10 No 1 Spring 1983 p. 30; **Takeshita** *FEER* 20 Oct 1983; **Tanaka** *Bungei Shunju* Nov 1974, *JT* 14 Oct 1974 and *Fin Tim* 11 Oct 1983; '**pledge**' Kimpei Shiba *Asahi Evening News*, cited in *Guardian* 22 Jun 1979; '**puppet**' *JT* 29 Feb 1980; **pneumonia** Sutsuta in *Chuo Koron* Jul 1978 and *Echo* Vol 5 No 3 Autumn 1978 p. 47; **Justice Minister** Takeji Kobayashi Jan 1969 *New Nation* 19 Feb 1970; **China textbook** *Sankei* 7 Sep 1982 and *Echo* Vol 9 No 4 Winter 1982 p. 13; '**disputes**' *Now You Live in Japan* (Research Committee for Bicultural Life in Japan, Tokyo 1975), see *JT* 22 Nov 1975; **hijack** Sunao Sonoda in *JT* 9 Oct 1977; **drowning** see *JT* editorial 12 Mar 1983; **Justice Minister** Tadao Kuraishi FEER 23 Nov 1979; **pharmacists** *JT* 10 Dec 1982; **perjury** Murata *JT* 25 Jun 1976; **Egawa** *Echo* Vol 6 No 2 Summer 1979 p. 11; **sugar** Ichiro Hatoyama 13 Sep 1977; **Tanaka** *JT* 10 Nov 1984; '**we don't go**' quoted in Gregory Clark *FEER* 20 Jul 1970.

Chapter 10: Naked Under Article Nine – Japan's Defences (pp. 128–138)

Times editorial 13 Aug 1985; **Nixon** in 1951, see *FEER* 31 Jul 1969; **Nakasone** *My Life in Politics* cited *FEER* 24 Dec 1983; **polls** *JT* 14 May 1984; '**a sin**' Shigeru Nambara in *Sekai* Jan 1964 also *JQ* Vol 11, 1964 p. 230; **Tanaka** at 1969 newspaper symposium quoted in Radha Sinha *Japan's Options for the 1980's* (Croom Helm London 1982) p. 209; '**It was necessary**' Michiko Hasegawa in *Int Her Trib* 14 Aug 1985; '*white man*' *FEER* and *JT* 10 Nov 1968; '**run away**' poll *JT* 14 May 1984; **Red or Dead** see Tsuneari Fukuda 'A Critique of Opinions on Defence' *Chuo Koron* Oct 1979 and *Echo* Vol 7 No 1 Spring 1980 p. 69; **Ishihara** *Jiyu* May 1972; **Kataoka** *Shokun* Oct 1979 and *Echo* Vol 7 No 1 Spring 1980 p. 96; **Shimizu** 'Japan, Be a State!' *Shokun* Jul 1980; **Inoki** *Chuo Koron* Sep 1980 and *Echo* Vol 7 No 4 Winter 1980 p. 87; **Nakagawa** *Shokun* Sep 1980.

Chapter 11: The Company is Eternal – Japan's Economic Structure (pp. 139–151)

Okita see Ikuhiko Hata *Bungei Shunju* Oct 1981 and *Echo* Vol 11 Special Issue 1984; **Economist** Norman Macrae 27 May 1967; **small car** Suzuki Motors see *JT* 30 Apr 1984; **Sweden** *Seiron* Apr 1977 and *Echo* Vol 4 No 2 Summer 1977; **Yomiuri** editorial quoted in *The Times* 17 Sep 1972; **suicide** in Takeshi Ishida *The Integration of Conformity and Competition, A Key to Understanding Japanese Society* (Foreign Press Centre Tokyo 1980) p. 16; **Morita** Los Angeles speech 24 Sep 1981; **bid** Minebea, see *Fin Tim* 4 Sep 1985; **capitalism poll** see *Echo* Vol 5 Special Issue 1978 p. 75; **Mitsubishi** Masaki Nakajima in *Int Her Trib* 6 Mar 1978; **financial centre** William Horsley in *The Listener* 12 Dec 1985; **Reischauer** *The Japanese* (Harvard Cambridge 1977) p. 194; **Amaya** *FEER* 29 Oct 1982; **Miyazawa** *Jiyu Shimpo* 17 Jul 1973; **Amaya** *Bungei Shunju* Dec 1980 and *Echo* Vol 8 No 1 Spring 1981 p. 92; **kyoso** *Fukuzawa* p. 202; '**Inhibited**' Akira Fukushima 'The Human Cost of Corporate Success' *Voice* Oct 1981 and *Echo* Vol 8 No 4 Winter 1981 p. 75.

Chapter 12: Bottom-Up Workaholics – Japan's Management, Labour & Science (pp. 152–171)

jobless see Radha Sinha *Japan's Options for the 1980's* (Croom Helm London 1982) pp. 116–22, and **doubling** Nomura Research Institute report see *The Times* 3 Sep

250 *Notes*

1985; **Kirkup** *Heaven, Hell and Harakiri* (Angus London 1974) p. 252; '**gardening**' Hyoe Murakami *Mugendai* No 32, 1977; **weeding** Tetsuro Morimoto *Sekai* Dec 1977 and *Echo* Vol 5 No 1 Spring 1978 p. 57; **Iida** paper at CULCON conference Tokyo Jun 1982; **Morita** quoted in excellent discussion by *Asahi Shimbun* writer Hiroshi Ando 'Has Japan Really Pulled Ahead?' *Voice* May 1980 and *Echo* Vol 7 No 3 Autumn 1980 p. 54; **Plath** *The After-Hours: Modern Japan and the Search for Enjoyment* (Berkeley 1964) p. 90; **Toyota** *JT* 22 Jul 1971; '**female**' Kenichi Imai *Kikan Chuo Koron* Spring 1980; '**Americans more loyal**' *Look Japan* (Tokyo) 10 Jun 1984; **Hayashi** *Daily Telegraph* 30 Jan 1982; **Nissan** Nobutoshi Ochi *Guardian* 3 Apr 1981; **Matsushita** *PHP* magazine (Tokyo) Jun 1981; **secretary** Richard T. Pascale and Anthony G. Athos *The Art of Japanese Management* (Simon & Shuster New York 1981) p. 137; **Sony** quoted in Malcolm Trevor *Japan's Reluctant Multinationals* (Pinter London 1983) p. 144; **Tsukamoto** *PHP* magazine (Tokyo) Oct 1981; '**mediocre**' Joseph Z. Reday letter in *The Economist* 12 Apr 1980; **Honda** *Guardian* 10 Jul 1967; **Morita** speech in Los Angeles 24 Sep 1981; **Nissan robots** Ichiro Shioji *The Times* 3 Nov 1981; '**front-line**' Tsuneo Iida *Chuo Koron* Jan 1978, also *Echo* Vol 5 No 1 Spring 1978 p. 106; **Tennessee** *The Times* 21 Jul 1984; '**I forced**' *Sunday Times* 6 Dec 1981; **Economist** Norman Macrae survey 27 May 1967; **Esaki** *Japan Times* editorial 1 Apr 1974; **poems** see Shuichi Kato *JQ* Vol 13, 1966 p. 480; **bread** *Landscapes* p. 41; '**originality**' Chiang Monlin *Tides from the West* (Yale UP 1947) p. 230; '**trying to fly**' Hiroshi Yamada *JT* 3 Oct 1983; '**slows**' quoted by Hidemasa Morikawa 'Engineers and National Prosperity' *Chuo Koron Quarterly* Spring 1976; **de Bono** *Fin Tim* 5 Oct 1971.

Chapter 13: Capturing the Regimental Colours – Japan's Foreign Trade (pp. 172–194)

Kipling *From Sea to Sea* Vol 1 p. 366 (he is quoting an English tea merchant in Kyoto in 1888); **sex** Donald Richie in *Experience* p. 56; **Sony** Morita speech in Europe 2 Feb 1982; '**yellow**' Democrat Representative John D. Dingell in closed House meeting Washington 26 Feb 1982, see *Int Her Trib* 25 Mar 1982 and *JT* 30 Jul 1982; '**prejudice**' *Asahi Shimbun* cited *FEER* 28 Nov 1980; **Connally** *Int Her Trib* 30 Oct 1982; **Morita** *Int Her Trib* 25 Mar 1982; '**cheats**' *Newsweek* cited *JT* 17 Jul 1982; **ambassador** Cortazzi *JT* 1 Feb 1982; **French** *Nikei Business* (Tokyo) 22 Feb 1982; **Dutch** see *Int Her Trib* 24 Sep 1979; **Nihon Keizai** *ibid*; **Ball** 19 May 1971 statement to Senate sub-committee; '**haulers**' Second Jones Report *JT* 17 Sep 1980; **Mondale** *JT* 11 Nov 1982; **Briton** Geoffrey Shepherd *World Economy* Dec 1981 p. 388; **settle** Ken Ishii *Int Her Trib* 21 Jun 1983; '**war**' Kazumi Masuda *JT* 17 Dec 1976; '**Why be nice?**' cited by Stokes *Int Her Trib* 17 Jan 1977; **Amaya** *Kancho Nyusu Jihyo* Jan 1977; **Olmer** *JT* 30 Jul 1982; **German** see Takashi Oshio *Chuo Koron* May 1982 and *Echo* Vol 9 No 3 Autumn 1982 p. 110; '**war**' *ibid* p. 105; '**never spontaneous**' Masaru Yoshimori *JT* 17 Jul 1982; **Economist** 7 Feb 1981; '**obscene**' see e.g. Christopher Huhne in *Guardian* 20 Sep 1984; **defining surplus** see e.g. Kenichi Ohmae of McKinsey in *JT* 5 Jul 1985 and *Economist* 6 Jul 1985, also Hajime Karatsu in *Echo* Vol 11 No 3 Autumn 1984 p. 26; **French** Perrin-Pelletier *Fin Tim* 12 Mar 1980; **Jenkins** Peter Dryer of *Journal of Commerce* (New York), speaking in Brussels Jun 1979; '**falsity**' Japan-US Economic Relations Group First Report Jan 1981 p. 16; **France** *JT* 20 Oct 1981; '**tearfully**' Kiyohiko Fukushima *Bungei Shunju* Oct 1977; **MITI** Kazuo Wakasugi *Int Her Trib* 25 Mar 1982; **Yomiuri** editorial 2 Apr 1965; **Edwardes** *The Times* 1 Oct 1981; **Okita** Press briefing of 13 Mar 1982 (Foreign Ministry) p. 28; **Economist** 12 Jun 1982; **Friedman** *Free to Choose* (Secker & Warburg London 1980); '**psychologically**' Hiroya Ichikawa 'Towards Better Japan-Europe Relations' for Japan Caravan in

Europe Feb 1982; '**Saracens**' *Fin Tim* 10 Nov 1982; '**impervious**' Leslie Fielding talk to US Chamber of Commerce Tokyo Apr 1982; '**societal**' Gibbon Report on US Far East trade, House of Representatives, Washington Dec 1981; '**outrageous**' Kentaro Koshiba *JT* 3 Feb 1982; **woolly** *Japan Task Force*, Japanese Chamber of Commerce, London Oct 1976; **sake** Tsunesuke Yoshimura *Int Her Trib* 7 Oct 1978; **Labour Minister** Toshio Yamaguchi *JT* 2 Jul 1985; **MOSS** William Horsley in *The Listener* 12 Dec 1985; **Action Programme** ibid.; **Rempell** *JT* 30 Jul 1978 and 23 Feb 1979; **Adams** 'Letters of Will Adams' in Sladen *More Queer Things About Japan op. cit.* p. 240; **Rotary** *Fin Tim* 12 Mar 1980; '**concubine**' *Bungei Shunju* Jul 1981 and *JT* 13 Jun 1981, also Amaya in *Journal of Japanese Trade & Industry* (Tokyo) No 1 Jan 1982; **LA Times** see *JT* 8 May 1984; '**raped**' *Guardian* 15 Jul 1982; **Fin Times** editorial 23 Apr 1982; **economist** J. Y. Bourlet *The Times* 30 Dec 1980.

Chapter 14: Betting on the Anglo-Saxons – Japan and the West (pp. 195–213)

Ohira *The Times* 14 Jan 1972; **Housman** *Collected Poems* (Cape London 1939) p. 111; '**a flaw**' Tadao Umesao 'Escape from Cultural Isolation' in *The Silent Power, Japan's Identity and World Role*; (Simul Tokyo 1976) p. 31; **Ishibashi** *On Unarmed Neutrality* (JSP Tokyo 1983), also *Echo* Vol 11 No 1 Spring 1984 p. 50; '**We came back**' letter to *Japan Times* 2 May 1981; **banker** *PHP* magazine (Tokyo) Sep 1983; **New York** *JT* 20 May 1984; **Prime Minister** Ohira and Nakasone are examples; **Yamagiwa** *Twelve Doors* p. 232; **Honda** cited in *Discovery* p. 116; **Natsume** quoted in Edwin McClellan *Two Japanese Novelists* (Univ. Chicago 1969) p. 13; '**People talk**' *PHP* magazine (Tokyo) Dec 1981; **Korean** June Silla in *Experience* p. 145; **Ishida** *JQ* Vol 8, 1961 p. 401; '**Englishmen**' cited *Condon* p. 118; '**brazenly**' Hisahiko Okazaki *Voice* Jul 1979 and *Echo* Vol 6 No 3 Autumn 1979 p. 40; **Kobori** *Shokun* Jun 1983; '**God on top**' *JT* 26 Aug 1984; **Diosy** *The New Far East* (Cassell London 1904) p. 291; **Allen** from a pamphlet 'Japan in the World of To-day'; **Romeo** Mitsuo Nakamura *Japanese Fiction in the Meiji Era* (Kokusai Bunka Shinkokai Tokyo 1966) p. 24; **anatomy** Genpaku Sugita *Discovery* pp. 29–30; '**science**' Shozan Sakuma *Sources II* p. 103; **Mori** see *JQ* Vol 12, 1965 p. 239; **Eeyore** fat man in Oe Kenzaburo's 'Teach Us to Outgrow Our Madness'; **Umesao** *Asahi Shimbun* Jan 1967 but see *Echo* Vol 2 No 1 Spring 1975 pp. 129–30; **Randolph** 'A Spenglerian View of Japan' *JQ* Vol 11, 1964 p. 96; **living standards** James Murdoch *History of Japan* (Kobe 1902), see Kanji Nishio 'Japan's Parallel Path to Modernity' *Chuo Koron* Dec 1982 and *Echo* Vol 10 No 1 Spring 1983 p. 69; '**Rescue**' Karatsu Hajime see *Int Her Trib* 13 Sep 1980; **Okita** 'Press briefing' (Foreign Ministry) 18 Mar 1982 p. 30; '**stingy**' Sasei Masamori *Shokun* Mar 1977; '**no choice**' Hisahiko Okazaki *Voice, Echo op. cit.* p. 39; **Brzezinski** *The Fragile Blossom* (Harper & Row New York 1972); '**golf**' *Fin Tim* 3 Oct 1980; '**rural credit**' Naomi Nishimura *JT* 5 Dec 1971; **Mushakoji** quoted by Seidensticker in *JQ* Vol 15, 1968 p. 492; **Tokutomi** *ibid*; **Tazaki** *The Times* 12 Oct 1981; **Kiku** *Guardian* 16 Jun 1984; **Maruyama** *Thought and Behaviour in Modern Japanese Politics* (Oxford UP London 1963) p. 85; **Korean** Silla in *Experience* p. 145; **Beasley** review of Reischauer's *The Japanese* in *The Times Literary Supplement* 18 Nov 1977; '**Lebensraum**' 'Traveller's Tales' in *FEER* 2 Jan 1971; **Kimura** *JT* 15 Jun 1982; **Nixon** a good account is in Frank Gibney 'The Japanese and their Language' *Encounter* Dec 1974 p. 35; **Ohira** see *Japan's Defence Debate* (Foreign Press Centre Tokyo 1981) pp. 14–5; **Suzuki** *Sekai* Jul 1979; '**commitment**' Takeshi Igarashi *Asahi Janaru* 5 Jun 1981; **Mushakoji** 'The Cultural Premises of Japanese Diplomacy' in *The Silent Power* (Simul Tokyo 1976) p. 35; **Regan** *Philadelphia Enquirer* 24 Mar 1982.

Chapter 15: Half-Hearted Elder Brother – Japan and the Third World (pp. 214–224)

Tang Chiang Monlin *Tides from the West* (Yale 1947) p. 230; **'indebted'** *JT* editorial 28 Aug 1982; **Matsui** cited in Maruyama *Thought & Behaviour* p. 95; **'wise no more'** *Landscapes* p. 273; **'Chinka'** see *FEER* 15 Aug 1985; **'cheeky'** Ashihei Hino *War and Soldier* (Putnam London 1940) p. 31; **'bayonets'** Prince Mikasa Takahito *Ancient Oriental History and I*, see *JT* 19 Jun 1984; **chauffeur** *JQ* Vol 12, 1965 p. 90; **Tanaka** see Murata in *JT* 6 Aug 1982; **Zhou** *FEER* 2 Apr 1973; **Okakura** *The Ideals of the East* (Murray London 1905), a book written in Tagore's home in Calcutta; **Fukuzawa** 'On Departure from Asia' *Jiji Shimpo* 16 Mar 1885 also *JQ* Vol 18, 1971 p. 318; **Tarui** see Kuo Hui Tai in *JT* 23 Mar 1977; **'central'** Toru Yano see *FEER* 4 Nov 1977; **'tense up'** Kazutoshi Hasegawa *Bungei Shunju* Sep 1977; **Tagore** Krishna Kripalani *Rabindranath Tagore* (Oxford London 1962) p. 256; **Okawa** *Sources II p. 289;* **'your voice'** *Rabindranath Tagore Centenary Volume* (Sahitya Delhi 1961) p. 340; **Nehru** *Toward Freedom* (Day New York 1941) p. 29; **100 Years War** Fusao Hayashi articles in *Chuo Koron* 1963, see *JT* 23 Jan 1964; **'Asian people'** Prof Ienaga in Lebra (ed) *Japan's Great East Asia Co-Prosperity Sphere* (Oxford London 1976); **Fujiwara** F. Kikan *Japanese Army Intelligence Operations in SE Asia* (Heinemann Hongkong 1983); **'martyr'** Minoru Suzuki *JT* 19 Feb 1980; **Lee** *FEER* 23 Mar 1979; **Hirohito** *Daily Telegraph* 7 Sep 1984; **pen-pals** *JT* 26 Mar 1984; **Miyazawa** *FEER* 10 Mar 1978; **'animals'** Clark *FEER* 28 Nov 1970; **Kataoka** *Shokan* Oct 1979 and *Echo* Vol 7 No 1 Spring 1980 p. 89; **Ambassador** Yoshihiro Nakayama *Fin Tim* 17 Mar 1977; **New Guinea** Shigeo Nagano see *JQ* Vol 19, 1972 p. 259; **Philippine** *Int Her Trib* 22 Sep 1981; **sayonara** Wee Mon Cheng *New Nation* (Singapore) Dec 1972; **Thailand** e.g. editor Noboru Onuki in *Seiron* May 1979, *Echo* Vol 8 Special Issue 1981 p. 84; **Kojima** *Pacific Trade and Development* (2 vols) (Japan Economic Research Centre Tokyo 1968–69); **Tokuyama** 'Japan's Role in the Pacific Era' *Ekonomisuto* 31 Oct 1978; **Mitsubishi** Chujiro Fujino quoted in John Halliday & Gavan McCormack *Japanese Imperialism Today* (Association for Radical E. Asian Studies, London).

Chapter 16: Conclusion: Finding the Staircase – Japan's Future (pp. 225–240)

railways see *JQ* Vol 8, 1961 p. 106; **Chinese** Hu Shih see *JQ* Vol 12, 1965 p. 28; **Oshima** *PHP* magazine (Tokyo) Oct 1983; **Asahi** 28 Jan 1972; **'in blood'** Seizaburo Sato, Shumpei Kumon and Yasusuke Murakami in *Chuo Koron* Mar 1976, also *Echo* Vol 3 No 2 Summer 1976 p. 90; **ego** Hideaki Kase *FEER* 22 Jun 1979; **architecture** Teiji Ito *JQ* Vol 13, 1966 p. 470; **'decadence'** Susumu Nishibe in *Echo* Vol 10 No 2 Summer 1983 p. 62; **Natsume** *Failure* p. 121; **'disinherited'** Arima *ibid*; **alarmists** Percival Lowell was one such, see *Letters* p. 83; **Isozaki** see *FEER* 31 May 1984; **Toynbee** *JT* 21 Oct 1968; **Bennett** in Dore *Aspects of Social Change* (Princeton 1967) p. 24; **Keidanren** Nihachiro Hanamura *JT* 4 Jul 1981; **Miyake** see *Guardian* 31 May 1984; **Kawai** *Interlude* p. 239; **Miyazawa** Peter Jenkins *Guardian* 9 May 1984; **Dore** *Aspects op. cit.* p. 21; **'superiority'** Kenichi Yoshida, Richard Hughes in *FEER* 4 Mar 1972; **Hirohito** quoted also by Hughes *FEER* 24 Oct 1975; **'We tried'** Hiroshi Ishikawa *PHP* magazine (Tokyo) Nov 1984; **gengo** *JT* 18 Feb 1979; **Aida** *Voice* Aug 1979 and *Echo* Vol 7 Special Issue 1980 p. 88; **surveys** *JT* 27 Jul 1979; **'regain'** Kiyoaki Murata *ibid*; **camouflage** Peregrine Worsthorne *Sunday Telegraph* 21 Mar 1982; **Yukawa** *JT* 1 Jan 1971; **Nakasone** *JT* 12 Aug 1985; **'mainstream'** Makoto Yasuda *FEER* 23 Jun 1978; **Nakayama** *JT* Jan 1980; **Mishima** Essay on Yang-Ying Thought, see *Interpreter* Vol 7 No 1 Winter 1971 p. 81; **Commune** Mose Matsuba (an LSE graduate) *PHP* magazine (Tokyo) Apr 1978; **'seashore'** Kenichi Takemura *The Times* 8 Nov 1982; **Fujita** *JT* 15 Jun 1982; **Yomiuri** quoted in *JT* 16 Aug 1983; **Amaya** quoted by Shinsaku Sogo, Culture Encounter Symposium Tokyo 22 May 1982;

geopolitics *Newsweek* 4 Jul 1977; **'porcupine'** *JT* 13 May 1981; **Uchimura** quoted in *Failure* p. 19; **Nakasone** *JT* 12 Aug 1984; **down-to-earth** Shigeto Tsuru *Asahi Janaru* 30 May 1980; **'duty'** Peter Peterson speech Tokyo Mar 1982; **Thatcher** speech in Tokyo *Asahi Evening News* 22 Sep 1982; **Reischauer** *The Japanese* (Belknap Cambridge 1977); **'nobility'** Tetsuya Kataoka *Shokun* Oct 1979; **Nakasone** *Chuo Koron* Jan 1983 and *Echo* Vol 10 No 1 Spring 1983 p. 22; **Amaya** *Bungei Shunju* Mar 1980 and *Echo* Vol 7 No 2 Summer 1980 pp. 58–60; **Nissan** Kazushige Sugiuchi *FEER* 12 Jun 1981; **Matsushita** *JT* 7 Jun 1981; **'stoical'** Japan Research Centre, see *JT* 18 Oct 1972; **Kusaka** *JT* 21 Jan 1980; **Johnson** *MITI and the Japanese Miracle* (Stanford 1982); **Economist** Norman Macrae 23 FEB 1980; **New Zealand** *Guardian* 13 Aug 1981; **pessimism polls** *JT* 10 Jul 1983 and International Institute of Geopolitics (Paris) survey *The Times* 2 Apr 1984; **'Suicide'** *Bungei Shunju* Feb 1975 and *Echo* Vol 2 No 2 Summer 1975 p. 9; **Mishima** to Donald Richie 1969, see *JT* 2 Dec 1970; **Fukuda** *JT* 15 Jun 1968.

Index